Nancy Spain, who was bo[rn] 1917, numbered Samuel [...] Beeton among her ancestors [...] aspects of which are clearly [...] the setting for *Poison for Teac[her]* [...] a variety of jobs – as sports commentator, BBC radio actress, and literary editor of a number of pre-War magazines. She served in the Wrens during the war, and after it established herself – via biography, journalism, detective fiction and highly successful broadcasting on both radio and television – as one of the most popular and celebrated of post-War personalities. With her lover, Joan Werner Laurie, she helped create *SHE*, a magazine which revolutionized women's leisure reading. Both Nancy Spain and Joan Werner Laurie were killed when the light aircraft carrying them to the Grand National in 1964, crashed close to the racecourse.

Alison Hennegan, the series editor of Lesbian Landmarks, read English at Girton College, Cambridge. From 1977 until its closure in 1983 she was Literary Editor and Assistant Features Editor at *Gay News*. She went on to become Editor of the Women's Press Bookclub 1984–1991 and in 1992 launched the specialist feminist Open Letters Bookclub, which she currently edits.

LESBIAN LANDMARKS

Lesbian writing is booming today – from the most rigorous of scholarly studies to the softest of soft-centre fiction – with special lesbian sections in many bookshops, crammed with volumes from the tiniest lesbian presses and the biggest publishing giants. In the midst of such plenty, it's easy to forget that it was not always so . . . .

Lesbian Landmarks is an exciting new series of reprints which illuminates the rich and eventful history of lesbian writing.

Their politics as varied as their prose and poetry, their ideas on gender as diverse as the genres in which they express them, the writers reprinted here span centuries, castes and cultures. Some were celebrated in their lifetimes but are now forgotten; others were silenced and exiled.

Amongst these authors you will find remarkable innovators in style and content. You may also find women whose far-distant attitudes and assumptions perplex or even anger you. But all of them, in their different ways, engaged in the long struggle to articulate and explore ways of living and loving that have, over the centuries, been variously misrepresented, feared, pathologized and outlawed.

The world these authors knew was often a world apart from ours; yet however unlikely it may sometimes seem, each of these books has helped to make possible today's frequently very different, confidently open lesbian writing. These, in short, are Lesbian Landmarks.

Nancy
Spain

Poison for Teacher

Introduction by Alison Hennegan

Our chief business is to be always running, as there is some place, on a time table, that we must be in *every minute of the day* and these places are often far apart, and no allowance is made for transit.

MARGARET KENNEDY—*The Constant Nymph*

Published by VIRAGO PRESS Limited, March 1994
42–43 Gloucester Crescent, London NW1 7PD

First published in Great Britain by Hutchinson 1949

Printed and bound in Great Britain
by Cox & Wyman Ltd., Reading, Berkshire

For
FAITH COMPTON MACKENZIE,
with love

CONTENTS

INTRODUCTION

There are two things that every foreigner used to know about the English. The first is that they are obsessed by their school- and college-days. The second is that Englishwomen write the best detective stories of all. To combine the two – *Alma Mater* and murder – makes supreme good sense, a fact joyfully recognized by mistresses of the Golden Age of detective fiction, from Agatha Christie to Gladys Mitchell, from Dorothy L. Sayers to Josephine Bell. Nancy Spain was particularly well placed to essay her own version of Murder Goes to School. An ardent reader of detective novels (which, unlikely though it may seem, she reviewed regularly in *Tribune*, by courtesy of Michael Foot, in the years immediately following the Second World War), she had also written four of her own before the publication of *Poison for Teacher* in 1949. Thoroughly enjoyable though the previous four had been, *Poison for Teacher* boasted a spectacular bonus: Hermione Gingold, the larger-than-life star of cabaret and revue, appears here thinly disguised as Miriam Birdseye, a most unlikely detective. Gingold was appearing by request – her own. Spain recalled:

> . . . one day in her dressing-room this legendary figure leant towards me and said (that purple voice husky with emotion), 'Put me in a book, Nancy. Oh, please put me in a book. I've always wanted to be in a book. Send me up as far as you like, but I do so want to be in a book . . .'.

And, finally, as far as schooldays were concerned, Spain had a most unfair advantage. Like her mother before her, she had gone to Roedean, perhaps the most mythologized of all English girls' schools.

Properly mindful of the joint demands of loyalty to one's School and the workings of English libel law, Spain was always at pains to distinguish Roedean from Radcliff Hall, the gloriously named fictional establishment which forms the setting of *Poison for Teacher*. Indeed, her affection for Roedean was so great that it briefly imperilled her affection for Noël Coward when he used the words of Roedean's Cricket First Eleven Song in *South Sea Bubble* and gave them to Vivien Leigh who 'used the *wrong tune*'. Miss Leigh had to endure Spain's singing the correct version down the telephone, and Miss Leigh, like Noël Coward when he had first heard Spain's rendering, wept bitter tears. But fond though Spain was of her old school, a reading of her exuberant autobiography, *Why I'm Not A Millionaire* (1956), suggests Roedean and Radcliff Hall were not always so comfortingly distinct as she claims. Both catered for the daughters of gentlefolk, but gentleness was the chief characteristic of neither. Both are situated on that stretch of the South Coast which in the interwar years was peppered with hundreds of independent girls' schools, some of which were simply bracingly eccentric, whilst others were lethally bizarre: more than two hundred of them closed their doors for ever during the Second World War. Both have a penchant for disastrous, not to say life-threatening, school plays: death does indeed strike during a Radcliff Hall rehearsal, but a Roedean Opening Night could be pretty strong stuff, as Spain's reminiscences of an ill-fated production of Euripides's *Trojan Women* make clear. The Greek army was played by members of the First Eleven who were a little above themselves, probably because Gertrude Lawrence, as Top Parent, was in the audience:

> Perhaps they saw themselves suddenly appearing with Gertrude Lawrence *and* Noël Coward in a *musical* version of C.B. Cochran's Trojan Young Ladies? Anyway, when the whistle blew the First Eleven went berserk. Heads down, chests out, they raced for Troy as though they were in the Olympics. Breast-plates burst, sandals flew and one spear caught with its top and bottom hard in the door where Cassandra was still calling down woe. And the entire Greek army fell with a reverberating crash into the school orchestra who were hard at it grinding out a Tone Poem by an Old Roedeanian called Greta Tomlin. The resulting crash in the timpani could be heard as far away as Falmer. And no one smiled.

Moreover, both schools boasted staff members with a gift for striking striking poses: Radcliff Hall, for instance, has the deeply unloveable Miss Devaloys, Roedean the altogether more enticing Miss Mellanby:

> Miss Mellanby was a very considerable character indeed, passionately loved by all her house and covertly admired by everyone else. She used to go riding on the Downs and could quite often be seen standing negligently about on the school terrace dressed in Jodhpurs, a remarkable thing in itself. Anyway, Miss Mellanby went to be head of Borstal in 1935 and Roedean made headlines in the *Daily Mirror*. She is now an Inspector of H.M. Prisons. And no one at the school could see why the rest of the world found this funny.

Perhaps most pertinent of all, both schools, as Miss Mellanby's career path demonstrates, had links with crime and might indeed even be said to exert an unfortunate fascination, curious in such select establishments, for the murderously minded. They included, in one instance, Spain's older sister Liz, who 'broke into the white marbled school chapel and drank the communion wine, and then in an advanced state of intoxication is supposed to have driven the Headmistress's niece, with a broken bottle, up on to the roofs'. Unsurprisingly, perhaps, Sister Liz left shortly afterwards and 'went to Mayortorne Manor, a perfectly *splendid* farm school run by Roger Fry's sister'.

More sombrely, Spain recalled that at Roedean '. . . various Brighton trunk murderers ran smartly through the grounds, leaving little trails of clues', and 'suicides flung themselves off cliffs almost daily. Roedean cliffs are almost as good for suicides as Beachy Head. But apart from that Roedean was really sad.' Note, by the way, that unnerving use of the phrase 'but apart from that'. Spain had her own ideas about the categories of comedy and tragedy and frequently disconcerts her readers by what she allocates to which.

Received ideas on Comedy and Tragedy weren't the only ones which gave Spain trouble. In life, as in her fiction, she had difficulty with a number of other conventional categories too: Family Life, Traditional Values, sexual 'normality' and the innocence of children, for example. At one level she fitted perfectly the expectations of her time and class: a spirited and talented sportswoman ('The idea of fresh air and running after a ball has always appealed to me strongly. Sister Liz says it is most unnatural. Maybe she is right'). She played lacrosse for

Northumberland and Durham, provided professional sports commentaries for the *Newcastle Journal*, brought the brio and enthusiasm which mark the best kind of amateur to her accomplished (paid) performances for BBC radio drama, and proved a perfectly splendid officer in the Wrens during the Second World War.

Once again, a perfect public school girl became, if not effortlessly at least inevitably, a perfect naval officer. Yet, as Sister Liz's wry observation on the deeply unnatural nature of women's field sports reminds us, there has always been an uneasy tension between the perfect English schoolgirl and the perfect English Rose: schoolgirls are *not* feminine as anyone who's spent the lunch-hour in an English playground knows. Those who have charge of them have sometimes wished they were not even female. 'Run about, girls, *like* boys, and then you won't think of them'. E. Arnot Robertson quotes her Sherborne Headmistress as saying in her aptly titled 1934 school memoir, 'Potting Shed of an English Rose'; a remark which Nancy Spain, never too proud to pilfer, appropriates for *her* fictional headmistress, Miss Lipscoomb, a woman whose own sex often seems uncertain: '"Silly Old Juggins", said Miss Lipscoomb, and sounded exactly like Arthur Marshall.' The reference to the much lamented Mr Marshall and his wickedly plausible evocations of the dottier sort of English Headmistress reminds us that, in the English comic tradition, at least, schoolgirls and their mistresses *aren't* always female. Witness, at the crudest level, the hordes of male medical students desperate to don gymslips and fake pigtails for the end-of-year revue – revues less polished than the remarkable performances of Miriam Birdseye (or those of her even more remarkable original, Hermione Gingold) but at one with them in their anarchic rejection of the arbitrary rigidities of gender.

Gingold's own rejections were notorious. In her hands cabaret became a licensed space in which a woman could say the unsayable: she pleased best when she outraged most. Gifted with an astonishingly mobile face (Spain said of her 'Hermione has become the most beautifully ugly woman in the world. She can actually radiate beauty for five minutes at a time and then ruin the whole thing with some fearful grimace, worthy of the gargoyles of Notre-Dame.'), she played the grotesque and glamorous off against each other, thus subverting both stereotypes of femininity. Herself irredeemably heterosexual, she became one of the most illustrious icons of British camp and for that a host of lesbian and gay admirers loved her. By bringing Hermione/Miriam into Radcliff Hall, Spain imports the Queen of Misrule into the heart of the school story – that genre which has traditionally proved a resonant source of parody and pastiche for homosexual writers and audiences ever ready to identify, not to say broadcast, the eternal homo-eroticism which runs as an often unwitting but (mercifully) relentless thread through tales of a traditional, English (single-sex) education.

There is comparatively little overt homosexuality in *Poison for Teacher*. But *hetero*sexuality is viewed through lesbian eyes, denied its usual privileges of 'normality'. Indeed normality itself, in all its usually accepted forms, is endlessly called into question, whether in cogent one-liners ('Mrs Puke, in common with lady Conservatives, liked a good crime' – a comment which must now seem sombrely prophetic), or in a sustained shift of perspective which renders the familiar unsettlingly alien and bizarre. Alternatively, of course, the supposedly alien can be rendered friendly and familiar: when Natasha and Miriam, unabashedly reading other people's letters, find themselves described variously as a tart and a witch. 'Natasha thought it was cosier to look like a tart'. 'Cosier', with all its overtones of domesticity, familial normality and an even slightly cloying warmth, 'tames' the word 'tart', removing the sneer and insult usually associated with it: one small example of a technique Spain employs repeatedly, and by so doing inverts conventional moral judgements.

When homosexual characters appear Spain's attitudes may at first sight seem mocking and unsympathetic. Poor Charity Puke, the Classics Mistress, yearns hopelessly and sometimes risibly for Gwylan Fork-Thomas, who teaches Chemistry. But when Gwylan sneers at Roger Partick-Thistle as 'an old woman', Natasha and Miriam snub her hard. Roger (Partick-Thistle is not his real name; an unfortunate incident involving Wolf Cubs in 1933 caused him to adopt a *nom de guerre*) is unmistakably a queen, and a screamer at that. But he is in effect a hero, not a butt; in this book homosexuality is part and parcel of human sexuality, *all* of which, hetero- or homosexual, is capable of being risible, ridiculous, bathetic and genuinely poignant. The overall effect is, most remarkably for the period, and indeed for *any* period, an unusual absence of moralistic judgements. And sex, regardless of its orientation, is allowed to be itself alone, not conditional upon marriage, stability or even love. 'Skip that', says Miriam sharply when Dr Lariat agonizes over the affection he did not feel for his sexual partners: 'No need for sex to be genuinely anything except sex.' Not a statement so often heard from a woman even today, let alone in 1949.

Indeed, in the historical context of the 1940s, sex, for homosexuals at least, was often safest when it was just itself. Gay men, such as Roger, were criminals solely by virtue of their sexuality, and would remain so until 1967 (unless, of course, they're under twenty-one, in which case the sexually active amongst them are still officially criminal). Stable relationships, with all the incriminating clutter of letters, photographs, and perhaps a shared home, paradoxically brought with them the dangers of 'evidence' in contrast to the comparative safety of casual sex with strangers. And although homosexual women have never been formally legislated against in England, their sexuality brought stigma and ostracism, and the possible loss of children in custody disputes. (What's changed?, I hear some of you ask.)

Like so many earlier books by homosexual authors, *Poison for Teacher* has at least two audiences: a fairly uninformed heterosexual one which will enjoy Spain's high-spirited romp; and an altogether more sophisticated and knowing one with which Spain shares jokes and allusions based on insider, gay knowledge. Most people, probably, would understand the opening joke, the name of England's most notorious lesbian author, Radclyffe Hall, re-spelt and newly applied to Miss Lipscoomb's tottering establishment. Fewer, probably, would pick up the allusion, encoded in Spain's reference to 'the other young ladies, whose errand had been sleeveless', to a once notorious, and banned lesbian novel, *Sleeveless Errand*. In-jokes of that sort are scattered through the text, mirroring the altogether larger injoke which Spain played weekly before a television audience of millions, with Gilbert Harding, the lovably irascible panellist and wit, with whom Spain flirted outrageously on innumerable panel games.

Harding's blustering geniality and self-consciously virile appearance were at odds with his homosexuality, which he concealed so painfully yet longed to be able to disclose. He once said the problem of homosexuality would disappear at once if every homosexual turned blue at midnight, thereby enabling homosexuals to identify each other and to demonstrate to the rest of the world how vast their numbers were. Questioned by John Freeman, one of the outstanding broadcasters of his generation, in the then shockingly hard-hitting and probing interview series, 'Face to Face', Harding shed tears when recalling his mother's death. For an audience so accustomed to the bluffly masculine Harding image, and so well attuned to psychological theories about homosexual men's 'unfortunate' attachment to their mothers, Harding's tears revealed a truth that could not be safely acknowledged either by Harding himself or by the audience. Those few seconds of television time marked a watershed, constantly recalled, its meaning rarely articulated.

Spain's appearance was as 'masculine' as Harding's. Shortly after the war she had revolted against 'the great heavy hairy tweeds and thick brogues which was *my* idea of the way ladies dressed in Northumberland. And I was sick of it . . .'. Instead, 'I cut my hair with a pair of curly nail-scissors and washed it every day in the bath. I decided then and there that I could never have another job that would demand little black suits and diamond clips. I decided that I didn't want to meet *anyone* who would make me put on a skirt.' Just *very* occasionally, it's true, she'd don formal female evening attire, only to be told by Noël Coward, with the rudeness close friends and gay brothers reserve for special occasions, that her dresses 'wouldn't deceive a drunken child of two-and-a-half'. But, in the main, she appeared before the camera in well cut tweed jackets, good shirts with elegant cuff-links, and dashing cravats around her handsome neck. As such she was a glorious inspiration and much loved proof of the possible, a heartening sight for a host of dykes, baby or otherwise, myself included. And for a gay audience her long-running and public flirtation with Gilbert Harding was equally warming: it playfully mocked heterosexual courtship whilst affirming the strength of a thoroughly genuine friendship between a homosexual man and woman. For those of you too young to remember British television in the Fifties, just believe me when I say that Spain brought thousands of lesbian viewers a sense of pure exhilaration and sheer relief. As ever with Spain, humour, a seemingly universal benevolence and an utterly relaxed self-acceptance enabled her to carry off a performance which might have wrecked others. The same qualities irradiate her autobiographical works, especially in her remarkably matter-of-fact writing about her partner, Joan Werner Laurie (the creator of *SHE* magazine) and the life they shared together.

Nancy Spain was already dead when the first stirrings of Gay Liberation began. She died when her light aircraft crashed on its way to the Grand National in 1964, and I still remember the shock of the Saturday evening news bulletin which told us so. She was not 'politically correct'; she and her books were the products of a particular time and class and although she shed an unusually large number of her period's prejudices, she retained others, and occasionally voiced them in her comic fiction.

Comedy, notoriously, often fails to travel, whether through time (history) or space (place and culture). In the almost fifty years since *Poison for Teacher* was first published few things have changed more than our attitudes to race and class. Some will find Spain's attitudes to the Jewish Dr Lariat and to Miss Lesarum, a woman of mixed race, offensive. My previous efforts to persuade feminist presses to reprint *Poison for Teacher* have foundered on that rock. Yet a closer reading softens the charges of anti-semitism and racism. Most comedy concentrates, initially, upon the *differences* between people, the traits and quirks which distinguish one from another. When used malignly, comedy never progresses beyond that point. Having first identified difference – whether in appearance, race, age, faith, whatever – it then persuades its audience to define difference as Danger: 'difference' becomes that thing most terrifying of all to timid and beleaguered minds: that-which-we-are-not. With its audience thus united against dangerous difference, comedy has frequently become a vicious weapon, turned as often against the weak and innocent as it is against the corrupt and powerful. Spain, however, was *intrigued* by human difference: for her it was a source of fascination and delight, rather than distaste or fear. The apparently racist and anti-semitic attitudes which readers of *Poison for Teacher* might be tempted to assume Spain endorses are overturned as the narrative progresses. In the end they prove just as unthinking and unfounded as Miss Fork-Thomas's assumptions about gay men and the hatred she believes they must arouse in 'ordinary decent people'.

Miss Fork-Thomas's mistake, of course, has been to assume that there is only one correct definition of 'decent' and 'ordinary'. Spain, her creator, could have no truck with such harshly confident certainties. She had taken too many hard knocks during her twenties and thirties as she struggled to find ways of dressing, looking, loving and being which 'fitted' her, even though they were often startlingly at odds with the conventions of the day. From that ultimately triumphant struggle she created a distinctive comic style. Hers was comedy written from a position of difference, casting an often quizzical glance at 'normality', yet refusing to replace its strai(gh)t-jacket with one of her own gay design. Resisting the easy tit-for-tat polarities of gay *versus* straight, she succeeded in producing a fictional world at once anarchic and humane. So far no other writer has produced anything quite like it.

Alison Hennegan, Dundee, 1993

Author's Note

I must apologize to the Sussex County Council for my impertinence in taking liberties with their coast line, tearing it apart in order to construct an imaginary landscape with two towns between Bexhill-on-Sea and Cooden Beach.

The towns of Brunton-on-Sea and Cranmer never existed anywhere but in my imagination. The school of Radcliff Hall is equally imaginary.

NANCY SPAIN.

CHARACTERS IN THE STORY

Natasha DuVivien	*An ex-ballet dancer*
Johnny DuVivien	*her husband*
Miriam Birdseye	*a genius*
The Hon. Miss Janet Lipscoomb	*the Headmistress of Radcliff Hall School for Girls*
Julia Bracewood-Smith	*a new girl*
Peter Bracewood-Smith	*a detective novelist, her father*
Mrs. Cluny	*his daily help*
Miss Phipps	*Secretary to Radcliff Hall School*
Theresa Devaloys	*French Mistress at Radcliff Hall School*
Gwylan Fork-Thomas	*Chemistry Mistress at Radcliff Hall School*
Miss Lesarum	*Mathematics Mistress at Radcliff Hall School*
Miss Zwart	*English Mistress at Radcliff Hall School*
Roger Partick-Thistle	*Organist at Radcliff Hall School, nephew to Miss Lipscoomb*
Gwen Soames	
Daisy Stuckenheimer	
Maud Stuckenheimer	*school girls*
Molly Ruminara	
Noni Postman	
Dr. Lariat	*Doctor to Radcliff Hall School*
Mrs. Buttick	*his housekeeper*
Gertie	
Greta	*parlourmaids at Radcliff Hall School*
Mrs. Grossbody	*Matron at Radcliff Hall School*
Miss Bound	*her assistant*
Mrs. Pont	*an accompanist*
Charity Puke	*Classics Mistress at Radcliff Hall School*
Mrs. Puke	*her mother*

CHARACTERS IN THE STORY

Sergeant Tomkins, C.I.D.	*of the Brunton-on-Sea Constabulary*
P.C. Beatty	
P.C. Jones	*also of the Brunton-on-Sea Constabulary*
P.C. Briggs	
Graham Micah	*chemist at Brunton-on-Sea*
Miss Try	*a Conservative agent*
Miss Helena bbirch	*formerly partner to Miss Lipscoomb, now principal of bbirch Hall School for Girls*
Mr. Bere	*senior partner of the firm of Fox & Fox*
Major Bandarlog	*of the Indian Army (retd.)*
Mrs. Bandarlog	*his wife*
A Pullman Car attendant	
Henry	*Owner of Grandy's Club, Brunton-on-Sea*
Black Market Bob	*a taxi driver*

Schools girls, visiting music mistresses, other residents of Brunton-on-Sea, Conservatives, and a white pekinese dog called Amy

BOOK ONE

BIRDSEYE ET CIE

CHAPTER ONE

"Of all the stinking, boring, belly-aching tunes," shouted Johnny DuVivien passionately, "*that* one jest about takes anyone's cake!"

He was a big, craggy, all-in wrestler in his fifties. Just at this moment he was very angry indeed with his lovely Russian wife, Natasha. It was a wet Sunday morning. They were both in the drawing-room of their house in Hampstead. Below the window, Hollybush Hill, suffering and dripping under February rain, made a sad background for the disintegration of their relationship. Natasha shrugged her shoulders.

"It is not a tune," she said coldly, "it is Stravinsky."

She half turned her head. Johnny sprang from his chair at the gramophone. It was happily giving out the confused and delightful fairground noises of the first act of the ballet *Petrouchka*. Until this moment Natasha's indifference had been complete.

There was a white pekinese dog called Amy in her lap. From time to time she gently pulled Amy's ears. But when Johnny exploded towards the gramophone it was obvious that she also was angry out of all proportion.

"If you are now going to try and take off that record," she said venomously, "I will kill you."

Johnny controlled himself with a great effort.

"Amy likes *Petrouchka*," added Natasha lightly. She kissed the dog on the top of the head.

"*Your dog!*" screamed Johnny. He was quite beside himself. He stamped over towards the fireplace.

"Do not be shouting like that, if you please," said Natasha, in insultingly even tones. Her nerves were leaping, raw-edged, at the uncontrolled notes in Johnny's voice.

She sat composedly in the window-seat, curled like a cat. Around her the drawing-room, with its silly little ikon, its elegant

French furniture, its Aubusson carpet, its artificial flowers (imperfectly dusted), reflected her personality. It also reflected the highlights of her career as a ballet dancer in the original Diaghilev company. Above the solid middle-class mantelpiece, for example, was a hideous flashlight photograph of the *corps-de-ballet*, taken, blinking, on the station platform at Monte Carlo. They looked singularly moth-eaten, and their fur coats had come out exactly like rat skins. By the door there was a glorious design for *Scheherezade* by Bakst. And framed in *passe partout* was a somewhat shaming programme of a Royal Command Performance in which Miss Natasha Nevkorina had appeared as one of the young ladies of the chorus.

There was also evidence of Johnny's activities. There were architect's drawings of his roadhouse (the Heeton Arms) in Yorkshire. There was a photograph taken at the opening of his London night-club (the Bag of Tricks) and an interesting police document (stolen) which showed that a famous pick-pocket had been arrested on the premises of his drinking-club in Shepherd Market.

The whole room had begun to get upon Natasha's nerves. It seemed to hem her in. She tucked the little white dog under one arm and looked furtively about her for a way of escape.

It was very many years since Natasha had danced in ballet. Still, her movements betrayed the easy mastery of the elements that is the inheritance of the dancer. Her lovely shining ash-brown hair fell to her shoulders. Her enormous hazel cat's-eyes looked balefully at her husband. She was sick of the sight of him.

"You are upset?" she said vaguely.

The first side of the record of *Petrouchka* wound to its close. There was a rhythmic click and whirr inside the gramophone, which then started happily upon the first side of the second record of the set. Johnny clenched his fists and banged them on his forehead.

"That *noise*!" he shouted. "I suppose you think," he went on, in a lower tone but still passionately, "that jest because I'm on'y an all-in wrestler an' night-club proprietor, an' Australian at *that*, 'at I've no *culture*? All *right*, then, so I'm common. So what? And who pays the bills around here?" he ended furiously.

Natasha buried her face on the top of the little dog's head. It was impossible to see what she felt.

"Amy is so *soft*," she said. To Johnny it was an adroit carica-
ture of her most maliciously inconsequent manner. "Did you say
something?" she concluded, with sudden exquisite charm, looking
up at him, fluttering her eyelashes.

Johnny flinched. He held out one enormous hand like a ham.
It shook and shook. He seemed to have difficulty in speaking
at all.

"I *said*," he mumbled, "that I pay the bills around here and
I'm common. I said I'd no culture. I said you thought yourself
very clever. I said——"

He stopped in the middle of this savage inventory. Natasha
smiled. Then she yawned, very delicately. She looked exactly like
the pekinese. In his heart Johnny longed and longed for her to
show him a little simple, uncomplicated affection. He had no idea
that this was all he wanted.

"You don't say any'hing?" he remarked uncertainly.

"Well, my poor Johnny," said Natasha gravely, "all of that is
perfectly true. But *I* am seeing no point at *all* in going on so about
it. You are behaving most extraordinarily. Amy and I are listening
to *Petrouchka*."

And Natasha adjusted her lovely head to listen all the more
clearly.

Johnny DuVivien stamped over to the fireplace. A tile cracked
as he walked on it. The noise was as sharp as a revolver shot.

"Hell!" he said. "You're *impossible*."

"Oh yes," said Natasha politely, "I am impossible."

There was a pause, filled only with the confusion and nervous
tension of *Petrouchka*.

"You have cracked a tile," remarked Natasha sweetly. "How
extraordinary you are."

II

Over luncheon the DuVivien's unpleasant quarrel began
again.

This time there was no background of *Petrouchka* to feed
Johnny's rage and add tension and beauty to Natasha's insulting
calm. There was, apparently, nothing to begin the argument
except their own intolerance. This was quite enough, however.

It all started again, this time over Amy, the pekinese. She had failed to be house-trained in the middle of Johnny's bed.

"That damned *dog!*" said Johnny angrily, as the door shut quietly behind the manservant. "It *is* six months old, sure*ly*? It'll have to be destroyed. . . ."

Natasha sat very still. Her plate in front of her was ignored. Amy, who had already been beaten, flattened herself engagingly against the floor and leered miserably at Johnny. She thumped her curly white tail on the floor and adjusted one ear with an ineffective paw. Lurching, she rose to her feet and sat up, quivering, in an attitude of supplication.

"How could *anyone*," asked Natasha wildly, "be being so *cruel* as to destroy a little dog who can do *that* and is just so sweet and soft as a cat? And with a tail exactly like ostrich feathers?"

"Ostrich feathers my ——!" snarled Johnny, and reached forward for Amy, who again flattened herself on the floor and cowered. Johnny was utterly surprised by all that followed. Natasha kicked him viciously on the ankle, snatched Amy to her heart and shot from the dining-room, moving with all the dangerous grace of a man-eating tigress. The door slammed behind her.

Johnny grinned ruefully and rubbed his ankle.

"Hell," he said to himself, "that's torn it!"

It is very much to be regretted that at this stage in his emotional life Johnny DuVivien continued to eat his luncheon.

Upstairs a door shut noisily, and Johnny still paid no attention, but helped himself to more green peas. Ten minutes later the front door crashed and sent him leaping to the window. He remained there like a stuck pig, staring down on the soaking path and garden. He was horrified.

His lovely, wilful wife, carrying a raw-hide suitcase, with Amy leaping and curvetting on the end of a lead, was hurrying down the garden path. She was shutting the garden gate. She was hailing a taxi. She was leaving. . . .

Johnny came to his senses. He ran downstairs, down the garden path to the front gate, to the taxi-rank, like a mad thing. The cold rain hit him a sharp blow in the face. Natasha had taken the only cab on the rank.

"Stop! Stop!" he cried helplessly, as the taxi twirled away from him. Natasha pulled up the window haughtily and sank back. She was obviously urging the driver to go faster and faster

III

When Natasha DuVivien leapt so melodramatically into the taxi that carried her away from Johnny, she acted, as she had always done, with the strictest integrity and on the spur of the moment. She had not the remotest idea *why* she had gone, nor *where* she was going; but at least *Johnny* would not be there. Nagging and suggesting that he paid for *her*, Natasha! He had really become impossible.

She scowled at the rain that made a glistening screen on the taxi windows.

"Where to, miss?" asked the taxi-driver. He slid back the little glass partition.

Natasha bit her lip. Where, indeed?

"I am hardly knowing," she said finally. "You see, I have just been leaving my husband."

The taxi-driver was delighted with her.

"Well, then, your boy friend," he said chattily.

"My boy friend," said Natasha, in sombre tones, "is *dead*."

"Lor'!" said the taxi-driver involuntarily.

He recovered himself and skidded ever so slightly as they paused for the traffic lights at Chalk Farm. "Got a girl friend?" he said at last, as the lights blinked from red and yellow and finally to green.

Natasha thought for a little as Amy attempted, most desperately, to dry herself on the uncomfortable and scratchy mat on the floor of the cab.

"There is," said Natasha eventually, "always Miriam."

"And where, if I may make so bold," said the taxi-driver, turning right-handed towards Kilburn, "does *Miriam* live?"

"Miss Miriam Birdseye," said Natasha, with great dignity, "is living in Baker Street."

"Aha!" said the taxi-driver, with a happy chuckle. "Like Sherlock Holmes."

IV

This was indeed the case. Like Sherlock Holmes, Miss Miriam Birdseye lived in Baker Street. And, like the master, she was making an attempt to earn, if not a pretty penny, at least an

5

honest living, as a detective. To this end she had put up an elegant oxidized plate that said *Birdseye et Cie—detectives*. To this end she had advertised in *Dalton's Weekly*, the *Exchange and Mart* and the *London Weekly Advertiser* that she would detect *anything*. To this end she had converted most of her house into a show-waiting-room for clients. She had only a slender idea as to how this should be done, so she had bought a lot of sofas and scattered them with *Vogues*, *Harper's Bazaars* and *New Yorkers*. Then she had been photographed by some famous stage photographers, surrounded by her favourite pieces of *bric-à-brac*, several American primitive paintings and a Marie Laurencin.

When Natasha arrived Miriam was hard at work.

"I have come to stay," said Natasha, as Amy bowed and pranced on the end of her lead.

"Thank God," Miriam had said, rather shakily. "Come in and lie down, dear. I am making out the bills for the detective agency."

Miriam was tall and thin and blonde and not very handsome. She was a genius who had earned £150 a week for a great many years in a series of intimate revues called *Absolutely the End*, *Positively the Last*, *Take Me Off* and *Hips and Haws* which had run and run and run near Leicester Square until poor Miriam was sick of the word 'revue'. Her ambition was to play Ibsen. Her misfortune was her sense of humour that would not allow her to do this. She liked young men, Delius, *Annie Get Your Gun* and Tchekov. She was a great darling and she adored Natasha. She had had the slightly crazy idea of becoming a detective with her manager of the moment, a young gentleman whom no one else had ever liked called 'Benjy'.

"Bills?" said Natasha vaguely. "I am never very good with these. However . . ."

Natasha draped her damp overcoat over a pretty little statue of a black boy that held an oil-lamp near the fireplace. There was a coal fire roaring happily away and several electric radiators were turned full on. The general effect was bizarre, but cosy.

Amy trotted to the centre of the room, yawned once or twice, and fell into a becoming sleep, holding her tail in her mouth exactly like a whiting.

"You must be telling me what to do, darling Miriam," said Natasha, picking up a little red notebook that lay on the floor. "I have just left Johnny."

6

"Oh, *good*," said Miss Birdseye. The matter was never mentioned between them again. "All this"—and Miriam sketched a broad gesture with her right hand—"is that brilliant actress Miriam Birdseye, who so wittily became a detective, going bankrupt."

"How?" said Natasha, startled. "I have five pounds," she added inconsequentially. "Shall you be wanting them?"

"Well, two ways, dear," said Miriam. "Slowly and now fast. Fast, since yesterday, when Benjy took the petty cash and went to Portugal."

"Oh, *lucky* Benjy," said Natasha, "to be in Portugal. Who was Benjy?"

"Well, dear," said Miriam, taking the notebook from her, "this has all the names and addresses of the clients in. Shall we say my *partner*, dear, and leave it at that? He was *hell* as a detective, I can tell you. And do you know"—Miriam opened china-blue eyes—"I don't think he was quite *honest*. Please don't let's mention him, shall we? Not, that is, if you are going to stay for some time."

And so the names 'Benjy' and 'Johnny' were expunged from their conversation. Miriam whirled the leaves of her notebook restlessly and eventually said to Natasha in bored and wearied tones that she could only conscientiously send bills to six of her clients.

"I owe money to all the others," she said. "Shall we put these six in the typewriter and post them? They're two drug addicts and three perverts and a very nasty divorce case."

She pointed to her shapely ankle, which was bound with an old piece of linen.

"I got *that* in the divorce case," she said gaily. "Climbing a lamp-post in St. John's Wood."

Natasha crossed the room to the typewriter, a big black office machine. It stood in the window on the left of an enormous looking-glass that took up most of the front wall. Beyond the windows was Baker Street. Buses passed occasionally and shook the house, otherwise it was very quiet.

"Of course, it is *Sunday*," said Natasha, in explanation to herself. She wound in a bill headed *Birdseye et Cie—we detect anything*. She looked happily at the rain which was still falling outside.

"But I feel so *gay*," she said out loud. "What have you been doing with the drug addicts and perverts, darling?" she remarked as she began to type.

Miriam, standing behind her, dictated names and addresses.

"Restraining them," said Miriam firmly. "For their relations, dear. It is very difficult to get perverts to pay their bills."

V

Twenty minutes later there was a heavy thump upon the door.

"Goodness!" said Miriam, clutching her throat. "A client. On a Sunday. That's queer, if you like."

"How do you know it's a client?" said Natasha, turning round in her chair. It was an exquisite little piece of Victoriana, neatly buttoned into navy-blue linen.

"Clients knock. Personal friends ring," said Miriam. "It says so outside."

Natasha recollected that this was indeed so.

It was most certainly a client. It was the Hon. Miss Janet Lipscoomb, of Radcliff Hall School for Girls, Brunton-on-Sea, Sussex. She strode into the showroom with an ashplant and a red draught-excluding jacket and brogues with big, fringed tongues.

"I am being persecuted," she said.

Amy pranced towards her, engagingly flinging her paws above her head and wagging her tail. She wagged all over.

"What a pretty little dog," said Miss Lipscoomb. "More like a moth or a butterfly . . ."

"She is not a dog. She is a pekinese," said Miriam severely. "Tell me about your persecutions."

"What form is it that they are taking?" said Natasha, helping her friend. Miriam looked at her gratefully.

"What form do what?" said Miss Lipscoomb. She leant her walking-stick against the little black boy and brought out an old-fashioned card-case. "This is me," she said, waving her card. "I can assure you I am not the imaginative type."

Amy stood on her hind legs and sank quivering into a sitting position. Her large, lustrous eyes were fixed upon Miss Lipscoomb's face. She was obviously making up her mind whether Miss Lipscoomb was the imaginative type.

8

"Revolting little dog," said Miriam absently. "Your persecutions, now. Tell us," she added.

"My card," said Miss Lipscoomb again.

"Oh," said Natasha, reading it, "a *school* mistress. Do look, Miriam. Isn't that so *splendid* . . ."

And Natasha, too, looked at Miss Lipscoomb with her large, lustrous eyes.

"I *like* girls' schools," said Miriam Birdseye. "This is my partner, Mrs. DuVivien."

Miss Lipscoomb, who had been looking oddly defiant and nervous, now pulled up the Victorian chair and sat upon it with her legs rather apart. Miriam kicked Amy behind a screen.

"Please to be telling us what is going wrong," said Natasha. "School-teachers are not always drug addicts, dear Miriam," she added encouragingly. "They are too poor, they say——"

"Thank God," said Miriam.

"Amen," said Miss Lipscoomb, and surprised them.

And then, quite unabashed by her bizarre surroundings, the head mistress of Radcliff Hall School began her story.

"It all began," said Miss Lipscoomb, crossing her legs rather high up and showing a lean leg dressed in a hand-knitted silk stocking, "in the Spring Term. Sickness and Lent, we always say——"

"Oh, so do *we*," said Miriam encouragingly.

"And right in the middle of the chicken-pox epidemic at a time when it all couldn't have been more inconvenient," said Miss Lipscoomb.

"Chicken-pox!" said Natasha excitedly. "Then this is a *real* school?"

"Of course it is, dear," said Miriam sharply. "Can't you see it is? Please go on, Miss Lip . . ."; she looked down at the card in her hand, shook her head and said "Not true," in a perfectly audible voice.

"Do be going on," said Natasha.

"Well, in the middle of the chicken-pox," pursued Miss Lipscoomb, "my partner, Miss bbirch, left——"

"bbirch?" said Miriam.

"Yes, *yes*," said Miss Lipscoomb testily. "Like Birch, but with two small bs, of course. Well, she left and took my fifty *best* pupils. And she opened in Cranmer. Just along the coast. bbirch Hall she called it."

"How awful," said Miriam, and meant it. But she added under her breath, "Should have been called bbirch hhall."

"Not content with *that*," said Miss Lipscoomb, her heavy face flushing a deeper crimson, "she took my elocution mistress and my dancing mistress with her. Imagine! A wicked, wicked thing."

"Elocution?" said Miriam vaguely, as though thinking of something else. "What a curious coincidence."

"And dancing," said Natasha. "But never be minding. Go on, *please*, good Miss Lipscoomb. Tell us more."

"And faster," said Miriam.

So Miss Lipscoomb went on. At some points in her narrative she was so overcome by the injustice of fate and so moved that she rose and paced restlessly, and made lunges with her walking-stick. This disturbed Amy, who barked and had to be shut up in a cupboard.

Miss Lipscoomb's story was usual enough. Flower-pots fell off roofs near her head. People wet her chalk so that it squeaked when she drew maps on the blackboard. Someone put a grand-father's clock in her bed and a small hedgehog in her bath. Some-one greased the stairs and she nearly broke her leg. Someone drew rude pictures on the blackboard and the English mistress left in a huff. Someone threw feathers on the fire in Main Hall just before prayers, and (if Natasha and Miriam would pardon a colloquialism) *stank* the place out.

It had all seemed *childish* until yesterday, when Miss Lipscoomb had found one of the ropes in the gym sawn half through. Just before she demonstrated 'Flying Angels' to IVʙ. This, Miss Lipscoomb thought, was *homicidal*.

"Or inefficient," drawled Miriam, leaning back in her chair. "You teach gym," she added, regarding Miss Lipscoomb through long false eyelashes like a pantomime horse.

"And fencing. And geography," said Miss Lipscoomb, sitting down abruptly.

"Ah!" said Natasha admiringly.

"And what is your proposition?" said Miriam, frowning hard.

"That you should come back to Radcliff Hall with me and protect my interests," said Miss Lipscoomb. "I *need* you. I tell you, I'll pay anything you like. I'm a very wealthy woman. I'll pay you your salaries if you like if you come as members of my staff. As well as your fee." There was a pause. "On the Burnham scale," said Miss Lipscoomb hastily.

Miriam wrinkled her nose at the word 'wealthy' and looked vague about the Burnham scale.

"But so are *we* rich," said Miriam grimly. "Very, very rich. You must tell us more and prove it is going to be interesting. Do your staff do a play?" she added, inconsequently polishing her nails.

"Yes," said Miss Lipscoomb, surprised. "They are rehearsing it now."

"What is it?" said Miriam, her eyes gleaming.

"*Quality Street*," said Miss Lipscoomb.

"We are *artists* and highly qualified," said Natasha suddenly. "And I do not really care for teaching kiddies."

"My gels are not kiddies," said Miss Lipscoomb; "and," she added cunningly, "there's the French mistress, Miss Theresa Devaloys. Someone tried, we think, to murder *her* a week ago. With a dumb-bell," she added.

"Murder?" said Miriam, with unholy gaiety. "We've never done a murder yet, *have* we, darling Natasha?"

"I should be hoping not," said Natasha.

Miss Lipscoomb laughed abruptly. Then she saw Natasha's look of astonishment and shut her mouth with a snap. She had good, fierce, white false teeth. Natasha took Amy out of the cupboard and went towards the door with her under her arm.

"Where are you going?" said Miriam.

"To pack," said Natasha.

"Excuse *me*, darling," said Miriam, brushing past Miss Lipscoomb.

"Oh, ha, yes, theatrical folk," replied Miss Lipscoomb.

Miriam said nothing, but she hung a little black notice outside the front door. It said 'OUT—GONE TO CRIME' in neat white letters. Then Miriam turned to Miss Lipscoomb with a frank, false, boyish grin.

"It's a deal," said Miriam, and held out her hand like a good Boy Scout. "Jolly d. of you to ask us, I think."

"Oh, by *jove*!" said Miss Lipscoomb, and coloured up.

VI

Natasha and Miriam did not have much time to discuss their new client during the next half-hour, when they were hanging about on the corner of Baker Street and Portman Square profanely screaming for taxis. They had agreed to meet Miss Lipscoomb in the Grosvenor Hotel, to catch the 3.45 to Brunton-on-Sea. Miss Lipscoomb was to buy the tickets. And when they were finally *in* the taxi, and swaying towards Victoria, Natasha was so *anxious* about dearest Amy (who had been left with Miriam's daily help, who was in turn to leave her at the kennels), and Miriam was so taken up with reassuring her, that they had no time to say anything more than "Very like Stephen Gorden, I think," and "I played in that once in the Basement Banned Theatre," before Miss Janet Lipscoomb came striding towards them through the dark hall.

"I've got your tickets; it's quite a jolly journey to Brunton," said Miss Lipscoomb. "The attendant always keeps the *coupé* for me and my friends on Saturday nights."

"So *gay*," murmured Natasha.

"Oh, we're often quite a jolly little party. At least, we used to be," said Miss Lipscoomb. "Before Miss bbirch . . ."

There was a second while Miss Lipscoomb registered heartbreak. Then she bravely lifted her head (in its wide-brimmed *sans-souci* gent's felt) as though to face a hostile world.

"—Miss bbirch and I and Hilda (that's Miss Zwart, the English mistress) and Miss Devaloys——"

"The French mistress," said Miriam, nodding.

"We kept it up the whole way down to Brunton, what with pontoon and whist and gin-and-limes, you know."

Miriam, whose reputation as a poker player was almost international, nodded gravely and politely and said pontoon was not *really* her game. Two men in scarlet hats picked up their luggage.

"Today (thank you, my man)," went on Miss Lipscoomb briskly, "there are only our three selves and Julia Bracewood-Smith. She is a new gel. Ju-li-*a*!"

Miss Lipscoomb called across the hall as though to an animal. A sulky over-grown girl of about fifteen rose to her feet. She had a pale, glossy face and a damp, black fringe. She was wearing the purple-and-white uniform of Radcliff Hall School. In passing, perhaps it is only right to say that the school was named more for the red cliffs of clay upon which it was built than for any other reason. Brunton-on-Sea possesses the only seam of red clay in Sussex.

"Here I am, Miss Lipscoomb," said Julia thickly, through a lump of chewing-gum.

"Daughter of Peter Bracewood-Smith, the son of the explorer, you know," explained Miss Lipscoomb in a quick undertone. "Just come back from Spain, the child has. Her father writes detective stories. Hurt her leg."

Julia limped towards them, chewing and scowling. She was a nasty sight.

"I have read them," said Natasha gravely, turning to Miriam. "The last one was being about a French governess who was being strangled in Paris, half-way up the Eiffel Tower. I was enjoying it. It was called *Death and the French Governess* . . . I will lend it to you," she said.

"Mum loathes detective stories," said Miriam.

"But this is more funny and malicious than detective," said Natasha. "The French governess, she pretends to be a member of the French aristocracy and is as snob as snob——"

"Mum *still* loathes detective stories," said Miriam, and turned her large pale blue eyes on little Julia Bracewood-Smith, who scowled back at her. "*Ugh!*" said Miriam, and shut her eyes.

Their progress to platform 15 and the fast express to Brunton-on-Sea was easy. They were unhampered by anything but Julia, whose shoelace came undone *en route*. When she had tied it she said who was Natasha? She did not, Julia thought, *look* like a schoolmistress.

"These ladies," said Miss Lipscoomb, "are nevertheless members of my staff. They will teach you dancing, dear, and elocution. Miss Birdseye——"

"I've seen Miss Birdseye before," said this odious child, rapidly transferring her chewing-gum from one cheek to the other. "I saw her twice in *Absolutely the End* and once in *Positively the Last*, and Daddy wouldn't take me to *Hips and Haws*—but I *went* just the same with our cook, Emma . . ."

"Good God," said Miriam piously. She turned to Natasha. "I should charge double, dear," she said, "if that child is in our classes."

Julia put out her tongue at Miriam. Miss Lipscoomb, fussing with the porters, did not see her.

"My name is Miss Nevkorina," said Natasha with sudden old-world courtesy. "And I shall teach you dancing when your leg is better. I am Russian."

And she smiled maliciously at Julia, whose mouth slowly fell open to remain fixed in imbecile adoration.

"Yes, thanks," said Julia. "It's all right really," and she kicked one heel against the other. "I like dancing. I danced in Spain. But I *loathe* elocution," she added.

Miss Lipscoomb was well out of earshot, signalling to the Pullman-car attendants. The men in red hats handed their luggage to the Pullman-car attendants (in white jackets). The Pullman car was called *Mabel*. They fell somewhat breathlessly into the *coupé* and Miss Lipscoomb ordered tea for four before anyone could stop her. The train, jiggling, ran slowly over the points out of Victoria. Natasha looked down with horror at the white tablecloth, the red jam, the toast and the little rattling teaspoons. Nothing got on darling Natasha's nerves quicker than little rattling teaspoons.

VII

Even when all the spoons were taken away and nothing else rattled, the journey was still a tiny nightmare. Miss Lipscoomb was apparently determined to bring Julia into all their conversations, and Julia was equally determined to remain out of them and say nothing at all. To please Natasha, Miss Lipscoomb spoke of the ballet (and rhymed it with 'Charlie') and looked upset and schoolboyish when Natasha used an advanced French swear word to describe the activities of Sadler's Wells. By East Croydon an uneasy silence had fallen upon them and Miriam was saying that "Mum's tum wasn't right." By Haywards Heath Julia had stumbled over their feet twice on her way to and from the toilet, and by Cooden Beach it was raining heavily, pattering against the windows with all the maniac intensity of a stage storm.

"A true sou'-wester," said Miss Lipscoomb, sniffing appreciatively at the nice warm air of the *coupé*. "We often have it blowy at Brunton."

Miriam said nothing, but she huddled her shoulders round her ears. Mum's tum evidently was still not *right*. There was a pause while Miss Lipscoomb leant forward to show them the lights of Radcliff Hall which would presently be twinkling on the headland.

"Just like *The Merchant*, Act III, Scene i," said Miss Lipscoomb with a happy laugh, turning as usual to Julia.

"So shines a good deed in a naughty world," said Miriam gloomily. "Suppose you haven't got a prospectus of the school that Natash—er—Miss Nevkorina and I can look at? That would give us some idea."

"For a monologue?" said Julia, under her breath, with a harsh adult laugh.

Miss Lipscoomb looked puzzled.

"But of course," she said. "What a good idea."

And she drew from her gentlemanly brief-case a sheaf of small prospectuses, printed on semi-art paper, with several much-smudged photographs. She dropped them into Natasha's and Miriam's laps. By the time she had finished they had three each.

"Ah," she cried. "We're *in*!"

The train thudded to a stop at a minute station where an oil-lamp called BRUNTON burned fitfully. "Better make haste," called Miss Lipscoomb laughingly over her shoulder. "It only stops here thirty seconds. Miss Zwart was once carried on to Hastings."

And, covered with suitcases, she plunged out of the train.

VIII

The results of their panic flung Miriam and Natasha breathless upon the platform, clutching prospectuses and handbags and very little else. The damp wind promptly twirled their coats open and the sea mist, cold and grey, blew inland over their heads. They said nothing.

"Never mind," said Miss Lipscoomb, coming towards them like an over-enthusiastic spaniel. "You won't have to *hoof* it. Not tonight we won't. We've got a taxi."

Miriam was very quiet climbing into the taxi, clasping her stomach with her two hands. Natasha held her hair down. The taxi creaked a lot and smelt of stale straw and moth-balls.

"Why," asked Miriam suddenly, "has Julia come to school in the middle of the term if she is a new girl?"

"And is she not rather *old*?" said Natasha.

The tall feather on Miriam's hat rasped itself against the roof of the taxi. Finally:

"Her mother died," said Miss Lipscoomb, "in rather sad circumstances this year."

"Oh?" said Miriam, interested. "What were they?"

"I'd rather not say . . ." began Miss Lipscoomb.

Julia Bracewood-Smith turned round from her seat beside the driver.

"Don't be a damned old fool," she said distinctly through her chewing-gum. "She committed suicide," she said chattily to Miriam. "I've just come from the funeral."

CHAPTER TWO

THE taxi stopped at dim buildings in the wet dark. Gravel had crunched under its wheels. They had passed a lodge and driven up about a mile of drive, and on their left they had observed a patch of lighted windows, described by Miss Lipscoomb as 'West House'. Instantly on their right there had been another smaller patch. "Staff wing," said Miss Lipscoomb.

"That means us," said Miriam, and began to shake with laughter.

There was a front door open in the dim building and golden light poured out to show wet, glistening steps and glimmering gravel. Miriam picked her way delicately over it to the front door. The taxi-driver clambered out, and so did Julia Bracewood-Smith. The driver unstrapped luggage. Julia limped up the steps and stood, glowering, in the damp porch. By and by they all joined her, and a small woman bounced out to greet them. She was a neat little figure in a neat little tweed coat and skirt, and she had a complicated hair-do.

"Pleased to meet you," she said, picking up a suitcase. She held out a friendly hand with blood-red fingernails at Natasha. "I'm Miss Phipps, Miss Lipscoomb's secretary."

Miss Phipps had a refined manner and a very slight Cockney accent. She was obviously extremely efficient and mildly contemptuous of Miss Lipscoomb. She went ahead of them, carrying Natasha's heaviest raw-hide suitcase (so she was obviously healthy), and as she went she tossed interjections and information over her shoulder.

"I suppose *that's* Julia Bracewood-Smith," she said.

"Yes," said Julia.

"*You're* to go over to West House," said Miss Phipps, not unkindly. "There's a prefect coming for *you*. Your dad rang up about six and says he'll be over to see you tomorrow. It wouldn't be right tonight when he's so busy with the rehearsals. *Mister* Bracewood-Smith lives in the village," said Miss Phipps, turning to Miriam. "So lucky to have him. So helpful about the staff play, bein' a writer."

Miriam said nothing at all.

"Miss Lipscoomb sent a wire about you both," went on Miss Phipps, "so we've had your beds airing in the staff wing since teatime. I'll take you over directly we've got rid of Julia. Ah, there's Gwen. Gwen, this is Julia Bracewood-Smith. Julia, this is Gwen Soames, the Head of the School."

Gwen Soames, who was a tall girl with a thick red plait and round blue eyes like pebbles, looked down her nose at Julia.

"How do you do?" she said. "We know your father. I hear you've hurt your leg," she went on, with a slight sneer. "How is it?"

Miriam and Natasha waited anxiously to see how Julia would cope with this encounter with a contemporary.

"*Shut up!*" said Julia passionately.

II

Miss Phipps hurried Natasha and Miriam away, as well she might. Clutching their prospectuses and their smaller suitcases, they followed her. Natasha began to lose her sense of humour as she wondered what sort of bed and what sort of room she would have to sleep in. The way to the staff wing was through a soaking-wet sunk garden. Even in the dark, Miriam thought, she could discern plaster dwarfs and plaster children lurching round plaster bird-baths. Natasha heard childish voices singing out of tune and the thump of a piano. Miriam swung along like a race-horse, far too fast for Miss Phipps, who had to trot to keep up with them.

The staff wing was a small red-brick house of two storeys. In the daylight, aggressively furnished with bright folk-weave and hessian and reproductions of Paul Henry's nasty Irish mountains and skies and beastly white cottages, it seemed, apart from a firm smell of Ronuk, almost cheerful. Tonight, with the windows battened against the storm and soaking wet towels lying on every window-ledge, it seemed to Natasha and Miriam just like a *crèche*. A *crèche* was the nastiest thing that darling Natasha could ever imagine.

They stood in the red-brick hall and Miriam stroked her nose and looked puzzled. Miss Phipps jumped up and down, trying to reach some latchkeys that swung dismally on a green-baize notice-board.

"Here, Miss Phipps, let *me*," said a man's voice behind them. Miriam and Natasha were surprised. The surroundings were not right for the male. An enormous man with a full black beard like a pirate reached over Miss Phipps' head and handed down the latchkeys.

"Oh, thank you, Mister Bracewood-Smith!" said Miss Phipps, flustered. "This is——"

"Miss Birdseye and Miss Nevkorina," said Natasha, slowly but firmly.

"I've been rehearsing," said Mr. Bracewood-Smith easily. "In the gymnasium. The staff play."

"*Quality Street*," said Miriam, with gleaming eyes.

"Ah . . ." said Mr. Bracewood-Smith, and bowed. "You know it, ma'am. The whimsies of the late Sir James Barrie make that instant appeal to mothers and daughters which is so desirable. No offence in the world, ma'am, and only a very little out of it."

Natasha stared at this curious man whose wife had just committed suicide, who chose, on a wet night, to come all the way from his snug hearth to rehearse a childish play with a lot of middle-aged spinsters. He wore a velveteen jacket (like a gamekeeper) and grey flannel trousers held up by a strap. The trousers seemed to have slipped very low. 'Perhaps he may be collecting material for his books,' thought Natasha. She flung back a lock of well-brushed hair and stared at him. She thought he seemed fat.

Peter Bracewood-Smith (author of *Death and the Archbishop*, 68,000, and *Death and the French Governess*, 9,000, and *Love and Murder*, 5,000) put his hands in his trousers pockets and looked back appraisingly. Natasha's artless, well-groomed beauty pleased him. A flame of interest leapt into his bold yellow eyes.

"I have been reading a *book* of yours," said Natasha, in her slow, childish voice. "I have been enjoying it so *much*. Your characters are *splendid* for a thriller. One can actually tell one from another."

The flame in Mr. Bracewood-Smith's eyes flickered and began to burn more steadily.

"Ma'am," he said gravely, with an ironic bow, "I am honoured. Shall I see more of you?"

"I do not know," said Natasha. "I am to teach dancing."

"Well . . ." said Peter Bracewood-Smith, astonished.

Miss Phipps remarked that the bedrooms were above and began to lead the way upstairs. Mr. Bracewood-Smith remained by the green-baize board, his hands still in his pockets, his mouth slightly open, the tip of his pink tongue showing between his white teeth amongst his beard.

"He's awfully nice," said Miss Phipps, shaking her hair-do a little out of place. "Since *he* came to help with the play there's never been a dull moment."

Natasha could well believe it.

"Now here," said Miss Phipps, flinging open an unstained oak door, "is your bedroom. Miss Tutt, the last dancing mistress, had it. She left that picture behind her."

Natasha looked over her shoulder and saw some Dègas girls at the practice-bar. This was over the gas-fire. There was a low, camouflaged folk-weave bed, cunningly concealed behind a folk-weave curtain in an alcove. There was a small wash-hand basin behind the curtain, too, and a milking-stool, painted white. There was a radiator that indicated central heating, another milking-stool and a bookshelf and a bureau of unstained oak. The windows were latticed and tight shut. Beneath them, already wet and dripping, were the inevitable towels. The gale flung itself unabated against the windows and they shuddered.

Miriam's room was the exact counterpart of Natasha's, except that everything that with Natasha was on the right was here on the left, and, instead of the Dègas dancing girls, there was *The Lark* by Van Gogh.

"Yes," said Natasha, looking round Miriam's room, "with the gas-fires lit we may be quite *cosy*. . . ."

"I find the central heating quite enough in *my* office," said Miss Phipps, pinning up a curl. "Ah well. I must be off. Lists to type. Dinner at 7.30 in the hall of East House. Anyone'll show you the way. Good night, all."

"Why, don't you live here?" said Miriam, a little desperately.

"Oh no," said Miss Phipps. "I dig in the village." And she hurried out and shut Miriam's door behind her.

III

Miriam sat down on a milking-stool and lit the gas-fire. It roared steadily for a minute or two and then settled to a steady purr. Soon the little room began to feel less damp.

"Let's read those pamphlets or whatever they're called," said Miriam. "There seem to be three. One with a picture of Mine Host side by side with the lamented Miss bbirch. . . ."

"Look at her amber *beads*," said Natasha.

"And one that starts 'The school is situated five minutes from the sea and ten or even twelve from the station', and one called 'Religious Services'. The second seems most relevant. Let's do that one first."

Miriam spread the prospectus on the floor and they read it together, occasionally pausing to giggle and say, "Don't understand, don't understand, don't understand" (Miriam), or "What are Gentlepeople? Do you know any?" (Natasha).

The prospectus went like this:

> The school is situated five minutes from the sea, and ten or even twelve from the railway station. It is a fine building (designed by the late William J. Locke) and carried out in red brick and Portland stone. It is a private school of the finest type, run by gentlepeople for gentlepeople, and public spirit is our motto.
>
> In addition to lawn tennis (which we play on our own lawn-tennis courts) and netball (on our own netball pitch), we can play hockey (on the Haberdashers' Usk School pitch, 20 mins.) and cricket in the summer. There are splendid opportunities for rambling, hiking, swimming and trout fishing, and in addition leather-work classes are conducted in the village by Mr. Bracewood-Smith.

(The last line had been heavily scored through by Miss Lipscoomb, who had written in, in ink, 'Substitute *Beekeeping and Knitting Classes, The Women's Institute*.')

> All subjects are taken up to School Certificate and University Entrance standard. The staff are fully qualified, most competent gentlewomen. The matron, Mrs. Grossbody, is a trained nurse and can deal with all aspects of health.

Then there was a list of the staff and their subjects:

English, Classics, History.	MISS HILDA ZWART, M.A. (LOND.).
French, German, European Literature, Spanish.	{ MISS THERESA DEVALOYS, B.A. (Oxon.).
Scripture, Gymnastics, Fencing.	THE HON. MISS JANET LIPSCOOMB (Dartford P.T.C.).
Chemistry, Biology.	MISS FORK-THOMAS, B.Sc. (Llandudno).
Classics.	MISS PUKE, B.A. (Reading).
Mathematics.	MISS LESARUM, B.A. (Oxon).
Dancing.	MISS TUTT.
Elocution and Drama.	MISS SPAWN, R.A.D.A.

"Miss Tutt and Miss Spawn," said Miriam, looking at herself in the glass and tossing back her mane of long, dry hair. "Oh, well. I suppose some people think Birdseye is a funny name."

"Oh *no*, Miriam," said Natasha politely. "Now let us read that one with the pictures of Miss Lipscoomb and Miss bbirch on it. Miss Lipscoomb is a very fine character, I think, because she is making me feel so tired already."

The prospectus with the portraits of Miss Helena bbirch in amber beads and Miss Lipscoomb dressed as a gym mistress holding a net ball said that Miss Lipscoomb was the younger daughter of the Baron Lipscoomb (cre. 1917) of Radcliff, Sussex. She had inherited the Hall on her father's death and had turned it into a school with the help of her friend and partner, Miss bbirch.

"You *can* tell them apart, can't you, dear?" said Miriam, looking at their pictures with her head on one side.

It had been formed in 1931 and had flourished ever since. In '37 an old Radcliff girl had swum the Channel. In '38 another had represented Poland in the Olympic Games. In the war no less than *fifteen* Old Girls had been killed in action. . . .

"At the same time?" asked Miriam, with her mouth open. "They do get about, don't they?"

"I do not know, it does not say," said Natasha. "And here is a little map of the grounds."

"That's what we want," said Miriam. "Mum's tum may not be *right*, but Mum is hungry."

At that moment there came a light, ironic knock on the door and a sweet and extraordinarily well-modulated voice said:

"Are you the two new members of the staff? Can I come in? Theresa Devaloys here."

IV

Theresa Devaloys proved to be a miniature pink-and-white model of a woman with a neat cat's face and hair cut in a fringe as for the 1920s. Her clothes inclined to frills and she wore *crêpe* taffeta blouses with little pleated fronts. Her feet also were tiny, and she was obviously proud of them. She sat on the edge of the bed and looked at Miriam quizzically. Then she looked at Natasha. Then she spoke.

"You don't," she said, "*look* like young and inexperienced teachers."

"We *aren't*," said Miriam, with a hideous leer.

"And neither, if I may be saying so, do you," said Natasha.

Miss Devaloys fingered her eyelashes and some mascara came off on her finger and thumb.

"I have the true teacher's vocation," said Miss Devaloys. It was impossible to tell whether she meant it or not. Her vowel sounds were curiously strangled, particularly her 'a's'.

"No," said Natasha gravely. "How *wonderful*."

"I was intended," said Miss Devaloys, "for a life of frivolous uselessness, but my family suffocated me with affection, so I took a position in the Ministry of Labour."

"So what?" said Miriam very quietly, and was not heard.

"And there I sat in a draught, and *then* I took my degree because my face had gone all frozen and I was *useless* for frivolity and I became teacher." There was a pause. "I like it," said Miss Devaloys, and put her doll-like head on one side.

"Sat in a draught?" said Miriam. "How awful. I sat in a draught once and got shingles."

"Your face is being all right," said Natasha doubtfully. "In fact it is quite pretty."

And so it was, in a queer sort of way.

"When I am excited," said Miss Devaloys, laughing, "one side of my mouth doesn't work."

Miriam looked at her for a minute or two and then said:
"Do you *get* much excitement in Brunton-on-Sea?"

"I make it," said Miss Devaloys, with a little tinkling laugh.
"I make it."

And she swung her feet back and forwards and sprang off
Miriam's bed with a rapid snake-like movement.

"The girls," said Miss Devaloys, "who *usually* come to Radcliff
Hall as dancing and elocution teachers are young and inexperienced. It is usually their first job after college, and some of the
poor dears are expected to teach needlework and sewing and
crochet, too."

There was a pause. Somehow Miss Devaloys sounded disappointed.

V

Nevertheless she conducted Natasha and Miriam through the
sunk garden towards East House. Miriam stubbed her toe in the
dark and swore, using a brief stock epithet much in use round
Seven Dials. In the dark, near them, Miss Devaloys giggled.

"It must be one of those concrete dwarfs," snarled
Miriam.

"But it *is*," said Miss Devaloys. "How did you guess? And
there are horrible little bird-baths with false stone birds on the
edge, and there are coloured gnomes peeping among the flowers."

"Who could it be who chose such things?" said Natasha.

"Why, who but *dear* Miss bbirch?" said Miss Devaloys. Her
silvery and malicious tones rang through the dark. "I wonder
she didn't take them with her."

"Too heavy," said Miriam shortly. Miss Devaloys' silvery
laugh rang out like a peal of little bells.

"Much more of *this*," said Miriam in Natasha's ear, "and little
Fairy Evil Thoughts will begin to get on my nerves."

On the drive in front of the door they met the heavy bearded
figure of Peter Bracewood-Smith once again. The light flashed
behind him for a second as he opened and shut the front door. It
lit up Miss Devaloys. He came forward and said:

"Ah, good, Theresa, I've been waiting for you. Can you
spare me a minute?"

Miriam and Natasha hurried on up the steps into the front hall of East House. Miriam carried her little map in her hand, and from time to time she consulted it.

"This is where we are, dear," she said, turning to Natasha; "look."

Maps meant nothing to Natasha and she said so.

There was a confused noise and trampling overhead. A dinner-bell rang, and the hall slowly filled with girls of varying shapes and sizes dressed in purple. They formed two silent lines. Some-one, evidently a prefect, called, "Silence there, you, you new kid!" and someone sobbed. Miriam hoped it was Julia Bracewood-Smith, but thought not.

The odious Gwen Soames came bullying down the line, her thick red plait bouncing behind her, her round eyes shining with authority.

"Yet," said Natasha, "I am seeing the point. If all these dear children were to be talking it would be hell's own delight."

Miriam said she thought so too.

"The staff dining-hall is in the centre of Main Hall," said Gwen Soames to them severely. "You can't miss it."

Rebuked, Miriam and Natasha hurried on. They passed the lines of waiting girls and came into a tall, bleak room with places for about seventy girls at ten tables of seven each. In the middle of the room, as Gwen Soames had said, was the high table for ten people. It was subtly different from the others, because there were pots of jam and special meat paste on it in neat piles, evidence of the existence of spinsters. All the tables were furnished with red-and-white checked runners and black bowls of marigolds. They were pretty nasty.

"Just the job," murmured Miriam, under her breath.

It speaks a great deal for the golden-hearted courage of this great figure of the English theatre that only at the smell of boiled mutton did she quail. She quailed now, as a vague smell of cabbage filtered in past the mutton. The room as yet was innocent of other human beings, but there was a dry bread crust under a chair left from lunch. Steadily tramping feet on the other side of the door grew louder.

"Miriam," said Natasha suddenly, "I am going away. Back to London."

"*Craven*," said Miriam. "Why, *anything* may happen."

It did.

Another door on their right burst open, and an exquisite young man with golden hair minced in. He was wearing a ginger tweed coat and a pair of whipcord trousers, and he had on a neat bow tie. He stood for a second aghast, staring from Miriam to Natasha and back again with a wild surmise. Then with a great cry he flung himself on Miriam.

"Goodness," he said, when they had embraced, *"what are you doing here?"*

"Roger Partick-Thistle," said Miriam. "This is Mrs. DuVivien."

"We are old friends," said Roger. "We met in Schizo-Frenia."[1]

Natasha remembered him and his friend Morris only too well.

"I am to teach these limbs of Belial English verse and how to speak it," said Miriam.

"Do you know any?" said Roger, and giggled.

"I know *Caviare comes from the Virgin Sturgeon*," said Miriam severely. "What are you doing here?"

"Miss Lipscoomb is my aunt, actually," said Roger, bridling. "But as a matter of fact, dear, I don't spend my whole *life* in your dressing-room. I'm the visiting music-master. I teach the *organ*."

And Roger leered.

At this moment, with a terrible clattering of feet, chairs, tables, knives, cups, swords and wands, the whole of East House crashed into the dining-room through one door and the whole of the staff of Radcliff Hall through the other. The girls came silently, but with flashing eyes and slavering lips. They were hungry. The staff came reluctantly, with lowered heads and their hands clasped in front of them in the old army 'At Ease' position. They were not hungry.

Here came Theresa Devaloys, with a wicked gleam in one eye, raking the ranks of children to torment them as she passed. And here was dark Miss Zwart, the English mistress, in glasses, carrying a copy of T. S. Eliot to prove her culture, in class and out of it. Here came Miss Fork-Thomas, the Welsh chemist. She had long bobbed golden hair like her own spaniel, or perhaps like Elizabeth Barret Browning. In the distance Winston Churchill, her spaniel, could be heard moaning and screaming, tied to the door handle. Finally, in an incongruous red dinner-gown that

[1] *Death Goes On Skis.*

fitted only where it touched, came Miss Lipscoomb, with a Bible to say grace.

She said grace.

And instantly, like the roaring of beasts loose after weeks of captivity, the snarling and worrying sounds of young English gentlewomen eating rissoles and bread-and-margarine filled the dining-room. Natasha clapped her hands to her ears. The whole thing was quite new to her. Miriam looked surprised.

"*I was expecting it to be boiled mutton!*" screamed Miriam to Roger Partick-Thistle. Miss Lipscoomb struck a hand-bell by her side. A hush prevailed. Roger was heard saying in a sibilant whisper:

"We had the mutton *days* ago. This is the last of it——"

"If anyone," said Miss Lipscoomb sharply, rising to her feet, "speaks above a whisper for the next ten minutes, the prefects have permission to tell them to *leave the room*."

There was silence for a second and then the noise began again. Sometimes discipline exploded and a hungry child would leave the room weeping. Eventually the rissoles were eaten and comparative peace descended.

"Tell me," said Roger to Natasha. "Why are you here?"

"Dancing," said Natasha briefly. "The rest takes too long to tell. Afterwards. In Miriam's room."

"Oh!" said Roger, surprised. "You left that nice dull husband of yours, then?"

"He was not being *really* dull," said Natasha. "But it was best. For a little while."

"He must miss you," said Roger politely.

"Oh, he does," said Natasha.

Miriam leant across Roger.

"Shut up, you two," she said. "I want to get all the dirt from Roger *afterwards*. Don't make these women suspicious. . . ."

And indeed Miss Fork-Thomas, who sat opposite, was giving a demonstration of ill-concealed curiosity as to why the head mistress's nephew should know these two new mistresses.

"Talk to that awful woman on your *other* side," said Miriam. "The one who looks like an ape."

Natasha turned her lovely head and observed Miss Zwart. She was trying to put a slice of bread and half a rissole and some cocoa in her mouth all at once. She gave them a swift poke with a fork and they all disappeared.

"Lor'!" said Roger, who had also been watching.

Natasha turned away from him and addressed Miss Zwart, who was chewing hard.

"You are reading a thriller, I can see," said Natasha cosily. "*Murder in the* something." Miss Zwart chewed and chewed and was unable to reply. "Is it a nice book?" said Natasha. "Who is the author? Are you enjoying it?"

There was a long pause of annihilating excitement while Miss Zwart swallowed everything that was in her mouth and reached for some more cocoa. She gulped a little and then spoke.

"I don't know what you mean by 'enjoy'," she said coldly, in intellectual tones. "And it is not a thriller in the accepted sense."

Natasha considered Miss Zwart with her head on one side and her clear hazel eyes like pools.

"I expect I am meaning 'funny'," said Natasha. "Is it funny?"

"What do you mean by f——" said Miss Zwart, and then checked herself. "It is *Murder in the Cathedral*, by T. S. Eliot."

Natasha laughed merrily and Miss Zwart was affronted.

"Is that what you mean by 'funny'?" said Miss Zwart.

"Please do not mind me," said Natasha. "I saw the word *Murder*, that is all," and she went on laughing.

After a time Miss Zwart grinned uneasily, but she did not join in. Then she asked Natasha to pass her some salt and looked around her for another rissole.

"Have you been here long?" said Natasha.

"I am not an old girl," said Miss Zwart suspiciously. "I was educated at a very good high school in Birmingham."

"I did not expect . . ." began Natasha. "*No*. What I wonder is how long you have been a member of the staff of Radcliff Hall."

Miss Zwart considered.

"I came here straight from college," she said. "I was assistant to Miss Pryce-Clark, the senior mistress, until a fortnight ago, when she left because——" She stopped, and then went on, "When she left."

"But your name is on the prospectus in print," said Natasha. "I have just seen it."

"Oh, is it?" said Miss Zwart, in innocent, girlish pleasure. "I heard Miss Lipscoomb was having it done. I should like to see that."

"I will show you," said Natasha, watching the shovelling movements that Miss Zwart made with the fork. "I will show

27

you now," added Natasha, "if you will tell me why Miss Clark left."

VI

"It was the drawings," said Miss Zwart. "The drawings of her and Doctor Lariat."

A plate of pink jelly and some prunes arrived in front of Natasha.

"How very nasty," said Natasha, stirring them with a fork and looking at them curiously. "What are they, do you suppose? And who is Doctor Lariat?"

"School doctor," said Miss Zwart. "You'll soon meet him. Don't you want your prunes?"

"It seems that they might be doing some good as *missiles*," said Natasha doubtfully. "Why? Are you wanting them?"

Miss Zwart said she was, and the plate changed hands, while Roger Partick-Thistle raised his eyebrows and said he did not care for persons who threw food about. Miss Zwart then ate the prunes.

"Doctor Lariat," said Natasha clearly.

Miss Fork-Thomas leaned forward, a lock of golden hair falling into her eye.

"The doctor," she said. "Do you know him too, then?"

"Why, no," said Natasha mildly. "I was told that he has been knowing the English mistress."

Miss Fork-Thomas smiled in a sophisticated manner and Natasha decided there was too large a proportion of knowledgeable adults on the staff. Miss Devaloys was an adult, even if she looked like a vicious child, and Miss Fork-Thomas also seemed to be an adult. It was disconcerting. In Natasha's experience school-teachers were innocent, childlike persons. Like Miss Lipscoomb, she added to herself, and glanced up the table at the head mistress, who was talking quite gaily to Miriam and Miss Devaloys.

"Of course," said Miss Devaloys, in explanation to Miriam, who had just suggested that Devaloys might be a Huguenot name, "I have royal blood in my veins. It is a corruption of De Valois, and not a Huguenot name at all."

"Oh, I see," said Miriam.

"I always find names so fascinating, don't you?" said Miss Lipscoomb.

"*Lariat*," said Natasha loudly. "Now *there* is a silly name."

"Oh," said Miss Lipscoomb furtively, looking down at her plate, "I suppose it is. . . ."

She seemed disinclined to discuss Doctor Lariat. And at that moment the light went out.

VII

The darkness was overwhelming and most frightening. Several of the younger girls began to scream. Only Gwen Soames kept her head and went to the fuse-box, and Miriam (who had stolen a large electric torch that she had seen lying in the hall) flashed it round her now. Someone had turned on the urns and the floor was running with red-hot cocoa. There was a strange apparatus in the fuse-box made of string and chewing-gum. It was something constructed by a clever, vicious child, perhaps. Or someone with a mind like one.

"*Who turned on the urns?*" cried Miss Lipscoomb in a terrible voice.

No one replied. It was a good hour before order was restored to the dining-room. Shaking with rage and emotion, Miss Lipscoomb led the way to her chintz sitting-room and here, sitting on the piano-stool, she addressed the staff.

"You see," she said, turning to Natasha and Miriam, "what I meant? It goes on *all the time. Lights* turned off in the middle of supper. It's . . ."—she groped for a word—"*dastardly*," she ended triumphantly.

"You don't suppose a fuse . . ." said Miss Fork-Thomas.

"Or a child . . ." suggested Natasha.

"Impossible!" snapped Miss Lipscoomb. "And little Daisy Stuckenheimer in IVв *parboiled*. This is the work of a fiend, not a child."

"Children are fiends, children are fiends," murmured Miriam under her breath.

"I think so, too," said Miss Zwart in a low voice. She had profited by the confusion and was eating a large slice of bread-and-butter. She was also covertly looking at her name in the school prospectus.

Only Roger Partick-Thistle retained true gaiety of manner, and much of this was due to the fact that he had borrowed his aunt's newly-worked-out time-table. Miriam had a full morning's work ahead of her on the morrow, he pointed out.

" 'Shakespeare and declamation, the VIth, 1st period. Verse-speaking and breathing, Upper IVA, 2nd period. The Junior School, last period,' " he read out mockingly. "How do you breathe verse, Natasha?" he added, turning to her.

"But you *must* have been listening to the Third Programme," said Natasha. "An intellectual boy like you. I think these persecutions at your aunt, poor Miss Lipscoomb, so offully serious. How long are they going on for nowadays?"

"Most of this term, dear," said Roger lightly. "I liked the sexy drawings, I must say. That was a good bit. Pity you missed that." He lowered his voice. "I think Miss Devaloys is responsible for the whole *thing*," he said.

"Why?" said Miriam sharply. "What makes you think that?"

"Well, dear, she's always so *pleased* when anything like this happens. Look at her now."

"But so are you," said Miriam sharply. "You're both just malicious, that's all."

But she looked at Miss Devaloys, who indeed was smiling all over her little face. As though compelled by Roger's personal magnetism, she looked up, caught his eye and crossed the room to talk to him.

"Ah, you bad boy!" she said, with a ripple of little silver bells. "Not wanting to play Ensign Blades. Making poor Miss Lesarum dress up in men's clothes."

"There's nothing she likes better," said Roger, "and I thought she was playing Valentine Brown."

"Who is Miss Lesarum?" said Natasha instantly.

"Teaches mathematics," said Miss Devaloys. "She's a half-caste."

"Oh, I say," said Roger, "that really goes too far. She's——"

"Certainly not white," said Miss Devaloys. "My dear boy, she looks like a West African native. *And* she's as queer as a coot."

"Well, dear," said Roger tartly, "there are coots *and* coots."

"Where is she today?" said Natasha, hoping to pour oil upon the argument. She did so most effectively. It burst into flame.

"With her Girl Guides," said Miss Devaloys finally, and that was that.

"I suppose," said Miriam, regarding Miss Devaloys with wary interest, "that you are playing Miss Phoebe? In *Quality Street*."

"Yes," said Miss Devaloys, inclining her head. "Peter Bracewood-Smith is producing."

"We are travelling down with his kiddy Julia in the train today," said Natasha, in her slow, soft, pedantic voice.

"What's she like?" said Miss Devaloys instantly.

"My dear, too awful," said Miriam, and Miss Devaloys roared with laughter. She did not sound one little bit like a peal of bells.

"Well, then," said Miriam, when Miss Devaloys had hushed, "if the wretched Miss Lesarum may not slap her thigh at you, who is your Valentine Brown?"

A parlourmaid came into the room and passed among them handing weak cups of cold coffee on a tray. To Natasha's astonishment Miss Devaloys blinked and jumped and blushed and spilt her coffee before she replied, in a meek little voice, "Doctor Lariat."

By the time that Miss Devaloys had recovered herself and had moved on to Miss Zwart, discussing little Daisy Stuckenheimer's burns, Miriam's tum was very far from right. She was wildly hungry.

"Thistle," she said to Roger, "is there a hotel near here where we can get a decent meal?"

Miss Devaloys asked Miss Zwart if she had been to see the plays given by the Company of Four at Hammersmith, and Miss Zwart said that Jean-Paul Sartre was the direct outcome of dialectic materialism.

"Yes," said Roger, without hesitation. "I'll drive you there."

"I want dinner," said Miriam, "and I'll pay for it."

Miss Zwart asked Miss Devaloys what she thought of *The Respectable Prostitute* and Miss Devaloys said did she mean *The Obedient Whore*.

"Pick you up outside the front door in two minutes' time," said Roger, and then in a louder tone: "Good night, Auntie."

He flung back his lock of golden hair (almost as long and golden as Miss Fork-Thomas's own) and Miss Lipscoomb looked up.

"Goin', Rodgy?" she said fondly. "Don't forget the choir practice tomorrow afternoon."

"No, Aunt Janet, I won't," said Roger, shamefaced.

"Rehearsal for Founders' Day," explained Miss Lipscoomb, turning to Natasha. "That will be at half term. We're all *very* busy preparing for it. I do hope it goes off well," added Miss Lipscoomb, with a little sigh.

"Oh, it shall, Miss Lipscoomb, it *shall*," said dear Natasha, and really meant it.

CHAPTER THREE

THEY drove briskly into Brunton-on-Sea, sitting upright in Roger's Austin Seven, petrol for which was allowed for educational purposes. They were unalarmed by anything on the wet dark drive except a leaf that blew against the wind-screen and an apparition that fled before them howling like a wolf. It wore a black slouched hat and a loose dark cloak, and was obviously Miss Lesarum saying good night to her Girl Guide patrol.

Roger drew up outside a hotel that seemed pleasant enough. "The Brunton," he said over his shoulder, turning off the engine. He opened the bonnet and removed the contact arm of the ignition. Then he ran ahead of them up the steps, his trousers flapping in the damp west wind. Natasha and Miriam followed, Miriam clutching her hat.

There was a clean white-and-red hall, with painted sofas and decent carpets. There was a dining-room vaguely discernible beyond an office, and a cosy barman's pantry. In the hall on one of the sofas, holding the hands of a young woman, was a stoutish, handsome young Jew. As they passed him, he said to her in thick, sobbing tones:

"But if you *allow* me to hold your beautiful hands and then perhaps to *caress* your beautiful——" He looked up as Roger passed, and the girl seemed displeased. "Hullo, Thistle," he said, in a quite-ordinary voice. Yet such was the respectability of Brunton-on-Sea that young Doctor Lariat only had a reputation for flirting.

"Hullo," said Roger, and then, with a slight pause, "Lariat."

He turned to Natasha to see if she had got the point. She had, and so had Miriam, so Roger hurried them on into the dining-room. As they went they could hear Doctor Lariat, with a return to his former manner, saying:

"I would have everyone *naked*, naked as dawn, nude as dew, fresh and untrammelled as morning itself."

"*Not* a very beautiful morning," said Miriam, and this for some reason convulsed our party. A waiter came towards them, and after some difficulty they succeeded in ordering pigeon pie and cabbage and mashed potatoes and apple pudding. He thought they were laughing at *him*. Miriam ate it all far too fast, without chewing, and the coffee came. It was about as bad as the coffee they had left behind them.

"Now, Miriam," said Roger, after an abortive attempt to obtain cheese, "why are you here?"

Miriam explained and Natasha interrupted whenever she began to exaggerate, but even so Roger found their story hard to believe. It was, after all, a little odd.

"But, Miriam . . ." he said. "*You* as a school-teacher. Shall you be yourself? Or shall you dress for it, dear? I mean in locknit jumper suits and that kind of thing?"

"I *might* wear a raffia hat and do a monologue," said Miriam. "Those children might not see the difference. A monologue on 'Speech'." There was a pause while Miriam considered herself and Roger began to giggle. "Yes. 'The v'owels are most important. And so, of course, are the con-sonants . . .'," she began in careful, experimental tones. She went on extemporizing brilliantly. Then they were interrupted.

Peter Bracewood-Smith, carrying a bottle of champagne under each arm, came storming towards them, his beard flowing behind him like that of the late W. G. Grace.

"Is one of you ladies Miss Miriam Birdseye?" he began passionately.

Miriam looked up, astonished.

"What*ever* is the matter, dear?" said Roger coolly, to Bracewood-Smith. "Why do you want to know?"

"I hear she insulted my daughter!" cried Bracewood-Smith explosively. "That is why. Said she was awful, sir. And I'll not stand for it, madam."

"Why, certainly not," said Roger, keeping his head admirably. "Now tell me, dear Othello, I bet that Miss Devaloys told you this."

"Why do you call me Othello, sir?" said Peter Bracewood-Smith. But he had seen Natasha and his temper became less fierce.

Natasha shook her head and murmured, "Pol Roger '29 is being my favourite thing," and Bracewood-Smith looked down at the tinfoil on the neck of the bottles complacently.

"No, no," he said. "You can't put me off. *Are* you Miss Birdseye? Did you say this about my daughter, and why do you call me Othello?"

"Because you are so ready to swallow any old lie told by anyone," said Roger. "Really, dear, some of you writers *are* stupid. What happened *was* that Natasha here said she travelled to Brunton with your charming daughter, and Miss Devaloys said she betted that she was awful. That is all. I heard the whole thing."

"And that is *right*," said Natasha. "Miss Devaloys is quite insulting." Natasha opened her eyes very wide. "It is not right the things she said."

"Goodness," said Roger, quickly and passionately. "What trouble that woman causes."

Peter Bracewood-Smith was pensive. A vein in the middle of his forehead pulsed and swelled as his temper slowly died. "I owe you an apology, madam," he said to Miriam. "Will you join me, perhaps, in a glass of champagne?"

And the merry pop of the cork and the foaming of the champagne into the glasses filled the next ten minutes in the agreeable way that champagne is inclined to do. Miriam's tum, as she now explained in childish tones, was now *quite* all right. Everyone became gay quite suddenly.

"Do you believe Miss Lipscoomb is being persecuted?" said Miriam earnestly. "She said she *thought* she was, after supper tonight."

"Why?" said Bracewood-Smith. "What happened at supper?"

"Someone turned the electric light out at the main," said Roger. "We thought it was a fuel cut at first. I'm surprised your chum Miss Devaloys didn't tell you when she made up that story about poor Miriam."

"I don't suppose she'd bother, sir," said Bracewood-Smith, "as she did it herself."

II

"But how do you *know*?" said Miriam, and "My poor *aunt*," said Roger, and "She ought to be being *stopped*," said Natasha.

"Lariat told me as I came in just now," said Bracewood-Smith. "*He* thought it was rather funny."

"Who was the girl with Lariat?" said Roger.

"Don't know, sir," said Bracewood-Smith. "And I don't suppose he does either."

"But some child is being *parboiled*," said Natasha. "From the urns. And it is all Miss Devaloys' fault."

"As if you cared," said Miriam.

"Well, Lariat said that she told him she was going to," insisted Bracewood-Smith. "They're very thick, you know." For a minute his lustful, yellow eyes looked puzzled under their great shaggy eyebrows. "*What* a menace she is," he said. "It's all because of that damned *Quality Street*, if you will forgive me, mesdames." He bowed gravely to Natasha and Miriam in turn.

"I have heard the expression," said Miriam gravely.

Mr. Bracewood-Smith laughed and poured out more champagne. No one attempted to follow his reasoning, or lack of it.

"Miss Lipscoomb must be told," cried Roger, who perhaps enjoyed making a little trouble himself. "I will drive these ladies back to the school and tell her. When is the dress rehearsal of your play? Nothing, *of course*, must be allowed to interfere with *that*," he said ironically.

"Of course not," said Bracewood-Smith, perfectly seriously. "Not that she's a very good Miss Phoebe," he said dreamily. "Lacks charm."

"When," said Roger patiently, "is the dress rehearsal?"

"Oh, tomorrow," said Bracewood-Smith. "After the choir practice," he added maliciously.

"Never mind that now," said Roger briskly. "My aunt must be told before she is any older."

"Do you suppose Theresa Devaloys was responsible for all the *other* things that happened? Like the drawings? *Lariat* said," Bracewood-Smith seemed to be considering, "that those drawings of him and Miss Pryce-Clark were the work of a maniac. A sex maniac, madam," he ended, looking wistful.

"Well, I expect she is," said Miriam cosily.

"Lariat ought to know," said Roger, and they finished the second bottle of champagne. I would not care to suggest that these ladies and gentlemen were at all drunk, but there is no doubt that they all felt better disposed towards one another as they left the hotel.

"Tell me, Bracewood," said Miriam, linking her arm with his as they stood on the top of the steps. "If you hadn't've met *us*, who would have drunk all that champagne with you, eh?"

"A curious thing about champagne, madam," said Bracewood-Smith, "is that one can usually find someone who does not mind drinking it."

III

Miss Lipscoomb was hurt and angry when they told her how Doctor Lariat had *said* that Miss Devaloys had *said* that she was going to turn out the lights during supper.

"It can't be true," said Miss Lipscoomb, pacing her drawing-room. "Why, she is a B.A. of Oxford University."

There were two chintz armchairs in the drawing-room, faded grey and pink and green. There were a number of good mats and a great many small skins belonging to animals like snow leopards, martens, badgers and skunks. They had all been snared or shot by the late Baron Lipscoomb, and his daughter would not have parted from them for the world. In front of the fire lay Miss Lipscoomb's revolting dog Scharnhorst. He was an angry, self-assertive, barking, worrying rough-haired fox-terrier with bad points. He smelt of fish and was worth, perhaps, fourpence. As Miss Lipscoomb paced and turned and paced, he growled, and Miss Lipscoomb said, "There, there, Scharny!"

"I am afraid it *is* being true," said Natasha. "She is, after all, a trouble maker. *See* what she is doing to poor Mr. Bracewood-Smith this evening about his daughter?"

"But why, *why*?" cried Miss Lipscoomb in a great wail, striking her forehead with clenched fists. "She *knows* what difficulty I am having just now in keeping the ship afloat. And yet *she*, an educated woman, deliberately tries to sink it."

"Perhaps she is standing to gain something by doing it," said Natasha, wrinkling her forehead.

"But I can't believe that anyone would *tell* if they were doing it," said Miriam.

"That is what *I* cannot understand," said Miss Lipscoomb. "It is *dastardly*," she said passionately.

"Well, it seems only right to ask her if it's true," said Miriam. "Why not get her? She can only deny it. I suppose she's in the school somewhere? She saw Mister Bracewood-Smith recently, so we know she isn't with him *now*."

"And anyway," said Natasha, "I do not think that he is *liking* her much."

"Yes," said Miss Lipscoomb obscurely. "You're right. Don't condemn a man till he's down."

She crossed to her brick fireplace (which was carved hopelessly into a motto that said 'OOst Woost Hooms Boost') and rang the bell. Presently a yawning parlourmaid appeared and said:

"Did you want something? I was just going to bed."

The parlourmaid's name was Gertie. She had a thin face and rimless glasses. "I was just going to bed," she repeated.

"Oh yes, please," said Miss Lipscoomb nervously. "Please pop across to staff wing and fetch Miss Devaloys. I want to see her urgently."

"It's pourin' cat and dog," said Gertie. "And I'll catch my death if I pop across."

"*I* will go," said Miriam suddenly.

"That's right," said Gertie chattily. "You two ladies have to pop over there any old how. I sleeps *here*. In the attic."

"I do not know," said Natasha (or could it have been the Pol Roger '29?), "that I am being so wildly interested in the sleeping arrangements of your servants. Nor," she added coldly, "have I ever been *popping* in my life."

"Yer nasty things," said Gertie, and left the room.

IV

Miss Devaloys' room seemed to be furnished entirely by yellow-backed novels by Colette. There was also a bookcase stuffed with André Gide and Proust and Rimbaud. In a low bookcase there was a tall volume of reproductions of lithographs by Toulouse-Lautrec. *Huis-Clos* (by Jean-Paul Sartre) was open on a low stool. A magazine called *The Theatre Underground* was turned back at an article on the effect of opium smoking on our younger playwrights. There was a smell of Turkish cigarettes. The effect was not so much of culture but of decadence. And sitting in front of the fire, smoking, was Miss Devaloys, reading *Quality Street* by Sir J. M. Barrie.

"Well, well," said Miss Devaloys. "Why not come in? What can I show you?"

Natasha, staring over Miriam's shoulder, suddenly said in a nasty tone that she did not much suppose *any*thing that she, Natasha, had not seen before. Miss Devaloys' thin eyebrows drew together in a line and the rouge stood out sharply on her cheeks.

"It is Miss Lipscoomb, the head teacher," went on Natasha, delighted to have penetrated Miss Devaloys' skin, "who is wishing to speak with you so urgently. In her drawing-room," added Natasha, "among the little beast skins."

"Why?" said Miss Devaloys. Her eyes were pale and cold, like fish. 'Perhaps they are most like the skin of *cod* fillet,' thought Natasha. 'Or hake.'

"We don't know," said Miriam. "She didn't say. Why should she?"

"But I tell to you a thing," said Natasha, "that Doctor Lariat has said to more than one person——"

"And we have *heard*," went on Miriam rapidly.

"That you are rigging up that apparatus with chewing-gum and string in the fuse-box for supper," continued Natasha.

"Well, why not?" said Miss Devaloys, yawning and stretching like a cat. "It's precious dull here." Her eyes were no longer cold and fishy. They sparkled with sudden life.

"And they are also saying that it was you who do the drawings. And throw the flowerpot. And grease the stairs. And saw the rope half in two to break Miss Lipscoomb——"

"Well, again, why not?" said Miss Devaloys. "And I'd like to see you prove it. Wait till *you've* been here eight years and then see what sort of pranks you get up to. . . ."

She stood up and put *Quality Street* on the table.

"Forgive me," she said, "if I ask you to leave my room. I rather want to *lock* it."

No words of mine can describe her offensive tone. Miriam flushed and started to speak; but Natasha, whose indifference to human beings was almost pathological, smiled sweetly and managed to imply, in her smile, that there would be nothing in Miss Devaloys' room worth stealing. It was Miss Devaloys' turn to blush, and she did not look pretty. She went clacking away down the passage to the stairs towards Miss Lipscoomb, her neat feet making clatters as she went. The door of her room remained half open behind her.

"*Good*," said Natasha, without hesitation, and in she went. Miriam followed her.

Beyond the French novels, and the works on sex and philosophy, and the cheaply bound modern poets, and the novels of Jane Austen, and *Vanity Fair*, and *The Old Wives' Tale*, and the litter of French exercise-books belonging to Form IV BR, Natasha had discerned a writing-table with a half-finished letter lying on it. She picked up the letter. Miriam looked over her shoulder. It said:

Helena, my dear . . .

"If there is being any more sinister mode of beginning a letter to a girl friend than 'my dear' I am not knowing it," said Natasha, and went on reading.

Helena, my dear,

Half my task is well accomplished and if all continues as I hope soon you may have it all your own way. Charteris, the auctioneer in Brunton, told Philip (that is Lariat, the man I told you of) that the Radcliff Hall School property is worth about £15,000 and some more for the good will, possibly. With your £10,000 and the £6,000 I hope to get from P. we should be, as the Americans say, in the clear.

Lip is absolutely on the hop, my dear, and has brought back two weird sisters from London who teach elocution (yellow cushion, as the children say) and dancing. Or so they are supposed. They are not at all the thing and we won't keep them on here as staff, I think, though that is up to you I suppose. Ose je dit la mienne? One looks like a tart and the other a witch. Perhaps they are Very Fond of Each other? Perhaps I am indiscreet, but life would be intolerable without gossip and gin and you, my dear. Perhaps these two new Teachers are the nucleus of a coven? And P. might be warlock?

"And then there is another piece in French about unnatural

vice," said Natasha, crossly, looking up. "This is truly an awful woman."

"Wonder what is happening with Lip, as she calls her, and where the horrid little thing keeps her gin?" said Miriam, without anger. "I suppose Helena is the fascinating Miss bbirch in the amber bbeads, the *femme fatale*?"

"I suppose this lady Iago will be her new partner in the new venture," said Natasha. "I expect she is being drunk just now, and before dinner too. Then each will betray the other. What hell are women. And in between how do the children get taught?"

"Can't imagine," said Miriam. "Sexy drunken piece." She laid the letter down. "Not that I care for myself as a witch . . ." There was a pause. "Which witch?" she said vaguely, as though it were an echo from the past.

Natasha thought it was cosier to look like a tart.

"Letter readers," she said, "are never reading good of themselves, as we used to say in Vladivostok. Much better, anyway, than an industrialist's mistress."

Miriam went to the window and pulled aside the folk-weave curtains. She looked down on the sunk garden and the dwarfs and bird-baths and gnomes. It had stopped raining and the moon came sailing through the clouds to throw everything in high relief.

"Come back," said Miriam, "to Miss Lipscoomb and see what has been happening."

V

Miss Lipscoomb was in tears and kicking a small skunk skin.

"She said I would be *ruined*," she wailed, "and that I could never run a decent school without Helena bbirch. She said I was *stupid*. She laughed at me. She said I had no humour. And when I tried to give her the sack she said *Quality Street* would be no good without her. And she was perfectly right, confound her."

"So what did you do?" said Miriam.

"I said she could stay till after, and then she sneered at my father and I lost my temper."

A heavy green glass ashtray, broken in five jagged pieces, lay on the cracked hearth to show how moved Miss Lipscoomb had been. The dog, Scharnhorst, crawled out from under the sofa and shook itself.

40

"And she is telling you that you are going mad, I suppose?" said Natasha.

"Yes," said Miss Lipscoomb, and sank into a chair. She put her head in her hands. "I think it is true," she said. "But how did you *know*?"

"*That's* an old one," said Miriam briskly. "I always used to tell my first husband he was going mad," she said. "In the end he *did*," she ended triumphantly. "Did you threaten her much?"

"I said . . ." said Miss Lipscoomb, with her eyes wild and hopeless and her hands suddenly limp and nerveless, "I said I could *kill* her."

She looked at the ashtray and the tile she had cracked with it.

"I am expecting that you could," said Natasha.

CHAPTER FOUR

NATASHA DuVIVIEN woke early the following morning and lay in her bed, warm and moderately comfortable. She listened to some interesting bangs and thumps and clangings. She was unaware of the dawn in the dim unchanging shadows of her alcove. The clanging was the rising-bell? Or the breakfast-bell, perhaps? It went by in the distance, a sound as dismal as church bells, summoning, no doubt, the faithful to *something* or other. It wasn't going to summon Natasha *anywhere*. She crawled disobediently under her sheets.

"I will not go to breakfast with those ladies," she said aloud.

The tumult and the shouting died. No more feet thundered clumsily overhead or past her door. No one came. So Natasha slept.

An hour later she became aware of another stranger, smaller noise (like a little scratching mouse) which slowly filtered through to her ears. And *then* there was a voice, harsh and strident:

"Miss Nevkorina? Is Miss Nevkorina there?"

Natasha came awake gradually, and, as gradually, said, "Yes." There was a pause.

"Well, what are you wanting?" said Natasha finally.

"Please, this is Daisy Stuckenheimer of IVB. We're waiting in the gym for you to teach us dancing."

'Goodness!' thought Natasha.

"Miss Devaloys sent me," began the shrill little voice again. 'She would,' thought Natasha. "It's nearly a quarter past nine," said the voice.

Natasha clambered carefully out of bed, shaking her feet.

"I shall be with you at 9.30," she said. "You are all to run round and round the gym without stopping until I come."

There was a little gasp outside the door.

"Without *stopping*?" said the voice, appalled.

"Without stopping," said Natasha firmly.

II

While she was dressing for IVB, Natasha wondered how much she had already missed of her daily round. Breakfast certainly and, perhaps, morning prayers. Natasha was sorry about morning prayers. She enjoyed people fainting and screaming and throwing fits, and she knew that dramas of this sort always punctuated morning prayers in girls' schools. Her stepdaughter Pamela had told her so. She wondered bleakly about baths as she washed herself all over in cold water. Yes, indeed. So this was the hell of being a school-teacher: the cold dawn, the cold water, the cold peremptory summons to do this or that.

Dragging back the curtains, looking out on a glorious Sussex morning, with navy-blue clouds dispersing round a bright golden sunrise, Natasha recalled the things that had happened to her yesterday. She decided she would make arrangements to live in the Brunton Hotel. Natasha enjoyed a little drama more than anything in the world, but even she felt that Radcliff Hall School had gone *too* far.

That Miss Devaloys was the villainess and that she and Miss bbirch were conspiring to acquire the school was obvious. But where did Doctor Lariat come in ('*There* is a sexy one,' thought Natasha, her mouth twisting. 'I wonder if this Theresa is his mistress'), or Peter Bracewood-Smith ('*How* I am allergic to beards!')? But whether Miss Devaloys suspected Natasha and Miriam of being Not Quite School Teachers was another thing. Miss Devaloys must have noticed Natasha being rude to her. One doesn't miss such things. And it was an unnecessary piece of impertinence to send Daisy Stuckenheimer for her.

Natasha glanced at herself in the looking-glass. She was nearly ready. She looked like a photograph taken for an expensive book on ballet behind the scenes at Sadler's Wells. She had not worn her practice-suit since 1934. She was delighted to see how well it still fitted. 'I have, if anything, *lost* weight,' thought Natasha complacently.

She wore a black tunic and black tights and a scarlet angora sweater that fitted her body like a snakeskin. Weed wide enough to wrap a fairy in. As she pulled on and tied her shoes (which had unblocked toes), Natasha determined to do *very* little dancing.

'How, I ask myself, can I be both teacher and detective?' said Natasha to herself complainingly. But she arrived at the gymnasium at twenty-five to ten and found thirty exhausted children crawling round and round it with their tongues hanging out. Daisy Stuckenheimer, covered with bandages, was bullying them from the platform.

"I am excused dancing, Miss Nevkorina," said Daisy, as Natasha came up to her, "because of my burns."

There was a thin, worried woman at the piano, who now stood up.

"I am Mrs. Pont," she said, standing up. "I am your accompanist."

III

Miriam faced the dawn *quite* differently, but only because she had a chance of looking at the school time-table.

"Declamation of Shakespeare—VIth."

Miriam had not gone to bed at all.

She had turned on her gas-fire and, sitting over it until 5 a.m., she had roughed out an astonishing little lecture called "What a Sixth Form Girl Can *Do* With Shakespeare". From five until six she had thought out gestures to accompany it, and from six until seven (when the first bell had sounded) she had dressed the part. "All of Shakespeare is not *quite* . . ." was a sentence that Miriam was particularly proud of.

Consequently she had walked over to prayers and breakfast in a splendid make-up that epitomized (Miriam thought) Enunciation and Controlled Breathing. She was rather sorry that Natasha was not there to see, for everyone else seemed to take it for granted. It consisted of a low-waisted mauve cardigan, trimmed with yellow worsted flowers, a dark-blue jersey with strings at the neck and a *splendid* shapeless mustard-coloured hairy tweed skirt that she had discovered in a cupboard outside her door. Miriam wondered who it belonged to and thought perhaps Miss Zwart. (She was perfectly right.) Her shoes and stockings had already been used in a revue sketch. She had brought them with her. They had last appeared in a monologue which she had performed in *Absolutely the End* called 'Novelist'. They were size nine and they strapped over the instep and fastened with buttons.

Among the other staff, at breakfast and at prayers, Miriam was quite indistinguishable. She melted among them, in her appalling protective clothing, like an animal in the forest.

Prayers were held in the gymnasium among coiled ropes and littered spring-boards and vaulting-horses of astonishing depravity of design. Miss Lesarum, in a costume so like Miriam's as to make it quite embarrassing, struck a few chords on the piano and the school (purple and white, and rank upon rank of it) burst into a throaty hymn. Miss Lipscoomb (navy-blue gym-tunic) read prayers and Miss Fork-Thomas (quite well-cut and becoming coat frock) read the lesson, and everyone muttered the Lord's Prayer. Julia Bracewood-Smith fainted and Gwen Soames took her out. Miss Lesarum played a very jolly march called 'Sons of the Sea', striking the notes with her putty-coloured wrists held very high, and sang the words under her breath as though she were a tiny bit dotty. Which indeed was the case.

Miriam, looking at Miss Lesarum's thick woolly hair from behind, reminded herself that she must get a black wig for her next revue and push a pencil through it. It is significant of Miriam's reaction to Radcliff Hall School that she was already contemplating a return to the stage. She suddenly glanced up as the music ceased, and realized that the last of the school was disappearing, marching furiously, through the swing doors of the gymnasium. She was standing alone with Miss Lipscoomb on a deserted platform.

"You have the Sixth Form first, Miss Birdseye," said Miss Lipscoomb kindly. "In Room 14. Shall I take you there and introduce you?"

"Take me," said Miriam abruptly. "But do not introduce me. *I* will do that."

44

"Jolly decent of you," said Miss Lipscoomb, "to be entering into the spirit of the thing like this."

"Yes, *isn't* it, dear?" said Miriam.

And so it came about that the first audience to see Miriam Birdseye's monologue, which packed the Diplomat Theatre for five years, from 1948–1953, did not laugh at it at all. They sat silently, cringing away from Gwen Soames or played noughts and crosses in the back row, while Miriam mouthed and gibbered in front of them.

"With Shakespeare," began Miriam, in a high and fluting treble, "you cannot be too careful . . ."

Miss Lipscoomb faded discreetly away from the door. Miriam had looked just like a real school-teacher.

IV

Miss Devaloys, like Natasha, began her day by missing (*a*) breakfast and (*b*) prayers. This was possible because she had nothing to do, officially, until 11 a.m., when she was due to take Gwen Soames and the rest of the Sixth Form for History of French Civilisation. It could hardly have been more of a swindle. Miss Devaloys dictated (in French) a series of essays which she had written many years before for a Swiss newspaper, and Gwen Soames and Company took them down in clear, legible hand-writing. Miss Devaloys did not even bother to correct their dictation.

It was ten o'clock on the morning of February 1st, and the sun glittered on Brunton and the sea beyond it. The roofs of East House and West House twinkled with drops of water left from the storm, the pool of water in the *art nouveau* bird-bath was deeper than it had been yesterday.

Miss Devaloys passed it on her way to the station. She was going to put some money on a horse.

Miss Devaloys, as they say, was a gambler. This morning she was going to put £2 on a double that she had worked out at Newmarket. Mr. Dewster, the stationmaster, who would put money on whenever you asked him, was a nice, companionable, fat man with very little to do. He greeted Miss Devaloys with the politeness that passes (in Sussex) for effusion. He said he had thirteen shillings which Miss Fork-Thomas had won yesterday on a horse called Cottage Pie. Mr. Dewster thought Miss Fork-Thomas ever so charming, too. The money was in an envelope, which Miss Devaloys might be so kind as to deliver. Miss Devaloys said she would, and she was pleased about the thirteen shillings.

"Goin' to stay out noice," said Mr. Dewster, in a rich Sussex accent. Miss Devaloys said she thought so, too, and went on to post her letter to Miss bbirch.

It *did* stay out nice all day, and this was just as well for Theresa Devaloys, for it was the last day she spent alive.

V

Theresa Devaloys always walked with a slight city shuffle, her eyes on the ground, as though she were bored or repelled by her surroundings. Quite often she was thinking of something else. Today, however, as she approached the school buildings, she appraised them as though she were already their part-owner. They did not look too bad in the sunshine. There was East House, with its conservatory flung out like a strong right arm in front of it. There was West House, detached and hideous. And there, in between the two of them, was the staff wing, like a tiny brick bandbox.

A smile that children in the Upper Fifth called 'cynical', and children in the Upper Fourth 'sarcastic', twisted Theresa's mouth as she thought about Miss Lipscoomb. She went to the staff wing to collect her notes. She remembered the envelope for Miss Fork-Thomas in her pocket.

In addition to teaching chemistry, geography, botany, physics, biology, zoology and nature study, Gwylan Fork-Thomas was the house mistress of West House. Her surface was serene and apparently efficient, undisturbed by emotional upheavals. No one would have accused her of inward turmoil or repression. It was even remarkable that she had put some money on Cottage Pie and won thirteen shillings.

Theresa, carrying the thick file called *History of French Civilisation* under one arm, stood in the doorway of her bed-sitting-room and looked at her watch. If she hurried she had time to deliver the thirteen shillings before her class started.

So she hurried through the sunk garden to the steps that led down into Miss Fork-Thomas' sitting-room. She stood in the french windows and her shadow fell ahead of her into the room. There was no one there. But for the lack of beast skins, the furnishings in the room were very like those in Miss Lipscoomb's house. There were a lot of books, modern novels in bright-coloured jackets, plays in uniform bindings, a great long shelf of detective stories. On the table a bowl of pink roses. *Roses* in *February!*

Theresa Devaloys was furious. She came slowly into the room, carrying the soft, chinking envelope in one hand.

"Gwylan!" she called in clear, unfriendly tones. Theresa stood with her head on one side, and her cold eyes jealously raked round Gwylan's cool parlour. The flower studies by Mrs. Fisher Prout, the Marie Laurencin, the tasteful *petit-point* footstool all made her see red.

Theresa never wished Gwylan any harm until this moment. Now she even stopped being glad that she had won thirteen shillings. Roses in February were *quite* out of place in a house mistress's sitting-room. They were *ostentatious*.

There was a visiting-card or something in a little envelope peeping out of the flowers. Perhaps whoever gave them to Gwylan had left them without her knowledge? Funny to leave a card in flowers when they had been arranged. A rich sentimental girl who had a crush for Gwylan? Theresa didn't care for *that*. Rich sentimental girls usually had crushes for Theresa. The elder Stuckenheimer girl, perhaps? Theresa took the card out of its little envelope and looked at it idly.

> *Gwylan, darling heart of gold, it will be all right. Trust me.*
> *Philip.*

Theresa went cold all over. 'Darling heart of gold'—Philip Lariat's name for *her*. Her nerves froze slowly along her arms, up her spine, in the nape of her neck, on the crown of her head. That all ladies were called 'darling heart of gold' by Philip Lariat when he had grown upon intimate terms with them did not occur to Theresa. Her hands shook with fury. She carefully put the card back into the roses and as carefully deposited the plump envelope on the table. There was a pile of letters on the writing-table. The top one, typewritten, was addressed to Miss T. Devaloys,

Staff Wing, Radcliff Hall School, Brunton-on-Sea, Sussex. It took her a good minute and a half to remember who this was.

"Save the cat the trouble of posting it, damn her!" said Theresa.

She slid it into the file called *History of French Civilisation*. She left the drawing-room by the french windows. She read the letter in the sunk garden. It was in Gwylan's hand. She had not bothered to conceal it. It suggested that *she* should leave Philip Lariat alone. It said that Philip really wanted Gwylan, but was too much of a gentleman to say so.

"But this is *pure* Llandudno University," said Theresa, reading it.

It ended, *If you do not leave P. alone, Theresa, it will be the worse for you.*

"Gwylan, heart of gold, everything will be all right, Philip," said Theresa savagely. She kicked at the bird-bath and hurt her toe. "Trust me, indeed. Well!"

Theresa's experience of the fickleness of human beings had been confined, during her thirty-nine years, on the whole to women. So there was a lot of femininity in Philip Lariat, was there? Well, it would be the worse for *him*. Theresa's unpleasant smile, that had in its time annihilated so many unhappy children, threatened the sapphire sky.

"We'll soon see who it will be the worse for," said Theresa, furiously and ungrammatically. "Philip or Gwylan. I've time to go and see Philip in his surgery this afternoon between two and three and I *will*." Theresa arrived at the Sixth Form, in a vile temper, five minutes late. For thirty-five minutes it was the worse for the Sixth Form. But, in the long run, it was the *worst* for Theresa Devaloys.

VI

Doctor Philip Lariat's surgery hours were from 10 to 11.30 in the morning and from 2 till 3 in the afternoon. He lived in a square house in the residential district of Brunton on the edge of the common. The house was called The Lawns, and he had an elderly housekeeper (Mrs. Buttick) who fed him well and kept him glossy.

His father, Mr. Emmanuel Lariat, a moneylender of Harrogate, had bought Philip the house and the practice as a birthday present. Emmanuel Lariat had originally been called Emmanuel Lazarus, and he had changed his name by deed poll before Philip's birth. Mrs. Lariat had died when Philip was twelve.

Mrs. Buttick was perhaps a little in love with Philip, but she thought it only right that the doctor should amuse himself with other ladies. And as for Miss Fork-Thomas and Miss Devaloys (whom she had observed in the distance), Mrs. Buttick thought them a couple of fools. Which was bad luck for the intellectuals.

When she answered the door to Theresa Devaloys at half past two that afternoon and observed her standing on the step, she sniffed.

"Good afternoon, Mrs. Buttick," said Theresa, with great charm. Mrs. Buttick resented it.

"There's plenty of people already to see the doctor," said Mrs. Buttick. This snubbed Theresa.

"Ah!" she said, and, "Indeed?" But Mrs. Buttick had withdrawn into the back parts of the house.

The waiting-room was also the dining-room, and it was draughty. It was furnished with a large polished mahogany table scattered with *Lancets* and *B.M.J.s* and *Punches*. Above the tiled fireplace was a photograph of a lady known to one and all as 'the first Mrs. Philip Lariat' who 'died in childbirth in Leeds'. Her death, Philip was fond of saying, with tears in his voice, had also killed "our child". These two characters were figments of Philip's imagination. He had bought the photograph because it was a nice picture of a nice woman, and he knew that a young widower was a more dependable thing than a young bachelor.

There were six people in the waiting-room when Theresa sat down and drew a copy of *Punch* towards her. There were two old men, a woman with a child and a shopping-bag, a married couple, blushing, and a young, nervous, sniffing lady with a bad cold in the head. This was the young lady whose hands Philip Lariat had been holding in the Brunton Hotel, but Theresa was not to know this.

Philip's well-brushed head came round the door. He said "Next!" and disappeared with one of the old men before Theresa had decided upon a plan of action. She now observed, with shrinking disgust, a calendar photograph of a wire-haired fox-terrier poised upon a chair, and called "A Doggie's Prayer".

When Theresa became the second Mrs. Lariat she would stop all that nastiness. Her mouth set in a thin red line, not unlike the British Infantry at Spion Kop. It is a curious fact that Theresa Devaloys, who was well-educated, sensitive, intelligent and a bit of a bitch, was determined to become the second Mrs. P. Lariat. And this in spite of the contempt that she felt for Philip. Theresa was an only child and, as I think I have said, she was inexperienced with men.

The crowd in the waiting-room melted by degrees, but not on account of heat. Theresa was left alone, shivering with the *Punchs* and a very small electric radiator. The door opened and there was Philip. He looked smug, she thought, in his navy-blue suit and his starched linen collar.

"Why, *Tessa* . . ." he began, and glanced over his shoulder. "Miss Devaloys," he corrected himself hastily. "What a—why——" He stopped again and pulled himself together. He had a nice, resonant, speaking voice. "Have you lost your memory and forgotten your part or something? I mean—we *are* to meet tonight at rehearsal, aren't we?"

He rubbed the palms of his hands together, and Theresa looked at him curiously. In spite of this gesture he was attractive to her.

By now they were in the consulting-room and hemmed in by his heavy desk, his swivel chair, his horsehair examining-sofa, his groups that showed P. Lariat at his University and St. Peggotty's Hospital. He was proud of his consulting-room. It was the sort of sound background that old-fashioned patients suffering from chronic bronchitis and heart disease preferred. Chromium plate and little white coats belong to diseases of the mind and the American movies.

"No," said Theresa gravely. "I was hoping to consult you professionally."

"Good heavens!" said Philip, and sat down on the edge of his desk. "Have a cigarette?" He pushed a heavy onyx box towards her and then produced an unhappy and tactless verbal gambit. "What are you complaining of?" he said.

Theresa bristled.

"My dear man . . ." she began. Then she steadied herself and went on in a light tone. "Very little, I suppose, that you can't put right. Time will tell the rest. Time doesn't press, truth does. Perhaps you had rather *not* deal with my case?"

"Why not?" said Philip angrily. He lit his cigarette. "What the hell is the matter, Tessa? I wish you'd smoke. Why are you looking at me like that? Is anything wrong?"

"A certain amount," said Theresa airily. "In my jolly way I'm going to have a baby."

VII

There was a pause.

"*Our* baby," said Theresa, and coughed.

"Abortion," said Philip, under his breath. He had turned the colour of ripe cheese.

"A marriage license," Theresa corrected him sweetly.

Philip slid from the corner of his desk and walked the room, swearing softly and biting his nails. He faced her with both his hands clenched in his trousers pockets, his cigarette thrown aside in a waste-paper basket.

"Out of the question!" he exploded. "I can't."

"Why the hell not?" said Theresa. She was no longer calm. There was a pause. Philip began his pacing again. There was no warmth in the sunlight outside on the lawn.

"Well . . ." he said, and then he blushed. "I'm married already," he said.

VIII

"*Philip!*" said Theresa, and then, "to Gwylan?"

"Good heavens, no!" snapped Philip. He began inventing. Lies came naturally to him. "A girl in Harrogate. We've been separated for years. What a rotten mess. Are you *sure* about the child?"

"Positively certain," said Theresa. "It is very disagreeable." A strange look of relief had come into her eyes. "You're lying, Philip," she said.

Under his breath Philip muttered, "So might *you* be lying . . ."

Twenty minutes later he said: "Yes, we've bought it this time.

You were right, Tessa." He licked his dry lips. He passed a hand over his hair. There was a pause.

"But I *do* know a man . . ." he went on. He washed his plump white hands in the basin in the corner. The words that he said were like stones dropping on concrete from a height. Theresa's face splintered with rage.

"I understand," she said coldly, "that there is such a thing as the Medical Register?"

Philip Lariat inclined his polished head.

"And I understand that doctors who perform or who recommend abortions for their patients, or seduce them, would not be regarded with favour by the Medical Council?"

Lariat's smooth, well-shaved jaw dropped.

"Oh, but I say, look here . . ." he began. Fifteen years had fallen from his face. His mouth was childish with sulky dismay. "You *can't* do this to me, Tessa—not to *me*, your *Pippy*?"

Theresa drew a hissing breath. She looked him straight in the eye like a snake.

" 'Gwylan, darling heart of gold, everything will be all right, only trust me, your Philip,' " she quoted angrily.

It was a perfect exit-line. She swept out, tossing over her shoulder the reminder that, "The rehearsal is at 4.30, don't forget, dear." The front door slammed behind her.

"Oh, damn and blast!" said Philip Lariat.

He sat in his swivel chair and put his head in his hands on his nice, solid desk. His nice, solid, middle-class practice, that depended so much upon his respectability, rocked around him like a ship in a storm. Lariat rated his security highly. A dealer in lies, he knew the truth when he saw it. Something would have to be done.

CHAPTER FIVE

TEN persons assembled in the gymnasium at Radcliff Hall School at 4.30 p.m. that afternoon for the dress-rehearsal of Act III, Scene i, of Sir J. M. Barrie's *Quality Street*.

They were Mrs. Grossbody, the matron, a soldier's widow in reduced circumstances, with a daughter, Peggy, in West House; Miss Puke, an indeterminate young lady hockey player who taught classics; Miss Phipps, the secretary whom we have already met; Gwen Soames; and Maud Stuckenheimer, the elder sister of parboiled Daisy.

There were also Miss Lipscoomb herself, vaguely self-conscious in a cravat and tights as A Gallant ("No time, y'know, to learn a longer part, but I like to do m'bit"); Philip Lariat, his looks much improved by the uniform of Captain Valentine Brown; Gwylan Fork-Thomas as prompter and stage manager, holding a very beautiful india-paper edition of the complete plays of J. M. Barrie (without cuts) and a much meaner acting edition (*with* cuts); Miss Lesarum, the dusky mathematics teacher, as Ensign Blades; and Theresa Devaloys as Miss Phoebe as Miss Livvy. Her hair was arranged in ringlets, she wore the white high-waisted dress necessary to the part. A pale-blue ribbon ran through her hair; she had on neat black slippers crossed by neat black elastic. She looked, as Miss Puke suddenly put it, "Twee".

Miss Puke did not look twee. Her uniform for 'Spicer the Bewitched' did not fit. A shako was provided by the costumiers to go with the tight white trousers and red coat. Miss Puke was uncertain whether to wear it. From time to time she discussed the matter with Miss Lesarum, who was wearing the counterpart of her costume. They looked like toy soldiers. Their tunics were far too big. Even upon their girl-guiding and hockey-playing frames it was obvious that the tunics would need to be padded out with newspaper. Although Miss Puke's and Miss Lesarum's mammas had often told them, in their time, that they did not take enough trouble about their appearance, they were both morbidly anxious about the set of their red tunics.

Philip Lariat, in the other main man's part, was of course undisturbed by clothes which he had hired (after a fitting) from Nathan. He stood in the middle of the stage, with time and confidence enough to admire the 'canvas pavilion' and the moonlit backdrop that Roger Partick-Thistle had painted in his spare time.

"It *is* very good, you know," Lariat was saying to no one in particular. "Thistle is an amazingly artistic young man. It looks *exactly* like a garden in the distance on a summer night. I must say, I give him best."

With his uniform Lariat had put on a slightly phoney but effective way of speaking, that gave each syllable too much weight and over-emphasized his consonants.

"Roger's family have always been artistic," said Miss

Lipscoomb. She swanked towards him, moving carefully in her tights. "My sister's boy Edgar teaches art at the Slade. His brother . . ."

"I remember the case," murmured Philip Lariat. His sad, oriental eyes followed Theresa Devaloys to the wings where she was chatting lightly with Gwen Soames and Maud Stuckenheimer. Peter Bracewood-Smith arrived with 'a bottle of cordial' for the great commotion scene. He held it up and described it as The Real Mackay. Everyone looked surprised.

"Why do they delay with the Cor-di-uller?" quoted Lariat self-consciously, as he took the bottle from him. "But, Bracewood, this is *John Haig*!"

"Oh well, you'll see we'll need it," said the producer wearily, "before we're done."

"Yes," said Philip Lariat, glancing round him, "but these are schoolgirls. . . ."

He jerked his head at Gwen Soames and Maud Stuckenheimer as Harriet and Charlotte, the wallflowers. They had been awarded these unpromising parts for the good of their characters. They sat on a bench in modified and ill-fitting versions of Theresa Devaloys' costume.

"Barrie is such *fun*," said Gwen Soames to Miss Devaloys.

"Do you think so?" said Maud Stuckenheimer tartly. She was a little sharp-faced intelligent Jewess like a Japanese painting. "*My* brother Tony says Barrie's as dead as the dodo."

Miss Devaloys sniffed and looked down her tip-tilted nose.

"I like my plays broad," she said. "I like everything broad. Even schoolgirls."

Maud Stuckenheimer, who was not broad, looked mortified.

"Where's the stage manager?" shouted Peter Bracewood-Smith, suddenly waving the bottle of whiskey.

"Here I am," said Miss Fork-Thomas coolly. She came towards the line of footlights. She looked elegant and efficient in her well-cut navy-blue dress. She was composed and unhurried. It was inconceivable, thought Theresa, Llandudno University or *no* Llandudno University, that she had written that stupid, emotional note.

Theresa, watching Gwylan, swung her little green silk reticule that went with her costume. Her ringlets bobbed and jittered. Then she bit her lip. Gwylan Fork-Thomas was wearing a pink rose in the bosom of her dress.

Natasha and Miriam, knowing nothing of the significance of roses in February, strolled in through the swing doors at the back of the gymnasium at the moment when Bracewood-Smith handed the whiskey-bottle to Miss Fork-Thomas.

"Take good care of it," he said.

"Well, I'll get a corkscrew," said Miss Fork-Thomas, "but I do think you might have opened it."

Bracewood-Smith handed up a corkscrew and bottle-opener combined and shrugged his heavy shoulders.

"Hurt my wrist," he said. "Shall we start? Harriet and Charlotte. You begin. Places, please."

II

Harriet and Charlotte shuffled to their places with Matron, who had played Miss Susan in *Quality Street* ever since Radcliff Hall School could remember. She was a dab hand at it now.

Roger Partick-Thistle was suddenly discovered in the wings, fussing around with a pot of paint. The new girl, Julia Bracewood-Smith, was also discovered crouched behind the arras and was shooed away by Philip Lariat. A sudden pop announced Miss Fork-Thomas drawing the cork of the bottle of 'cordial'.

"They've set that stage very quickly and well," said Miriam to Natasha, staring up from the body of the hall.

"Miss Lipscoomb is telling me that the hired man puts it up with the footlights whenever this is happening."

"Does it happen often, dear?" said Miriam, her eyes gleaming.

"It is happening perhaps once or twice a term for different plays, they say," said Natasha. "Plays at schools are good. They are getting reported in the local papers. That is why Miss Lipscoomb is so fussed about perhaps losing Miss Devaloys before this one."

Miriam found a lukewarm radiator belonging to the system of central heating and perched upon it, her long legs dangling inelegantly.

"Wild horses," she said, "wouldn't drag me away from this, dear. How I wish something would happen and *I* could play . . ."

She sounded as wistful and stagestruck as a child of fifteen. Natasha found it endearing.

"Ladies, *please*!" shouted Peter Bracewood-Smith, already

55

angry about something or other. "From the beginning. *'Are we so disagreeable that no one will dance with us?'* Harriet."

And Harriet (Gwen Soames), as always startlingly disagreeable, started on what can now be described as the fateful act of *Quality Street*.

III

For a dress rehearsal it went swimmingly.

Miss Puke, as Spicer, came and went. Matron, as Miss Susan (and much here depends upon Miss Susan), played her scene splendidly. Miss Lesarum (mathematics and Ensign Blades), over made-up with Number 5 to show Blades' 'apple cheeks', missed a cue, was admonished, and blushed a dirty purple. Theresa Devaloys, as Miss Phoebe as Miss Livvy, whipped in and out, being ever so funny, and everyone hoped she would get a laugh on the night. Miss Lipscoomb as A Gallant and Miss Phipps, her secretary, as An Old Soldier, then gave an incredibly bad performance of their little scene, rehearsed by them daily for the last three weeks over the morning typewriter. Mr. Bracewood-Smith did not admonish them, but he fidgeted a lot.

Then came the commotion. Valentine Brown rushed on, carrying the 'half-fainting Miss Phoebe' and laid her on her 'couch of chairs'. Ensign Blades, very late on cue again, entered with the 'cordial'.

"Oh no, for God's sake, Miss what's your name!" bawled Bracewood-Smith from the middle of the gymnasium. "That will *never* do. This is the one cue in the whole act that *matters*. It must go pat. It really must. Mountin' tension. Discovery any minute now, an' so on. Please take it over again. Cue, please, Valentine. *'You have over-fatigued yourself.'* Miss Phoebe, *'I remember.'* "

On the stage, Philip Lariat told Miss Devaloys she had fatigued herself.

"I remember," said Miss Devaloys.

Nothing happened.

" *'Blades enters with the cordial'!*" screamed Bracewood-Smith, dancing up and down in the darkened gymnasium like a mosquito in a tank. "Hey! Miss Thing! *'I remember.'* That's your cue!"

"Oh—er—sorry," said Miss Lesarum, in her deep voice.

"Thought you meant take the *scene* again. Umph. I remember," and then she entered, jauntily, with the cordial.

"*No*," said Bracewood-Smith, spacing his words very carefully as men often do in a rage. "You-will-please-enter-like-a-young - man - in - love - and - unsuccessful - at - that - and - not - like-a-principal-boy."

"Er . . ." said Miss Lesarum. "Yes. Sorry."

"*Take* it again, *take* it again," said Bracewood-Smith, with a wearied theatrical sigh. " '*Why do they delay with the cordial?*' "

"Why indeed?" murmured Miss Devaloys, prone on her chairs. "I heard someone say it was John Haig."

And so they took it again. And again. And again. Sometimes Ensign Blades muffed her first cue, sometimes her second. Sometimes the 'cordial' reached Miss Phoebe and she knocked it back. Once it got as far as Miss Phoebe handing it to Miss Susan; but Bracewood-Smith made them do the whole thing over again, from Blades' entrance, before poor Miss Susan could drink any. By the time they were ready to proceed with Act III, Miss Devaloys had drunk what appeared to Natasha and Miriam to be a tumbler and a half of Scotch whiskey and poor Matron (owing to Theresa's greed) had had none at all.

"Theresa always had a head like teak," said someone near them. It was Miss Fork-Thomas, holding the book. "I slipped down," she said to Miriam and Natasha, in explanation, "to look at Roger Thistle's *moon* from the front. He's touched it up, you know, and got a new baton on it. He thinks he needs another lime."

"It looks good," said Miriam. "Funny how very young men always fuss about their lighting."

"Not as much as old women," said Miss Fork-Thomas brightly.

"Is Miss Devaloys really drinking all of that whiskey?" said Natasha in her slow, soft voice. "And is it whiskey?"

"Apparently," said Miss Fork-Thomas coldly, annoyed that they had not laughed at her joke. Miriam thought it offensive. "The same answer to both questions. I opened the bottle myself. Quite an easy one. It smelt like whiskey."

"Didn't you have any?"

"I drink gin," said Miss Fork-Thomas.

On the stage Miss Devaloys was faltering, " '*Should they see my face it will be idle to attempt to deceive them.*' " " '*Idle indeed,*' "

57

snapped Matron. " *'Phoebe—the scandal. And you a school mistress!'* "
There was a heavy undramatic pause.

"Well?" said Bracewood-Smith irritably. "Miss Phoebe?"

Miss Devaloys shook her head.

"Prompter?"

" *'That is it, sister,'* " shouted Miss Fork-Thomas clearly. " *'A little happiness has gone to my head like strong waters.'* "

Someone tittered, and on the stage Miss Devaloys raised one hand to her head and repeated the words, " *'Gone to my head like strong waters.'* "

"Yes indeed," said Miss Fork-Thomas, her mouth set like a rat-trap.

"I do feel funny," said Theresa Devaloys vaguely. "I never forgot that line before."

" *'My dear, stand still and think,'* " said Matron, proceeding briskly with her part.

" *'I dare not, I cannot,'* " said Miss Devaloys. "Oh, dear!"

And she put her hand to her head, rose to her feet, saw the lights of the floats and batons reel around her like stars, and she pitched forward on her face.

"Good heavens!" said Matron.

"House lights!" shouted Bracewood-Smith in a most professional manner. Evidently Roger turned them on, because they came up immediately. Bracewood-Smith went on shouting. "*Doctor!* Lariat! That looks like a real faint."

Lariat, his face white and chalky under his make-up, hurried on to the stage. His dolman swung from his shoulder. He knelt beside Theresa Devaloys. The dolman got in his way a little and he swore. His first movement was odd. Natasha, who was used to faints, had expected him to thrust Theresa's head between her knees. Miriam, who was used to drunks, expected him to dash cold water in her face.

Instead he rolled back one of her eyelids with his finger and said, "Oh *no*, oh no, oh *no*," in a quick and childish voice.

"What d'you mean, man? Spit it out!" snarled Bracewood-Smith. "What's wrong, you fool? What's wrong?"

Lariat stood up in his scarlet tunic, with his ridiculous dolman swinging, in his white trousers and his hessian boots, his handsome commonplace face altered by fear to dignified immobility.

"She's dead, that's all; she's *dead*," said Lariat.

CHAPTER SIX

THE confusion that followed this sentence is quite indescribable.

Gwen Soames screamed. Maud Stuckenheimer used a dreadful word that she must have picked up in the holidays and Miss Lesarum burst out laughing. Miss Puke, most surprisingly, showed herself to be quite able in a crisis. She began to give Miss Devaloys artificial respiration. Miss Phipps said, "I think I hear the 'phone," and left the room, looking extremely odd. No one tried to stop her.

"Rubbish!" said Mrs. Grossbody, the matron. "It's a faint. Let me look." She elbowed Lariat on one side, remarking that she had always *said* he was too young to be the school doctor. "Dead, indeed," she repeated scornfully. "Never heard of such a thing. . . ."

Neither, apparently, had Gwylan Fork-Thomas. She stood between Natasha and Miriam, utterly stunned. Natasha and Miriam, who, let us face it, had seen things like this happen before, advanced towards the stage in a state of cold curiosity. Gwylan Fork-Thomas remained exactly where she was.

"Dead?" said Natasha. "It is not *true*. But what can she be dead *of*?"

"Heart failure, possibly," said Philip Lariat, recovering himself and more annoyed by Mrs. Grossbody than he would have cared to admit. "It was a bad heart, you know. She was consulting me about it only this morning."

"She never mentioned it to *me*," said Miss Lipscoomb belligerently. "And I think we should go on trying artificial respiration."

Miss Puke looked up from her labours, with a large drop on the end of her nose, and said she did not think it was much use. "Funny, she smells," said Miss Puke. "Kind of *musty*."

"I think you should go on just the same," said Miss Lipscoomb sternly.

"Oh, so do *I*," said Natasha, and turned eagerly to Miriam. "I have never seen it done before, you know," she said.

"I'm afraid, dear," said Miriam, "that Doctor Lariat is right. In spite of all that Matron says, don't you think we ought to take her to her room?"

Roger Partick-Thistle appeared in the wings and used the

same awful word that Maud Stuckenheimer had used and dropped a pot of paint.

"Quite," said Bracewood-Smith. "Can't leave everything hangin' about here, now can we, Miss Lipscoomb?" He had remembered that he was the producer. Miss Puke cowered away from him and Miss Lesarum hid behind a curtain.

A bell shrilled in the distance and the tramping feet of kiddies coming to their lessons came nearer and nearer.

"The Lower Fourth are due here for singing any minute now," said Miss Puke. She stood up and shifted uneasily from foot to foot. Miss Lipscoomb suddenly said there was not a moment to be lost.

"Well, for God's sake do something, then," she said, most unfairly to poor Miss Puke. "Send for the police or something."

"Police?" cried Matron, with a little scream. "What for? You heard the doctor say it was accidental."

"I said no such *thing*," snapped Philip Lariat. "The nearest I came to saying *that* was that poor Miss Devaloys might have had a heart attack. Valvular lesions. Yes. She might have died *any* time. I actually brought some dope over with me for her . . ."

And Philip Lariat reached into the bosom of his scarlet tunic and drew out a small flat bottle containing a number of capsules. He hid the label with his thumb. Natasha craned but could not see it.

"Will it be all right to move her, then?" said Miss Lipscoomb timidly. To everyone's surprise and some people's indignation she addressed the new Russian dancing teacher, who did not reply but merely nodded her head over the footlights.

"Anyway, dear," said Miriam suddenly, "if she really *is* dead, I don't think it's in the best of T for us to stand around in groups *arguing* about it. And I think we ought to drop the curtain."

The curtains came together with a stealthy, mocking swish. The hand of Partick-Thistle still moved silently in the darkness behind the stage.

"Time enough for arguing," said Maud Stuckenheimer suddenly and clearly, "when we're collecting the threepences for the wreath."

And she giggled.

"*Really*, Maud!" snapped Miss Lipscoomb.

II

In the end Lariat and Bracewood-Smith carried poor Theresa Devaloys off the stage, through the music wing and the sunk garden that she hated so much, to her own room. She was very light. Lariat was very moved. He chewed at his thick, well-shaped underlip and tried to control himself.

"Nasty business this is, Smith," he said, with his head on one side, listening to himself. His voice *sounded* all right.

They laid her on the bed. Bracewood-Smith was staring out of the window.

"Jolly nasty," said Lariat.

"Eh?" said Bracewood-Smith and jumped. "It would suit my book jolly well if she had died of heart disease, y'know," he said wistfully. "I suppose there ought to be a police autopsy, though? Funny it is, being mixed up with this sort of thing, y'know, after havin' written about it so often. Not a bit like books, the real thing is. No."

The rather stuffy little bed-sitting-room seemed smaller than ever now that there were two men in it. The blue-black, inky twilight that always comes at four o'clock on a Sussex evening had made the windows blank squares of mystery. Lariat pulled the curtains. They rasped together along an expanding curtain rod.

"Different deaths, different circumstances," said Lariat profoundly.

"I expect," went on Bracewood-Smith, taking a large pipe from his pocket and biting nonchalantly on it on the stem, "that accidental death would suit Miss Lipscoomb. *She'd* like the whole thing tidied up for her Founder's Day. I couldn't care less."

"As a novelist," said Lariat, suddenly and rather nastily, "don't you want to see truth and justice served? You're in a very good temper all of a sudden," he added, "compared with at rehearsal."

"Nervous work, rehearsals," said Bracewood-Smith, and filled his pipe. "Justice might be interesting to watch. Truth? No. *Nothing* is served by the truth in *my* profession." He turned to Lariat with a rather engaging grin. "It's an occupational disease, novelist's falsehood," he said; "like miner's phthisis. I expect Miss Lipscoomb will be glad to see the back of this young woman," he ended reflectively.

61

"Oh, what *rot*!" said Lariat explosively. "Miss Lipscoomb is half-way to being ruined already. Theresa was jolly bad as Miss Phoebe, but no one else could play the part."

And he took off his ridiculous tunic and began to examine Miss Devaloys for the second time that day.

"Perhaps," said Bracewood-Smith, scratching with a match, "as it *has* put paid to Miss Lipscoomb's Founder's Day——"

As he spoke the door handle rattled furiously, and Natasha DuVivien, her eyes gleaming like a cat's, her lovely hair wild and floating, stood panting in the doorway. She was very angry.

"I am hearing every word you men are saying," she said, "and *I* am Russian. *White* Russian, and so I do not care how I am getting my facts."

"No lady and proud of it," said Bracewood-Smith, and lit his pipe. He gave the impression, now and always, that he was not quite sober.

"I am often learning a lot from listening down keyholes, and I tell to you once and for all, and I say it to you here, that Miss Devaloys is *not* being a heart patient and you are knowing it, you *sexy little man*."

Philip Lariat drew himself up and looked like something very small out of *The Prisoner of Zenda*.

"Oh yes," hissed Natasha irrelevantly, "the Guard of Peter the Great are being never less than six foot six, and always Irishmen. Doctor Lariat," she went on, with drama, "go tell that about the heart disease to the marine coroner. I myself am ringing up the police."

"Look here, madam," began Bracewood-Smith, blowing blue, oily smoke all around him and raising one fleshy hand. "If this is not death by misadventure but is death by someone's design, the deceased's or some other . . ." He spoke ponderously, looking admiringly at Natasha.

"You are speaking quite differently to me than you are speaking to Doctor Lariat," said Natasha, "and I am wondering *why*. Miss Lipscoomb," she added inconsequently, "would certainly keep her Miss Phoebe alive until after Founder's Day play. *Then* she would be murdering her."

There was a pause while the two men digested this remarkable piece of syntax.

"This she richly deserved, sir and madam," said Bracewood-Smith, and smiled. "She was in a scheme, you know, with Helena bbirch to purchase all this property and swindle poor Lipscoomb out of quite a lot of dough, as they say."

Bracewood-Smith bowed gravely to Natasha who said she had been knowing this for some time. She looked from the handsome commonplace young Jew back to the bearded Elizabethan adventurer.

"Eh?" Lariat was taken aback. "*You* don't let the grass grow under your feet, do you?"

"I am hoping not, *I* who dance for the great Diaghilev."

"No?" said Bracewood-Smith, his eyes wild with excitement. "Did you really?"

III

Miss Phipps, dressed in her appalling Chelsea Pensioner clothes as An Old Soldier, hurried to her little office in East House. No one else, she thought bitterly as she went, was aware of their duty towards (*a*) their employer, (*b*) the children in their charge and (*c*) the unhappy dead. Mildred Phipps was determined to do the right thing. She picked up the telephone in her office and, trembling a little, asked for the police-station. There was a terrible pause. Then a voice spoke in her ear.

"Streamline!" said the voice.

It took Miss Phipps some time to explain that she did not, in fact, want the taxi-rank, but a policeman. And by the time that she had told the operator what had happened and the operator had managed to get the police-station to reply, someone in the Brunton exchange had dropped her earphones, screaming, "Lor', the Radcliff Hall girls are being murdered!" down a perfectly good trunk line from Tunbridge Wells to Dublin. This is the curious sort of hook-up that occurs daily at Brunton-on-Sea. Dublin had a third leader about it in the *Irish Times* next day.

The policeman who took Miss Phipps' message breathed heavily, but otherwise showed no emotion.

Miss Phipps had by this time acquired a more effective unhurried metallic delivery. Sergeant Gourlay handed the message on to Brunton's C.I.D. sergeant, a bright young man who believed the worst of everyone and thought life extremely funny. He had a little bristly fawn moustache like a paint-brush and bloodshot eyes. His name was Sergeant Tomkins. He was a Cockney who had married a wife with a weak chest, and was consequently forced to spend the rest of his life in Brunton-on-Sea telling old ladies the time.

"Miss Phipps, school seckertery at Radcliff'All, says someone's bin murdered."

"No?" Sergeant Tomkins pulled his soft hat into a becoming spivvy angle. He twitched his natty dark-green tie straight. "Girls' school. Just the job. We c'd do with a nice murder."

He ordered the big black Wolseley and drove over to the school. He looked pathetic, somehow, as he stood on the top step and rang the bell. He was so well brushed in his reach-me-downs. The stout young policeman in uniform at the wheel looked less pathetic but more stupid. Miss Lipscoomb's other parlour-maid opened the door to him.

"So you've got a murder on the premises?" began Tomkins chattily. "Your Miss Phipps rang me. I'm from the police-station. Sergeant Tomkins."

The parlourmaid fled screaming before him.

IV

Miss Phipps apologized for the parlourmaid and her own appearance in the same breath.

"She's only new since Gertie's going, and we were rehearsin'," she said, as she led the way energetically through gymnasium, music wing and sunk garden. Sergeant Tomkins said that *did* make a difference, and then felt vaguely embarrassed by the Lower Fourth, which rose to its feet as Miss Phipps and Sergeant Tomkins passed through its (collective) singing lesson. Mrs. Pont, quivering at the piano, struck a bar or two of 'Charlie Is My Darling', and the Lower Fourth began to sing, shrilly and wildly, out of tune. The curtains on the stage were still drawn against intruders. No one but Miss Phipps and the remainder of the cast, and now Miss Lipscoomb's new parlourmaid, Greta, knew the truth.

Greta, drinking a very strong cup of tea with the East House cook and kitchenmaid, began to sob less wildly. She told them her story and they did not believe her. Greta was given to invention. Even the sight of uniformed Constable Beatty, motionless and pink at the wheel of the Wolseley, dimly lit by starlight in the dark drive, did not convince the East House cook and kitchen-maid peering up through the basement grating. They had been interrupted in a game of fourpenny whist, and they said they preferred this to Greta's whimsy-whamsies.

" 'E's come about that there Scharn'orst's licence," said the cook comfortably. "An' was tryin' to be funny. Trouble with you, Greta, is you'll believe *anything*."

And the kitchenmaid said she had no sense of humour.

V

Sergeant Tomkins and Miss Phipps arrived in the staff wing when Natasha and Lariat and Bracewood-Smith were still arguing in Miss Devaloys' room. Miss Phipps showed Sergeant Tomkins which the door was, and then fled most basely. She left him to introduce himself to these three ill-assorted personalities. Tomkins, however, was equal to anything. He shut the door behind him.

"Tomkins is the name," he began cheerfully, taking off his hat, as he would have put it, 'in the presence'. "Sar'nt Tomkins, C.I.D. Good lady there, Miss Phipps, thinks there has been a murder . . ."

He jerked his sandy head at the door behind him and said, as he looked from poor Miss Devaloys on the bed to the three fairly cheerful faces that surrounded him:

"Well, we've got a *body* anyway, an' that's something. Moved, though. That's a pity. Teacher, I understand. Anyone care to tell me?"

His common sense and steady insensitivity were most reassuring. Lariat replied:

"The lady was Miss Theresa Devaloys, languages mistress here," he said. He had been kneeling by the bed. He stood up and brushed his knees. "I am a doctor."

"Oh, I know *you*, Doctor Lariat," said Tomkins happily, taking a fountain-pen out of his waistcoat pocket. "Introductions unnecessary. *An'* I know Mr. Bracewood-Smith, too, if I may say so. I'll just take your names an' occupations, though, if you don't mind."

He looked at Bracewood-Smith, who said, "Novelist—*well*, detective-story writer," and looked ashamed and cross.

"Always beats me," said Tomkins, bringing a flat shorthand notebook out of his jacket pocket, "why you fellers write about crime without knowin' one damn' thing about it. The *bloomers* you make . . ."

Natasha began to laugh. She *liked* Sergeant Tomkins.

"I don't know you, miss," said Tomkins. "You a teacher, too?"

"Yes—I mean *no*," said Natasha, who had a healthy respect of policemen. "I am a detective myself. I am being hired by Miss Lipscoomb to protect her interests. I am *Russian*, but a naturalized British. My husband, Mr. DuVivien, is British, that is. I . . ."

Dr. Lariat and Peter Bracewood-Smith remained unnaturally unmoved by this information.

The remarkable Sergeant Tomkins said he understood perfectly and wrote it all down at a fair speed in longhand in his notebook.

"You callin' yourself by your married name while here, miss?" said Tomkins. "No. Miss Nevkorina. Oh. And the name of your agency?"

"Birdseye et Cie," said Natasha, a little shamefaced.

Tomkins took this very well, too.

"My partner, Miss Birdseye, is also here," went on Natasha, taking heart. She felt secure with the brisk, unimaginative little man opposite her.

"Not Miss *Miriam* Birdseye?" Tomkins was incredulous at last. Natasha nodded. "Not Miss Birdseye the actress, who had all them burglaries in her house in Baker Street an' used to keep 'er fur coat in the oven? Miss Birdseye of *Positively the End* and *Absolutely the Last* or whatever them revues was called?"

"You are been knowing her?" said Natasha, confused.

"Ma'am," said Tomkins, "I investigated them burglaries. When I was attached Marylebone. Before Mrs. Tomkins's chest got so bad. I'm a fan of Miss Birdseye's."

All of which made Natasha feel much better; but there is no doubt that Doctor Lariat, who had never heard of Miriam Birdseye, now began to feel restless and provincial. Bracewood-Smith also moved about restlessly. It is a curious fact that novelists, when presented with romantic facts in real life, usually refuse to believe them.

"Well, sirs an' madam," began Tomkins, "perhaps I c'n collect preliminary statements from you three an' interrogate the other witnesses later. Save time."

"The doctor *says* he believes it is an accident," said Bracewood-Smith.

"Still 'ave to be an inquest," said Tomkins. "Next, please?"

"The doctor has been saying Miss Devaloys has a *weak heart*," said Natasha, and *glared*. "It is, I can be assuring you, *quite* untrue."

But as Natasha started upon this rather foolish speech, based upon those amateurish intuitive perceptions that passed, with her, for detective work, a terrible cry shook the staff wing from end to end.

"Gawd!" said Sergeant Tomkins.

He turned a little pale. A trampling of feet was heard on the stairs, a breathless clatter of urgency and horror, and Roger Partick-Thistle came tumbling into the bed-sitting-room.

"It's Matron!" he gasped. "Mrs. Grossbody!" He flung his hair back. His violet eyes were staring with horror. "My dears! She must have swiped that bottle of whiskey that you left down there. And she's passed out. I mean literally passed out. I thought at first she was dead *drunk*, my dears, but she's not. She's dead. . . ."

And Roger Partick-Thistle sank upon the little milking-stool and buried his beautiful face in his thin white hands. He sobbed and sobbed and sobbed.

BOOK TWO

SERGEANT TOMKINS, C.I.D.

CHAPTER ONE

"Actually, it's this bottle of whiskey now that interests me," said Sergeant Tomkins.

He sat at a table in the library, next door to the conservatory in East House, and read through the statements of the persons at the *Quality Street* rehearsal. The library was a little useless box of a room containing unpleasant works of fiction locked into wire-fronted bookcases that looked like rabbit-hutches. A girl in East House called Barbara Porlock had once broken into these rabbit-hutches and stolen a book, had been found out, and had been named ever afterwards 'Spitty Picklock'. There was nothing else remarkable about the library. An entrance led out of it, up two steps, into the conservatory.

Sergeant Tomkins had transcripted their statements in long-hand. They made neat slim dossiers headed variously, 'Natasha Nevkorina, Mrs. DuVivien, 44P Baker Street, W.1, dancer (retd.)'; 'Miriam Birdseye, 44P Baker Street, W.1, actress (retd.)'; 'Philip Lariat, M.D., F.R.C.P., The Lawns, Brunton-on-Sea'; and so on. The information contained in them is exactly contained in chapters one to six of this story.

They littered the table in front of him. His energy and intelligence were unflagging. Sometimes he pulled at his little moustache to wake himself. Had it not been for his bloodshot eyes no one would have suspected him of being tired.

"This bottle of whiskey, now," repeated Tomkins.

It was 1 a.m. A horrid scene had just taken place over Mrs. Grossbody with a stomach-pump. Her life had been saved and she had been delivered to the Cottage Hospital by police ambulance. It had then continued to the mortuary with the remains of Miss Devaloys. Everyone was looking their age. The stage had been examined. The bottle had been dusted with powder from an insufflator and had shown the finger-prints of Peter Bracewood-Smith, Miss Fork-Thomas, Miss Devaloys, Matron and a lot of smears.

"Now, *you* provided the whiskey, sir," said Tomkins to Bracewood-Smith. His voice was interested, not at all accusing, and Bracewood-Smith looked sleepy as he suggested there must have been a switch. "We'll have it analysed, of course." Mrs. Grossbody had left perhaps four fingers of whiskey in the bottle. "Now who opened it?"

"I did," said Miss Fork-Thomas wearily. "It's all in that bosh —er—*statement* that you were writing."

"Bosh it may seem to you, ma'am," said Tomkins. "Murder is a serious business. Any experience with bottles? I mean, would you 'ave noticed what this one was like?"

"Well, the *tinfoil* was intact," said Miss Fork-Thomas, rebuked. She looked puzzled. "If *that's* what you mean. And the cork didn't crumble or anything. Actually, I *have* some experience with bottles. I'm a chemist."

"And it came out with quite a loud pop, darling, for a whiskey-bottle," said Miriam to Sergeant Tomkins, who said, "Thank you, madam," and wrote it down.

"Well now, sir," said Tomkins, turning to Bracewood-Smith, "where did you purchase this whiskey? Was it Black Market or anything? Might it have been wood alcohol? Hooch? Don't mind replyin'. *My* concern ain't with Black Market, or your morals, at the moment. . . ."

"I *think* it's one I had from Drawhurst, the wine-shop in Brunton-on-Sea. I'm almost *sure* it wasn't hooch," said Bracewood-Smith. "But we writers, you know, we drink more than we should, I'm afraid. I go to more than one place." And again he suggested that the bottle might have been switched.

Tomkins wrote down 'Drawhurst' and frowned at his fountain-pen, which had thrown up a most unpleasant blot on the paper.

"Where else do you go, sir?" he said respectfully.

"Devilboger and Wine Sippers (Brunton) and a man I know near Hastings," said Bracewood-Smith. "But I've never had hooch from any of them *before*."

"When do you think you got this bottle?"

"It was one of three, I think, from Drawhurst. My quota for the quarter. Sore point. Everyone wants whiskey. Wish I drank gin."

"Everyone wants gin just as much," said Miss Fork-Thomas sharply.

"One of three, you *think*," said Tomkins frowning. "Don't you *know*?"

"No, I *don't*," said Bracewood-Smith angrily. "Does it matter?"

"Yes, I think it *does*," said Tomkins.

There was a pause while Bracewood-Smith tugged at his beard and failed to remember.

"Drawhurst will know," he said finally. "You ask *him*."

"Thanks very much, sir, I *will*," said Tomkins gravely. "I don't think we can do more with the first tragedy tonight," he said thoughtfully. "Now then," he added briskly, "the *second* nearly tragedy."

There was a little gasp of exhausted horror that ran round the circle of ladies and gentlemen sitting round him at the table. Miss Lesarum moaned and laid her black woolly head on her arms. Miss Puke said something about Mother ringing up to see where she was. (Miss Puke and Mrs. Puke lived in a bungalow called Woodmansterne in Brunton Old Town.) Miss Lipscoomb asked if she mightn't change. Doctor Lariat, who had returned from the Cottage Hospital, said angrily: "Here, I *say*, I might be wanted. Confinement . . ." and then fell silent. Only Miss Fork-Thomas, Bracewood-Smith, Natasha, Miriam and Roger Partick-Thistle did not say anything. Tomkins referred to his notes.

"Now you, sir," he said briskly, turning, incredulous, to Roger. "Mr. Partick-Thistle."

Roger's eyes were bright and unfatigued. He minced forward and sat in the high-backed chair that Tomkins had set at his elbow. Tomkins made a little hieroglyphic by the side of the margin in his notebook and began.

"Name, Roger Partick-Thistle. Occupation . . . ?"

"Well . . ." said Roger, considering and passing his thin hand over his bright hair. "I *suppose* I am a *dilletante*, dear. I mean I do lots of things. . . ."

Sergeant Tomkins didn't doubt it.

"But I get *paid* at the moment for being a schoolmaster. Yes . . ." Roger rolled his eyes and looked like a horse about to bolt. "Young ladies are *quite* safe with me. I teach them a little music— the organ, you know. And I take some extra pupils for drawing."

"Drawing and music master," wrote Tomkins firmly.

"Chelsea, dear, when I'm in London," said Roger nervously, again rolling his eyes. "But again, you see, *here* when I'm not. . . ."

"What is being the matter with Thistle?" said Natasha to Miriam. "Can he be drunk, perhaps?"

"I expect he's frightened," said Miriam.

"Oh yes. I see what you *mean*," said Natasha earnestly.

"Now it was you, was it, who found Mrs. Grossbody sufferin' from the effects?" said Sergeant Tomkins.

Roger turned a face of tragedy upon him.

"Can't I see you *alone*?" he said dramatically. "And not in *public* like this?"

"All right." Tomkins looked vaguely annoyed. "You ladies and gentlemen," he said, turning to them, "can go home or do as you wish." Oddly, no one but Miss Lipscoomb moved. Roger turned to Miriam, who was obviously Policeman's Pet. "Would you and your partner care to step along of me and Mr. Thistle into the conservatory, like? It may be interesting."

He got up, and so did Roger.

"Good night, sirs and mesdames," said Sergeant Tomkins. Dismissed, the company went about its business. In this friendly and untroubled way Natasha and Miriam (for no better reason than that Miriam was once burgled) were made free to the most secret and confidential interviews of the Brunton-on-Sea Criminal Investigation Department. Miss Fork-Thomas considered it a highly irregular proceeding, and I have no doubt that she was right.

II

In the conservatory, when the noise of tired, angry feet and furious muttering had died away, Tomkins sat down on a wicker-work chair and turned back to Roger.

"Well, sir? Please describe 'ow you found Matron—er—Mrs. Grossbody, and do it quickly."

Tomkins was quite suddenly in a bad temper, and Miriam was sorry for Roger. There were wickerwork chairs for all of them, but only Natasha relaxed. Roger began quickly, rather as though he were used to giving police evidence.

"Well, it was the same night, you know, the Night of the First, like you've already *said*, dear, and poor Miss Devaloys was taken away by Bracewood-Smith and Lariat. I was still messing about on the stage. I admit I was in a bit of a rage, dear, on account of I was *disappointed*. I thought, 'No play. No one will see Rodgy's little bit of nonsense!' I'd designed the scenery, you see, and there was quite a *well-known* London *manager* coming to see it," went on Roger, looking imploringly at Tomkins.

"Hm," said Tomkins.

"And I was trying to think who might play Miss Phoebe." There was a pause. "I'm not really heartless, you know, mum," he said, turning to Miriam, "I was *ever so sorry* about Miss Devaloys, I was really. It's just"—he turned back to Tomkins— "that this production means so *much* to my Aunt Janet. She needs the publicity so *badly*——"

"Get on with the story, Thistle, and don't A about," said Miriam.

"Yes," said Roger, and drew a deep breath. "Though now we're missing the two principal female parts I don't know *what* we shall do." There was a pause. "I might play Miss Phoebe myself," he said brightly.

"Don't be silly, Thistle, Sergeant Tomkins can't stay here all night," said Miriam, like Nanny. Roger looked hurt.

"Go on, please, it is so *interesting*," said Natasha, and Roger giggled and continued with the narrative.

"Well, there I *was*," he said, "biting my lips over *Quality Street*, and I suddenly heard . . ." He turned to Tomkins again. "You must imagine, Sergeant, the whole of the Lower Fourth singing a selection from the *Student's Song Book* in a most repulsive way, all off-key: 'Billy Boy' and 'Charlie Is My Darling', and a hundred other little ditties in praise of young men . . ."

"I heard 'em," said Tomkins.

"And then, right across this caterwauling, dear, I heard the most awful noise, just like this . . ." And Roger, drawing a deep breath, went: "Glug! Glug! Glug!"

"Pretty," said Miriam, with her head on one side.

"Couldn't A with you, M," said Roger. "So I said to myself, 'Behind the arras?'—*Hamlet*, you know, dear—and I pulled it— the arras, I mean—and there was the good Frau Grossbody, with the whiskey-bottle, my dear. *Matron*. Like any old rat."

"How did she look?" said Tomkins sharply.

"Exactly as when you saw her, dear," said Roger triumphantly, as one who would say, "*I* don't move *my* bodies about." "Eyes shut, bad colour. Musty smell. What d'you think it is?" he went on excitedly. "Opium?"

"I really can't say, sir," said Tomkins. "That's for the police-surgeon to decide."

"Who is being the police-surgeon?" asked Natasha.

"Not the Lariat young man, I hope," said Miriam.

"The police-surgeon is Doctor Fortescue, madam," said Tomkins, refusing to be drawn. "You're all very bright for this time of night," he said, and looked at his watch. "It's nearly 2 a.m.," he said.

"We're all night birds here," said Roger, and leered.

Miriam, in her role as Nanny, said, "Now, now!" automatically, with the inflection that implies, "It will all end in tears, Master Roger."

"I think you ought to go to bed, you know," said Tomkins, getting up, "just the same. I'll be along at nine in the morning. Nothing I can do really till I've compared your statements. We seem to know *how* the good lady died, but we may be mistaken. Tomorrow I shall be startin' (I hope) on *why*."

"I am thinking Mrs. Grossbody was so obviously an accident," said Natasha thoughtfully.

"Facts first, theories afterwards," said Tomkins, as though he were quoting Emily Post. He put away his fountain-pen and notebook. "How's that for a motto, madam?"

"I will think it over," said Natasha slowly.

"Good night, all," said the irrepressible Sergeant Tomkins, and he clapped his smart gent's felt on the side of his head and shuffled all the statements together into rather a battered brief-case. He joined Constable Beatty in the Wolseley. They drove away back to the station. The headlights stabbed a narrow white path for them. Half-way to the town the headlights lit up the vast, hunched figure of Peter Bracewood-Smith plodding home to his conventional writer's cottage above the coastguard station.

"Among the dead marines," said Tomkins gaily.

And when he returned to the police-station he found that there had been two robberies and a barrow-boy smash and-grab job and someone had complained about a man on the cliffs who pestered schoolchildren. But all these things belong to another story.

III

Peter Bracewood-Smith's bungalow, Gull Cottage, was, as we know, on the red cliffs above the coastguard station.

It was a lonely spot, unmenaced by human beings or women committing suicide for their demon lovers. Only the postman, the daily help, the baker, the butcher and the milkman, with bicycles and little vans, took the trouble to come there. The daily help, like the midwife, had a bicycle.

Bracewood-Smith disliked visitors; but like all writers, he was inconsistent. He would suddenly feel gregarious; then he would get up and lurch out of his house down the cliff path to Brunton-on-Sea.

He was a curious figure. His heavy shoulders were usually hunched round his ears, and his velveteen jacket strained across them. His black beard flowed in the wind, the turn-ups of his trousers were always damp and shabby. He was wild and peculiar. Oddly, he was generally liked.

He was intelligent and hard working, untroubled by high-brow considerations. He had four shaming pen-names to which he admitted (Ron Berkeley, Edward Belvoir, John Pytcheley and Sam E. Sussex). He even wrote love-stories, calling himself Mavis Chare, for the women's magazines. He wrote very fast and glibly straight on to the typewriter, in double spacing on quarto sheets. He sent his manuscripts straight to the publisher as he typed them. There were seldom errors in spelling, punctuation or typing. P. Bracewood-Smith's errors were all errors of taste. He wrote excruciatingly badly.

The bungalow had a bedroom, a sitting-room, a spare bedroom, a kitchen, a bathroom and a dining-room. When Julia Bracewood-Smith came to stay with her father she slept in the spare room. Before her mother's death she had lived with her mother in Queen's Gate and had gone to day-school for gentle-people (at her father's expense). Mrs. Bracewood-Smith had money of her own, which paid for the flat in Queen's Gate, but Peter made her a large allowance. 'Mavis Chare', 'Ron Berkeley', 'Edward Belvoir' and the rest of them made him about £2,000 a year.

He stood now at 7.30 in the morning, combing his beard in the bathroom. He stared down the cliff path at the postman tacking towards Gull Cottage on his bicycle.

He heard the letters fall through the letter-box on to the mat, and finished dressing before he went to pick them up.

He put on a thick seaman's sweater with a roll collar and a pair of navy-blue serge rating's drop-fronted trousers. Biting on an empty pipe, he knelt in the hall and fingered his letters. One from his agent with a cheque in it. *Good.* One from his solicitors. Not so good. The baker's bill. The butcher's bill. Only to be expected. One . . . He thrust them into his trousers pocket and went to the kitchen. He made tea and grilled two kippers and read the letters, which got covered with toast crumbs.

Mrs. Cluny, the daily help, came at nine. Provided he got through breakfast before she came and began to take off her coat and hat all over him, he could escape into the work-sitting-room and shut himself away in the luxuries of *Death and the Principal Boy.*

The bungalow had been let to him, furnished, at four guineas a week four years ago. The owner had never intended to live in it, so it was unpleasant furniture. There were stained-oak settles, tables and chairs, bevelled looking-glasses on chains, divan beds and nondescript rugs. Peter Bracewood-Smith did not notice them. He lived exclusively in the half-world of his thoughts, at this moment with characters from *Death and the Principal Boy.* He only emerged from this *demi-monde* during licensing-hours, when he surveyed Brunton-on-Sea through a pleasant haze of whiskey. This made it bearable.

Before he sat down behind his typewriter he stood at the window and stuffed his pipe far too full. He glared out at the sunrise. Another beautiful day.

From this point he could see all Brunton below him. There was the curving beach of golden shingle and grey sand, the contours of Beachy Head, the groins and the breakwaters (black and angular), the silver winter tides, the pale-green summer sea. The *horrors* of Brunton—the Sally Lun and the Copper Kettle Tea Shoppes, the nightmares of attached and semi-detached villas and the private hotels that were mere concoctions of turrets, battlements, pinnacles, spires, towers and olde oake signs—were hidden from him by merciful mist and blinding sun. They were too far away for him to see in detail. He could just see the twin oxidized domes of the Brunton Hotel. He could just see the roofs of Radcliff Hall School . . . There was something he ought to remember. But *what?*

His mind was already "in the stalls of a deserted theatre . .
Trixie Duncan bent and straightened a wrinkle on her fleshy
thigh . . . tights . . . Bonzo Buckman, the comedian, with a
twisted face and a reek of alcohol . . . the curtains went up with a
swish . . . Trixie screamed, 'You swine, you swine!' "

What ought he to remember? He dragged his thoughts away
from Trixie Duncan and Bonzo Buckman and went to the
kitchen. Something about . . . *yes*—the whiskey!

IV

He crouched and opened the little cupboard he used as a
cellar.

He still had two full bottles, both from Devilbogers. He had
that boring old bottle of white wine (Had that now for *months* and
months. Must do something with it. Cook with it, perhaps?) and
that half of gin. And there were all the empties! What a lot of
empties.

He got them out and tipped them tinkling on to the kitchen
floor. There were three empty gin-bottles. (Funny. Who drinks
as much gin as that?) Two empty bottles of claret. (Remember
buying that claret in Paris in 1946? Before the travel ban shut
down? Remember the things the customs officer said?) And
empty whiskey-bottles. *Oh, lor'!* There were fifteen of them.
Drawhurst must send his van to fetch them away, fetch them away,
fetch them away . . .

"Good morning, sir."

The voice was high and brisk and maddening. Not like Mrs.
Cluny's at all. Bracewood-Smith groped his mind ('*How* sluggish
is my mind before ten') back from the floor to the window and
concentrated.

"May I come in, sir?" said the voice. "Sergeant Tomkins
here."

V

The sergeant sat in the sitting-room. Mrs. Cluny had arrived
and now went banging about in the bedroom next door.

"Drink?" said Bracewood-Smith automatically.

"Don't mind if I do," said Sergeant Tomkins. "If you can spare it."

There was a pause while Bracewood-Smith wondered about policemen not drinking on duty and thought this acceptance rather sinister, and then the whiskey sputtered into the glasses and annihilated thought. Oddly, the glasses were clean. There was another pause as Bracewood-Smith poured water into them.

"Bungho," said the sergeant.

"Good health," said Bracewood-Smith.

"Well, sir," said Tomkins, opening his brief-case and taking out papers, "got your statement here. Just necessary for you to read it an' sign it. Says what you told me last night concerning the death of Miss Devaloys. In police language, like . . ."

Bracewood-Smith wiped his eyes and blew his nose and read it through.

"That seems about it," he said. "Funny," he added. "I knew her quite well. . . ." And he signed it.

"Good oh," said Sergeant Tomkins. "Results of the autopsy aren't yet known, but that whiskey of yours, sir, the *weapon*, as you might say . . ."—he looked sharply at Bracewood-Smith, who seemed to be giving an imitation of a sleepy lion—"it contained seventy per cent of a narcotic belongin' to the barbituric group. For sleeping-pills, it's usually used. Reckon about fifty of 'em must've been used. If we find traces in the corpse it's murder okeydoke."

"Fancy! Someone must have doctored it," said Bracewood-Smith. He drank the remains of a glass of whiskey rather noisily. "Hope there's nothing wrong with *this* bottle."

"Tastes all right," said Tomkins. "I see you were having a decko at your empties," he added.

"Yes," said Bracewood-Smith, and yawned. "I must have 'em taken away."

"C'd *I* have a go at 'em? I've no warrant, of course, but it would save me time in tracing that particular bottle."

"Of course." Bracewood-Smith's eyes strayed back to his desk and his typewriter. "Can you do it alone?" he said politely. "I've some work to do."

He was already on his feet.

"Thanks very much," said Tomkins. "Yes, I can do it alone. Just one thing, though, sir. Any idea if Miss Devaloys had enemies? Sorry to disturb you. Thanks for the drink."

"Not at all," said Bracewood-Smith, gravely and politely. He held the door open and repeated vaguely, "Enemies?"

Mrs. Cluny, a hard-faced young woman in her thirties, emerged from the bedroom wearing a print overall, and sniffed.

"Mrs. Cluny," said Bracewood-Smith very politely, "this gentleman is from the police. He will look around. Allow him to go anywhere he wants and take anything he wants."

Mrs. Cluny looked surprised. Bracewood-Smith turned back to Tomkins.

"Enemies?" he repeated. "Oh, absolutely not."

And he re-entered his sitting-room and shut the door. Presently they heard the key turn in the lock.

VI

Tomkins went into the kitchen. He put his waterproof on a chair. He wiped his hands and began upon the whiskey-bottles. There were five *John Haigs*. One was called (on very small labels pasted on the back) *Les Caves de France*, another was called *Wine Sippers* (Brunton). The other two were unmistakable Drawhursts. The remaining whiskey-bottles were *White Label*, something called *Rare Old Liqueur* and something Very Scotch with a picture of a haggis with a tartan bow on it that said, '*A Wee Drammie an' a Haggie an' another Wee Drammie*'.

"Hooch," said the cynical Tomkins, and sniffed the neck of the bottle. It smelt of cork and copper filings and sawdust. "*Hooch*," repeated Tomkins.

By and by Mrs. Cluny came and stood over him with her arms akimbo. She said:

"Call yourself very smart, disturbin' respectable folks."

Tomkins was a foreigner (Cockney), so Mrs. Cluny distrusted him.

"You silly Sussex," he said pleasantly. "No holdin' you. So smart you'd cut yourselves."

This for some reason pleased Mrs. Cluny.

"Got a bit of old sack or something? For me to take this lot away in?" said Tomkins. "Put in the back of the car?"

"Some folks," said Mrs. Cluny bitterly. "Drivin' round in motor-cars," she added, in a darker tone, "spendin' our good money." But she found a little sack called 'Fertilizer' at the back of the cupboard, and Tomkins dropped the bottles into it. They clashed together.

"What's he like?" he said, and jerked his head at the sitting-room door. The rattle of the typewriter now shook the whole bungalow. "Bashin' out masterpieces," said Tomkins wistfully.

"Queer," said Mrs. Cluny, and sniffed. "Fact is, though, he's regular. Pays up. Quite the gent."

"Where's he sleep?" said Tomkins.

VII

The bedroom had a double bed, now neatly made; a horrid stained-oak press containing a tweed suit and a city suit and four pairs of filthy grey flannel trousers; a chest of drawers; a chair and a bedside table with a reading-lamp.

The Loves of Frank Harris and Jean-Paul Sartre's *The Reprieve* lay beside the bed. *The Rock Pool* by Cyril Connolly had been thrown into a corner. There was a copy of the *New Statesman* folded up and used as a window wedge. There was a complete set of uniform Kipling in a badly made book-trough on top of the chest of drawers. When Tomkins opened one of the drawers, *Zuleika Dobson* was lying among the underwear. With the sweaters and pullovers was a book called *Mamzelle of the Remove* by Mavis Chare.

Tomkins had a thing about girls' school stories, and he stole *Mamzelle of the Remove* while Mrs. Cluny was doing the bathroom. He dropped it into the sack on top of the whiskey-bottles. Except for the scattered books (which Mrs. Cluny had evidently been told not to touch) the room was unremarkable. There was a half-full tumbler of water by the bedside, a pipe and a box of tobacco. Some matches. On the window-ledge there was another tumbler, sticky with old whiskey and (possibly) sugar. There were aspirins, a bottle of liquid paraffin, a pot called 'The Ointment' and a bottle of black, thick cough-mixture. Tomkins put the cough-mixture and the dirty tumbler in the sack. The cough mixture had a label that said 'Micah and Son, Chemist, Brunton-on-Sea.'

"Goo'-bye, going now," said Tomkins, and put his head into the bathroom.

"Don' you want to see the dining-room?" said Mrs. Cluny suspiciously.

"Well, if you insist," said Tomkins.

"Nothin' to see *as* you can see," said Mrs. Cluny, and Tomkins went whistling down the garden path to the police-car. It is significant of Tomkins' incredible vitality that he now had a different driver. Beatty, the other, had retired to bed, whacked, at 3 a.m. Tomkins had not been to bed at all.

"Strike the iron w'en it's hot, Jones my boy," said Tomkins.

"Yes, Sergeant," said Jones, and then, respectfully: "How was he?"

Jones was a nice, fresh-faced local boy, known to one and all as 'Casey'.

"Wuzzy," said Sergeant Tomkins. He turned round. He could just discern the gorilla shape of the detective-novelist at the window. For a second a red cavern appeared among the beard as though Bracewood-Smith attempted a social smile. "Wuzzy," repeated Tomkins firmly. "Funny thing," he added, "I don't believe Mrs. Cluny knew anything about the murder at all."

CHAPTER TWO

"You were very late home from rehearsal last night," said Mrs. Puke.

She faced her daughter, Charity Puke, teacher of Latin and Greek and therefore a clever girl, across the breakfast-table accusingly. Charity had been known at every school where she had attended and taught as 'Pukey', but this did not stop her mother calling her by her proper name on all occasions.

Mrs. Puke was a querulous, difficult lady in her sixties, much messed about with old shapeless garments of mauve and a mouse's nest of beige hair. At the sideboard, Pukey shrugged her heavy shoulders and growled that no wonder she was late, Mother, when Miss Devaloys had been murdered.

"You speak so indistinctly," said Mrs. Puke, "and in such a *grunting* sort of way, I almost understood you to say that someone was *murdered*. So you see, Charity, how you must take care. How your girls can hear you in form *I* don't know."

Pukey took a kipper and sat down. She said very loudly and distinctly that Miss Devaloys *had* been murdered and could she have some tea, please. Her mother poured the tea and handed the cup without complaining of her daughter's rudeness. She was stunned.

Their two-storeyed bungalow, Woodmansterne, was over-furnished and stuffed with relics of Mrs. Puke's better days. Warming-pans, bellows, antique fireguards, little brass ornaments for hanging on cart-horses (though heaven knows why, for no Puke ever kept a cart-horse), silver snuffers, a knick-knack table (containing medals and the late Major Puke's revolver)—all these things littered the sitting-room. The bellows were particularly redundant in Woodmansterne, a house warmed entirely by gas-fires.

"Miss Devaloys *murdered* . . ." Mrs. Puke repeated. She sat with the teapot poised. She gathered her tippet of hand-embroidered crocus-coloured wool about her. "I can't believe it. Now if it had been Miss Fork-Thomas . . ."

Mrs. Puke paused dramatically.

Alas, the unhappy Pukey nourished a forbidden friendship with Miss Fork-Thomas. Not unnaturally she preferred evenings spent in the drawing-room at West House, even when she had to read aloud to the elder girls, to evenings spent in Woodmansterne, under the framed photographs of Mrs. Puke and Major Puke, R.E., on their wedding-day.

"Oh, do shut *up*, Mother!" growled Pukey. She buttered a piece of toast and put too much marmalade on her plate.

"If *that's* the sort of manners you learn from your new friends . . ." began her mother menacingly.

"I suppose you mean does Gwylan take too much marmalade?" snarled Pukey, suddenly angry.

"Oh, Charity, Charity!" whined Mrs. Puke. "How can you speak to your mother like that? Oh, I don't *know* . . ."

Pukey, who was a good-natured (if unattractive) lump, was very upset and thought that she had been very unkind to her mother.

"But I must hurry," she said, when she had apologized, "or I shall miss prayers."

And she raced upstairs to her bedroom, where her treasures, all gathered together in a tiny suitcase, were hidden by lock and key from Mrs. Puke's jealous eye. One might have used this adjective about Mrs. Puke altogether, but her eye was particularly jealous.

Pukey's treasures could hardly have been more pathetic. There were her sleeping-pills, two of which she took when she needed them, without Mrs. Puke's knowledge. There was a photograph of Gwylan taken on that picnic on August Bank Holiday that she and Pukey and Doctor Lariat had gone on a year ago. Pukey's car had been used and therefore Pukey had gone, too, because Lariat's was in dock. Gwylan treated Pukey's car quite as though it were her own, and Pukey was glad that she should. When the basic ration had been withdrawn, however, and Pukey had not been allowed a supplementary, it was noticeable (Mrs. Puke said) how Gwylan's affection for Pukey had waned. Pukey wished for Gwylan's happiness. Now that Miss Devaloys was dead, *surely* Gwylan and Philip would get married right away? Pukey was longing to be Gwylan's bridesmaid. In fact Pukey was a sweet, simple, mentally arrested girl.

Also in the suitcase were relics of her innocent past. There was a prayer-book inscribed *To Charity from Monica* (a friend who was up with her at Cambridge), and there was a photograph of 'Bill, yours ever'. Bill was a plain frank young man with an open neck shirt and an Adam's apple, who stared straight into the camera lens and now sold carpets in India. Pukey had played lawn tennis with him in a tournament at Scarborough. And there were letters from Gwylan (very precious) and a letter from Bill (fairly precious) and a postcard from Monica, who had got married and now lived in the U.S.A.

Pukey never left this suitcase at home because her mother was inclined to poke about, resenting the corners of her daughter's mind where she was not invited. Mrs. Puke was indeed difficult. She was not interested in bridge or politics and therefore had no friends of her own, and when Pukey made friends they were not good class.

Bill was a cad. Monica was common. Gwylan was . . .

"Well, she's *Welsh*. And that's quite enough. Even if she didn't go round in that silly, furtive way with that young Doctor Lariat." This fragment of the last serious row she had had with her mother rose now from Pukey's little attaché-case to torment her. It even seemed to distort the cherished photograph of Gwylan and Philip, taken by Pukey. Mother spoilt *everything*.

Pukey shut the lid of her attaché-case with quite a vicious

snap and turned to the head of the stairs with it under her arm Mrs. Puke began screaming:

"*It's gone the quarter!* What will Miss Lipscoomb think? Do you want to spend your life *begging on the streets?*"

Mrs. Puke did not scream these questions as though she wished for information.

"Oh, shut *up*, Mother!" said Pukey. She rattled downstairs. "Miss Lipscoomb will think I'm damned good to get to prayers at *all* after having been kept up all night, questioned by that policeman."

And Pukey bolted out of the house and slammed the door behind her, while Mrs. Puke, baulked, sat upon a carved oak settle of singularly hideous design. It blocked off most of the hall of Woodmansterne.

"Oh, oh! She is so selfish," moaned Mrs. Puke, and began to cry. "And she uses such bad language. She doesn't love me at all. And she didn't even *say* whether she'd be in to supper."

And Mrs. Puke, who found everyone in Brunton-on-Sea so common, discovered to her annoyance that her daughter had told her absolutely nothing about the murder. She put on her hat and set out for the shops half an hour earlier than usual.

She was to attend a strictly non-political lecture in the house of the local Conservative agent at 4.30 that afternoon. It was by the distinguished author Mr. Peter Bracewood-Smith, and it was entitled *Crime and the Individual*. Mrs. Puke, in common with lady Conservatives, liked a good crime.

II

"Where now, Sergeant?" said Jones admiringly. "Don't you want any breakfast?"

The big black Wolseley turned down High Street, Brunton. It passed Miss Puke, peddling furiously up the hill to Radcliff Hall School, the attaché-case bouncing slightly in the wickerwork basket on her handlebars. It passed Mrs. Puke, bouncing down-hill on foot to the fishmonger.

"Breakfast?" said Tomkins vaguely. "Oh no. I'll have a coffee later. A minute saved this end of the job'll mean a coupla days *that* end. An' don't you ever forget it."

Jones said that he wouldn't.

"Micah," said Tomkins. "The chemist."

Jones turned out of the High Street and halted the car opposite J. Micah, pharmaceutical and dispensing chemist. J. Micah had been dead for some years. Graham Micah, his son, and Mrs. G. Micah, his son's wife, now ran the business. They were bright, brisk, fully qualified chemists, passionate amateur photographers. They lived in a flat above the shop and sometimes took members of the staff of Radcliff Hall School as paying guests. There was a close liaison between Mrs. Micah and Miss Lipscoomb. They were Conservatives, although Mrs. Micah (who was 35) was a Young Conservative. Graham Micah and Mrs. Graham Micah both hoped to attend Bracewood-Smith's lecture that afternoon. It was early closing day.

Graham Micah was brushing the step as they drove up. He smiled toothily at Sergeant Tomkins. He wore a white coat.

Behind him the enchanting elegance of an up-to-date chemist glittered and blazed in the morning sun. The remedies for asthma and bronchitis, the Cow and Gate food, the patent spinach in its coloured tin, the kiddies' icky bicky pegs, the cardboard replica of the Kodak girl, the sponges, the hair-brushes, the rows and rows of cold cures (like poker chips in little boxes), the trays of pastel-coloured cosmetics in vulgar cardboard boxes—all these had no effect on Sergeant Tomkins. He walked briskly into the dispensary beyond the shop, taking everything else for granted. Mr. Micah followed him.

The dispensary was connected with the Micahs' flat by a small hideous staircase, covered with a brilliant oilcloth that showed a vivid green Grecian urn upon a crimson ground. Everyone who lived in the flat had to pass through the shop and the dispensary to reach the street. There was no separate street door.

Tomkins deposited his chinking sack on the bench among the tiny weighing-machines, the distilled water, the drawers marked 'Tinct.' and 'Pot.' and 'Bism.' and 'Silt.' and 'Supht.'

"Here on business, I see," said Mr. Micah, rubbing his hands briskly together. "Police business, I mean."

Graham Micah was tall, and possibly consumptive. Kipling would have expected him to write verses on the white wrapping-paper. He kept a little gas-jet burning all day for the sealing-wax for the parcels.

" 'Fraid so," said Tomkins. "Looks like murder, this business up at the Hall. French teacher. You got a paying guest now?" he added, jerking his head up at the ceiling with a gesture very like a cock sparrow.

"Yes, oh yes," said Micah carefully, his mouth falling slowly open. "Mr. Partick-Thistle. He's usually here four days a week, but since they've been rehearsing it's been all the time. Funny. He didn't tell us about . . ." Mr. Micah paused and coughed, "the French teacher. But there, he usually comes in late."

"Nice young man. Drugs," said Tomkins briefly. He unpacked his empty bottle of cough-mixture.

"Now that you mention it I have noticed that his eyes . . ." began Micah. He spoke rapidly and in an undertone, occasionally glancing over his shoulder at the staircase. "Mind you, I don't suppose it's more than an occasional sleeping-tablet . . ."

"Pretty regular, if you're askin' *me*," said Tomkins. "Do many people in the town take sleeping-pills? You *are* the only chemist, aren't you?"

"Well, yes," said Micah, with some pride, "we *are*. Brunton air is good for sleep, but some people need a little extra. We have *some* prescriptions deposited with us, of course; repeats of fifty or twenty-five at a time, you know, renewed by the doctor when necessary. Patent compounds of opium and barbituric. You know the kind of thing."

"Do they have to sign the poison-book?" said Tomkins.

"*We* copy the prescriptions," said Micah, surprised. "You ought to know that," he went on chattily, "and you a policeman."

Micah flipped open a heavy book bound in patent leather with brass corners. He opened it, with Tomkins straining over his shoulder to see. The prescriptions were copied in a beautiful copper-plate hand and the names of the subjects were inscribed in red ink.

"Lovely writin'," said Tomkins. "Can I have a look?"

He carried the book over to the window.

"*Mrs.* Micah," said Micah proudly. "She's *very* artistic."

"Yes, indeed," said Tomkins.

The names that leapt at him from the paper as he flipped through page after page and month after month were all well known to him. There was Major Banderlog, the old fool who was always complaining about noise and dogs' filth, who lived in the Indian quarter beside the pier. There was old Lady Fondant, who was half dead anyway, and very unkind to her lady companion. There was Mr. Intrikit, the manager of the

Brunton Hotel, who went in for spiritualism and witchcraft and black magic. And there were other names, more significant to this story and much better known to you and me.

There was Miss Lipscoomb. There was Miss Puke. There was Miss Fork-Thomas. There was (a very recent entry) Roger Partick-Thistle. And there was the dead woman, Miss Devaloys herself.

"Hullo, 'ullo, 'ullo," said Tomkins gaily, copying out the names. "These school-teachers seem to be a sleepless lot, I must say. *And* your P.G."

He turned to Micah, who grinned and bowed at what he considered vaguely must have been a joke. Micah was a rare sort of human being: a lover of accuracy, who had once said to his wife: "The trouble with me is I have no humour. I can't see a joke." And his wife had said it was just as well, because who wanted a humorous chemist?

"Does Lariat get his supplies from you?" said Tomkins briskly.

"Yes. Yes. I don't know if they're *all* he gets, of course," said Micah. "Naturally, all the prescriptions he makes out for Brunton people would come here. We're the only chemist for miles."

"Good," said Tomkins. He laid his cough-mixture bottle on the table. "That one of yours?" he said.

Micah said it was. "Certainly. Oh, Mr. Bracewood-Smith. Oh yes. The novelist. We have a special supply of Alka Seltza for *him*."

"No sleeping-pills?" said Tomkins.

"Not that I remember," said Micah. "Isn't he in the book?" Tomkins shook his head.

"What's in the cough mixture?" he said.

"Oh, just the usual," said Micah casually. "We keep a great big supply of it here ready made up. We draw it off by the half pint."

"Just like beer," said Sergeant Tomkins.

"Pardon?" said Micah. "It's one of our old bottles," he went on, examining it. "We haven't used that shape for at least a year. Everything's screw tops now."

"Oh well," said Tomkins, "Mr. Bracewood-Smith can't have been suffering much with his chest."

"Can't have been suffering much at all," said Micah gravely, and he nodded his head at the unsold tubes of Alka Seltza that stood behind him.

"Always nice to know," said Tomkins, and turned to leave the shop.

He almost collided with Roger Partick-Thistle. Roger was a neat conventional figure in a sombre suit. His head was bare and careless with its usual unconventional beauty. Roger hurried out of the shop behind Tomkins, walking on his heels.

"Goin' to London or something?" said Tomkins wistfully. He looked at the young man's smooth shoulders and his hard, clean white collar.

"No," said Roger. "I didn't think I *could.*" He recovered himself. "I mean, dear, that I thought you wouldn't want us to leave *at all.* Until you've apprehended someone."

Tomkins looked surprised.

"Oh no," he said. "*You* can go to London if you want. Only wish I could. Why the glad rags, though, if you'll excuse me?"

"I thought," said Roger, surprised, "I thought when there was a murder, dear, that we were all kept under supervision, dear, until the arrest. The glad rags, as you so wittily call them, are by distress out of respect. For the dead, you know."

"*We?*" repeated Tomkins. He frowned and his little sandy eyebrows were cross and bristly. "Who d'you mean by *we?*"

"We, dear?" said Roger carelessly. "Why, the *suspects*, of course."

III

At what stage in this Wednesday morning the astonishing Sergeant Tomkins visited his Chief Constable and made his report on the case I cannot say. I only know that he was sitting doing what he was pleased to call Having A Coffee, in Epsom's the teashop and baker in the High Street, at half past eleven in the forenoon, with a silly self-satisfied smirk on his face. He was eating two madeira cakes with the coffee, and when Natasha and Miriam came in he was pleased to meet them.

Miriam, of course, greeted him like an old friend and almost kissed him on both cheeks. Natasha was more reserved. But both ladies were agreed that they would have a coffee with the sergeant.

Sergeant Tomkins ordered it. When he was away, Miriam snatched his madeira cake and ate it, swallowing quite a lot of it whole (this being her custom). Natasha said that she reminded her of Amy, the pekinese, and then became Slav and sad "because of missing the little dog", and Miriam was quite glad when Tomkins came back and told them that the Chief Constable wanted him to have a go. At the murder, he explained.

"Not but what," he went on earnestly, eying the last crumbs as Miriam brushed them from her lap, "it isn't really a case for the Yard by rights. But there, miss, you know what these provincials *are*. . . ."

Miriam, who had buried one husband and had two still living, bridled like a boa constrictor when Tomkins called her 'miss'.

". . . Conceited as hell. Full of local pride. Must show East Kent or some such place . . ."

Miriam was now heard to say indistinctly that Brunton-on-Sea wasn't Provinces, as it wasn't even on a fifth-rate music-hall circuit.

"Oh, come, miss," said Tomkins, suddenly silly Sussex himself. "Sarah Bernhardt once stayed here. And we've got the Repertory. Ever so good they are. Home Counties, *we* are."

Miriam sniffed.

"Everlasting *Quiet Wedding* and *Dear Octopus* and *Fools Rush In*," she said.

Natasha said what could be being nicer unless it was *Autumn Crocus* or *Call It a Day*, and the Sergeant now observed a distinct lowering between his two table companions. He attempted a change of subject.

"Not teaching, this bright morn?" he said ponderously.

Miriam's gargoyle scowl would certainly have been torn down by Cromwell for obscenity.

"Detecting much, darling?" said Miriam, and struck him playfully on the knee. He recoiled.

"I only meant why are you both out before lunch," he said nervously.

"We are not, they tell us both, to be teaching at *oll* until to-morrow morning," said Natasha slowly, "and so we are both feeling we should be having a little freedom. Cream buns and freedom," she added wistfully, as the sergeant's second order, four cream buns filled with life-giving synthetic cream and vanished jam, arrived with three cups of coffee and a bright young waitress in white.

"Particularly," said Miriam, rolling her pale blue eyes, "as we have agreed to play Miss Susan and Miss Phoebe in Miss

Lipscoomb's Founder's Day play. Mrs. Grossbody will not be well enough to play Miss Susan. Miss Devaloys is, of course, dead."

Sergeant Tomkins was startled. Closer scrutiny would have shown that he was appalled.

"Goodness," he said. "Miriam Birdseye, straight at last, and as Susan Throstle. Cor!" He drank his coffee and sighed deeply. "If they bill you it'll be a sell-out."

Miriam cast down her eyes and simpered.

"Miss Lipscoomb has ordered three-inch billing from the *Brunton Observer* and everyone is going to pay for their seats," she said.

"And we are going to get a percentage," said Natasha gaily.

The sergeant choked in his cup.

"And now please tell us, de-ah boy," said Miriam, choosing her moment, "all about your *lovely* murder."

IV

The sergeant drew a deep and confidential breath and lowered his voice. He glanced round Epsom's, which was deserted but for a woman in a turquoise head-scarf and pram, and a child in gumboots buying sponge cake, and old Mrs. Puke in a corner. Then he began to speak. His uneasy cocksure manner had gone. He was all intelligence and sensibility and intensity of purpose.

"Look here, Miss Birdseye," he began in a low hoarse whisper. "I wouldn't tell this to anyone but you. Not even my wife. Fact is, I'm worried. This is one of these fancy inside jobs, like. Not my tea. Don't care for it at *all*. How the 'ell can *I* get inside a girls' school and tart about pickin' up motives? An' that's what it's goin' to amount to."

"Why?" said Natasha, and caught Miriam's eye.

The lady with the pram went out, and the child bought its sponge cake. Old Mrs. Puke got up and moved a little nearer to them. She had recognized the sergeant because he had once called on her during the war about inefficient black-out.

"Well, look here," said the sergeant, utterly forgetting his conspiratorial whisper. "Here's the stage." He turned a plate upside down and put a teaspoon on it. "Here's Miss Devaloys," he said.

"Dead," said Natasha, in a pleased, childish voice.

"Dead," agreed the sergeant. "An' here," he went on, "are all the cast of this play."

He turned to Miriam and asked her if she knew the play at all, and Miriam said she would soon, as she was quick study. She elegantly held her nose for a second or two.

"I quite agree, miss," said Tomkins. "I see you know it. Well, I got it out of the public library an' had a look. Murderer must of been someone who knew Miss Phoebe was goin' to drink this cordial. An' who had opportunity of doctoring same. *Therefore* probably someone concerned with the Founder's Day play. Or wouldn't you say?"

"Couldn't A with you, M," said Miriam, and slowly spread her cream bun across her chin.

"Well, first there's two wallflowers in this scene," said Tomkins, licking his finger and turning up a copy of *Quality Street* bound in pale blue with a white label. Stamped across each page in purple was 'BRUNTON PUBLIC LIBRARY. DO NOT TAKE AWAY'.

"Gwen Soames and this nasty little Jewess," said Natasha.

"I hate Gwen Soames," said Miriam passionately. "She made a fool of me in elocution. I hope she did it."

"Hardly grounds for murder," said Tomkins sensibly. "And both young ladies are under twenty-one."

"Doesn't mean a thing, dear," said Miriam. "Lots of children are homicidal."

"Well, these children'll have to show access to poison an' motive to destroy Miss Devaloys before I can get a British jury to swallow them. No, miss; sorry, I don't think it's likely." Sergeant Tomkins sounded genuinely sorry, as though he wished to please Miss Birdseye. "Then there are the other small parts. There's Miss Lipscoomb an' Miss Phipps, her seckertery. Miss Lipscoomb takes sleeping-pills. I have evidence."

Miriam looked angry.

"Don't be ridiculous, darling," said Miriam. "So do I take sleeping-pills. That doesn't mean a thing either. Miss Lipscoomb obviously had a low-grade male mind and would therefore use a meat-chopper. Not *poison*, dear. Poison's a woman's weapon."

Tomkins said, doubtfully, that he saw what she meant.

"That sort of loose psychological conjecture won't do for the police," he added firmly. "No. We mustn't jump to any conclusions. Miss Phipps, so far as I know, don't drug. She don't look or act like it, for one thing. She *may*, of course," he added unhappily, "and buy them somewhere else, like London."

"But she is not looking like it," said Natasha. "That one does not. But I will find out for certain. A school secretary would be unlikely to be using any but the local chemist and getting the rake-off."

Tomkins regarded Natasha with admiration.

"Sound," he said. "Sound. Then there's Ensign Blades, the mathematics mistress (no information about pills) . . ."

"I'll get it," said Natasha happily.

"And Miss Puke (Spicer the bewitched), who takes slumber-well. I've evidence to that effect. And Doctor Lariat with access to the whole poison-cupboard, and that washes up the cast."

"But the producer, the prompter and Roger Partick-Thistle?"

"They all take 'em," said Tomkins callously, "of one kind or another. So until I get the motives straightened out, you see how it is?"

They both saw how it was, and Natasha became excited. She leant across the wickerwork table with the pink glass top and her hair fell forward over her eyes. She tossed it back.

"Since you are knowing Miriam and seeing how anxious to be helping she is and I also, and since kudos is not a thing we are wanting, you——"

"Would let us help," said Miriam.

"Well, with the *motives*," said Natasha. She laid one lovely white hand on the sergeant's arm and looked up at him through her lashes. There was a pause while he turned a little pinker and breathed a little faster.

"Darling, I'm *good* at that sort of thing," said Miriam, and she too put a warm hand upon the sergeant on the other side.

"Oh, lor!" said Tomkins. But he was not displeased. His little moustache was still full of vitality.

"Tell you what, miss," he said, patting Miriam's hand. "Try. You bring in some proven motives with corroborative evidence for these people against Miss D. and Mrs. G. an' then we'll see if'n I can use them, shall we? Not," he added cunningly, looking at Natasha, "but what I don't doubt you won't manage anything *valuable*."

"You are *mean*," said Miriam angrily. "I can tell you *one* right away. . . ."

And completely abandoning all ideals of fair play to the client,

Miriam told Tomkins how Miss Devaloys had plotted to destroy Radcliff Hall School and Miss Lipscoomb and to rebuild it in her own image with the help of Miss Helena bbirch. And how Miss Lipscoomb had then thrown the ash-tray at her.

"For the honour of the school," said Tomkins, and chuckled. "Now that's a motive appeals to yours truly. Crazy about school stories, I am. Got one off Mr. Bracewood-Smith but I promise myself not to read it till the case is cleared up. . . ."

He wrote down the facts that Miriam had told him in his notebook. "We won't take a statement about them till we know if it's necessary," said Tomkins. He made a face as he wrote Miss bbirch's name. "Don' fancy popping along to interview *that* old bit of fluff," he said. "So let's hope it ain't Miss Lipscoomb. Have to prove that she doctored that whiskey or even knew of its existence, or substituted a bottle of her own. Gor', what a game! My fowls are the doctor and the boy, Partick-Thistle."

"You are *mean*," wailed Miriam. "Poor Rodgy! Why?"

"I do not like thee, Doctor Fell," said Tomkins. "An' Thistle's a friend of yours, is he? Oh well. Go ahead and clear him. Point is," he added, writing a little list on a blank page in his notebook, "all these people present. Those with crosses we *know* had access to sleeping-pills, probably in large enough quantity to cause death. That one with the motive written in we know the motive."

"Your grasp is astounding," said Miriam, without sarcasm.

The list looked like this:

Miss Lipscoomb. X. For security. Deceased menaced her living. Nothing known against Mrs. G.
Bracewood-Smith
Fork-Thomas   X
Partick-Thistle   X
Miss Puke   X
Miss Lesarum
Doctor Lariat   X
Miss Phipps

No one in the party observed Mrs. Puke, who now rose to her feet and slipped out of Epsom's into the glittering High Street. She had a trouble-making expression on her face.

Natasha and Miriam got up and the sergeant gallantly paid his bill. On the broad window, below the sign '*Epsom, Fancy Cakes and Morning Teas*', was a pink bill pasted neatly with sticky corners.

It announced that Peter Bracewood-Smith, author of etc., etc., was due to lecture on *Crime and the Individual* in the hall adjacent to the house of Miss Try, Conservative agent to the constituency of Brunton. At 4.30.

"Oo, look, it's old Pol Roger '29," said Miriam gaily. "If he's talking about crime let's go, instead of going to *A Matter of Life and Death.*"

"I am a fan," said Natasha; "and what is a Conservative?"

"I haven't seen one for years," said Miriam.

CHAPTER THREE

MRS. PUKE, poised on the kerb a hundred yards above Epsom's the pastrycooks, wondered which way she could turn with her priceless information. Truthfully, she would not *see* anyone who would be interested in this piece of scandal until the meeting at Miss Try's at 4.30 that afternoon. She did not know whom she might seek out. She was not popular and she knew it, but such pieces of gossip did not often come her way. A large black Rover, driven by Doctor Lariat, drew up beside her. The doctor's handsome, mobile face was all recognition and charm. Old Mrs. Puke was a nice heart disease.

"Why, look," he said, in his nice open boyish way. "How about a lift to the top of the hill? Might do that ticker of yours a bit of good."

Mrs. Puke, although certain that the late Major Puke would have called *his* heart a 'ticker', would much have preferred that the doctor should refer to *hers* as The Heart. Yet, after a little conversation about the inconvenience she was causing him, she climbed into the Rover and opened fire with her port guns.

"I think it's very *furtive* of Charity to take sleeping-pills—slumberwell, or whatever they're called—without telling me, her mother. Why, it gave me quite a shock. . . ."

"Oh?" said the doctor. He smoothly let in his clutch. His sad oriental eyes glanced sideways at the withered old hands, clenched with old-fashioned garnets, that grasped the shopping-basket. "So Pukey takes slumberwell, does she?"

At the nickname, Mrs. Puke winced and determined to show this common young man no mercy.

"Do you mean to say that you don't know, Doctor? That it wasn't *you* who prescribed it?"

"Why, yes; wait a second," said Lariat, altogether too casually, noted Mrs. Puke sourly. "Don't get excited. I believe I did. She wasn't sleeping so well that time after she got so anxious about you. *That* was it now, wasn't it?" he beamed. He was all polished efficiency and well-organized memory once again.

There was a pause while the doctor blew his horn to warn some repulsive leaping morons of children, escaped from school at their lunch-time. They burst across his bows, yelling, from the elementary school. As the Rover waited at the traffic lights, old Mrs. Puke swung out of the line of battle into the wind, trained her starboard guns and fired.

"This Sergeant Tomkins is very clever, they say. I'm glad he's in charge of the murder, Charity tells me. Though I *must* say enlisting the help of two of the teachers at the Hall, and one of them a foreigner——"

"What's that?" Doctor Lariat's face turned from a healthy pallor to a cheesy green.

"Didn't you *know*?" Mrs. Puke was gleeful. "To ferret round and collect motives. . . ." She looked up cunningly through old horny eyelids and began brilliantly to extemporize. "*Charity* tells me these ladies have a list of all the *suspects*. Seemingly Miss Lipscoomb is top of it, poor thing."

"Goodness!" said Doctor Lariat, and began to stutter. "That doesn't seem proper police procedure, now does it?"

"Oh, I don't know," said Mrs. Puke airily. "If they catch Miss Devaloys' *murderer* I dare say *any* methods are justified. Though *that's* a Jesuitical point of view," she said kindly, "which you wouldn't understand."

Lariat's handsome Jewish nose flushed a little and his speech became ever so slightly thicker.

"However was this list made out? Whoever could they put on it?" he said. He stopped the car by the gate of Woodmansterne.

"Oh, everyone at the rehearsal, I understand," said Mrs. Puke briskly. She began to get out, dripping mauve scarfs and woollen turn-back gauntlets and an old leather purse with a brass catch to it. "*How* clumsy of me. I'm so sorry. Thank you. But of course only those with access to the *poison*, as I suppose we must call it. A nice thing, I must say. Murder at the Hall. *Disgusting*."

Nevertheless Mrs. Puke did not seem disgusted as she skipped towards the neat dark-green gate of Woodmansterne. Lariat sat frozen and horrified. His hands in their smart new washleather gloves were motionless on the wheel, his face was no longer plump and prosperous.

"Well, very many thanks for the lift, Doctor."

"Not at all," said Lariat automatically. Then he suddenly leant forward. "Mrs. Puke," he said nervously, through the car window. "Mrs. Puke, do you know who *else* was on the list? Besides Miss Lipscoomb?"

Mrs. Puke considered. She put her head on one side and looked very much like a parrot. Then she fired her broadside.

"Why, Miss Fork-Thomas was on it," she said venomously, "of *course*. And I understand there was no love lost *there*. And *you* were on it, Doctor, naturally. Oh, and some others. But the sergeant didn't seem to think them important. . . ."

Lariat said nothing. Then he very slowly lifted his black Anthony Eden hat.

"Thank you," he said humbly. "Thank you. Good-bye."

He drove slowly away.

Old Mrs. Puke, tittering slightly, walked into Woodmansterne to cook herself two nice greedy fillets of real sole for her lunch. She had made young Lariat *hop*.

"That'll learn *him*," she said, as she slapped dripping into her frying-pan. "That'll learn him to play fast and loose with school-teachers. Two of 'em at once. . . ."

The fat sputtered and fumed and smoked.

"Using Charity's car to take his girl friends joy-riding, with Black Market petrol. . . ."

Mrs. Puke dropped in the fillets of sole. They dwindled and crisped in the fat as though they were damned and she was the Evil One, with complete dominion over them. As indeed she had.

II

Walking uphill to Radcliff Hall from Epsom's, with stiff sore legs and bad tempers, Natasha and Miriam encountered Miss Lesarum. She was swinging gaily along in her Girl Guide uniform, looking, as Miriam pointed out, just the job. That lean look on her harshly modelled face Miriam kindly attributed to her natural hunger for the school luncheon. She *was* curiously like a West African native.

"Well," said Miriam chattily, "isn't this all *awful?*"

"Ugh!" said Miss Lesarum, and nodded. "It is. Except, of course, *you* can't feel it as *we* do who have been associated with the Hall so long."

"No," said Natasha. "No. That is something to be being grateful for."

They turned in at the great black gates. They were neatly labelled GO SLOW. RADCLIFF HALL. Miriam and Natasha were trotting to keep up with the loping stride of Miss Lesarum.

"Why," said Miss Lesarum gruffly, "I've been here ever since Dad died, and that must have been eighteen years ago. Dear me! And I'm an Old Girl, you know. . . ."

She spoke smugly.

"Goodness!" said Miriam, and was dumb.

"It is *such* a fine record," said Natasha, with sincerity shining in her enormous hazel eyes.

"Isn't it?" said Miss Lesarum, with simple pride.

"And I expect you know everyone so *awfully* well," said Miriam.

"And can probably say just quite, quite when Miss Devaloys first came and how she was received here and all that," went on Natasha with a flash of inspiration.

They were now walking up the ragged, pot-holed drive towards East House. Hedges of tamarisk guarded it. Pine trees gloomed around West House on their right. Miriam was thankful that she could not see the sunk garden and the plaster dwarfs.

" 'Course I can," grunted Miss Lesarum. "She's nothing like so senior as me. For length of service, I mean. Compared with me and Forky."

Natasha noted that Miss Lesarum considered her work at Radcliff Hall in the nature of a long-service commission in the Wrens.

"Has Forky been here long too, then?" said Miriam, prancing over a pothole full of water.

"Exactly the same length of time as me," said Miss Lesarum proudly. "For she was a kid teacher my first term in the Sixth. Her first job when I was head of the school. Her first job. Oh yes. Forky and I got on *jolly* well. . . ."

"I didn't like Miss Devaloys either," said Miriam. "And I only knew her for a day or two. Now you——"

"Endured her for *three years*!" cried Miss Lesarum passionately. "She was foul to all of us. I hated her." Then she added, with incredible naivety, "I always thought that she was jel. of Forky getting West, you know, when Miss Helena——" Miss Lesarum stopped and pulled her Guider's hat straight upon her woolly mop of hair.

"This would be being Miss bbirch," said Natasha, and nodded.

"Yes. When Miss bbirch went. But that business over Philip Lariat about evened things out. Well, I must pop," concluded Miss Lesarum startlingly. "Can't hang around, eh, now can I? Forky'll *murder* me if I'm late for lunch."

And she disappeared, galloping, through the pine trees towards West House, leaving Miriam and Natasha helpless on East House doorstep.

"No," said Miriam wistfully. "I'm afraid we can't only count the business with Philip Lariat as a motive. I don't suppose Miss Fork-Thomas would murder anyone just for intense dislike."

"Yes, she is civilized, that one," said Natasha. "Or apparently so. I wonder if Miss Lesarum knows just how strangely her last remark is sounding."

III

Miriam opened the front door. The usual lunch-time milling about was going on inside. Maud Stuckenheimer passed them, rolling her eyes, pushing some of the younger girls into line. Miriam suddenly put her head down and plunged through the semi-darkness and the mass of snorting, kicking schoolgirls. She arrived (more or less) safely in the dining-room. Natasha crossly massaged an ankle.

"It is this *Gwen* Soames," said Natasha. "I am *positive* she kick me. I will show her."

Natasha sulked.

Miss Lipscoomb entered through the other door and came towards them. She wore a grey silk shirt with a high semi-stiff collar and a dark-green tie and she seemed cheerful.

"A significant *occurrence* has *occurred*," she said. "Miss Devaloys' diary has been found."

The other door flew open and the room quickly filled as she handed Miriam an exercise-book bound up in green-and-purple-marbled boards.

IV

After luncheon, escaping from the horrible noises of the released and screaming young ladies (and also from the horrors of lukewarm coffee in Miss Lipscoomb's sitting-room), Natasha and Miriam ran through the sunk garden to Miriam's room. Natasha passed the plaster dwarfs with her eyes shut, which was considered by Miriam to be affectation. They examined their prize. It was a good thick book. It was labelled, unashamedly enough, *Theresa Devaloys*.

It began amiably in French, as one of Miss Devaloys' little articles for the *Engerdine Post*. It was all about the significance of the University of Grenoble in European education. Miriam, reading and translating in a loud clear voice like an electric bell, suddenly said she thought it was very dull. Natasha took it away from her and turned it upside down and began at the back. Here it started with a school song, evidently to be sung to the tune of 'Stars and Stripes'.

> We're the Girls of the Lower Remove
> The Best Lower Form at St. *Saviour's* . .

"Well," said Miriam, after Natasha had been singing for a minute or two, "that's all very well, dear, but it isn't even a school song of Radcliff Hall. Rather off the point, pet. Is there anything else?"

"Only a list of *names*," said Natasha slowly. "In columns. With questions, marks and prices. Oh, and remarks written in short-hand. Pitman's shorthand. And sometimes there is being a sentence very small and fine in red ink, done with mapping-pen."

"Like what?" said Miriam. "And how do you know what it is if it is in shorthand?"

"I am learning it once. It is easier than Russian," said Natasha simply. "Well. Like *Major Bandarlog*. £20. *Beats wife*, and *Mr.*

Intrikit has affaire *with barmaid?* £10 *or even less*. And then she has written *Never worth it for a tenner* in pencil."

"Let *me* see," cried Miriam. And she spread the book open on the floor and crouched over it, crooning. "Fancy you speaking in shorthand, pet," she said. "Translate."

And Natasha, speaking very slowly, translated the weird hieroglyphics, looking so much like Arabic and yet, as Natasha so rightly said, *so much* easier than Russian.

Miss Lipscoomb	Also might drag up that old Swiss business. But unnecessary. Speak to Charteris about acreage.
Bracewood-Smith	
Fork-Thomas	Write to Fox and Fox.
Lady Fondant	Footman, seen with on downs? £50.
Partick-Thistle	*News of the World*, 29.1.35? 10£ p.m.
Puke	
Lesarum	Positive about parents now Sergeant Gurkha Regiment/Englishwoman. Any money better than none.
Phipps	23 Overstone Drive, Brunton.
Lariat	Positively no dead wife.

"It is a blackmailer's notebook," said Natasha excitedly.

"With records of transactions. What a bitch!" said Miriam.

Natasha said wait, how could Miriam be sure?

"My dear, of course I'm sure. 1935 was the year Rodgy was Assistant Grey Wolf at a Wolf Cub pack near Brighton. That was the year he changed his name to Partick-Thistle."

"Oh," said Natasha, "I see."

"10£ p.m.," said Miriam thoughtfully. "Ten pounds a month, I expect. Poor darling Rodgy. What a silly boy."

Natasha quite agreed. "Let us be finding him," she said, "and getting the details before Sergeant Tomkins is beastly about him. And who are Fox and Fox? And what does that arrow mean?"

"I don't know," said Miriam. "They sound like bookmakers. Something to ask Fork-Thomas, perhaps? Charteris is the auctioneer, of course. I remember that one . . ."

And there was a knock on the door. It was Miss Phipps. She burst in, panting slightly. Her well-cut wool taffeta blouse rose and fell. Her elaborate hair-do bounced in the light wind of her coming.

"Run all the way," she announced gaily. "Miss Lipscoomb

wants everyone in the gym *immediately*. He's got Doctor Lariat and Mr. Bracewood-Smith and it's quite disrupted the time-table and IVB have had to give up gym *again*. And he has another bottle of whiskey and a corkscrew and we're to do the whole thing over, and if it wasn't for Miss Zwart being a Plymouth Rock there'd be no one to teach at *all*, so we've set the whole school an essay. And naturally you'll have to do your parts."

Miriam growled that she didn't know her part yet and who was *he* anyway?

"It must be being the dear Sergeant she is meaning," said Natasha, who had listened with grave care to Miss Phipps' message.

"That's right," said Miss Phipps, and spun round to go out of the room.

"*Miss Phipps*," cried Miriam, after her, "*who lives at 23 Overstone Drive, Brunton?*"

Miss Phipps gasped. Her face sagged. She became fifty years old. Deep lines suddenly appeared in her face, running from her nose to her chin. She slammed the door and faced Miriam with ghastly courage.

"——!" she said. "Can't the lot of you leave a poor girl alone to earn her living? He's my *nephew*, I tell you. Can't an auntie look after a nephew, if her sister, her *favourite* sister, *his* mother's dead? That's what I told that bitch Theresa Devaloys and that's what'll do for *you*, too——"

"I think you are so *right*," said Natasha soothingly.

"You keep out of this, you dirty Russian," said Miss Phipps passionately. "No better than you ought to be, obviously. And suppose I had gone wrong, as they call it, where'd the shame be? And if you don't damn' well mind your own business you'll get a taste of what I gave Theresa . . ."

"Yes, dear, yes," said Miriam blandly. "Go on. What did you give Theresa?"

"Oh!" said Miss Phipps. She sank into a chair and covered her face with her hands. "What have I said?"

CHAPTER FOUR

Miss Phipps' little outburst delayed their arrival in the gymnasium by fifteen minutes. She had to be soothed, and given an aspirin in warm water, and Natasha and Miriam had to discuss the tiny illegitimate child-size skeleton in Miss Phipps' cupboard. This they managed to do as they ran along. Miriam complained fretfully that 'all this exercise' was making her legs too thick.

"But oll those school-teachers are having skeletons," said Natasha, vaguely surprised.

"I think it's *awful*," panted Miriam. "She's afraid, poor sweet, of getting the sack, I suppose. . . ." Miriam was incoherent. "I must say I think Theresa Devaloys was *hell*. . . ."

"What I am wondering is how far she is actually going with her bloddy notebook. Perhaps she has only actually been black-mailing Phipps, for example, and Phipps give her the flea in the ear," said Natasha. She paused with her hand on the swing door of the gymnasium.

"But obviously, darling," said Miriam. "That's what Phipps meant when she said she would give *me* what she would give Theresa Thing. I mean it was *obvious* . . ."

"You are generous," Natasha said. "An unkind lawyer could have been making this remark mean anything. But *anything*."

"Don't lose your head, dear," said Miriam, "I'm not an unkind lawyer."

And she passed into the gymnasium.

II

A large member of the Sussex Constabulary rose from a chair, creaking, and murmured that Sergeant Tomkins was up by the stage. He also said (in a hoarse whisper and accusingly) that it was past 3.30. They saw Miss Phipps come through the swing doors on to the stage from the back. She had come through the music wing. Natasha and Miriam now observed their friend Sergeant Tomkins, a small dejected figure, sitting among the footlights.

"We are so offully sorry to hold things *up*," said Natasha. She swept forward like royalty, only perhaps with more grace.

"All right, miss. I like a bit sit," said Tomkins. His active lack of sleep had begun to tell on him. His eyes were red-rimmed as well as bloodshot. His manner was indomitable.

"What we're chiefly gathered together *for*," he said, standing up. He raised his voice and swung it about the room. "What we're chiefly gathered together for," he repeated, "is to find out exactly the movements that bottle of whiskey passed through after it entered the gymnasium. That is why," he added, "I have mustered you all here so that you may check each other's statements and so we will all be agreed about this rather important matter. Constable Briggs, who is an expert shorthand writer, will take down the substance of the discussion, and I must warn you we may require to use it in evidence."

Natasha and Miriam glanced around them. Drawn up in the gloomy shade by the ribstalls, against the vaulting-horses under the draped ropes, were Miss Lesarum, Miss Lipscoomb, Maud Stuckenheimer, and Roger Partick-Thistle. On the stage, talking in nervous undertones, were Miss Puke and Gwen Soames and Miss Phipps. The two men, Lariat and Bracewood-Smith ("Who are causing most of this trouble, let us face it," said Natasha, looking at them), were huddled together as though for warmth and protection on the far side of the room. Miss Fork-Thomas joined them as the sergeant began to speak. She laid a hand on Lariat's shoulder, and he seemed grateful and comforted.

"I may say," said Tomkins chattily, with a slight lapse from his parade-ground manner, "that the cause of death in the case of this lady was a very large proportion of Slumberwell, which in the opinion of the police-surgeon was contained in about fifty tablets or capsules. It is a patent sleeping-draught much in use in this town. It is only issued under a doctor's prescription, usually in *forties*. I may say"—and here the sergeant allowed himself a discreet little titter—"it appears to have been taken in a very large quantity of alcohol."

Maud Stuckenheimer was heard to say that people who drank hooch quite often went blind, and her brother Tony knew a fellow in Tunbridge Wells who——

"Now that raises a point," said Tomkins, spinning round on his little feet. "This whiskey was of the same high standard which we expect from John Haig. The cork and tinfoil were perfectly intact when Miss Fork-Thomas, the stage manager, drew the cork. Or so you have said, madam?" He spun back again to Gwylan Fork-Thomas, who removed her hand from Lariat's shoulder but otherwise looked composed.

"That is so," said Gwylan, as though practising for police evidence.

"And you stick to that, madam?"

"I do."

"And you realize the importance and the implications of this answer?"

"You mean, I suppose," said Gwylan bitterly, "that I was the person best qualified and with the best opportunity and the easiest access to this bottle, and that I probably introduced the slumberwell?"

Tomkins said nothing, but his bright little eyes watched Gwylan Fork-Thomas. A faint Welsh intonation had crept into her speech, otherwise unruffled and smooth as usual. It betrayed her. So she was not as calm as she sounded.

"Oh yes, I realize all that, look. But I am not a conjuror. And I seem to remember that someone was at my elbow when I drew the cork."

There was a pause, while the ripple that had run round the gymnasium died and each one present looked at his neighbour.

"I can't, however, recall whom this might be," said Gwylan Fork-Thomas wearily. She rubbed her forehead with one slim hand. Then she looked round the gymnasium, and it was obvious that her gentian-blue eyes were no longer undisturbed. Charity Puke, standing on one leg, leaning against the Swedish horse, suddenly started upright and blushed a firm and unbecoming crimson. She folded her arms.

"Me," she said in a deep, anxious voice. "It was ... er ... me."

Sergeant Tomkins rustled some papers and said good, that was just what he hoped to find out; and Miss Lipscoomb said, "I, dear, I," and caused Constable Briggs some trouble with his notes.

"And did you see me put anything into this whiskey or the glass that I poured it into?" said Gwylan coldly. "Because if I did you *must* tell the sergeant, you know."

"No—er—no. That is . . ." said Pukey, "*no*."

"No," said Briggs, and he and Sergeant Tomkins wrote it down.

"We'll check on this," said Tomkins, "with your movements, miss," and he went gently on with his narrative. Pukey, who had looked as though she wished to say something else, now grunted and put her hands in her pockets.

"That's the staff with the crush on Fork-Thomas," said Miriam to Natasha. "Is Fork-Thomas mentioned in Theresa's testament?"

"There is this Fox and Fox that Theresa was to write to," said Natasha doubtfully, "with this little line."

The sergeant in loud clear tones was now repeating the scene from *Quality Street* that is so well-known to us. Miriam tip-toed (although she would soon be required upon the stage as Miss Susan) towards Fork-Thomas and Lariat. They were standing hand in hand. Bracewood-Smith sat crouched on the floor and hugged his knees and said nothing at all.

As Miriam came up to them Lariat dropped Gwylan's hand and hissed at Bracewood-Smith:

"Aren't you disturbed at all, Bracewood? Damn it, man, you brought the stuff in yourself."

"Why should I be?" said Bracewood-Smith casually. "*I'd* no motive to kill the girl." And he whistled under his breath and through his square strong sound teeth a little number out of *Annie Get Your Gun* called 'The Girl That I Marry', and Doctor Lariat did not appear to care for it at all.

III

Sergeant Tomkins was calling over the names of the cast and everyone was answering to them. Miriam said "Here" when he said "Miss Susan", and then she stood beside Miss Fork-Thomas in the gloom. She said to her, gently, that she thought Miss Puke was possibly lying.

Miss Fork-Thomas turned her head and said that was obvious, wasn't it? This disconcerted Miriam, who said that sort of thing made it so confusing for the police.

"Yes, doesn't it?" said Miss Fork-Thomas, with an amiable smile. "Now look," she added, teasing. "Can I stop the foolish girl testifying for me? Now can I?"

"No," said Miriam, in a tone that meant 'Most obviously, yes', and plunged to the attack. "Who are *Fox and Fox*?" she said, fairly loudly. In the dark there was a little noise, as though someone gasped.

"I've no idea," said Miss Fork-Thomas eventually. Her voice was curiously level and even. "They sound like bookmakers and house-agents," she added quietly.

"Or solicitors," said Lariat, entering into the spirit of the thing. "Why do you want to know?"

On the stage Sergeant Tomkins called everyone to get into position for the start of the scene, please. Miriam went on cosily talking.

"*I* see them as solicitors," she said. "Very, very old family solicitors. In butterfly collars."

"Miss Birdseye, please!" said Tomkins, with more than a hint of displeasure. Miriam went towards the stage slowly and pouted. People sat up and began to take a little notice. Perhaps Miriam wouldn't be Policeman's Pet much longer, and that would make a nice change.

IV

"Now then, as I understand it, this scene commences with the two wallflowers, Harriet and Charlotte, one on each side of Miss Susan—that is, Miss Birdseye," announced Tomkins in gentlemanly tones.

Gwen Soames and Maud Stuckenheimer rose and shuffled forward. Maud remarked that she thought that it was the sticky limit that she should be a *wallflower* in the only murder case she might ever have to do with in her life.

"Let's hope so, Maud," said Gwen Soames, in shocked tones.

"Oh, *you*!" said Maud, and put out her narrow muscular tongue. She had not yet acquired that facility of repartee considered so desirable by her brother Tony and his circle. Maud and Gwen sat on their bench. After some delay Miriam joined them. She said rapidly that although she did not yet know her part as well as *Matron* it would be all right on the night and they were both a couple of little devils. Which upset Gwen Soames.

"Now, commence from the commencement, please," said Tomkins again. And so they did.

The scene could hardly be said to go with a swing. Whenever the sergeant sprang up and asked where the whiskey was, and whose entrance was next from the whiskey (or O.P.) side, Miriam heaved a great sigh and reached into her bosom to scan her part. She had it typewritten with cues on loose sheets of quarto paper. It was disconcerting to Gwen Soames and Maud Stuckenheimer, but on the whole the young ladies bore with Miriam very well.

The answer to Sergeant Tomkins' question was always the

same. No one had touched the whiskey. It had stood (with its attendant tumbler, into which perhaps four fingers of whiskey had originally been poured by Miss Fork-Thomas) on a small green-baize table screened from the main hall of the gymnasium and also from the music wing. It had been shrouded by the curtains and it had stood there all the time.

These curtains were a curious blend of old gold and string colour and were considered 'very artistic'. They were the gift, as it so happens, of Mrs. Stuckenheimer, mamma to Maud and Daisy. They had been most efficient at shrouding the whiskey from the view of all.

Thereafter, as the scene progressed, the tumbler was lifted by Miss Lesarum in her capacity as Ensign Blades and carried on the stage, where it was tossed off by Natasha as Miss Phoebe, in full view of everyone. Miss Lesarum then took it away and filled it up again, perhaps four times. Maud Stuckenheimer suddenly realized how *very sinister* this was and caused a slight diversion.

"And who ordered these replenishments?" said Sergeant Tomkins.

"No one," said Miss Lesarum, fidgeting. "I mean, it wasn't necessary, I just did it myself without being told.'

"Ah! . . ." said the sergeant, and Miss Lesarum became very upset, too. By the time that Maud Stuckenheimer's hysteria had been soothed and she had been slapped roughly and maternally on the back by Gwen Soames, and by the time that Miss Lesarum was also happy again, Tomkins wound himself up for one of his public outbursts.

"That," he said, tangling participles as though they were rambler roses, "seems to preclude the possibility *of* some person having been placing the poison, already in solution, in this glass. Matron's indisposition would also be pointing to the entire contents of the whiskey-bottle having become poisoned between the drawing of the cork and its final consumption."

There was a deep and heartfelt pause, and Miss Fork-Thomas said plaintively that *that* had always been obvious, and Doctor Lariat said shut up, Gwylan, and not to annoy the man any more.

"Incidentally," said Tomkins, roused and rather vexed, "since my theory depends upon the fact that this bottle was securely corked and the seal unbroken, where is the cork?"

Everyone in the gymnasium looked (and was) surprised. Yes indeed, where was the cork?

Miss Lipscoomb turned to Miss Puke and said, "Good point, good point," and Miss Phipps said irrelevantly that for a professional actress Miss Birdseye wasn't showing up very well. And everyone sighed with relief when Gwylan Fork-Thomas produced a cork from the pocket of her navy-blue dress. This, she now pointed out, was the same dress that she had worn at the rehearsal.

"That's a lucky thing," said Sergeant Tomkins. "But you ought to have handed it over sooner, miss."

"Yes," said Gwylan.

"And why didn't you replace the cork in the bottle, miss?"

"I don't know," said Gwylan wearily. "I just don't know."

"Oh, very well," said Tomkins, and shrugged his shoulders. It was obvious to everyone there that Gwylan wasn't doing too well.

"This must be the tinfoil, too," said Gwylan suddenly, producing another little object from the same pocket. "I expect I put *that* there for the hospital. We collect silver paper in West House," she explained with a cold bright smile, full of charity and good works. Sergeant Tomkins stared.

"Do you?" he said. He glanced at the cork. It was much mangled by the corkscrew. He put cork and tinfoil in an envelope and laid them carefully on the floor with his notes.

"Now then," he pursued ponderously, "at Miss Devaloys falling unconscious to the floor, where were all your positions?"

If he had hoped for some outstanding reaction, Tomkins was disappointed. Most people looked nervously at their feet and one or two shuffled them.

Tomkins' painstaking reconstruction of the movements of the cast about the stage around the whiskey-bottle recalled nothing that we do not know already. Miss Phipps had gone to telephone and she now said so, glaring for some reason at Miriam. Miss Lipscoomb and Miss Puke (after Miss Puke's vain attempt at artificial respiration) had gone to hold back the Lower Fourth singing-class with Mrs. Pont, the accompanist and singing-teacher. Lariat and Peter Bracewood-Smith had carried Miss Devaloys away.

"Very wrong of you, if I may say so, sir," said Tomkins, suddenly severe. His tone implied, 'We'll never have you as police-surgeon if you go on like that, you know'.

"I'm sorry," said Lariat.

"It was *so* awkward," said Miss Lipscoomb imploringly, "what with the little girls being due any minute and what with trying to keep it all a secret . . ."

"There does seem to have been very little trouble, and I must say I was summoned very quickly," said Tomkins, as though to reassure this important ratepayer. "Ah well. P'r'aps it won't look quite so bad in the evidence. P'r'aps the judge won't go for you, ma'am."

And he winked again. Again Natasha and Miriam were aware of the extraordinary vitality of Tomkins. Miss Lipscoomb looked quite gay again.

"And he has on a pink-and-blue paisley tie today, dear," pointed out Natasha inconsequently to Miriam.

Roger Partick-Thistle repeated his evidence about poor Matron and the arras with fewer 'my dears' and hardly any parentheses. Someone said that they heard Matron was due for discharge from the Cottage Hospital and Sergeant Tomkins, who was a little light-headed with lack of sleep, realized that he had lost his command of the proceedings. He promptly called it a day.

"You may go if you wish," he said, and sat down again amongst the footlights.

Miss Lipscoomb bustled out. She said over her shoulder to Bracewood-Smith that she had *just* time to see the school hand in its essays to Miss Zwart before she went to hear Mr. Bracewood-Smith's most *interesting* lecture. Bracewood-Smith smiled amiably (as befits a successful novelist) and pulled his beard. He shambled to his feet, looking very like a bear as he did so, and shook imaginary dust from his elbows.

"What essay is that?" asked Sergeant Tomkins, wrinkling his eyebrows.

"Set to the whole school on account of all the staff being at your rehearsal, darling," said Miriam. "Subject, 'My Happiest Day'. Too macabre." And Miriam shuddered.

"If you don't know your part any better than *that* by next Thursday, miss," said Tomkins, "this play is going to be a *flop*."

"I know the *whole* of Act I already, and so does Natasha," said Miriam severely. "Don't be silly, dear. Show him Theresa's testament, Natasha."

And the two ladies crowded round Tomkins together. He

went quite bristly with pleasure. They pointed out to him the page of the entries that they considered to be blackmail records. The sergeant whistled and said he wasn't at all surprised about Major Bandarlog and Lady Fondant and Mr. Intrikit. Apparently he, too, could read Pitman's shorthand.

"'Ad me eye on that there Major for some time," said Tomkins bitterly. "Causes us more trouble than anyone else living in Pondicherry Parade. Always a complaint about something or other. Tell you what." The sergeant sucked his teeth and giggled. "I'll 'ave Briggs there go an' interview Bandarlog. Do them both good. Ask him if he beats his wife, Briggs."

Briggs advanced creaking towards the row of footlights and said the sergeant wasn't half a one.

"What do you make of Miss Fork-Thomas' reaction to the words 'Fox and Fox'?" said Miriam. "*That* happened when you were ticking me off, dear, so you see. What do you suppose they are? A double act? On the halls? Swinging by their teeth and singing *Tosca*?"

"Conjurors," said Tomkins without hesitation. "Conjurors and ventriloquists. Oh, *definitely*."

"And that's why I like him, dear," explained Miriam, turning to Natasha.

"Oh, get on with you, Miss Birdseye!" said Tomkins. But he looked pleased. He stooped and opened the envelope with the cork and the tinfoil in it. He held the two objects in the palm of his hands. They were short square hands with very small ginger whiskers on them.

"Be holding on, please," said Natasha suddenly, and laid her hand (a long smooth hand trimmed with neat scarlet finger-nails) on his sleeve. "Be holding on. That is not John Haig foil at *all*. That is Gordon's gin."

And indeed it was. Natasha was perfectly right.

V

Sergeant Tomkins confessed that he was puzzled. He wrinkled up his little face and looked from Natasha to Miriam and back again.

"What I want to know really is 'ow the 'ell that stuff *got* in this whiskey at all!" he said explosively. They were still standing on the stage beside the square table that Miss Lipscoomb used to hold her Bible and Prayer Book at morning prayers. Miss Phipps had officiously moved the table back into place as they stood there talking. "It stands to reason," said Tomkins fretfully. "No one could possibly dissolve all those capsules before they arrived here, and then pour the stuff *in* without being seen. I mean, it's not *likely*. . . ." And he ran his square hands with their broken, bitten finger-nails through his hair. "And they can't *all* be lying," he concluded angrily. "Proper gum tree, that's what it is."

"Oh yes, isn't it?" said Natasha.

"Miss Puke was," said Miriam suddenly. "Lying, I mean, not a gum tree."

"Oh, *you* noticed that, did you, Miss Birdseye?"

"So did Fork-Thomas," she said. "She told me so."

"These *school*-teachers," said Natasha.

CHAPTER FIVE

MEANWHILE, Charity Puke walked back to West House with her friend Gwylan Fork-Thomas. A Sussex sunset, all pink and diffused light and gun-metal clouds and other shadowy splendours, lay ahead of them.

"Of *course* I'll take Winston Churchill for his walk, Gwylan," said Pukey fondly, "if you want to go to Mr. Bracewood-Smith's lecture. Honestly, I don't want to go one little bit."

"Don't you? Oh well," said Gwylan. "It's very kind of you." Gwylan was obviously thinking of something else. "He *whines* so if he isn't absolutely worn out by six. And that gets on my nerves," she added. Pukey lurched a little among the potholes in the drive. She turned one of her thick ankles. "Be careful, dear," said Gwylan sharply.

"Sorry," said Pukey roughly.

They reached the door of West House. The pine trees grew all round it, pressing closer, even pressing out the last grey-and-pink light of dusk and sunset. It was well past four o'clock. At the door-way the golden spaniel, Winston Churchill, came cavorting to meet them, shaking his golden ears. Gwylan promptly became quite fond of him, just because she was to be free of him for an

110

hour or so. She fussed over his lead and collar and even reminded Pukey not to let him eat stones.

"Of course I won't, Gwylan," said Pukey earnestly. Her untidy bob blew all about her foolish, kindly face. "I *always* treat him just as you do and hit him for all the same things. Why, Gwylan, I'm nearly as fond of *him* as I am of *you*."

"Good," said Gwylan lightly and handed over the lead.

She stood in the doorway of West House and watched the well-groomed golden dog and the unkempt young woman lolloping down the drive towards the damp countryside. There was already a small clue to Spring in the air.

Gwylan turned into her smooth, well-decorated drawing-room. Only an infinitesimal responsibility awaited her this evening, or indeed on any other evening. She had to say good night to her prefects. After that she was as free as air.

Gwylan had what is known as a genius for deputization. It meant that she never appeared to do a stroke of work. Many people thought she was lazy, and perhaps they were right. Yet how could that powerful concentration (with which Gwylan so purposefully bent others to her will), how could all that be called laziness? It had required someone as selfish as Theresa Devaloys to remain unswayed by Gwylan.

II

Gwylan's prefects were waiting for her in her drawing-room. She stood poised for a second in her serene white-painted doorway and looked them over. They were a poor-looking lot. There was a red-haired foxy-faced girl from Pontefract, a Jewess, a Portuguese and a dull dentist's daughter. The girl from Pontefract and the Portuguese both had a crush on Gwylan. It is a sad fact that the human judgment (however keen) may so easily become warped by personal considerations that Gwylan truthfully believed that these two girls were quite nice. She called them both *intelligent* and had once told Miss Devaloys that the Portuguese had excellent taste in artistic matters. Miss Devaloys had sniffed.

"Good night, Miss Fork-Thomas," said Noni Postman, the red-haired girl from Pontefract. "I hope you enjoy the lecture. I *do* wish the Sixth *had* been allowed to go."

"I wish that too, thank you, Noni," said Gwylan. She left

young Miss Postman in a transport of delight for the evening, trying to figure out whether Forky had *meant* anything by this remark.

"I wondered if I might borrow another book, please, Miss Fork-Thomas, and thank you for the *Bridehead Revisited*, it was ever so good, I think," said Molly Ruminara, the Portuguese. "But a thriller this time, if you don't mind." She spoke English well, without much trace of accent.

"Just help yourself, Molly," said Gwylan, and turned her back on her. Molly had a new boil this evening. "And do tell me which one you've taken," she added, in the silvery and hospitable tones that all the prefects but Molly and Noni called 'putting on the Ritz'. "Then we can have a jolly good *discuss* after, can't we?"

"Oh *yes*, Miss Fork-Thomas," said Molly. She crouched on the floor by the bookcase like an ape.

"Good night, Miss Fork-Thomas," said the dull dentist's daughter, whose name Gwylan could not remember. Gwylan said good night rather coolly, and I really cannot blame her.

The room emptied. Only Molly Ruminara remained, running her fawn, prehensile hands up and down the shelf of thrillers. It was a well-stocked shelf. There were all the vintage Agatha Christies (and even some of the non-vintage years), there was *A Surfeit of Lampreys* by Ngaio Marsh, and *Death in Ecstasy* by the same author, there was the complete Dorothy Sayers' Whimsey saga. And there were also, in the cheap and vulgar dust-jackets, brightly coloured as no human beings, or skulls, or glasses of fizzing poison, or revolvers could ever (luckily) look, three books by P. Bracewood-Smith. Signed by the author.

"Can I take two, please, Miss Fork-Thomas?" said Molly Ruminara. "I do read ever so fast. Although it is against your rules."

"If you like," said Gwylan vaguely, still looking out of the window. "Which two do you want?"

"Oh, thanks awfully. Sorry. May I take *Strong Poison*, by Sayers, and *Death and the French Governess*, by P. Bracewood-Smith?"

"Do," said Gwylan, even more vaguely. "The Bracewood-Smiths aren't in the same class as the Sayers, of course, though."

How she wished the child would go. Her adolescent devotion was really too touching . . . or perhaps she honestly only wanted

something to read, in which case she could go and go *quickly*.
"Good night, Molly," said Gwylan firmly.

"Good night," said Molly, and the drawing-room door shut behind her with the faintest of clicks.

Gwylan, standing by the window, unclenched her hands. Nervy, that's what was the matter. Perhaps an aspirin . . . ? No, a drink would be even better. She opened the nasty *art-nouveau* cocktail-cabinet and mixed herself a drink. A very, very strong pink gin. It would no doubt have interested Sergeant Tomkins to know that she mixed her drink with Gordon's gin.

III

Tomkins went into the Brunton-on-Sea police-station swaying wearily. He went upstairs to put his papers away. He hardly noticed the ugly beige-and-green tiles that lined the staircase. He paid little attention to anything but his feet, which were now so swollen with fatigue that they felt four sizes too large for their ready made gent's suede shoes (dec. toecaps, 39*s*. 6*d*., seven coupons). The little corn on his little toe gave him gyp.

"Time I got some sleep," said Tomkins, who always used his feet as a barometer. He pushed open the door of his office. He found Police Constable Jones sitting behind his desk. On the little hard chair that was kept for visitors there was a visitor. It was old Mrs. Puke. She was wearing a very nasty hat trimmed with mauve and purple flowers.

Jones got up and came forward.

"Sergeant," he said, "Mrs. Puke has some evidence of motive in the Radcliff 'All School case. She thinks she ought to tell you personally. She thinks we ought to have the facts."

And Jones went out and shut the door.

Tomkins opened his eyes, which had closed at the sight of Mrs. Puke's hat.

"How do you do?" he said. The words came from many miles away as though he were talking in his sleep. "No more trouble with your window curtains, I'm sure?"

Mrs. Puke obviously considered this impertinence. She folded her lips tightly and clasped and unclasped the metal clip of her handbag. They had got off to a bad start.

"No, thank you," said Mrs. Puke.

"*Now*," said Tomkins, and slid his notes into the top drawer of his desk and locked it. He sat down and tried to stop thinking about his feet. "What is it that you wish to tell me, madam?"

Mrs. Puke looked down and looked up and was ruffled. Then something got the better of her annoyance and her eyes gleamed nastily. She began to speak rapidly and viciously. She said (as usual) she had the whole thing from her daughter Charity Puke, a mistress at the school. Tomkins, who had seen Pukey, knew at once how much value to set on Mrs. Puke's evidence.

"Yes. The young lady who is so good at artificial respiration," said Tomkins, and wrote 'N.B.G.' on his blotting-paper.

"I beg your pardon?" said Mrs. Puke.

"Nothing," said Tomkins. "Go on, please, madam."

So Mrs. Puke went on. She said that However Clever a doctor Was, he Hadn't really Behaved like a Gentleman to that poor Miss Devaloys. She said as early as last *October* he had been playing fast and loose one against the other. Surely the sergeant didn't think that right? Amorality in a doctor——

"Please, madam," said Tomkins. "Against the other? What other?"

"Why," said Mrs. Puke, surprised and angry, "Miss Fork-Thomas, my daughter's *friend*; that's how I *know*."

"Oh!" said Tomkins. "Go on."

So Mrs. Puke explained what an awful state her daughter Charity had got into last October and how her health had suffered and how she had thought at first it was just girlish invention. The sergeant knew what girls were and Tomkins leered. Since then she had an opportunity of speaking to the doctor about it. Speaking her *mind* too, if the sergeant didn't mind her saying so. . . .

Tomkins, whose knowledge of trouble-making old ladies was about as extensive as anyone's in Great Britain, said oh yes.

"And in your opinion, madam," he said, and began to lose his temper, "this Doctor Lariat was playing one against the other, and Miss F. Thomas was very jealous and angry with Miss Devaloys?"

"Yes, *yes*," said Mrs. Puke. "I'm perfectly certain of *that*. I know She doesn't Look Emotional, but I can assure you, Sergeant, my daughter Charity——"

Sergeant Tomkins said he saw what Mrs. Puke meant.

"And you'd be prepared to say all this in evidence before the court, madam?" said Tomkins, and again wrote 'N.B.G.' on his blotting-pad.

Mrs. Puke bridled. She didn't know about *that*. She had thought it was her duty to come forward as a private person with any facts she——

"*Yours* are not facts, madam," said Tomkins sharply. "Yours are theories. Or even *hearsay*. I'm sorry. And if you can't produce it in court, it's no use to *me*, madam. Good afternoon."

And he stood up and blinked his little bloodshot eyes as he did so. His wearied brain refused to listen or to register the connecting words in the outburst which now flowed all around and over him. Every now and then a savage noun sprang out of the narrative and exploded against his ears and he was forced to hear it. Otherwise he paid no attention.

"Extraordinary thing . . . rudeness . . . public department . . ." apparently said Mrs. Puke rapidly as she stood up. ". . . Complaint . . ." went on Mrs. Puke. ". . . Question in the House . . . Secretary of State . . ."

She was by now at the door and speaking even more rapidly, her voice rising to a shrill, whining scream. Tomkins' eyes shut again as he opened the door for her. Threats like 'Home Office' and 'Chief Constable of the County' and 'I'll break you' sprayed round him, as from a flame-thrower. They failed to rouse him.

"That's right, madam," he sighed. "You do that."

And he shut the door behind her and remained for a little while, holding himself up by the door handle, leaning against it on the inside.

There was a little black-enamelled hospital cot in the corner of the office. It had been left over from fire-watching. Tomkins looked at it longingly. Then he very slowly took off his shoes and his jacket. His toes instantly uncurled and crimped like an oyster in hot milk. He rolled his jacket in a ball and put it on his chair. He put the shoes together under the chair. Then he limped to the bed and folded up on it like a clasp-knife. Everything went smooth and merciful and black. He passed out.

IV

Gwylan Fork-Thomas drank her drink slowly and lit a cigarette. She was perhaps not altogether unaware of the slanders on her name that were now sliding round Brunton. She smoked her cigarette rather faster than is usual. She inhaled angrily and coughed once or twice.

She went over the facts as she could see them, isolating them, trimming them down, differentiating most exactly between what had appeared to be and what actually was the case. She remembered everything that had happened on the night of the rehearsal. Gwylan's laziness (if it were laziness) lay only in physical undertakings. She merely loathed anything that bored her.

There was nothing boring about the death of the wretched Theresa. It had happened right under her nose and because she had opened a bottle of whiskey. And it looked to her very much as though that sharp little sergeant was making out a case against her.

She lit another cigarette and poured another drink and looked at her watch. It was half past six. Pretty soon Pukey would come bounding in with Winston Churchill. She wanted above all things to avoid Pukey at this moment. Soon, too, everyone else would be returning from Bracewood-Smith's lecture and her peaceful interlude would stop. Gwylan grinned sardonically. She must make the best of it.

V

At twenty to seven she went to the telephone and rang up Doctor Lariat. She was told by Mrs. Buttick that the doctor was out. She told Mrs. Buttick that she would be walking over to talk to him. Mrs. Buttick sniffed.

At a quarter to seven Pukey came in with Winston Churchill, very tired and muddy, and Gwylan had already gone. Winston Churchill instantly fell asleep in his basket under the desk. On the desk there was a note for Pukey that said:

Thank you very much. Have a drink if you want one. I don't know what time I shall be back.

Gwylan.

Pukey was disappointed. She put the note in her pocket and didn't have a drink. She went across to the music wing and played the piano for some time, because she did not want to spend the evening with her mother. She played Couperin, Debussy and a little Mozart.

CHAPTER SIX

NATASHA and Miriam hurried down the hill towards Hereitis, Miss Try, the Conservative agent's, little house. Behind it was a Nissen hut where Peter Bracewood-Smith's lecture was to take place. Miss Try had inherited the hut from the R.A.F., during the war, in some obscure fashion.

They could just see Miss Lipscoomb and Miss Phipps ahead of them. Miss Lipscoomb was wearing a broad-brimmed black hat like a sombrero. Miss Phipps was wearing a head-scarf. Their chins were going furiously up and down as they talked to each other.

The evening was curiously still and luminous. Brunton, as a South Coast resort, is chiefly given over to health-giving gales and storms. Miss Lipscoomb's remarks came clearly towards them through the air.

"I really *do* think," she was saying, with all the incorrigible enthusiasm of the old-fashioned school-teacher, "I really do think *everything* is going to be all right."

"Provided Miss Birdseye learns her part," said Miss Phipps sourly.

"Aren't people *awful*?" said Miriam, as they approached the neat front gate and path of Hereitis. Miriam had thrown off her school-teacher's garments as 'too handicapping when there might be gentlemen'. She appeared in a very elegant little suit with a bolero in broad black-and white checks, and over all she wore a snow-white, spotlessly clean, naval officer's duffle coat with a hood. It is to be feared that no one would have suggested that she was either a school-teacher or a Conservative.

"Aren't people awful?" said Miriam. "So little faith."

II

Miss Try, heavily outlined against the dim yellow electric light, welcomed them in the doorway of the Nissen hut. She was a firm, busty figure. She was an ex-W.A.A.F. officer who had been a Conservative agent before the war. Now, she had no objection to being known as 'Squadron Officer Try'. She was a member of something called the Malcolm Club and consequently often appeared in Air Force blue, much decorated with the O.B.E., the Defence and Victory medals. She had an excellent opinion of herself and also of Lord Woolton and (possibly) Winston Churchill. She was, she said, pleased that Natasha and Miriam could come. Then she smacked Miriam on the shoulder (which Miriam did *not* care for) and said, "An old Service type?"

"*Type* I can stand, but not *old*," said Miriam, edging away.

Inside the Nissen hut there was a certain amount of confusion. There was (as Squadron Officer Try said) a good turnout. There were the chairs, spread about in ranks, and there upon them (or dragging them about the floor to speak more intimately with their friends) were the Brunton Conservatives, apparently entirely ladies.

They filled the hut with their bulky musquash coats and brown political hats. Miriam pointed this out to Natasha and whispered that at Labour Party meetings there were no men either and the ladies wore exactly the same uniform. Natasha, whose main preoccupation in life was clothes, wondered why. She suggested that possibly the Conservatives wore the coats to give the impression of a vast assembly? Miriam shrugged her shoulders, and said anyway the effect wasn't becoming. Squadron Officer Try rose to introduce the speaker.

III

In spite of the billing about the NON-POLITICAL aspects of the meeting, Squadron Officer Try's introduction was wildly full of propaganda. She spoke at some length about 'Central Office' ("Whatever this may be," said Natasha) and something called the Political Truce of which 'Transport House' had taken advantage. It was also, apparently, *up* to Miriam and Natasha to contribute as much as they could Jolly Well Afford to party funds. And there had been a Rotten Turn Out at the Member's Tea Party. And they ought to be Ashamed.

"And now," said Squadron Officer Try, "*Per Ardua Ad Astra.* I really must introduce our speaker and Leave Shop. Mr. Bracewood-Smith, whose picturesque figure (if I may call it so) we often see striding about our little township. He is to speak to us tonight on his very own subject, *Crime and the Individual.* Mr. Bracewood-Smith."

IV

Peter Bracewood-Smith, as novelists go, was only a moderate speaker, dealing in paradox rather than in logic, and in shocks rather than good, sound information and provocations.

"Crime," he began, "is entirely a matter of individual taste. We are all criminals at heart. . . ." There was a ripple of annoyance, quickly checked, among the audience. "Some of us have the courage to follow our inclinations. Others have not. These last tend to take their crime at second hand, inside the covers cf the who-dun-its, and so swell my bank balance. . . ." A titter, graciously checked by Mr. Bracewood-Smith. "Between these two sections of society is a nasty sneaking majority who dare not commit murder, but kick the cat. Who dare not rob banks, but get off buses without paying for their tickets. Who dare not set alight to their house or motor-car for the insurance money, but cheerfully accept a double ration of butter from their grocer if he offers it to them. . . ."

Bracewood-Smith paused and glared round his audience, now thoroughly embarrassed.

"*Such* petty sneak thiefery and gangsterism," he cried passionately, "is not, thank God, my concern tonight. Man is born to crime as smoke drifts upward. . . ." He flung back his great head, and using his fine bass-baritone as though it were all the brazen trumpets of the Judgment, he declaimed the first lines cf 'Paradise Lost':

" '*Of man's first Disobedience and the Fall* . . .' "

"The man's a fanatic, dear," said Miriam suddenly to Natasha.

Natasha started. She had been deep in a dream, adapting a raglan sleeve in her winter overcoat.

"What?" she said.

"*Fanatic*," said Miriam, more loudly. "Thinks everything's run for *him* personally. *I'm* not a criminal. *I* don't cheat the buses. I think he's mean. I don't kick cats or read thrillers."

"*But* you would accept double butter," said Natasha, wagging her head. "So perhaps this will be a Communist talk after all?" And Natasha sighed.

"Sh!" said a cross lady in eyeglasses in front of them, and, "Sh!" said the whole of the front row, turning round. "Sh!" said

Miriam instantly, turning to the rows behind her. Bracewood-Smith finished with 'Paradise Lost'. He gave a pat on the head to Milton as he passed and began to speak about the awful ape-like ingenuity used in the writing of detective novels.

"Of course," said Bracewood-Smith, his eyes blazing with interest and excitement, "the most perfect trick of *all* (one played so often by G. K. Chesterton in those irritating Father Brown stories) is that Things are not what they Seem. I mean, no man comes to the house (except the postman) and the murder is then committed by him. The diamond was hidden in a lot of other diamonds, so no one found it. The unbreakable alibi. The use of the murderer narrator. The injection of poison through a cracked egg to make an omelet. Things are never what they seem. At least, in fiction."

Bracewood-Smith paused and glared along the rows of flat-faced Conservative women. Even Squadron Officer Try had begun to pay attention. Even the cougher in the back row had stopped coughing.

"In *fact*," said Bracewood-Smith, with an unpleasant sneer, "or so the *police* tell us, everything is always what it seems. The most obvious suspect is your man. Crimes are always committed for a good reason and usually by homicidal maniacs. No one hides a diamond among a lot of diamonds. He takes it to Amsterdam in a tiny black bag and is consequently picked up by the Customs. The murderer is always the bloke with the motive who found the body. . . ."

An Independent lady (perhaps a Liberal) in the back row now became bored and said to her neighbour so what? She had heard all this much better put before, and everyone else had read *Strong Poison* and the *Murder of Roger Ackroyd* and the *News of the World*, too. Her neighbour said yes, she quite agreed, but do *hush*.

"So it follows, if only in fact," said Bracewood-Smith, apparently winding up to a terrific peroration, "*if only* in real life some criminal would employ the methods of Sayers and Christie and Chesterton he would . . . he would . . ." He paused and added in a tiny little voice with rather a silly giggle, "Why, he could get away with *murder*."

The Conservative ladies laughed heartily and were much relieved. Only the Liberal lady and Miriam were displeased. Miriam particularly was furious. She sat scowling heavily, her lips drawn up into a vexed pout. "Not a murderer, not a murderer, not a murderer," she muttered under her breath.

The lecture drew on through a barren waste of Bracewood-Smith's experience of life until Squadron Officer Try looked at her wrist-watch and said, "Any questions?"

Yes, there were questions. A lady in the back row had a copy of *Death and the Archbishop* she wanted autographed, and Bracewood-Smith began to beam through his beard like a dog. The Liberal lady then got up and asked if he had read Gross on *Criminal Investigation*? And Bracewood-Smith looked annoyed and said that wasn't necessary, surely, for a man with a B.A. in Law (Oxon.)? The Liberal lady said thank you, she had only wanted to *know*, and sat down leaving an unpleasant flavour about the meeting. In the pause that followed, darling Natasha rose slowly to her feet.

She looked extremely beautiful in this appalling setting. Her neat tweeds showed her slender shoulders to great advantage. Bracewood-Smith, appraising her from the platform, said, "Yes?" in a kindly tone.

"I am only wondering," said Natasha. "It is only perhaps a matter of opinion I ask for . . . you may not care to answer. . . ."

Mr. Bracewood-Smith said he was flattered, madam, to give his opinion on any subject at any time, and seemed to swell visibly upon the platform.

"Yes," said Natasha. "Then your opinion is what in real life is being the most motive for murder, would you say?"

"I should think to obtain *security*, madam," said Bracewood-Smith. "After all, that is why we *all* commit murder. It is why a country goes to war. It's a paradox, of course, madam, but I understand that Mister Average Citizen does not enjoy taking life. Or so they tell me. And it is only the hunted stag that dares to rend the hounds."

"Oh," said Miriam scornfully, from her seat. "That old menace-to-society stuff."

"I beg your pardon, madam?" said Bracewood-Smith invitingly.

"I only *said*," remarked Miriam, rising to her feet and tossing back her mane of yellow hair, "I only *said* that murderers always thought they were quite different from anyone else and that society was always *at* them, menacing them."

There was a ripple of applause among the musquash coats.

"In your opinion, then," pursued Miriam, "in this nasty murder at Radcliff Hall the murderer's motive must have been to obtain his own security?"

"Oh, undoubtedly. Or *hers*. I mean, *I* think so, madam. Don't you?"

Miss Lipscoomb dropped something on the floor and bent to pick it up.

"I don't know, I don't know, I honestly don't know," said Miriam wildly. She sat down to a buzz of real excitement and interest.

V

As a result of all this, the interlude that followed (for cakes and tea in the drawing-room of Hereitis) was (as Squadron Officer Try said) "quite one of the best". Mr. Bracewood-Smith received his cheque and drank several cups of tea and said very little more.

But all the ladies all around him went on with the discussion on What and Who were Crime and Criminals and whether a Crime against Society was also a Crime in the Sight of God. And several ladies asked if Mr. Bracewood-Smith had read the new Agatha Christie and didn't he think it was awfully good? But for the most part, in little scattered whispering groups, the Conservative ladies continued the discussion of the motive behind the Radcliff Hall murder. Most people favoured the *crime passionel*, but would not believe that *nice* Doctor Lariat capable of such a thing. Then one lady (in a black hat and therefore very memorable) said in a meaning voice that all school-teachers were *most* peculiar and someone said, "Hush, Miss Lipscoomb is over there," and the lady in the black hat said that was just what she meant.

The evening had certainly been a success. There was a high emotional tension about that seemed to suggest that lunacy would break through any minute. Conversations were carried on in whispers. Even when Mr. Bracewood-Smith left the house, with his nerves all on edge and tingling, the Conservative ladies did not relax. Almost, they felt, if they went on talking long enough they would solve the whole thing.

But eventually they went away, and Squadron Officer Try cleared her drawing-room and began to run the Hoover over the carpet where the cake crumbs and cigarette ash had dropped. It was a nice carpet. It had come from the R.A.F. mess at Ocherlochty.

VI

Natasha suddenly remarked that she knew there was danger in the air.

"My back is crawling with it," she said.

"Very disagreeable for you, dear," said Miriam lightly. She had had a little experience of Natasha's psychic moods. She stood and looked at her under the faint clouds that sailed in overhead from the English Channel. "What do you suppose it is?" she said. "Shingles?"

"If I knew I should not be crawling," said Natasha simply. And she shuddered eloquently.

"What you need is a *drink*," said Miriam. And she led the way to the Brunton Hotel, where they both spent an hour (which has absolutely no bearing on this story at all) with Mr. Intrikit, the manager. They discussed the existence of their gross or materialistic selves, their etheric selves and their aura. Natasha's aura, apparently, was *pink*, and Miriam's (not so easily discernible) was a rather *chic* puce.

At about ten minutes to nine they left the hotel and wandered, vaguely intoxicated and therefore less aware of *nuances*, away from Radcliff Hall School towards the sea front. They had a singular reluctance to return to duty. The moon had risen. It lit the dim lengths of the Marina Parade with a mild phosphorescent glow.

"I am supposing," said Natasha, "that we should go back to that bloddy school and learn our parts."

Miriam agreed without enthusiasm.

"It looks so peaceful, dear," she said. "You'd never suppose that people did murders much round here, now would you, dear?"

Natasha said she wouldn't, but then she was actually thinking everything rather odd always. And what about that old beast in the beard, Bracewood-Smith, who said everyone was really murderers all the time? What did Miriam think?

"*Life* is jolly odd anyway," said Miriam, begging the question. "*I* don't know why people get murdered at all, I'm sure. Now, *I've* never been murdered."

"I have, however, been shot at," said Natasha proudly.

"But missed," said Miriam.

"But missed," agreed Natasha regretfully.

They were now approaching the very grand hotels (product of the warped fancy of an Edwardian jobbing builder called Strawberry) that make up the whole of the Brunton sea front. The hideous contours of the Lipscoomb Hotel (after Baron Lipscoomb, upon whose estate it had been built) threw a frightening shadow on their left. The Hotel Trafalgar, complete with jolly flagstaff and roller and neat, sanded paths, was a little less repulsive on their right. Because Brunton was out of season, all the hotels were dark and gloomy and abandoned. No lights shone and twinkled along the parade. The pier, too, was a mere skeleton of blackened girders, without mystery, without romance. A little wind blew in from the sea, where the waves came hissing over the shingle.

"Tell me, Miriam, what are you thinking about? Who has been killing off everyone like this, and why?" said Natasha, and she put her hands in her pockets. The light hair lifted all along her forehead.

"If you want my *guess*," said Miriam, "which you probably don't, dear, *I* should say Gwylan Fork-Thomas."

And this was no doubt why Miriam was so very upset when she went into the little wind-shelter that lies on the parade below the Hotel Trafalgar. For sitting in the opposite corner, thrown into a distressing relief, was Gwylan. The whole of the back of her head had been blown away. Apparently by an army revolver.

BOOK THREE

IN SEARCH OF A WIFE

INTERLUDE

THAT same afternoon Johnny DuVivien sat miserably in his empty house on Hollybush Hill, Hampstead. He considered his lovely, absent, wilful wife, Natasha.

She had left him almost a week now, during which time he had tried to keep himself occupied. He had bought a derelict ski-ball alley. He had paid a firm of detectives large sums to try and find his wife. He had turned the ski-ball alley into a night-club called The Bird Cage Walk. It had been depressingly successful and he had even hired an elderly actor to play the part of Charles II all among the little cages. But it had made no difference to his state of mind. Natasha was the only thing in his life that had ever mattered. And she was no longer in his life.

Often, when she had really been in the house quite near to him, maddeningly playing highbrow gramophone records, or sitting remotely on the window-seat, reading Virginia Woolf and Osbert Sitwell and Evelyn Waugh, he had wished the house had been truly empty. Then he could have played the sort of records that *he* liked. 'I'm Just Wild About Harry', or 'Tiger Rag', or a 'Selection from *Oklahoma*'. Natasha was detachment itself, and quite often did not address a remark to him for hours and hours and hours. But he had never imagined anything like this echoing desolation. All she had left behind her, it seemed, that had any personal significance at all, was a cheap Swiss mass-produced white scarf. Johnny folded it sentimentally and slept with it under his pillow.

He had often been exasperated by Natasha in the past. He had been driven mad by her endless, tantalizing telephone conversations, all about nothing at all—or worse, all about Virginia Woolf, Osbert Sitwell and Evelyn Waugh. Now he would give anything to have that exasperation back, to hear her voice again. He was very, very miserable. He did not even know where she was.

He got up and crossed to the window. Damn the window! It was so *pretty*. It was *all* Natasha. Her little muslin curtains, her linen blinds (trimmed with lace like a little girl's drawers). It had nothing to do with him personally. Yet it had so much to do with *them* both, and their relationship, that his heart winced and felt sore again as though someone had stabbed it. Why, there was even a book, lying on the window-sill where Natasha had left it: a book of poems.

Poems. Oh, hell! Johnny opened it. A verse leapt at him from the page:

Il pleut dans mon coeur . . .

"Aw, shucks!" said Johnny DuVivien.

He slammed the book across the room.

It hit a wrought-iron standard lamp and fell with a little crash in the grate.

Johnny went to the telephone and viciously dialled a number.

"Bag of Tricks!" said a voice almost immediately.

"Hullo yourself," said Johnny morosely.

"Oh, baws, baws!" said Eddie the barman (for it was he who had answered the telephone). "I been tryin' to ring you *all* the mornin'. I've news for you."

"So what?" said Johnny rudely.

"I've seen madam," said Eddie.

There was a ghastly pause in Johnny's bloodstream. His unstable heart gave a convulsive leap. It went on beating heavily in his throat. He swallowed it desperately and hiccupped.

"When? Where? How?" he said eventually.

"When did yah get back, baws?" said Eddie maddeningly.

"*When did you see madam?*" screamed Johnny.

"Hey, hey! Temper, temper!" said Eddie.

"Sorry, Eddie," said Johnny.

"That's better," said Eddie. "About a week ago."

"Where was she, Eddie? What was she doing? How did she look? Oh, Eddie, Eddie! Did she look *well*?"

"Relax, baws, just relax," said Eddie.

He began to speak very coldly and carefully, punctuating each sentence with unnecessary dashes and full stops.

"She - was - on - Victoria - platform. The - Hastings - and - St. - Leonards-platform. She-looked-very-well. She-was-wearin'——"

"Never mind what she was wearin'!" cried poor Johnny. "Was anyone *with* her? Was she with a man?"

There was another silence, while Eddie, who had never appeared more half-witted to Johnny, apparently racked his brains.

"No," he said finally. "But she was with that there actress. Miss What's-'er-name."

"*How the hell do I know?*" shouted poor Johnny. "Natasha knows a million of 'em."

This was in fact the case.

"Wall," drawled Eddie, "there was a kinder striding lady spinster with a school kiddie an' a walkin'-stick."

"My God!" said Johnny. "What can she be up to?"

"That all, baws?" said Eddie wearily.

"Isn't it enough?" said Johnny. "I'll ring you back if I think of anythin' more."

He put the receiver back and wandered around the drawing-room, kicking chairs and tables, pushing cushions straight, occasionally grinning sardonically at the sepia photograph of his lovely wife.

"So you were well a fortnight ago, were you?" he said savagely. "I wish to heaven I knew where you *were* and what actress you were with."

For there were certain actresses of whom Johnny DuVivien disapproved.

II

Johnny was sometimes represented (even by his most intimate friends) as a clod. He was, nevertheless, a man with a high percentage of objective intelligence. He was practical and unimaginative. The high intellectual heights meant nothing to him. But over little matters like missing keys and handbags and lost spectacles and 'where did I last see my ration-book?' Johnny was superb. He outpointed Saint Anthony on straight detective work of a routine nature.

Looking for his errant Natasha was going to be quite difficult, but he would accomplish it. Like it or not (and he was almost sure that Natasha was going to *dislike* it), he would find her. Why, perhaps the silly little thing (it was in this way that Johnny regarded his accomplished wife) might get run over. Or get into danger. Women with walking-sticks. Perhaps they were hitting her with the walking-sticks even *now*. . . .

Johnny paced round the room.

The copy of Verlaine knocked against his foot as he passed the fireplace and he sent it flying. Books, books, books. Books couldn't help him now. Or could they?

He glared accusingly at the bookcase that had once seemed to absorb all Natasha's time. He saw *Whitaker's Almanack* and *Bradshaw* side by side. *Whitaker's Alman . . . Brad . . .* why, damn! Perhaps books *could* help.

He snatched up the *Bradshaw* and opened it viciously, almost breaking its back. St. Leonards and Hastings express, eh?

Hastings, Bexhill, Brunton, Cranmer, Cooden Beach, Eastbourne, Haywards Heath, East Croydon. He ran a stubby thumb along the names of the stations. Wait a minute. Maybe he was getting some place. He ran at the telephone like a wild bull.

III

"Eddie! Eddie!"

"Baws, baws," wearily.

"What time er day did you see madam in this *galère*?"

"*Galère? Galère?* Whatcher mean, *galère*?"

"Gallery, hell, gallery. 'S French."

"They wasn't in no gallery, baws, they was in Victoria," said Eddie patiently. "On platform number 13."

"Skip it," said Johnny angrily. "What time did you *see* them?"

And Eddie considered endlessly, while Johnny bit his nails.

"It was tea-time," said Eddie finally. "Yes, baws, it was tea-time."

IV

There was a 4.45 express to Hastings that stopped everywhere after Eastbourne. Johnny shut the *Bradshaw* with a snap. He glared at his watch. It was three o'clock. By damn! He could catch it. His heart flew into his mouth. He glared round him and picked up the *Whitaker*. Girls' schools on the South Coast. Cor. There were *hundreds*. How could he narrow the field?

He plunged at the telephone again.

"Bag of Tricks," said Eddie's voice.

"What colour was that-a school kiddie wearin'?" said Johnny without preamble.

"Hell!" said Eddie involuntarily. But he added "Purple and white" in an undertone, as though the words were being forced out of him.

"Thanks," snapped Johnny. He slammed back the receiver. And once again someone rushed to Victoria to catch the 4.45.

V

"Excuse me," said Johnny, settling into the Pullman car. "Do you often travel with this train? The 4.45, I mean?"

The Pullman-car attendant raised surprised, bald brows.

"Everywhere Mabel goes I go," he said.

"Mabel?" said Johnny.

"Yessir, Mabel," said the attendant. He whisked white table-cloths about and laid teaspoons and sugar-basins on them. "Mabel, my car. I had Pansy for a time, but she got involved in a *collision* at Eastbourne. I've been going around with Mabel for six months now."

"You got a good memory?" said Johnny. He looked him up and down. The attendant swayed to the rhythm of the train and continued to look surprised.

"Dunno, sir," he said, as he swayed. "Dunno, I'm sure. What d'you want me to forget? You? How much is it worth?"

"Hell, no," said Johnny. He took a ten-shilling note from his note-case and laid it flat on the table. "Hell, no. Want *you* to try an' remember. Uh-huh. Two ladies an' a lady with a walking-stick. An' one school kiddie. School kiddie in purple. Purple an' white."

"Purple, sir?" said the attendant, eying the note. "Wouldn't that be Roedean, sir? The Brighton line, that would be."

"*No*," said Johnny. "It would *not* be Roedean and it would be *this* line. One of the ladies," he added sadly, "would be very beautiful."

The attendant grinned broadly.

"Oh, I know the party you mean," he said happily. "Queer lady quite often goes up an' down on this line. Usually has a *lot* of other ladies with her. School-teachers, I think."

" 'Sright," said Johnny, puzzled. He handed over the ten-shilling note. "You've seen her lately? On this train down from Victoria?"

The attendant frowned.

"Thank you, sir," he said vaguely.

"Better still," said Johnny. "Maybe you can't remember the date. Who could, damn it? But you might remember where she gets off? This lady an' her party? What *station*, I mean."

The attendant balanced the tray on the table with the tips of his fingers.

"Oh yes," he said. "Oh yes. I remember. Those ladies got off at Brunton-on-Sea. We're due there at half past six. I'll give you a call. Oh, thank you, sir. Thank you, really. It's far too much. . . . Very kind of you, I'm sure."

CHAPTER ONE

At twenty minutes past seven that night Mrs. Grossbody sat up in her sick bed in the Radcliff Hall sanatorium and rang the bell for her assistant, Miss Bound. Miss Bound was a penniless out-of-door girl. She looked as though she should have dressed in white kennel-coats, but on the whole she wore cotton dresses and a heavy, long tweed overcoat, summer and winter. She was a very, very wholesome girl indeed and took everything very, very seriously.

Since Mrs. Grossbody had been so nervously incapacitated by the amount of barbituric she had consumed (and since her life had been saved in the Cottage Hospital by Doctor Lariat's stomach-pump), Miss Bound had officiated in her absence.

Miss Bound had handed out extra milk, and salt-and-water gargle, and bull's-eyes to take away the taste. She had also taken temperatures and felt necks for swollen glands each day between five and six. So far she had only found one gland the size of a pea in Andy Pratt's neck and only one girl (Daisy Stuckenheimer, as usual) had put her thermometer on a hot-water bottle and had earned an illicit day in bed. Also, a rare thing for the Spring Term, there had been no epidemics.

These duties, as anyone may see, could not truthfully be described as arduous, and very little responsibility went with them. Yet each day since she had returned to the sanatorium Mrs. Grossbody had run the whole gamut of the human emotions, and had nearly gone black in the face wrangling with Miss Bound over Andy Pratt's gland. Mrs. Grossbody was an advocate of Proper Care and a Stitch in Time.

So when Miss Bound heard Matron's bell she dreaded it. She hurried up the stairs from her little sitting-room. She came into Matron's room.

"You wanted me, Matron?" she said, and ducked her head.

"Yes, yes," said Mrs. Grossbody restlessly. She leant on an elbow and pointed to the little white chair that stood beside her on the bedroom mat.

The room was white and hygienic and simple, with another bed in the corner. It was one of Mrs. Grossbody's most furious complaints that she had not been allowed to sleep in her *own* room (warm and brown and full of photographs of nursing chums) because there would have been no bell to ring there for Miss Bound.

There were ten bedrooms in the sanatorium, all with two beds in them, enough to deal with quite a stubborn epidemic of German measles or chicken-pox. All the rooms were the same shape, with pitch-pine floors and two broad windows and a commode hidden behind a green puckered silk screen. Mrs. Grossbody picked restlessly at her sheet.

"I'm uneasy in my mind," she said.

"Oh *yes*, Matron," said Miss Bound fervently. She was not yet used to Matron's perpetual uneasiness of mind. "Why not have a cigarette? They're jolly good for settling one. *Jolly* good."

And Miss Bound held forward a battered packet of Gold Flake, while Matron drew in her mouth to a thin straight line and shuddered ever so slightly.

"My stomach," she said bitterly, "is supposed to be upset. Really, Miss Bound, I should have hoped after five months' experience with a fully qualified person like myself you would have known better."

"Sorry, Matron," mumbled Miss Bound, and folded large rough pink hands over the packet of Gold Flake in her lap.

"I do not wish to *add* to my uneasiness," went on Mrs. Grossbody severely. She wore a pink swansdown bed-jacket which looked a little foolish.

"Of course not, Matron. Sorry," mumbled Miss Bound again.

"No," said Matron, turning back in bed to stare out into the deep inky-blue twilight of Brunton-on-Sea. "I am uneasy about Miss Fork-Thomas."

Miss Bound looked up in dumb surprise. She had expected a little more fuss about Andy Pratt's gland. She said nothing, but went right on looking astonished.

"Miss Fork-Thomas left here at twenty minutes to seven," said Mrs. Grossbody. "Well, after I'd listened to the six o'clock news and Dick Barton hadn't yet started. She went *that* way."

Matron pointed savagely in the direction of Doctor Lariat's house, across a piece of waste land.

"And she hasn't come back," she concluded in some triumph.

"Oh?" said Miss Bound. "Ought she to have?"

"Well, in the first place she didn't ought to have left her house at this time of night at all," said Mrs. Grossbody, snapping her eyes and speaking rapidly. "Miss bbirch, in *her* day, would never have dreamt . . . Ah, well. . . ." Mrs. Grossbody heaved a deep sigh for the good old days. "And in the second place, that piece of common there has a very bad reputation. Yes."

"What sort of reputation?" said Miss Bound, and swallowed a sigh in her turn. "Do you think a nice cup of tea would settle you? Or Ovaltine? Or coffee? Or cocoa?"

"Ovaltine, I *think*," said Mrs. Grossbody, giving the matter her whole consideration. "But not for a little while. Perhaps at about ten o'clock, *dear*?" she added falsely.

"Yes, Matron," said Miss Bound, and tried not to fidget. She had left a book called *Anthony Adverse* downstairs in her sitting-room and wanted very much to go back to it.

"That piece of waste ground," said Mrs. Grossbody, lowering her voice, "*is known as Lover's Loose.*"

"No?" said Miss Bound. "How *awful*."

"And once, though this was before *your* day, Miss Bound, poor Miss Pilkington, the carpentry teacher, was going back home in the evening and she was *knocked* down there and *set upon* . . ."

"And robbed?" said Miss Bound stupidly.

"And *raped*," said Mrs. Grossbody, as who should call a rape a rape. "Most distressing. However, Miss Pilkington had her little hacksaw with her, and she defended herself, and at the inquest they said the saw marks on the man's legs were as deep as anything you care to mention, Miss Bound, and very, very conclusive."

"Inquest?" said Miss Bound. "So she killed him, then?"

"No, no," said Mrs. Grossbody crossly. "In the magistrates' courts, or whatever they're called. And now," she ended in tones of purest misery, "I have been lying here waiting and watching for Gwylan Fork-Thomas going out across Lover's Loose, waiting for her to come back. But she doesn't. They never do." There was a pause. "Say something, dear," added Mrs. Grossbody kindly.

"Perhaps they come back some other way," said Miss Bound finally.

"Certainly *not*," snapped Mrs. Grossbody. "I am quite certain, no matter *what* you say, that all is not well with Miss Fork-Thomas."

"Sorry, Matron," said Miss Bound.

"If Ovaltine is the only sensible thing you can suggest," said Mrs. Grossbody, "you had better fetch it."

"Yes, Matron," said Miss Bound. And she stood up and shook her untidy, ragged hair out of her eyes. "Shall I pull your curtains?"

And she moved towards them, and inevitably clumped a little with her feet as she did so.

"Certainly *not*," said Mrs. Grossbody. "I wish to see what time Gwylan Fork-Thomas *does* come back from Doctor Lariat's house."

II

Tomkins, awakened from the deep smooth sleep of exhaustion by the thundering on his door, pulled on his shoes and put on his jacket. He opened the door and listened, exasperated, to the story that Constable Beatty had to tell him.

"Well?" he snapped. "Is the Wolseley outside an' tickin' over? Where's Miss Birdseye now? Who's with the corpse?"

"Miss Birdseye is in the office, Sar'nt," said Constable Beatty, stiffening angrily. "I understand from 'er that that Russian lady, Miss——"

"Nevkorina. Yes. *Get* on," said Tomkins savagely. "So she's with the body, is she?"

"So Miss *Birdseye* says," said Beatty sulkily.

III

Tomkins did not talk in the car. He sat beside Miriam, bouncing about on the back seat, trying to keep his mind awake.

He had heard her story (and very quickly and well she had told it, too) and both of them had drunk cups of strong hot black tea without sugar or milk. Then Tomkins had mysteriously disappeared into a tiled locker-room and had come out furiously towelling his head. The whole thing had taken less than five minutes.

The parade was still deserted. The Wolseley made very little noise. Opposite the hideous outlines of the Hotel Trafalgar Miriam could see the shelter. Then she saw Natasha standing in front of it. Her head was slightly bowed. Her hands were clasped. They stopped beside her. Natasha looked up.

"I am so *glad* you came," she said. "So very glad."

Tomkins bounced out of the car. He began his examination, drawing chalk marks on the seat, dictating to Beatty, who took down everything he said, repeating it more slowly as he did so. These two men had worked together before on many smaller cases, usually robbery or Black Market offences, and they were used to each other. But the effect of their twice-repeated and prosaic running commentary upon the earthly shell of Gwylan Fork-Thomas was more than disconcerting. It was weird. Miriam was overcome. Whatever Gwylan's shortcomings, she had been an urbane and not unattractive human being, with intelligence and taste. She had been a bitch, of course, but it was awful to hear a bitch discussed in terms like these.

"Very little blood indeed, they must look for that later!" said Miriam savagely, turning to Natasha. "Contents of *handbag*, forsooth!"

"But, *Miriam*," said Natasha, "we are supposed to be *detectives*, darling. You too should be being interested in the contents of handbags. It is the very first thing." There was a pause. "Now *I* find this *fascinating*," said Natasha bravely, and without much conviction.

"You're very heartless," said Miriam, and scowled. "And you must have a stomach like teak. Also, I think you are lying."

"I am detached," said Natasha lightly. She followed Tomkins into the shelter. "As a matter of *fact*," she added, "I am very, *very* sensitive."

Miriam growled.

"Lipstick, letters (examine those later), gold cigarette-case, pigskin wallet, handkerchief, tinfoil, purse containing fifteen shillings and fourpence."

"How much in the wallet, Sar'nt?" asked Constable Beatty, licking his pencil.

"Upwards of ten pounds," said Tomkins. "So it's not robbery with vi'lence. Tinfoil?" he repeated in a puzzled tone. "Nor grievous bodily harm."

"I should have thought," said Natasha, in her low gentle voice, "that to blow off someone's head with a revolver was grievous bodily harm."

"Tinfoil," said Tomkins again. "That's odd, isn't it?"

He sat back on his heels.

"Huh," said Beatty with sardonic humour. "The whole of this case is wrapped up in tinfoil, one way an' another. What sort of tinfoil's this tinfoil?"

"The lady said she kep' it for the hospital," said Tomkins, smoothing it out. "But it's all crumpled . . . John Haig," he said, as the letters and trade mark came into view. "It's Johnny Haig."

"So what?" said Beatty.

Natasha was silent, wrinkling her smooth forehead.

"What are you able to deduct from that, dear?" said Miriam. "I expect you'd find that Miss F.-T. simply put the thing in her *bag* at the rehearsal instead of her pocket."

Tomkins turned. His round face was again alight with intelligence.

"Well, miss, I dunno what you'd say, but it's this lack of blood, see? I've seen fellers killed lots of times by blowin' their bloomin' brains out before now, an' there's always plenty blood. So this wasn't done hereabouts, see?"

Miriam, who had evidently overcome her scruples, or had had her perceptions blunted by contact with the rude police, now wrinkled her nose and composed herself to listen.

"Go on, please, dear Sergeant Tomkins," said Natasha. "You are saying that poor Miss Fork-Thomas' head was blown off somewhere else?"

"Well," said Tomkins, "for what it's worth I should say that this Miss Fork-Thomas was quite a clever woman. An' I sh'd say she'd know I was makin' up a case against her."

"Were you, dear?" said Miriam, surprised. "How *awful*."

Tomkins shrugged his shoulders.

"But she was nobody's fool. Like all these Welsh she used 'er loaf, see? An' when she'd figgered out who *she* thought the murderer *was*, she 'opped out when everyone was at the Conservative meetin'. And she goes, without sayin' anything to anyone, to call on this bloke. The one she thinks is the murderer, see?"

Natasha said she saw, and Beatty said he supposed the sergeant thought it was a man on account of the weapon used? Tomkins nodded and said that wasn't conclusive, of course. Beatty said who wasn't at the meeting? He turned to Natasha.

"Curious way you have of putting things, dear," said Miriam coldly. "*Lots* of people *weren't* at the meeting. Don't be silly."

"I am knowing one, though, who wasn't, and I see what this gentleman means," said Natasha.

"Oh, for heaven's sake!" said Miriam testily. "*Who* wasn't at the meeting particularly, Natasha?"

"Doctor Lariat," said Natasha. And both policemen stood very still.

V

"This *bloke*, as you are calling him," said Natasha slowly, "although I think that is a very disagreeable word. Was it necessarily at his house that Miss Fork-Thomas was going to meet him? There might have been a rendezvous. And he might have been a woman. Surely it might still have been *any* of your original suspects? I am supposing your theory to be fact," she said kindly, and for the benefit of the sergeant, who looked a little cross.

"Thank you, miss," said Tomkins ironically. He wiped his forehead with the back of his hand and bounced on the soles of his feet. He looked spry once more, but not as healthy as usual. "Wish the ambulance'ld hurry up," he said petulantly. "I don't think it's *likely* a woman would own or borrow or use an army revolver. 'Owever, since you insist. Yes, a woman is possible, obviously. And, yes, a rendessvouss is possible, too."

"I suppose a lot depends on where we find your blood an' *if* we find your blood, Sar'nt," said Beatty wistfully.

The sergeant corrected him with a little snort of laughter.

"The deceased's blood, I 'ope," he said severely. "And the weapon. Don' forget that," he added brightly. "Myself," he now said, with a sort of grim briskness that Natasha found oddly reassuring, "*I* am going to call on the doctor."

Natasha and Miriam became a little embarrassed, unsure if it would be in order for them to attend this party. The police ambulance appeared quite suddenly, and Tomkins and Beatty fussed about and superintended its departure for the police-station. Natasha and Miriam politely turned their backs and began to talk quietly to each other. The peacefulness of the Brunton Esplanade was disconcerting.

"Who are these homicidal school-teachers you have up your sleeve?" said Miriam.

"And *what* are you thinking about?" she said crossly, five minutes later, as Natasha still remained silent and did not answer her question.

"I was thinking," said Natasha in her usual slow drawl, "about Fox and Fox."

INTERLUDE

I T was not yet utterly dark when Johnny emerged, blinking, into the cold damp wind that blows for ever round the railway station at Brunton-on-Sea. A phlegmatic old gentleman took his ticket and waved an oil-lamp in front of his feet. Johnny hesitated uncertainly in the teeth of the gale.

"There's a school here wears purple and white," he said finally. He stubbed his toe on a milk-can that clanged wickedly in the shadow. "Damn!" he said.

"Mind them cans," said the old gentleman. "Can't replace *them*. Ah. Purple and white. That'll be the College."

"College?" said Johnny, rubbing his foot against the calf of the other leg. "What college? And I cain't replace my *toes*."

"Radcliff'All," growled the old gentleman. "Clumsy. No call to swear. *I* always keeps a civil tongue in *my* 'ead. Proper masterpiece."

The wet wind snarled round Johnny's ankles and took all the fight out of him. He moved from foot to foot.

"Sorry," he muttered

"No offence," said the old gentleman.

"There's a *club* here, at all?" said Johnny. He licked the damp salt from his lips. "Where I can buy a drink?"

"Club?" shouted the old gentleman, instantly in a raging temper. "Pubs ain't good enough for you, I suppose. The likes of *me*. There's hundreds of pubs. Clubs, indeed! There is that *Brandy's* Club on the front. By the pier there. By Pondicherry Parade. Brandy's for the likes of you. Black Market. Spivs an' soaks. . . ."

The old gentleman withdrew into a noisome cupboard called *Brushes*. A yellow trolley bus whirled up out of the darkness. It stopped opposite the railway station, clicking and whirring. The darkness had increased considerably in the last two minutes.

"Go to the sea front?" called Johnny.

" 'Course 'e does!" screamed the demon old gentleman, lifting the window of his cupboard. "Wastin' all our time!"

Johnny sprang on to the platform beside the conductor.

"You know Brandy's Club?" said Johnny. He searched his pockets for a penny.

"Terminus," said the conductor laconically.

It was not entirely accurate to say that Brandy's Club was the bus terminus. It was, however, near enough for the bus conductor to point to it morosely and say, "Where the lights are," before the trolley bus went plunging and whispering away towards Cranmer and Bexhill and Cooden Beach.

Johnny stood for a second feeling quite wifeless and homeless. He had no luggage, no change of clothes, and there was an obvious storm beating up from the sea. All he had in his trousers pocket was Natasha's white scarf worked on with edelweiss. They had bought it last year in Schizo-Phrenia.[1] The sea hissed and dragged and muttered very near at hand. It pulled and tugged at the shingle. The light had not quite gone from the sky. His desolation of the morning returned. Johnny squared his shoulders. Action would blot that out. Johnny grinned.

He pushed the wooden doors of Brandy's Club and stepped blinking into the usual South Coast drinking-box. A radio gramophone moaned on his left. Several couples were dancing rather inefficiently round a tiny floor. There was a nasty, semi-circular

[1] *Death Goes On Skis.*

bar decorated with strange plaster masks of pierrots and their female equivalents. There were one or two tall stupid-looking young men with big moustaches leaning on it. There was a young lady in a rusty black dress with a little apron carrying a tray about. A young gentleman in a white coat undulated delicately towards him.

Johnny squared his shoulders and watched him carefully. Ah. To be sure. Must have been in one of his own joints one time.

"How d'y' do?" said Johnny genially. "Name's Orr. Ion Orr. Seen you in my London place sure*ly*? The Bag of Tricks? No. Wait a minute. The Cholmondeley Club."

"Pronounced Beefeater," said the young gentleman instantly, and smiled. He showed good, regular teeth. "Of course I know you. Mr. DuVivien, isn't it? Why, I'm a member of your club."

Johnny realized that he was very hungry and thirsty indeed. "Do you want a drink, Mr.——"

"*Orr*," said Johnny firmly. "Yes, I surely do. But I want food even more."

"Can do," said the young gentleman. He turned on his smile again. "Why not join me? And my friend? I'll rustle up food for you in my office in two seconds."

He undulated back across the room and Johnny followed, compelled, as a beagle follows the forbidden rabbit. The young gentleman paused by a table.

"This is Mr. Bracewood-Smith," said the young gentleman. "Mr. Bracewood-Smith has had a hard day. *Lecturing*. This is Mr.——"

"Orr," said Johnny. "Ion Orr of Melbourne, Australia."

Johnny teetered on his heels and looked at Bracewood-Smith. He was leaning back on a greasy little sofa. One enormous foot, in a dirty brogue, was supported above his knee. His great shoulders strained through his dusty velveteen jacket. His beard had cigarette ash and dust in it. He was not a pretty sight.

"Ha!" said Bracewood-Smith. "Have a drink."

He waved a large hand at the young lady in black. She came forward and hovered while Bracewood-Smith tried to persuade Johnny to drink gin.

"Sorry," said Johnny toughly. "Never touch it. Sorry to say I'm a brandy drinker."

"Sorry, sir?" said Bracewood-Smith. "There's nothing to be

sorry about in that. A sorrier sight is a man who will *not* drink brandy. Yes, indeed. That's all I can say."

Outside, the English Channel roared and surged and worked itself up to high tide. The wind sighed and whined and a spatter of rain fell against the window behind Johnny's back. Johnny shivered. He felt that he was wasting his time. What could this ponderous bearded beast have to do with Natasha?

"Two double brandies," said the young lady in black, and went away before anyone could change his mind.

"Guess I c'd be sayin' a whole lot more," said Johnny, "in praise of brandy."

"Ah . . ." said Bracewood-Smith. A wild light appeared in his eye. He leaned forward. He intoned solemnly:

"What do they know of heaven, sir, who only seek the stars?
  We, too, can reach those heights, my friend, who sit in public bars.
  On gin and with martini, yes, and with lager beer.
  We too can wander starwards with our feet in sawdust here."

"Gin and martini and lager beer," repeated Johnny. He made a face. "Pre-tty cool comfort." He felt vaguely hot and sticky. He found himself wiping his forehead with something. It was the scarf from his trousers pocket.

Bracewood-Smith seemed vexed.

"I wrote that when I was very young, sir," he said tartly. "Very young indeed."

"Should hope so," said Johnny. "Thank you, dear."

He turned and took his brandy from the tray that the young lady held under his nose. At this moment the scarf, unobserved by anyone, fell between them on the sofa.

"D'you know a school hereabouts," he went on chattily, "called, let me see now, Radcliff Hall?"

Bracewood-Smith didn't hear. Johnny was just going to repeat his question when there was a dry rustle at his elbow. The young gentleman in the white coat had come back. He seized Johnny's shoulder with a hand that felt long and thin. He dug his nails into Johnny's flesh.

"Ow!" said Johnny. He wriggled round, shaking off his hand. "Ouch! What's wrong?"

"Nothing," said the young man. "Nothing at all. Your food's ready, that's all."

But he signalled frantically with one eyebrow.

"Ah . . ." said Johnny. "No Radcliff Hall, eh?"

"Oh *yes*," hissed the young man. He put his pale pink face on a level with Johnny's. His breath smelt sweet and stale, of soft-centred sweets and cachous. "Not in front of *him*. Sends him off his nut. . . ."

And he nodded sideways at the distinguished detective-novelist who was not paying either of them the slightest attention.

"Not really sane on the subject," said the young gentleman, pulling gently at Johnny's sleeve.

"Add to these, moreover, the bright lights and the song,"

went on Bracewood-Smith ponderously, rolling his brandy round and round his tongue,

"The joy of those old soaks there, who suddenly feel strong,
Who feel young blood run through their veins, who suddenly feel fine.
Oh, think upon these blessings, friend, e'er you condemn our wine."

"He doesn't seem very sane on any subject," said Johnny quietly, looking at him.

"And which of us, sir, is *that*?" said Bracewood-Smith, suddenly disconcertingly awake. He rolled his great cat's eyes at Johnny, who became acutely embarrassed and thought once again (and how wrongly, only we know) that this fellow could have nothing to do with his dearest Natasha.

"I should like you to meet my young friend, sir. A pleasant character. Partick-Thistle by name."

"Partick-Thistle by nature, too," hissed the young gentleman in the white coat in Johnny's ear.

Johnny's mind made a sideways and backward jump. Partick-Thistle, by God! Surely *that* was the name of the young man they had met in Schizo-Phrenia at the winter sports?[1] Perhaps he *was* on the right track after all. But above all he didn't want to be recognized.

"Thanks," said Johnny. "But, by golly, I'm hungry. Surely you'll forgive me if'n I eat? I'll be right back. . . ."

[1] *Death Goes On Skis.*

Bracewood-Smith dismissed him with a gesture like Imperial Caesar's.

"Help yourself, sir," he said. "To be sure, to be sure."

And Johnny went, leaving behind him his white scarf. He did not notice his loss until some hours later. By that time Peter Bracewood-Smith had already blown his nose on it several times, taken it home and had left it on a chair in his kitchen.

CHAPTER TWO

DOCTOR LARIAT's house seemed a series of dark pools and stretches of shadow. They could discern, but only dimly, its ridiculous paved path, its lawns and its little bell strip. "Marked *Night and Day*, just as though Cole Porter lived there," said Miriam, in cold contempt.

Tomkins, standing on the top step, asked Miriam if she could make out which was night and which was day, and finally rang both bells together.

"I think that was silly, dear," said Miriam, with a prodigious yawn. "I mean, *both* of them can't be right."

Instantly the window above them opened and a passionate head, crowned all with curlers, emerged into the night and squeaked and gibbered like the Roman dead. Mrs. Buttick, disturbed.

"Nothing's so urgent but it can't wait," said Mrs. Buttick. "Some folks always fancy they're dying."

The head popped back. The window snapped shut. Tomkins leant wearily against the door jamb.

"Must be her party piece," he said sardonically. "Good thing no one *is* dying instead of just being dead."

Miriam and Natasha said nothing. They felt a little cold and tired and shocked. After all, as Natasha now pointed out to the stars, *they* were not policewomen and it was past eleven o'clock.

"*And* highly irregular," said Tomkins, with a smirk. "Here's someone."

The slip-slop of feet inside the door stopped abruptly. A light was switched on. The door latch was fumbled. A bolt was shot. The door opened about two feet. They expected Mrs. Buttick and her curl papers. But it was Doctor Lariat. He was fully clothed. He had obviously not yet been to bed.

"Yes?" he said sharply. "Who? Come in."

"The police," said Tomkins firmly, and entered.

"Oh, goodness!" said Lariat weakly, holding the door for Natasha and Miriam. "*More* of it? Never at an end. Oh well, come into the consulting-room."

He led the way through the dark hall and through the silent waiting-room. He switched a light on ahead of them and the waiting-room sprang into relief. The *Tatlers* and the *Punches* seemed like dead things, unopened on the table.

"Come along, come along," he called testily. "Don't waste time. Mrs. Buttick will be wondering who you are, in any case."

The tone of his voice said plaintively, "*Do* let us avoid scandal."

He stooped and struck a match. The gas-fire roared and flickered and settled to a steady purr. Some acrid fumes struck Lariat's throat and he coughed and his face became thin and dry and rather pathetic. He looked young and helpless and he seemed to have lost weight in the last week. His collar was a little big for him. He rubbed his hands together as he turned from the fire and tried to adjust his smile.

"Well?" he said, and faced them, thrusting his hands deep into his trousers pockets. "*Now* what?"

"Er . . . now," said Sergeant Tomkins, measuring him with his eye. "Would you mind sayin' what time Miss Gwylan Fork-Thomas left here tonight, please?"

Lariat glanced at the clock. He went slightly white in front of his ears. Then he blushed most obviously and, as obviously, clenched his hands tightly in his trousers pockets.

"Oh, for goodness' sake," he said fretfully. "How do *I* know? What's the time, half past eleven? Late for calling, in all conscience."

"Ah, so she *was* here, was she?" said Tomkins triumphantly. "Thanks for *that*, anyway."

Constable Beatty flicked open his notebook and licked his pencil like an automaton and began to write. Lariat looked from one to another and his eyes grew wider and wider.

"What *can* you mean?" he said angrily. "*Certainly* she was here. About seven o'clock, I suppose. *I* don't know how long she stayed, or when she left. After all, she was my *fiancée* . . ."

"N.B. 'was'," said Tomkins, and Beatty growled.

Lariat evidently did not hear this, because he went on, more and more angrily:

"Why, damn it, man, even in a town like this, where so many people have minds exactly like sinks, I suppose a man can have his *fiancée* in for coffee after supper, or *can't* he? And what the hell are these two ladies doing with you, might I ask?"

"*Was*," said Tomkins in horrid triumph. "You *did* mark that 'was', Beatty?"

Natasha and Miriam stood their ground as Lariat angrily looked them over Then he glanced at his desk. Below the university and hospital groups, under the silver photograph frame that contained his father, on the desk was a half-finished letter. Beside it there was a ring. There were several balls of crumpled paper lying about on the floor. There was a stain of ink on Doctor Lariat's finger.

"Been writin' a letter, have you?" said Tomkins truculently. He moved towards the desk. "Mind if I read it, eh?" he said.

Lariat exploded.

"Good heavens!" he said. "I really think this is too much. Why the hell should I? In any circumstances whatever? You've far exceeded your authority already. I've been very patient. Damn! Damn! It's bad enough——"

He stopped and bit his lips. For a moment it looked as though he were going to cry. His full, childish lips trembled. His dark, prominent eyes filled with tears.

"Poor fellow!" said Miriam Birdseye suddenly. "Poor chap!"

"Be waiting just a little minute, Sergeant," said Natasha suddenly. "Please wait a minute. I am thinking that the doctor is trying to tell you that Miss Fork-Thomas is coming here this evening to break off their engagement."

Sergeant Tomkins looked at Natasha and back at Lariat and shrugged his narrow shoulders.

"That so?" he said aggressively.

"Yes," said Lariat. "Yes, it is. Certainly. What do you mean, *is* that so?"

"What I said," said Tomkins. "So *you're* goin' to tell *me* that *you* don't know that Gwylan Fork-Thomas is dead? Eh? That's a likely one, that is."

In the silence that followed this appalling and brutal remark, Natasha saw the sweat bead up on Lariat's forehead. His face went taut and strung. It worked most dreadfully. He collapsed in his chair in front of his desk. His hands were shaking.

"Dead?" he said. "Dead? I don't believe you. Why *should* I

believe you? You come here to mock me. I'll not stand it. . . . Why should I stand it?"

He laid his hands flat on the desk ahead of him. Evidently he tried to stop them shaking.

"Dead?" he said, in a different tone, suddenly childish. "*Why* dead? How?"

He turned his head, moved it stiffly and looked at Natasha. Then he visibly stiffened and every emotion but anger left his face. He became an adult and a doctor again. He looked remote and detached.

"You, madam," he said to Natasha. "You seem to have a modicum of sense. Tell me why this man says that Gwylan is dead."

II

Natasha did her best. She put her head on one side, and she used every note in her lovely soft voice to soothe and coax and comfort the stricken young man. He sat very still and very watchful. Only the flickering of his large dark eyes following the movements of her mouth betrayed the violence of his concentration.

"What the sergeant is saying is so true, I am sorry," she began, in some confusion. "My friend here, and partner, Miss Birdseye, and myself, we are finding poor Miss Thomas in a shelter on the front. Quite dead."

"You're sure of that?" said Lariat coldly, turning to Miriam.

"Quite sure," said Miriam woodenly. "No doubt at all."

"But how . . . who . . . ?" began Lariat, fumbling with the fountain-pen on his desk. He dabbed at the ring with the fountain-pen and the ring rolled over, winking mockingly.

"How? With a revolver. Who? Well, you tell *us*," said Tomkins briskly.

"Revolver," said Lariat stupidly. "I don't know anyone with a revolver. . . ."

III

Sergeant Tomkins spent a frustrated quarter of an hour questioning Philip Lariat before he gave up with a snort of contempt and rage. Lariat sat with his head bowed all through the questioning. Sometimes he made some pointless monosyllabic reply. He was obviously deeply shocked, or else his mind was absolutely elsewhere.

"May *I* be asking a question?" said Natasha suddenly.

"If you like," said Tomkins ungraciously.

Doctor Lariat looked up with surprise and pleasure when he heard the tone of Natasha's voice again. Miriam felt sorry for him.

"Doctor Lariat," said Natasha. "You, a doctor, will be a psychologist also. This is quite certain?"

"I suppose so," said Lariat, surprised and obviously glad to be talking about an impersonal subject. "One wouldn't get very far as a doctor without it. Psychological insight, I mean."

"Ah!" said Natasha. "Then you will be understanding me when I say I have no shadow of reason to tell you these things which I am surmising with my heart."

"Women's reasoning is as good as men's," said Lariat testily. "It merely works *quicker*, that's all. Don't malign yourself. Most women leave out logical links that they consider unnecessary to their thought processes. . . ."

And he smiled quite pleasantly. He no longer seemed a creature of despair, snarling savage and meaningless replies. He seemed unafraid and intelligent. He linked his fingers together and leant back in his chair.

"Now *is* that phoney or not?" said Miriam, more to herselt than Sergeant Tomkins.

"Well, first," said Natasha, in caressing tones, "I think you *have* been plotting to kill Miss Theresa Devaloys and someone else gets there first. Is this so?"

IV

Tomkins gave an astonished gasp. Beatty sucked in his teeth and said: "Oi! Definitely irregular, miss."

"Madam and I," said Lariat, suddenly and coldly, "do not deal with the law. We deal with truth. She speaks with her heart and her instinct. And I shall repay her by trying to tell her the truth. Or as much as I know of it."

For a moment or two this young Jew was not without dignity.

He smiled and seemed to draw farther and farther away from his emotions.

"Yes," he said. "That is quite true. I hoped for an opportunity of murdering Theresa Devaloys. I can't think it matters that I tell you this now. It may be of assistance over Gwylan. For you to find out how these people all reacted on each other. Including me. Because I *didn't* kill her, you know."

His handsome dark eyes looked all the time at Natasha, who now drew a deep sigh.

"*I* cannot tell whether you have done this thing or not," said Natasha. "But that you plotted it, I am certain. Now, please, why did Miss Thomas break the engagement? She is being in love with you all along, I think?"

V

Lariat did not speak for a minute. He looked down at his hands and folded them. Then he glanced at Tomkins, standing aggressively on his hearthrug, at Beatty with his notebook propped on the mantelpiece, at Natasha and Miriam in his consulting-room chairs.

"I know you have no warrant," he said coolly. "My statement at this point may be long-winded, but it may clear the air. You may act on it how you wish. It is *weird* how one's life becomes tangled with other people's. I *have* been foolish. One's will to destroy is a very tricky thing. There is absolutely no knowing what may happen when three people let loose unlimited powers of potential misery at each other."

Sergeant Tomkins cleared his throat.

"Excuse *me*, sir," he said, "but my colleague an' I are pretty busy. An' as you say, we have no warrant. We've got no time for professional language. Make it simple, make it snappy. Make it so Miss Birdseye here can understand it."

And he smirked at Miss Birdseye, who looked affronted.

"I," she said coldly, "can understand *Freud* when I hear it, dear."

VI

"Very well, then," said Philip Lariat, looking up at his college groups. "To understand anything about *my* part in this horrible business you will have to understand us. Myself and Theresa and Gwylan. And *I* do not really understand myself. So you see."

He turned his hands in a helpless little gesture, palms face upward, and swung round in his chair towards Natasha.

"Tell us then as much as you understand," said Natasha and smiled like a young angel.

"I am weak, I suppose," said Lariat, as though talking in his sleep. "And conscious of my social inferiority. Being a Jew, I mean. So I am fascinated by the sort of woman *you* would call a bitch."

He nodded at Miriam, who said that all women were bitches at heart and he didn't need *her* to tell him that.

"All that ruthlessness and detachment and that intellectual power," said Philip Lariat as though he were calling up the dead. Natasha's large hazel eyes grew wide and troubled as she looked at him. "And, so often, allied with that is verbal dexterity and the lightness of a shallow heart. And cruelty. Goodness, yes. And cruelty."

"Well, dear, yes, rightly are they called bitches," said Miriam. "But admitting their fascination for you, what then?"

"Well . . ." Lariat linked his hands behind his head and swayed back in his chair. There was pain in his face, but curiosity as well. "Theresa Devaloys was like that. It was her wit and her intelligence that attracted me first. And her waywardness and her inconsequence. Her insincerity, if you like." There was a pause and Lariat looked very uncomfortable indeed. "Also," he said slowly, "she was a lady, you know. And, of course, I am not a gentleman."

Miriam sniffed. This sort of humility always failed to move her.

"That sort of intelligent person is very seldom found in Brunton-on-Sea," he said to Tomkins. Tomkins said just the same there were plenty of ladies and gentlemen in Brunton and would he please cut the cackle?

Lariat sighed.

"And how are you meeting her at all at first, La Belle Theresa Sans Merci, or whatever you are calling her in your laughing way?" said Natasha lightly.

"You have some of the same qualities, madam," said Lariat reflectively, looking at Natasha in what Miriam afterwards described as 'a very sinister way'. "The inconsequence. The intelligence. . . ."

"Now look, dear," said Miriam briskly. "My chum is very nice and very intelligent and very sweet, but skip *her*. Tell us why you decided to murder Theresa Devaloys. Because you aren't a gentleman?"

Lariat sighed again.

"My *affaire* with Theresa began about two years ago," he said. "It was such a hot summer. There was nothing to do but drive around the country in my car and go swimming. Very few people were ill. I wasn't very busy. And we ate delicious meals. Theresa was a good cook," said Lariat wistfully. "Mrs. Buttick went away every week-end. I was happy. It was a good time."

Lariat traced a pattern on his desk with his forefinger and looked very sad. His mobile face slid into a tragic mask.

"We had fun," he said. "We laughed at the same things. . . ."

Natasha, who had never yet observed Doctor Lariat do anything but smile and smile and smile, like a dog, found this hard to believe. She inclined her head as Lariat went on.

"I suppose she got sort of sick of me," he said. "She often said she only liked people who were funny and amused her. I suppose I didn't learn enough new tricks or keep up to date with the latest intellectual fashions. I suppose I was altogether too stationary for her." There was a little pause, while poor Lariat contemplated the inadequacy of a rather common G.P. who had not read Proust or Rimbaud or Jean-Paul Sartre. And he sighed again. Natasha imagined very well how Theresa had played on his nerves and his sentimental Jewish heart.

"She wouldn't ever let me *quite* go," he said. "But she used to mock at me and be unkind. But then I found how jealous she could be."

For a minute that tragic, chalky mask slipped sideways and for a second there sat there a naughty, grinning little boy like a faun.

"I played her up," said Lariat triumphantly. "*Avec les girls de la village*. She was always kindest when she thought she was losing me. And then, oh, heavens," said Lariat, and he truly groaned, "I stupidly thought I could play her up with Gwylan Fork-Thomas."

"That was a damn' silly thing I tell to you," said Natasha explosively. "This Gwylan. She is being just such another as Theresa."

"Oh, I know, but her thing was Science and no one can put on the Ritz with Science with me. I soon found out about Gwylan.

I thought I was getting Civilization and the Scientific Mind with all that beauty (she *was* beautiful, you know, like a Botticelli), and lots of the wit I admired in Theresa."

"Listen, dear," said Miriam bitterly. "A nice quiet lady is what you want."

"I only want to be left alone," said Lariat, like a caged beast, showing his teeth.

"I see your point, dear," said Miriam easily. "But fancy a doctor not knowing that one can't escape from one emotional relationship into another."

Lariat blinked.

"I suppose that's what I thought I *was* doing," he said. "At the time I just thought I had Theresa's measure. I just thought I could bring her to her senses. But, of course, I reckoned without Gwylan. Theresa would have called me back from the ends of the earth, I think. And what was so awful, I would have *come*. Luckily, Gwylan had a tame girl friend called Puke . . . Charity Puke. . . ."

"Ah," said Tomkins. "Mrs. Puke's little girl, Charity."

"Mrs. Puke. Yes," said Lariat, with a sudden change of manner. "A nice heart disease. Well, Pukey used to pinch hit for Gwylan and me. Take Theresa off for the afternoon in her motor to Glyndebourne, and so on. She's a good sort, that girl. I hope no harm comes to her." He looked up with a sudden start of horror. "She'll be upset about Gwylan," he said. "She had a Thing about her."

"Leave that now, I beg, and be concentrating," said Natasha. "I am judging you only by what you tell me. And all this is happening last autumn and winter?"

Lariat nodded.

"So at this point, when things between the three of us are getting so complicated, I say, like a fool, and really to please Theresa, who's playing Miss Phoebe, that I'll take a part in this damned play they're putting on. *Quality Street*. That was sticking my neck out, I can tell you."

"Yes," said Natasha, and nodded.

"I can't explain what my feelings were. I still can't think what I hoped it would do for me. I can't understand why I acted as I did. I can't even say if what I felt for either of them was genuine affection."

"Skip that," said Miriam sharply. "No need for sex to be genuine anything except sex."

"Morals no concern 'f mine," mumbled Tomkins automatically.

"I felt myself going deeper and deeper into a sort of hell where nothing mattered. I even forgot about keeping the practice unharmed and my name respectable. I wasted a lot of money, too," he said suddenly, looking startled. "It was all a symptom. And this was the point when Theresa decided to bring things to a head. She was determined to marry me, you know. . . ." There was a pause, while Lariat stabbed at the wood with his forefinger. "Her big idea was that herself and myself and Helena bbirch (Miss Lipscoomb's ex-partner) should go into partnership and run a school together. She was putting through some very tricky negotiations to buy Radcliff Hall. She said she could persuade Miss Lipscoomb to back out of the possession. She *said* she could put up £6,000." Lariat stared round him at the ring of unsympathetic faces. "I was reluctant," he said. "I'm a doctor and not a tame schoolmaster, even though I *am* common."

There was a pause.

"So Theresa allowed herself to become pregnant," he said calmly.

There was no one there unshocked. Natasha (whose dislike of children and child-bearing was deep and sincere) was horrified that Theresa Devaloys could have done anything so disgusting. Miriam, whose dislike of Doctor Lariat was now tempered by admiration for his evident virility, thought he was being callous. Tomkins and Beatty were plainly jealous. Lariat sensed hostility in the atmosphere.

"I *mean* that Theresa found herself with child and insisted that I was the father," he said hastily. "By this time I'd made up my mind. I'd recognized Gwylan as my Good Angel. . . ." Miriam winced. "And she didn't make me feel inferior," went on Lariat.

"Anything being less like a Good Angel than the late scientific Miss Fork-Thomas *I* could never have been finding," said Natasha coldly.

"Couldn't be phonier, dear," said Miriam, agreeing. "Make him say some more, Natasha."

"We are now, I am thinking at all events," said Natasha, with some kindness and a certain amount of mockery, "reaching the point where you decide to do away with the bitchy Miss Devaloys (probably because you are passionately dependent on her and resent this) and then marry this Good Angel of yours and live together in Science ever after?"

Lariat looked down at his hands.

"The afternoon that Theresa told me about the child," he said, in a low voice.

"Your child," said Tomkins sharply.

"That isn't proved," said Lariat firmly. "I did have this insane impulse. I think I had obviously been disintegrating to the point of a nervous breakdown for some time."

"Really don't wonder, darling, do you?" said Miriam.

"So I put up some cyanide capsules in a little bottle and marked them Amyl Nitrite. Like for a heart case, you know. It shouldn't have been difficult."

"My lor'," said Tomkins, appalled. "And you sit there and tell us this? Lariat, you're mad!"

"Yes, I sometimes think I am, too," said Lariat simply. "But between the two of them I didn't know if I was coming or going."

Tomkins could well believe it. There was a long pause while Constable Beatty's pencil squeaked despairingly across the paper and Miriam clicked her tongue and wondered where Theresa Devaloys had been going to get her £6,000. Natasha looked pityingly at Philip Lariat. He now sat with his head bowed.

"Well," he said finally, "you know what happened, more or less. I left here with murder in my heart. . . ."

"And cyanide in your pocket, pet," said Miriam briskly.

"Yes, yes, I said so, didn't I? And then that rehearsal started."

"And *you* say someone forestalled you?" said Tomkins, and he did not attempt to conceal his sneer.

"Yes," said Lariat. "That's what I say."

"A likely tale," said Tomkins.

"The only thing that is being in Doctor Lariat's favour is this, that Miss Devaloys was being killed by barbituric," said Natasha.

"So what?" said Tomkins, watching Lariat. "*His* precious capsules might just as well have been barbituric. We've only *his* word they were cyanide."

VII

"Truly," said Lariat, "I *do* see that my story wouldn't make a nice impression on a jury. But I hope I won't have to tell it to them. *Do* look at the facts. As Valentine Brown I never did anything but hold the fatal whiskey in its beastly tooth-glass. And although a cyanide capsule *could* have been dissolved in that whiskey I couldn't possibly have got enough barbituric into the glass to kill a person. And it would be silly to waste time with barbituric if one had cyanide. See what I mean?" he ended.

"Tcha!" said Tomkins explosively.

"I think a jury might believe him, Sarge," said Beatty, suddenly.

"Oh, teach your grandmother to suck Australian eggs flown to this country by air," said Tomkins angrily.

"I do not think," said Natasha, "that those sort of eggs are very nice, even for grandmothers."

Lariat burst out laughing.

"Shut your mouth, *you*," said Tomkins angrily. "Suppose you tell me about your feongcay's visit here this evening. Did you have any insane impulses about that, eh?"

"I was coming to that," said Lariat. "All this has made me very thirsty. Do you mind if we have a drink?"

"Cyanide and soda," said Beatty gloomily.

"Oh no," said Lariat, blithely, moving towards the cupboard. "John Haig."

VIII

Constable Beatty clutched his throat and clucked. Natasha and Miriam said they never touched whiskey.

"Only gin and brandy and champagne," said Natasha rapidly.

"I'll take whiskey and water," said Tomkins. "Thanks."

Lariat handed the drinks round. The glasses tinkled agreeably. Everyone relaxed a little.

"This evening," said Lariat, drinking his whiskey rather fast and making a wry face. "Well, *this evening* Gwylan appeared about seven in a rather maddening mood of renunciation. She said all sorts of cutting things, and told me she didn't want to marry me at all. Also, she said that you"—he nodded at Tomkins—"were making out a case against her. Is that so?"

"Yes, I think so," said Tomkins, and finished his drink. "Yes, certainly. Yes. That was so."

"Well," said Lariat, "what could *I* do?"

"You do so *many* things," said Miriam, "and all of them violent, dear. What did you do *this* time?"

"Nothing," said Lariat. "I accepted what she said, of course. I respected her wishes. I took back the ring. Then she left. It was a bit of an anti-climax," he said. "I showed her out," he added, as an afterthought.

"Which way is she going?" said Natasha. She wrinkled her forehead and looked puzzled.

"I can't say," said Lariat, frowning. "No, I honestly can't say."

"Can't you, then?" said Tomkins and stood up, looking like a little rubber ball. "Mind if I have a squint in your garage?" he said. "You know I haven't got a warrant."

"Garage?" said Lariat, surprised. "Of course, if you want to. Come the outside way and then we won't wake Mrs. Buttick again."

He got up. Tomkins and Beatty moved towards him.

"At what time was your car last out today, sir, if you will pardon me?" said Tomkins.

Lariat stared.

"I haven't been out since five," he said. "Mrs. Buttick will tell you."

Tomkins bowed ironically, implying that the evidence of a faithful retainer was inadmissible in a Court of Law. The doctor went ahead of them to the garage. In the distance, at sea, at five-minute intervals, the winking light of the Brunton light-buoy made everything bright.

"Nice thing, that light-buoy," said Tomkins, suddenly chatty.

"Yes. It's timed with the coastguard station," said Lariat. "But I expect you know that."

He switched on the garage light and opened the door for them.

IX

It was bare and clean and newly whitewashed. The Rover, glossy and invulnerable as a wood louse, lay there demurely. There was a bicycle and a coil of rope, a hose and a stirrup pump, left over from the war. There was a long-handled incendiary scoop, an inspection lamp, and two cans for petrol.

"Kind of isolated you are here," said Tomkins, still in the doorway. He looked across the patch of scrubland and common that came up to the edge of The Lawns. "On the edge of Lover's Loose here, aren't you?"

"Yes," said Lariat easily. "Nice and handy."

"Who is being your nearest neighbour?" asked Natasha suddenly. She shook back her hair in the light wind that came in from the sea. "That must be being the lights of Radcliff Hall up there." She pointed.

"Yes," said Lariat. "That's Radcliff Hall Sanatorium. I've got old Matron, Mrs. Grossbody, in there recovering from shock. That's my first neighbour *that* way. There's nothing that way" —he pointed west—"until you come to the coastguard station and Bracewood-Smith's frightful little bungalow."

An exclamation from Beatty, who was scrabbling at the back of the garage, brought their heads sharply round.

"What is it, man?" said Tomkins, angry and startled. "Cough it up!"

"It's blood, Sarge," said Beatty. "Blood on this bike."

INTERLUDE

" 'At's a pretty average lunatic character," said Johnny, jerking his head back towards Bracewood-Smith. He was in the office of the young gentleman in the white coat, in Brandy's Club, on the esplanade.

He jerked his head at the bar behind them where it lay beyond a dark-red frieze curtain. Someone had put on an old record of a *Showboat* selection. The young gentleman in the white coat hummed the melancholy refrain.

" 'Only make believe,' " he sang gently, " 'I love you. For to tell the truth, I *do*.' Mr. Bracewood-Smith is a drunk and a nut and all those things, dear. And the very mention of Radcliff Hall is enough to send him berserk. He smashes things, dear. A lovely quiet feller."

The office was small and dusty. The curtains were drawn. The windows behind the curtains evidently backed on to the pier. The noise of the sea was now louder than the gramophone, which faded away as the red frieze curtain dropped back into place. There was a table laid for one with a fairly clean white tablecloth. There was a plate of bacon and eggs, a loaf, a great mass of butter and a plate of spring onions on the side.

"Heavens!" said Johnny, and paused. His big shoulders seemed to fill the little room. "That looks good. Sends him clean off, does it? Why's 'at?"

"Has a daughter at the school, dear," said the young gentleman. "And, by the way, my name's *Henry*."

"Oh?" said Johnny. "Why should that upset him? Cain't he pay the fees?"

Johnny straddled the little chair. He drew it towards the table, almost riding it as though it were a Grand National entrant. He began to eat, bolting his food. He ate in the American manner, balancing his knife on the plate while he shovelled the food into his mouth with the fork.

"It isn't so much *that*, dear," said Henry, and sat down beside him. "There are all sorts of things going on at the moment. Bracewood-Smith gets into a rage about them most nights."

"Oh?" said Johnny. He spoke through a mouthful of food, chewing steadily. "Such as what?"

"We-ell . . ." Henry considered him with his polished head on one side. "Suppose you tell *me* what you're doing here in Brunton, dear? I mean, you might be a *newspaperman*. Or a Ministry nark. Or what?"

Johnny stared round for inspiration. He saw a cheap little oak desk littered with bills. Bills *without* little sticky labels and orange stamps, and therefore *unpaid* bills. He saw a lot of Income Tax—Private—Inland Revenue envelopes, unopened, and another from the G.P.O. marked 'Telephone Account—Final Demand'. 'In fact,' thought Johnny sardonically, 'Henry's gotten himself into a pretty bad way.' He helped himself to mustard.

"I was thinkin'," he said lightly, "of buyin' a little place like this on the South Coast. Hey? What you say? Is it up for sale at all?"

Henry stared at him, unbelieving. His careful assured manner fell from him like a cloak. His cultivated voice deteriorated in all directions. He began to speak the impurest form of Cockney. Johnny suddenly began to like him.

"You want to *buy* this place?" said Henry. "Gawd a'mighty. You cawn't want to buy this blooming white elephant."

"Sure do," said Johnny gaily.

A quarter of an hour later, when Johnny had examined the lease and the caterers' bills, and the various outstanding accounts that Henry felt himself quite unable to meet, he felt he was a little nearer to broaching the subject of Radcliff Hall.

"Well, now," he said. He leaned back in his chair and drank a cup of unpleasant inky-black coffee, "what sort er clientele, iı any? All *I* know about Brunton-on-Sea is it's gotten a school in it called Radcliff Hall that sends an old maniac into a flat spiral."

Henry giggled. He swayed forward on to his hands. He sat on them, rocking to and fro. He looked quite different. His old, tiresome bantering manner had returned. Johnny instantly hated him.

"That old maniac, as you call him, dear," said Henry, "is about the only regular we have. Can he *drink*!"

"Dunno," said Johnny sourly. "Can he?"

"Oh, don't be silly, dear," said Henry. "Of *course* he can. Why, tonight he arrived here howling like a wolf after this lecture he'd been giving to these Conservatives, and bought *two* bottles of our whiskey to entertain that Partick-Thistle boy . . . and I *honestly* don't think he's interested in anything but the drink, dear. Odd, isn't it?"

Henry rolled his eyes while Johnny flinched and said it was indeed odd.

"Well, have a drink yourself," said Johnny crossly.

"I don't mind if I do," said Henry. "What do you want to know about Radcliff Hall, dear?"

Henry leant forward and peered intently into Johnny's face. Once again Johnny felt the creamy sweetness of Henry's breath and felt quite ill. He suddenly decided that he could not bear to confide his secret humiliations to this unwholesome little stranger. It is, after all, difficult enough to tell anyone that one's wife has left one because she is sick of the sight of one.

"Chiefly, I suppose," said Johnny rapidly, "if it's a decent school or not. I'm thinkin' er sendin' my youngest kiddie there. Er . . ." He looked wildly round him. "Er . . . *Joan*," he ended lamely.

"How old is Joan?" said Henry, with the bright inhuman glance of a basilisk.

"Er . . ." said Johnny again, and, "*twelve*," he added firmly.

"Oh, then I expect it'll be all right," said Henry, in his worst gossiping voice. "Miss Lipscoomb's going through a very sticky patch just now, *I* can tell you, dear. That's the head mistress who owns it. A great deal of misfortune. Oh yes. Miss bbirch, her *partner*, leaving and all, *that* was the first thing. And then all those sexy drawings and things, to say *nothing* of the murder——"

"Murder?" Johnny sat bolt upright. He set down his coffee-cup. He slopped a little in the saucer.

"Why, yes," said Henry easily. "So you're *not* on a newspaper. I don't suppose it's reached *London* yet. But *that's* one of the nicest selling points of *all*, dear. Radcliff Hall. Murders laid on every term. Last one was the French mistress, a Miss Devaloys. Or so they say."

"Hell, do they?" said Johnny. And his mouth fell slowly open.

"Shouldn't let *that* put you off, dear, about Joan," said Henry, patting him affectionately on the arm. "I should think your daughter will love them. Children always love a good murder."

CHAPTER THREE

"ALL bikes look alike to me," said Tomkins, and stepped blithely into the garage. His feet rasped the roughcast floor and put Miriam's teeth on edge. His stocky, bouncy figure was reflected in the polished surface of the car as he passed. As usual, he seemed quite undismayed. "Let's have a look," said he.

It was a lady's bicycle and old-fashioned, standing high at the saddle and the handlebars, with a light coating of rust. There was the tattered remains of a white-and-green dress-guard flapping miserably round the rear mudguard. There was a flat japanned luggage-carrier. On the handlebars was the lower half of a bell, much disintegrated. And there was a wickerwork shopping-basket.

The shopping-basket was red and dismal, dripping, dreadful. Beatty stood and stared at it and dabbed it with his pocket handkerchief.

"'Sblood all right," said Tomkins.

"Someone might have been carrying *rabbits* home," said Miriam.

"Or liver," said Natasha gravely. "Liver is so *dreadful*, it makes such a mess . . ."

"Mighty big rabbit," said Tomkins, without turning round. "Whose bike is this?"

"I . . . er . . . don't know," said Lariat, who had gone very white. "Perhaps Mrs. Buttick's."

"Your own garage and a bike in it and you say you don't know whose it is?" said Tomkins, with withering contempt.

"Oh no, darling; be *fair*," said Miriam instantly. "I once had a motor-bicycle and a case of shotguns and a stuffed buffalo head all in *my* garage, and *I* never found out who any of them belonged to. Except the stuffed buffalo," she added, after a minute. "That turned out to be Thistle's. Roger Partick-Thistle's," she explained, turning to the sergeant.

"I was forgetting all about *him*," said Natasha. "Dear Roger! I haven't seen him *all day*."

Tomkins touched the basket with his forefinger.

"Still sticky," he said. "Care to analyse it, Doctor?"

"Find out what blood group it belongs to, do you mean?" said Lariat, with a nervous cough. "Why, yes, if you like. I'll go and get a couple of slides. The microscope's in the consulting-room."

He turned away, left the garage, went towards the house.

"Hold on," called Tomkins after him. "Wasn't it your job during the war? Blood transfusion for district? Collecting supplies from donors and all that? In Brunton, I mean?"

Beatty caught his foot and trouser on one of the bicycle pedals and swore bitterly. Lariat stood still to reply, looking defensive and nervous. Natasha, carefully watching him, had the impression that something unexpected had happened that he did not understand. The bicycle, perhaps?

"Yes," he said. "I was responsible for collecting donors and so on."

"Then you will remember," said Tomkins slowly, "what blood group your late *fiancée*, Miss Fork-Thomas, belonged to?"

II

"This is just going to go on getting more and more sinister," said Miriam, in the garage. She sat on the edge of the running-board of the Rover. She pouted angrily and was obviously very, very cross. "I loathe all this talk about blood."

Miriam's hatred of blood transfusions dated more or less from the spectacular failure of her musical version of *Dracula*, in which she had played the Countess (The Un-dead) a year or two before. Her resemblance to a lady vampire was only superficial.

"I think I shall go home," she said.

"You cannot be going just now, Miriam, when everything is becoming more and more dramatic," said Natasha. "Even though Miss Fork-Thomas *was* a universal donor."

"Group O," said Miriam coldly. She began to sing under her breath:

> "I rented a quite delightful crypt—
> And welcomed a slight intrusion;
> And the B.B.C. had me write a script
> On my methods of blood transfusion:
> But J. B. Priestley
> Thought I was beastly,
> Complained, and caused some confusion.

"I never could see why *Dracula* didn't go down in *Hull*, dear."

"Can't you?" said Natasha vaguely. "I suppose we will have a little *search* up and down the highways and byways and everyone will now be looking for more bloodstains of poor Miss Fork-Thomas amongst the grass. Perhaps it *is* rather nasty."

"And I expect they'll start with Lover's Loose," said Miriam, gathering her overcoat round her. "Well, dear, I *am* going. I have my public to think of. The Upper Fourth wouldn't care for my eyes to be all *cerné* at elocution tomorrow."

"Dearest Miriam, so public-*spirited*," said Natasha. "Now I really could not be caring less about what the Sixth Form and that filthy Gwen Soames thinks of me at the National Provincial dancing."

"In God's name," cried Miriam, "what is National Provincial dancing?"

"It is a sort of Morris dancing without the knee-bells," said Natasha, and Miriam shuddered.

"Very nasty," agreed Natasha.

"Nasty is as nasty does, miss," said Constable Beatty, coming through the garage door. "That blood in the basket *is* Group O. And as someone has bled heavy and pretty recent there the sergeant supposes——"

"Miss Fork-Thomas?" said Miriam.

"That's what the sergeant supposes, miss," said Beatty.

"I'm g-going," said Miriam, standing up. "I've had quite enough." She shook herself. "Aren't you coming, Natasha?"

"No," said Natasha. "I am staying. I wish to be a real

detective and learn all about clues and everything. Mr. Beatty has *promised*——"

Constable Beatty whickered. Miriam shrugged her shoulders.

"It's a long walk up to Radcliff Hall," she said wistfully. She rolled one large pale-blue eye towards the Wolseley where it stood demurely outside the gate.

"About ten and a half minutes I'd say, madam," said Beatty, unmoved.

Miriam went tripping away on her high heels. She seemed cross about something.

III

Apparently Miriam's ghastly news had preceded her. In her bed-sitting-room in the staff wing she found a little note in Miss Lipscoomb's untutored hand. It was addressed to Miss Birdseye, L.R.A.M. ("What do I suppose that means?" she asked herself.) She opened the letter.

Dear Miss Birdseye [said the note],

I have some rather shocking *news that I cannot write to you, but the police have* told me *that* poor Miss Fork-Thomas *will not be returning to her duties.*

In the circumstances, therefore, I must appeal to your Public Spirit to accept, for my sake, the appointment of house mistress to East House at a salary of min. £270 p.a. (£20).

Yours sincerely,
Janet Lipscoomb.

IV

"You are meaning, are you not," said Natasha, "that Miss Fork-Thomas was wheeled about on this bicycle while she is being dead? With her head in the basket?"

"So the sergeant thinks, miss. Carried down from wherever she was killed like, and pushed along, do you see, and finally parked in that there shelter where you and Miss Birdseye found her."

"She must have been being killed not very far from here, then, do you suppose?" said Natasha.

"Your guess is as good as mine and the sergeant's, miss," said Beatty.

"Oh *no*," said Natasha, shocked. "No one can guess as well as the *sergeant*."

Beatty had taken off his peaked cap, and his pleasant country face was already pink and perspiring from too much thought and too much running about.

"So everything is looking rather unpleasant for the poor dear doctor, is it not?" said Natasha.

"*Huh*," said Beatty, which caused a silence between them. Beatty looked at Natasha's pale and upturned profile. He wondered how ladies felt who looked as beautiful as that.

"Penny for 'em, miss," he said, finally, heavily.

"I am thinking," said Natasha, "about some people called Fox and Fox. Perhaps they are a team of music-hall artists or solicitors or chartered accountants, or even gentlemen's outfitters. Sergeant Tomkins has not heard of them."

"Sergeant Tomkins is a London man, miss," said Beatty.

"We have found them in the blackmail notebook which has been so *conveniently kept* by the late Miss Devaloys."

"Ah," said Beatty, and scratched his head.

"I am believing that Miss Devaloys was expecting to get £6,000 from Fox and Fox quite very shortly."

"Ah," said Beatty again. "Like unclaimed relatives in the *News of the World*, like?"

"Just like," said Natasha.

There was a cosy silence between them, neatly punctuated by the flattering, darting beam of the Brunton light-buoy.

"Fox and Fox, now," said Beatty. "There'd be a firm o' solicitors of that name over to Cranmer. Nice old family firm they are."

The light-buoy flashed twice before anyone spoke again. Then Beatty went on.

"There hain't been a Fox in the firm now ten years," he said. "Mr. Bere, he's senior partner. Main Street, Cranmer. He'll tell you what you want to know, miss."

"I thought," said Natasha, "solicitors were not talking about their clients?"

Beatty laughed.

"How do you suppose they get any business if they don't gossip, miss?" he said.

"Then," said Natasha, "someone else must be taking the Sixth Form in National Provincial dancing, that is all."

V

Tomkins announced that he would comb Lover's Loose for bloodstains. He was vexed to find that his pet, Miss Birdseye, had gone home. He was also disconcerted when Doctor Lariat put on a tweed overcoat and produced an enormous and expensive torch and said *he* would come instead. In Tomkins' mind Lariat was once again Suspect Number One. A man who admitted murderous intentions towards one lady might well have had murderous intentions towards another.

Tomkins and Beatty also had torches.

They fanned out into a straight line with Natasha on the outside left and Lariat on the outside right. Tomkins and Beatty were in the middle. They beat slowly up the middle of the field, catching their ankles in brambles and barbed wire. When they came to the top of the field and began to beat all the way back again, Tomkins firmly retraced the ground that Lariat had covered. Lariat did not seem to mind.

He did not, as it so happens, appear to be concentrating at all. He slouched along in a daze, stabbing the dark night ahead with his torch, hardly picking up his feet, occasionally stumbling, and always biting his lip. Tomkins, perhaps, had justification for his loss of faith.

Even so, it was Lariat who made the discovery. He swung his torch in a wide spectacular arc. He shone it on a patch of grass, clotted all over with little white fragments.

"I think . . ." he said gruffly. "I think . . . this is . . . what . . . we're looking for."

His voice was full of uncertainty and fear. Tomkins approached. Natasha's scalp crawled and shivers ran up and down her back.

"Looks it," he said. He sounded as though he thought it was a curious thing that it was *Lariat* who had picked up the evidence.

"Now all we want," he said truculently, "is a revolver shell. C'n you produce *that* for us too, Doctor Lariat?"

The wind suddenly began to sigh through the mean grass. The waves, dragging at the shingle, seemed nearer and still nearer. A drop of rain fell with a heavy smack on Natasha's upturned face. Another plopped on to Tomkins' wrist.

"Better make 'aste," said Beatty suddenly. "Going to rain properly."

"We found it just in time, then," said Tomkins. And he still looked suspiciously at Lariat.

"Better cover it over," said Lariat. "We were just in time."

His voice sounded dead, without intelligence in it.

Tomkins now looked puzzled. But he took off his sea-green sports coat and began to spread it over the grass.

"Where are we *being*, exactly?" said Natasha.

Lariat swung his torch. The first thing he lit was the back of the coastguard station. The second was Gull Cottage, Peter Bracewood-Smith's bungalow.

VI

The rain came down at high speed. It hissed in the grass and blew in from the sea in great wet gusts. Tomkins, in his shirt-sleeves, was already soaking wet. His shirt clung to his chest in dark patches.

"Bracewood-Smith's place," he said. "He'll have some whiskey anyway. Might have a bit of galvanized iron or a sack or some-'hing, an' I can get me jacket back. That'll be more efficient an' watertight, too. We'll knock him up."

Natasha, her hair already soaking, was glad to hear of any shelter. Lariat jumped the railing of Gull Cottage and stood in a flower-bed to help her over. He lifted her confidently, one deferential hand under her elbow.

"Thank you," said Natasha gently. "I have never been seeing the inside of an author's house. But I have been reading this man's books during a long time. Have *you* ever read one?"

"No," said Lariat shortly. "I never read detective stories. They appear to me to combine all the worst faults of the cross-word puzzle and the Grand Guignol, with none of the compensations.'"

"Oh, *so does Miriam think so*," said Natasha earnestly.

"No, honestly," said Lariat. "I've no time for any reading.

Theresa. She was the one for detective stories. Crazy about them. Intellectual exercise, she called 'em.''

Lariat laughed shortly and harshly, but he sounded more happy.

They stood in the porch of Gull Cottage, their coat collars turned up against the rain. Lariat's hair already lay in a dark, damp streak on his forehead. Natasha's oval face was wet and shining. Above them, from a dormer window, a light shone.

"Not asleep yet, then," said Lariat, and nodded up at it.

"No," said Natasha. "We could, perhaps, ring?"

There was a bell-pull on their right, connected, by a series of far-fetched olde worlde rusty linkes, with the interior of the house. Natasha pulled it, and an old chime of Swiss cow-bells gave an agonized imitation of several cows falling over some Alps.

"Goodness!" said Natasha. "What a curiously unmusical noise."

Doctor Lariat attempted to jam the bell chain with his handkerchief. Indoors the bells rang and clattered and tripped each other up in a frenzied tangle of Bs, B sharps and B flats. Sergeant Tomkins approached them, dripping wet and very angry.

"What you waitin' for, with a light on? Let *me* ring."

And before anyone could stop him he gave the bell another tremendous tug. Once more the appalling noise broke out and Gull Cottage rang with mad Swiss scales.

"Gawd!" said Tomkins, standing looking up at the lighted window with his hands on his hips. "Hope we haven't *another* corpse on our hands. That noise ought to wake John Peel. Anyone fancy a climb?"

VII

No one fancied the climb; but Tomkins accomplished it, wearily tearing holes in his gent's shirting as he did so. Natasha and Lariat stood below, their upturned faces wet and milky in the rain, their eyes vague and wide, watching him. They caught their breath when he slipped. This happened rather often.

"There's either no one *in* that room, or else he's dead or drugged or something," said Lariat, suddenly afraid.

"Oh *no*," said Natasha. "Please God not. No more drama. I am so *bored* with it by now."

Above them Tomkins kicked in the window and disappeared with a little tinkle of broken glass.

"So *ruthless*," said Natasha admiringly.

"What can you see, Tomkins?" shouted Lariat. But there was no reply.

VIII

Tomkins stood inside the window on a white-painted wooden chair with a cane seat. He was in the spare room. It was a little stuffy room beside the bathroom. Even the storm, rising furiously from the sea, roaring in through the broken pane of glass, did not air it. There was a sickly, creeping atmosphere, stale and unpleasant.

It had walls made of three-ply and beaverboard. It was ill-furnished. The curtains were too short for the windows. They were made of red-and-white checked gingham and they flapped dismally in the wind. There was no carpet. There was a chest of drawers with a looking-glass. The glass was so badly cracked that the mercury backing showed. There was a narrow divan bed. The light came from a bedside light which threw a pool of yellow light on the pillow.

In bed was Roger Partick-Thistle, fast asleep. His beautiful face was flushed. One golden lock dangled in his eyes. He was breathing heavily.

Tomkins crossed the room and smelt his breath. He was drunk all right. The smell of whiskey was formidable. Tomkins made a face.

The young man's clothes were scattered all about the floor. His trousers were rolled into a ball, fallen behind the bed. A shirt had been thrown violently against the chest of drawers. There was a forlorn pair of shoes, still laced, on an old and threadbare mat.

Tomkins looked down at Roger again. One long and graceful arm, white and slender as a girl's, lay outside the bedclothes. He was evidently stark naked.

"Obviously sleepin' off a drunk," muttered Tomkins. Confused words, shouted from below, filtered through the window. He remembered his companions, getting wet outside. He tip-toed out on to the landing.

He suddenly felt guilty. His mind began to frame the evidence he would give when he was accused of irregularity of conduct. No, your Worship. I was of the opinion that further deaths by misadventure might well take place in that fatal neighbourhood. I am not of the opinion that I overstepped my authority as a police officer. . . . As he went, a board creaked violently.

The landing was still. Tomkins stole downstairs to the front door. He shot back a bolt. He lifted a chain. He turned the yale lock. So old man Bracewood-Smith was afraid of burglars? Well, anyway, he was afraid of something.

Lariat and Beatty pressed in, followed by Natasha. They shook themselves like retrievers.

"Well?" said Natasha. "Why are you being so *long*? Where is Mr. Bracewood-Smith? Why didn't he reply? What *was* that light?"

"That light was Mr. Partick-Thistle, the chemist's lodger, sleeping off a whiskey jag," said Tomkins. "I didn't try to wake him. I don't know where Smith is. I haven't been in his bedroom yet. Thought I'd better get *you* in out of the wet."

He leered at Natasha, who felt reassured.

Beatty ambled forward into the kitchen, looking for something to use as a cover. Natasha tried the door of Bracewood-Smith's workroom and failed to get in. It was locked. She sat on the stairs and shook each of her feet delicately, like an animal. Lariat and Tomkins began to argue about the expediency of waking Bracewood-Smith.

"No, honestly, we ought to find out if he's home, anyway," said Lariat finally. "I think it's madness to leave without finding if he's home. Why, man, he may have heard a *shot*. With all those bloodstains outside his gate? You'd be *mad* to waste this opportunity."

Tomkins scowled at him. Lariat's efforts to shift the suspicion from himself were (Tomkins thought) puerile.

"Sit on the stairs with Mrs. DuVivien," he said. "I'm going up."

And he trotted lightly upstairs, lifting his feet as daintily as Amy, the pekinese puppy. Natasha sighed. She remembered her little dog so *clearly*, with her pretty ways. She hoped that darling Amy was happy. Lariat sat still, holding his head in his hands.

IX

Natasha supposed when daylight came that fear would go on the wings of the morning. When the sun rose, perhaps the absorbing misery and bitterness that seemed all around her would depart. And what would remain? Would everything be broad and sunlit once more?

Or would none of them be able to relax? Would they still be caught up in this insane arthritis, always worrying, always afraid of being found out? Would there ever again be gaiety to meet half-way with gallantry?

"Now what," said Natasha angrily to herself, "is making me think thoughts like these ones? It is this house," she added. "It is horrid."

Upstairs a window banged. Everyone shuddered. Natasha said, "Hail Mary." It seemed that all the angels of evil were loose and flying in that house.

Tomkins stood at the head of the stairs, licking his dry lips. He had caught the general *malaise*. His eyes were too wide open.

"His bedroom door is locked," he said slowly. "I thumped and banged and nothing happened. And then I heard a window slam shut. So I came to see. . . . "

No one listened to his explanation. Outside the storm was rising. Rain rattled on the windows and the house creaked and strained. Tomkins sat above them on the fourth step; his wet tie made dye marks on his shirt. His ego was quite punctured.

"Could do with a warm," he said. "House is cold."

He shivered and turned his head sharply to look behind him. And then he gasped.

Staring over the banisters, looking more like a wild beast than anything, was Bracewood-Smith. He was bare to the waist. His beard mingled horribly with the great curly mat of hair on his white chest. One of his yellow eyes was half shut. He looked like Pan. His hair and his beard and his torso were shining and glistening wet.

"How," he said, in his slow, thick voice, "how did you get into my house?"

168

INTERLUDE

Johnny DuVivien leant on the window-sill of his hotel bedroom. He felt very old and sad. But, he thought, there was something to arriving in a seaside resort out of season. At least he had got himself a room on the sea front.

Idly he regarded the sea, heaving and tossing, phosphorescent in the light of the corporation's gas. The street lamps looked exactly like sea monsters, prehistoric monsters, holding mantles in their nasty teeth. Maybe they were *meant* to look that way. He looked beyond them at the few people who were still walking about outside. They hurried along the cold, damp, windy pavement, wishing, no doubt, that they were safe and warm indoors. He hardly saw them.

Earlier there had been a big black closed Wolseley and an ambulance; and before them, in the dusk, what seemed to be a miner, pushing a sack of coal on a bicycle. He hardly noticed them at all. He was thinking so stupidly and so sentimentally, he was so utterly absorbed in his dreams, that these figures had only been a mirage to him. They were, perhaps, shadows reflected in a pool. Even the most obvious manifestations of the world had ceased to exist.

Tomorrow, in the daylight, when he was less confused, he would have time and energy enough to figure out the whole thing. Maybe. *Then* he would understand if Natasha fitted into all this at *all*. He would call at Radcliff Hall. He would ask to see over it. Tonight he was too tired to think any more.

Yes. He would ask to see over the school. That was it.

Little Joan Orr (aged twelve) began to take shape in his mind. She *must* be delicate, he thought, turning away from the window, taking off his jacket, emptying the pockets, disposing loose change, notecase, watch, pocket handkerchief, on top of the chest of drawers.

Otherwise why should she go to school at all? Delicate and difficult, that was Joan. Sheer terror with governesses. No governess can hold her.

He clambered slowly between the sheets. The embrace of the hotel bed was cool and hard. Perhaps even a little damp? There was a very small area of warmth round the stone hot-water bottle. Johnny turned, creaking, on his side. He put out one hairy arm and turned out the light.

With the light out his loneliness was less obvious. In the dark Natasha might even be in that other bed. Snoring very slightly.

Johnny turned on to his back. It was at this moment that he missed the scarf. Then he dismissed the thought.

Why, perhaps he was nearer to her than he had been for *days*. It was all Lombard Street to a peanut that she was in the same town. Poor Johnny sighed unhappily and fell asleep.

CHAPTER FOUR

"O H, so Bracewood-Smith looks *awful* undressed, dear, does he?" said Miriam.

She and Natasha sat side by side at the long, empty staff breakfast-table. It was early, but the school had already breakfasted and left, leaving a trail of toast crumbs and marmalade and torn envelopes and letters.

"What a pity," went on Miriam. "I quite fancied him. Like the Monarch of the Glen, dear? Yes, I see he might."

Natasha stabbed at a grape-fruit with a small spoon and filled her eye with juice. She looked sad. She dabbed at her eye insecurely with a table-napkin.

"I am quite unable to tell you, Miriam, how much I wish that you had been staying last night," said Natasha in her slow smooth voice. "You would have found something so smart to say to Pol Roger '29. As it was, he was being so very, very angry. Just being waked up at midnight would not account?"

Miriam looked up and shuddered delicately. The strange, bitter cup of coffee that she had just drawn, only faintly steaming, from the urn, was unpleasant. She put it down and sighed.

"What was Roger Thistle doing there, do you think?" she said. "A lot of total strangers in my house at midnight, making the stair-carpet wet, would account for a lot of my crossness if it had been me. Do you think they clean the inside of the urns with metal polish?" she added. "That would account for *this*."

She rapped her coffee-cup with her forefinger.

"How else did Bracewood-Smith seem?" said Miriam.

"Besides angry and wet?" said Natasha. "He said he had been

out on the roof when we asked him . . . but I expect that was British sarcasm. He was not making so much sense, let me face it, Tomkin tell him of the blood that we find, but *practically* on his lawn, but on his lawn. And he says, 'No motive,' and will we please leave at once."

"I see his point, I must say," said Miriam inconsequently. "Especially that bit about the motive. I have thought of a *most* sinister thing about our dear client," she went on, in a very quiet voice. "Read this little note."

And she thrust the letter from Miss Lipscoomb into Natasha's hand. When Natasha had read it, and covered it lightly with grape-fruit juice, Miriam said she had just thought Miss Lipscoomb was possibly killing off all the members of her staff so as not to pay their salaries. Miriam's eyes were wide with fear and sincerity as she said this, and she waved her arms so indignantly and angrily that she knocked over a small vase and a breakfast-cup. Natasha started to expostulate and to point out what bad economics this would be in the long run. Miss Puke came in and stared Byronically round the room, so they talked about the weather.

"I find I cannot take the god-damned Sixth," said Natasha, finally to Miriam. "I am going to a place called Cranmer where the blessed Beatty has found a definite Fox and Fox."

"I call that most unfair and selfish and un-public spirited," cried Miriam. "Why, I would not leave IVв for all the Foxes in the world."

Natasha said that elocution was different.

"Does anyone else know about Fox and Fox?" snapped Miriam.

"No," said Natasha, adding in a thoughtful tone: "I shall tell Gwen Soames to teach them 'My Lady Bellamy'."

"Who is Lady Bellamy?" said Miss Puke, seeking after truth. "No letters for me?"

"I do not know," said Natasha, "and I hope that Gwen Soames does not know either." There were no letters for Miss Puke.

"What time is the Cranmer bus?" said Natasha.

"In ten minutes," said Miss Puke. "I biked up. It's usually about five minutes after me."

"You *are* selfish, Natasha," said Miriam crossly. "Leaving everything and rushing off to Cranmer like that. Besides, I want you to tell me whether to accept this offer." She rapped Miss Lipscoomb's little note. "I can't accept, can I? Even though you do think mud of my theory?"

Miss Puke turned her back in a very gentlemanly fashion. Natasha's mouth was full and she did not reply.

"Miss Fork-Thomas," said Miss Puke, "hasn't been in, has she?"

Miriam's hand, holding her coffee-cup, shook so much that she could not put the cup back into the saucer.

"No," said Natasha.

"Very, very late," said Miriam.

"I must go," said Natasha, pushing her chair back. "I must not be missing that bus. Good-bye, Miriam. I should say yes, because it is your duty and an honour and because you are getting *so very* public spirited." And Natasha fled most basely from the echoing dining-room.

Miriam hiccupped with rage.

"Touch of indejaggers?" said Miss Puke sympathetically.

II

As Natasha ran down the drive towards the lodge gates she could hear the beating engine of the Southdown bus. It was going to take her away from Radcliff Hall for a whole day, bless it.

It was most lovely weather. The rain had long since stopped. Little beads of raindrops shone and twinkled everywhere. Under the ragged pine trees at the gate Natasha waited, and hoped that the weather would not break again until the evening.

The Cranmer bus drew up and stood, vibrating and creaking. Miss Lesarum alighted, wearing, monotonously, her Girl Guide uniform. There were also one or two other members of the staff, who Natasha only knew by sight, carrying for the most part music-satchels and violins in canvas cases. These were the visiting music staff, whose day this was. And all day long, in Natasha's absence, Radcliff Hall would rock and swing to the sound of violins and flutes at ten extra guineas a term.

Natasha clambered on to the bus in an excellent frame of mind. And the first person that she saw was Roger Partick-Thistle.

III

Natasha made no attempt to speak to Roger. He was dressed as a young American with a white shirt and a hand-painted tie and a very nasty red-plush hat. It was the sort of hat that is left unsold in the shop windows in the Charing Cross Road. He had no socks on. He was staring gloomily at his lean brown ankles, crossed one over the other. He held the hat on one knee.

Natasha sat beside him. She looked out gratefully at Sussex, streaming past on either side of her. They came into the long three miles of grass-covered delta that surrounds the little market town of Cranmer. It has been silted up by the River Cran for years and years. The River Cran winds to the sea through these dry, salty marshes and also through a rash of holiday bungalows that is called Sheringsey Bay on the map. Natasha watched lambs, three weeks old, going about heavily, almost tiny sheep. She watched rooks hopping clumsily. She watched the great white clouds (thunderheads, the Americans call them) as they sailed inland on the south-west wind. She did not think *once* of Roger Partick-Thistle, glum beside her.

"I suppose," he said suddenly "that you are thinking me absolute *hell* because I got drunk with Peter Smith last night and couldn't walk back to that chemist's?"

Natasha, who probably cared less for the debauches of others than anyone else in the world, opened her eyes very wide and stared at the beautiful face beside her. Roger's eyes certainly looked faded, and there were deep mauve shadows round them. If anything, they improved his appearance.

"I beg your pardon?" said Natasha politely. "If it is making you *happy* to get drunk I am *so sure* that it is the best thing."

"It doesn't make me happy," said Roger. "I get drunk because I *am* so miserable."

"Well, then, that is very *sad*," said Natasha, with some resignation. She looked out at a windmill spinning in the fields on her right. "Either way it is not *my* business."

Roger giggled.

"Just," he said, "what I was expecting to have to tell *you*, dear."

Natasha paid no attention, and Roger was slightly piqued.

"You are very nice for a woman, Natasha dear," he said.

173

"And it may sound foolish to you, dear, but I should have cared very *much* if I had lost your good opinion. I *like* people to like me, you see."

Natasha, who had always had the very lowest possible opinion of Roger Partick-Thistle, was rather touched by this naivety.

The bus swayed to a stop, and was instantly filled with a lot of angry, leather-faced ladies carrying baskets and hens tied together by the feet. They clambered over Natasha's legs and two of the stoutest of them sat on Roger, crushing him sideways. They began to shout to each other about money, and the weather, and their mutual friends, and money again, and even more weather. Roger, with his beautiful mouth about half an inch from Natasha's ear, turned sideways to avoid complete annihilation.

"Excuse me, dear," said Roger, wriggling.

"You had a pleasant evening, I hope?" said Natasha politely.

"Well, no, quite honestly it wasn't a pleasant evening," said Roger. "Peter was so *cross*."

One of the ladies put a hen in Roger's lap and shouted, "Went to *Mrs. Miniver* lars' night!" in his ear.

"Yes, that was what I was telling to Miriam this morning," said Natasha gravely. "But how did it happen? Because Mr. Bracewood-Smith was lecturing to us all about crime and the Conservatives in the Air Force ladies' hut until at least eight. Or I think. And then Miriam and I, we were talking to Mr. Intrikit about our auras until closing-time."

"No, we went to the repetwar!" shouted the ladies' friend.

"Do you know Intrikit too, dear?" said Roger. "My *dear*, his daughter is the *talk* of Brunton. Such a horrid girl, all *covered* with horse manure and riding masters."

"Mr. Intrikit told Miriam and me that she is merely *horse mad*," said Natasha gravely.

"Bestiality," said Roger. "Delicious." And he inhaled the rich air about the ladies on his right. "I met Peter Smith," he added, suddenly, "of all places, in Brandy's Club. I have a *louche* little friend who is manager there." He rolled a violet eye at Natasha.

"How nice," said Natasha vaguely.

"And then this extravagant man comes in (I suppose from that squalid little lecture) and we all drink a Jeroboam of champagne."

"Government champagne?" said Natasha.

"Well, yes, I'm afraid so, dear," said Roger, and pouted. "But a Jeroboam is an awful lot of anything. And after the gin I drank with my chum . . . do you know . . . I couldn't stand? Wasn't it awful?"

"Indeed yes," said Natasha. "I always prefer to stand, myself."

"And I couldn't face the idea, you see, of getting through the dispensary at Mr. Micah's. I have to go through *all* those repellant bottles and jars and Icky Bicky Pegs every night, drunk and sober. And I should *inevitably* have brought them *pouring* on to my head."

"Oh, so should I," said Natasha, with grave sympathy.

"Oh *yes*. And Mr. Micah and that nonconformist wife of his would *not* have understood, dear. And I like being their paying guest, you know. And it is nice not to quarrel."

"Cosier," agreed Natasha.

"So Peter (and he was pretty plastered too) said I could come home with him."

"What time are you leaving Brandy's Club?" asked Natasha. "And how did you get there when you couldn't walk?"

"Wasn't it ingenious?" said Roger, with his silly giggle. "He put me on a lady's bicycle belonging to my *friend* and pushed me up the hill on that. Peter is so kind, isn't he?"

"He sounds kind," said Natasha. Her mind made no attempt to grapple with these confused images.

"*Wot we want 's some steady rain and none of this a wind,*" said a lady on Natasha's left.

"I am on my *way* to Cranmer," said Roger. "To buy Peter a little present to apologize. What do you suppose he would like? You are so *intelligent* about gentlemen, Natasha." There was a pause, while Natasha remembered that the famous Helena bbirch now also lived in Cranmer. "I would never have thought," he ended casually, "that the old man would have been so *altruistic*. I passed out outside his gate and don't remember a damned thing until this morning, and he never says a word about it. But I wasn't sick, thank God," he ended triumphantly.

"Oh, *good*," said Natasha gravely.

There was a pause.

"So I suppose," added Natasha, "that you didn't know anything about any of *us* having come wetting Mr. Bracewood-Smith's stair-carpet until this morning?"

"No," said Roger. "Peter said this morning you'd all called, dear. Apparently I broke the window in my room, too. Wasn't

I *awful*?" Roger sighed deeply and gave another maddening giggle. "A drunken *thing*," he ended finally, and polished his horrible hat with his elbow.

IV

So (thought Natasha) although Roger Partick-Thistle had been with Peter Bracewood-Smith most of the night (from closing-time until the early morning, he had been too drunk to hear revolver shots and too drunk to hear them all ringing the doorbell. And Peter Bracewood-Smith had not been so drunk (although 'pretty plastered').

But where was the point of it? As Bracewood-Smith had said so angrily (drink always accounts for anger, of course), no motive. He was (apart from his insane dabbling in amateur theatricals) minding his own business in Brunton-on-Sea. Natasha sighed and extricated her bag from Roger Partick-Thistle's thigh and apologized.

Even Theresa Devaloys' notebook had not provided him with any sort of link. Natasha wondered if the little line had meant Fox and Fox should apply to Bracewood-Smith. How odd. Natasha suddenly felt sorry (of all people) for Doctor Lariat, tangled up, going deeper and deeper into other people's lives. As though he were wreathed in river weed. Paddle your *own* canoe, Lariat, thought Natasha, and sat upright.

Natasha's mind often overflowed with nonsenses like these.

They were bouncing through the sunlit street around Cranmer's market cross. Bicycles were piled against the kerb, sunblinds were pulled down over fish-shops. Scarlet lobsters lay carelessly about blocks of ice. Great piles of pink shrimps, and kippers all in cellophane, proclaimed the fact that Cranmer (once one of the most flourishing fishing villages in Sussex) now had its fish brought just the 300 miles from Scotland. The spring sunlight poured down on bicycle-shops, hung all with stiff yellow mackintosh capes and black mackintosh trousers legs. Chromium plate winked furiously and *Estelle* (*Court Hairdresser*) received clients every half-hour.

Yet in the centre, its beauty unspoiled by the litter of bicycles flung against its flanks (as though the Roman legionaries had carelessly abandoned spears and swords) stood the magnificent fourteenth-century Cranmer market cross.

The bus drew in among whitewashed parking-lines. They were opposite a Trust House, shuttered round a cool and shadowed courtyard.

"Do let us have luncheon, Natasha darling," said Roger suddenly. "Do let's. And then you can tell me why *you* have come to Cranmer."

He showed his pointed teeth for a second. Natasha said that would be delightful.

"Let's have it there, then," said Roger, waving a beautiful hand at the Trust House. "A quarter to one in the bar?"

And then his beautiful golden head went mincing away among the jostle of housewives and labourers and hikers and postmen and farmers. Natasha, arrested on the warm pavement, wondered why he had 'made a thing' out of lunching. Then she told herself that if she were going to fuss about people with Opportunity to kill these ladies and no Motive she might just as well pick on Partick-Thistle. After all, the sergeant had said he was recovering from a *whiskey jag*, and here was Roger telling the whole bus that he had been drinking gin and champagne. It did not make sense.

Natasha asked a policeman for Main Street.

V

Main Street ran north and south from the Market Cross. Everything in Cranmer was arranged like a flag around this common centre. Main Street was a pleasant-enough Regency Street, with bay-fronted houses and round-bellied windows. Here and there a brass plate proclaimed a house of professional standing. A cat or two crossed the road or rolled happily in the gutter or stretched and scratched against the palings.

There were area steps, too, nicely brushed and sanded. Natasha, peering at the brass plates, saw that there were doctors, dentists, veterinary surgeons and a Commissioner for Oaths. There was also Bunderton and Jacob (turf commissioners) and a big concreted garage called The Market Cross, Ltd. (Prop. T. Soper).

Natasha crossed the road and looked on the shady side for Fox and Fox. Eventually she found them, installed in a fair, sandy house with a black front door and the smallest brass plate Natasha had ever seen. In the wide bay window Natasha could see a lady with a typewriter, probably copying leases and documents with words in them like '*inter alia*' and 'messuages'. And all, reflected Natasha gaily, without *any* commas at all.

Natasha rang the bell and the lady got up from her typewriter. Somehow Natasha had not expected this. She felt, obscurely, guilty.

VI

"Is Mr. Bere free? My name is Mrs. DuVivien. I am afraid I have no appointment," said Natasha, all in one breath.

The lady from the typewriter who opened the door was little and friendly. ("Like Nanny," said Natasha to Miriam, describing her afterwards.)

"Oh," said Nanny, listening carefully. "Mr. Bere *is* free, as it so happens. Come in, Mrs. DuVivien, and sit in my room while I tell him you wish to see him."

And she showed Natasha into her front typing-room and disappeared.

Now I cannot hope to explain Natasha's peculiar and moody impulses. I only know that the moment that Natasha sat down in that pleasant room, all dominated by an angry oil painting of 'Fishing Boats on the Cran, 1846', she knew that she must dissemble. So she breathed a sharp prayer to her guardian angel (whom she had always believed to be a benevolent old gentleman called Saint Stanislaw of Lwow) and asked for him to intercede for her over her deceit. The ends, Saint Stanislaw always told Natasha, justified the means.

"Mr. Bere will see you now," said Nanny, reappearing in the doorway. She wore a dark-green overall and looked cool and pleasant.

"Ah, dear Saint Stanislaw, help me and bring me luck," said Natasha to herself, following the green overall.

VII

Mr. Bere lived at the top of an elegant white-painted Georgian staircase, all white-panelled. On the walls were prints of Brighton (the pavilion with figures in the foreground, the chain pier with gayer figures in the foreground) and an enormous signed engraving of the famous *Pas de Quatre*. Grisi, Grahn and Cerito. Natasha forgot the other lady's name. She wondered what the hell sort of gentleman Mr. Bere would turn out to be. (Taglioni, *of course*.)

"Mrs. DuVivien, Mr. Bere," said Nanny, and melted away at the door.

Natasha stood on a smooth carpet in a room the exact shape of the one downstairs. In the window was a desk, and behind the desk was a young-old man with grey hair and a well-cut tweed suit. The sunlight penetrated on this floor. Something to do with reflection from the other side of the street. There were roses on the desk. The air was full of the smell of them.

"My word," said Mr. Bere involuntarily, as he saw Natasha. "Do sit down. I hope I can help you."

"Oh, so do *I*," said Natasha.

"Who sent you to me?" said Mr. Bere amiably. "Have a cigarette?"

"I do not smoke," said Natasha, and looked as though she were going to cry. She felt as though her heart were being wound tighter and tighter. "Mr. Bracewood-Smith, the detective-novelist," she whispered finally.

VIII

"How wise not to smoke," said Mr. Bere smoothly, lighting a cigarette himself. "A filthy habit. So you know old Peter, do you? Nice, isn't he?"

"Oh yes," said Natasha, and felt her heart start beating again. She began to compose her fantasy. "He is telling me you have been his lawyer for . . ."

(Natasha pronounced 'lawyer' to rhyme with 'Charles Boyer'.)

"Fifteen years," said Mr. Bere, dropping his dead match in his big green glass ash-tray. He looked down into Main Street, and the smoke of his cigarette wreathed itself round his head. "Fifteen years. Not, of course, that I can handle *everything* he does. Authors are so impulsive, aren't they?"

He handed Natasha a nice professional smile.

"Oh yes, *indeed*," breathed Natasha fervently. "But so generous. So altruistic. Such a *brain*," she ended weakly.

"Quite," said Bere, and frowned. "Certain lack of *depth* in old Peter, though. Pity. I'm a Cambridge man myself. Feel he wastes himself on those detective stories and girls' school stuff. His is not a true creative genius, as you probably know," went on Mr. Bere, "and he *will* knit in people from real life into his books. And then, what can you expect?" He looked at Natasha triumphantly. "Then he gets into trouble," he ended casually. "Well, what did you come to see *me* about, eh?"

"Oh!" said Natasha, with a great leap in her chair. "Oh, I came to . . . er . . . to make my will."

IX

Natasha and Mr. Bere were very well pleased with each other's appearance. They spent an amiable ten minutes discussing Natasha's possessions. These did not seem so very many when Natasha thought about them.

There was Amy the pekinese, and a block of rather tiresome shares that were re-invested every ten years in Government gilt-edged. And there was the house on Hollybush Hill in Hampstead and a half-share in all Johnny's, her husband's, terrible night-clubs and road-houses. Johnny had preferred that she should have her own money, rather than he should pay her an allowance.

"Well," said Mr. Bere, at this point, learning that they were separated, "obviously you will be returning to this extraordinary man, your husband?"

Natasha was silent, and after a moment said that she did not know about *that*.

"In any case," she added, "I wish to be leaving it all to him in trust for my step-daughter, Pamela. So I cannot see that it matters much about the details?"

"Oh, rather," said Mr. Bere uncomfortably. He looked out

of the window. "Well, I'll have that drawn up and sent to you. Where shall I send it, Mrs. DuVivien?"

There was an agonized silence between them while Natasha stared over his head with dilated eyes.

"I am staying at the Brunton Hotel, Brunton-on-Sea, c/o Mr. Intrikit," she said firmly. "But I thought wills are having to be witnessed. Can I not just come here and be signing it?"

"Oh, quite," said Mr. Bere, and moved restlessly. "Of course. Are you lunching with anyone?" he said wistfully, as Natasha stood up and pulled on her white gloves.

"Yes," said Natasha boldly. "With a Miss Fork-Thomas. A friend of mine. A school-teacher. Do you know her?"

"No," said Mr. Bere, with a sweet professional smile. The name obviously meant nothing to him. "I'm afraid I don't."

(So the arrow *has* applied to Peter Bracewood-Smith.)

Natasha thought Sussex a wonderful county where nothing got into the papers. Mr. Bere came to the white-panelled door. He inclined his head most humbly as he opened it for her.

"Ah, well . . ." said Natasha. "You might have joined us. Perhaps we can be having luncheon when I come in for signing my name?"

"But of *course*," said Mr. Bere. "I am looking forward to it."

And when Natasha passed Taglioni, Cerito, Grisi and Grahn on the stairs she winked at them most shamelessly.

X

In the street, when she was retracing her steps towards the Market Cross and the Trust House, the big clock on the cathedral clicked and buzzed and whirred and struck the quarter after twelve. Half an hour before she need meet Roger Partick-Thistle. Half an hour to try and sort out these new ideas.

Natasha's instinct always worked in this disorderly way, flinging up startling messages to her sensitive and receptive mind. It had now presented her with a gambler's certainty without a shadow of evidence or proof. She saw herself, against a black backdrop, moving to slow music dressed in a *chic* white night-dress (with the new look) radiantly opposed to Evil. Evil, for this little *pastiche*, wore a pair of dirty pyjama trousers and a black beard and carried a cheque for £6,000. His yellow eyes shone like a cat's in the dark. But how could Natasha, all unarmed (except with her native intelligence), trap this monstrous animal?

She approached Cranmer cathedral. Natasha's taste was entirely baroque and she found it a tiresome pile of frozen Gothic built upon Norman foundations. To say nothing of the fact that it was housing what Natasha called 'The Anglican Heresy'. (Darling Natasha also spoke of it as "Crawling with dog-tooth mouldings and indecent gargoyles and Saxon murals that are leaving *nothing* to my imagination.") But it offered her sanctuary. She entered.

Natasha sat in a little wooden chair, harnessed to its neighbour. And her hazel eyes, that should have been turned upward to the beauties of vaulting and the elegancies of a decorated clerestory, were shadowy as she turned them inward instead.

She remembered Miss Devaloys' notebook, and she took the facsimile page from her handbag and looked at it under cover of a prayer-book. Yes, now she looked at it again, it *was* a debatable point as to whether the entry 'Fox and Fox' was opposite Miss Fork-Thomas' name or that of Bracewood-Smith.

"How careless this Theresa has been being," said Natasha angrily at this point, and startled a verger who was hovering round her.

So Theresa, in her tortuous way, must have Had Something on Bracewood-Smith. And all was grist that came to Theresa's mill against buying the school for herself and Lariat and Helena bbirch. Natasha now found herself believing the doctor's story. She felt an odd compassion for Theresa, whose tortured jealousy had worked out these blackmailing plots to secure her sentimental future. What hell ruthlessness could cause! But *surely* there was nothing that Bracewood-Smith wanted to conceal that was worth £6,000?

Natasha could not imagine any vice, however perverse, whose hushing up was worth £6,000. It could not even do much harm to a *novelist* (Natasha thought mud of novelists) to be connected with stray waifs or golden boys like Roger Partick-Thistle.

Natasha wished she had had the nerve to ask Mr. Bere more about his uncomfortable client. Perhaps she should have had luncheon with him after all. Natasha was suffering from a form of conceit, based upon her immediate past.[1] She was sick of

[1] *Death Before Wicket. Murder, Bless It. Death Goes On Skis.*

enforced confessions and spectacular and unresolved endings. She wanted no more murderers committing suicide or leaping screaming into Broadmoor. Nothing short of the Old Bailey and a darling judge in a black cap would satisfy her. It is quite possible that Natasha hankered after a gracious appearance in the witness-box. Possibly in hyacinth blue. Yes, hyacinth blue would be exactly right for a witness for the Crown.

But to achieve this she would have to find some connection between Theresa Devaloys and the £6,000 and Bracewood-Smith.

"A little document," said Natasha, "signed by *him*. That is what I want. For corroborate."

She went over again and again all she knew of Bracewood-Smith. He had an unpleasant daughter called Julia. His wife committed suicide. There might be something there.

Natasha would look him up in *Who's Who*. Or find out who his wife was.

The whirr of the clock announced the three quarters and struck them lazily.

Perhaps Roger knew the man *quite well*? She got up from her little seat and went to the door where the spring sunlight lay smooth and innocent and unrevealing, bland.

The roar of the Southdown buses twirling and turning ahead of her hardly disturbed the peace at all. Natasha dropped half a crown in a box called 'For the Organ Fund' and crossed the road to luncheon.

INTERLUDE

THAT morning poor Johnny DuVivien must have missed Natasha, his wife, by the merest whisker of time—by a little less than five minutes.

Ironically enough, this was due to his physical energy and not to his mental laziness. For, instead of climbing like everybody else on to the Southdown bus and riding up to Radcliff Hall, he walked, snuffing the air like a three-year-old. He waved an ashplant that he had bought in an oddments shop on the sea front opposite Brandy's Club. He strode happily along the centre of the camber, inhaling and exhaling in long, boring breaths. He was quite a little menace to traffic.

By the time that he arrived at Radcliff Hall the bus had over-taken him and passed him. Miss Puke had arrived on her bicycle. Natasha had climbed into the bus and gone on to Cranmer; the visiting music-mistresses, with their terrifying canvas-covered 'cellos and violins, had bolted up the drive. There was no one in sight when Johnny came to the lodge gates. He read the notice, 'Go Slow—Radcliff Hall'. He grinned. He started up the drive.

As he progressed, his spirits slowly dropped. In spite of the bright sun the trees dripped yesterday's rain on his head as he passed. He saw the sinister bird-baths and the plaster dwarfs. He very nearly threw away his ashplant. He wished he had not come. He pulled himself together and rang the front-door bell. He waited. The trembling Greta appeared.

"Can I please see Miss Lipscoomb?" said Johnny. He leant on his walking-stick with a debonair self-confidence he was very far from feeling. "Can I see the head mistress?"

"What name, please?" said Greta.

She went ahead of him, into the dark hall where Natasha had so often recoiled at the stale smell of mutton. Johnny, too, recoiled. He failed to associate his darling Natasha with any part of this sinister, stuffy house. This was not altogether unreasonable of him. For example, there was a yellow glass door-knob to the front door. There was also a painted glass panel in the front door showing a young lady in blue, holding a crimson urn.

"The name's Orr," said Johnny quickly. "Ion Orr."

There was a dark oil-painting of a monk with a barrel of beer on the wall above the hall table. Johnny did not care for it.

"This way, please," said Greta.

She shut the drawing-room door firmly behind him. Johnny was left quite alone amongst the little beast skins. He sat miserably on the sofa, clutching his hat between his knees. He felt like hell. Something held him rooted there. Something stopped all his natural inclinations to read stray letters. He did not get up to examine the school time-table. He could see it (although he did not know what it was) lying on Miss Lipscoomb's desk. Above it a surprising little procession of green jade elephants walked along the top of the desk. These did not attract him either.

It was, perhaps, a pity that Johnny remained a slave to these gentlemanly instincts. The three words, 'Dancing. Miss Nevkorina' would have meant quite a lot to him.

"Ah, Mr. Orr, very good of y'," said Miss Lipscoomb in her best social manner. She swept into the room like a gust of the warm south. "Sorry to keep y'. *And* can only give y' half an hour even so."

"That'll be grand," said Johnny, rising to his feet in sections, his long arms looking more like an ape's than usual.

"Got Matron in bed, to add to everything," said Miss Lipscoomb indefatigably. "Well, what can I do for y'?"

She sank on to the sofa beside him, showing her teeth.

Johnny looked at her and failed to hide his distaste. He had never liked long, pinched, tinted noses, or broken veins in ladies' cheeks. He had never yet seen a lady who wore a gentleman's necktie with *panache*.

"Was lookin'," he said finally as he stared at Miss Lipscoomb, "for a place to send my little Joan. Turned twelve. Vurry, vurry difficult kiddie."

Miss Lipscoomb picked up Johnny's ashplant and toyed with it. A ray of hope shot a little hysterically through Johnny's mind. Walking-sticks . . .

"Jolly decent stick," said Miss Lipscoomb wistfully. She put it between them on the sofa. "You must be the only parent in England wanting to send a gal to Radcliff Hall at this moment. D'y know that? Hey?"

"Did hear some'hing," said Johnny cautiously, leaving his sentences unfinished. "But I didn't attach . . . on'y the porter at the railway station . . . after all . . . I . . ."

Miss Lipscoomb clapped her hands.

"*Noblesse oblige!* Good man!" she cried. "Shows you're sound. It certainly does. Well, show you round the school, eh?"

"Thanks vurry much," said Johnny, trying to get a grip upon himself. He stood up. He felt that the whole interview had escaped him. He had almost forgotten his reason for coming. He had ceased to have any identity.

"Sure," he added vaguely, as Miss Lipscoomb swept him towards the door. "Sure. That will be swell. Crazy to see over schools. . . ."

"Ha!" cried Miss Lipscoomb, with a sudden, astonishing flash of humour. "You'll be crazy all right if you see over this one."

And she led the way, talking, and gesticulating with the ash-plant which she had appropriated.

. . . . .

"I'm vurry anxious," said Johnny cunningly, as they approached the gymnasium, "to have my little Joan learn physical trainin'. The specialist says it's due to such lacks—of dancin' an' so on, you know, ma'am—that she's gotten herself so peculiar."

Miss Lipscoomb idly loosened a rope and ran one strong muscular hand lovingly up and down its surface. She laid the walking-stick on the top of a radiator.

"What sort of *peculiar*, poor little soul?" she said kindly. "I have a great affinity with *peculiarity*," she added.

"Have you!" said Johnny involuntarily. "Oh, well," he went on quickly, in the wearied tones of the good father, "she kills things. You know. Beetles an' so on."

"I have had just such another problem child all this term," said Miss Lipscoomb proudly. She reached up the rope and sprang lightly into the first climbing position. Johnny was appalled. A child looked in through the gymnasium doors, gave a faint scream and scuttled away. "Julia Bracewood-Smith," remarked Miss Lipscoomb, swaying about three feet above his head. Johnny watched her, open-mouthed. "Started by breakin' dolls an' so on. Just like your Joan. Eventually went too far. Now *we've* got her."

"Is that the daughter of that big beast—um, *feller*—in the beard?" said Johnny, as Miss Lipscoomb alighted at his feet in the position known as curtsey sitting.

"Yes indeed," said Miss Lipscoomb. She got up and wandered on towards the stage at the far end of the gymnasium. "No idea Mr. Bracewood-Smith was so well known. This is for our play." She indicated the stage with a wave of the hand. "I don't suppose you care for school plays?" she said wistfully.

"No," said Johnny.

"Oh!" said Miss Lipscoomb, disappointed. "And this," she went on, with more of a flourish, "is our music wing."

The moaning of 'cellos and flutes and the rattle of fifteen inadequately tuned pianos showed that the visiting music staff were hard at work.

"But do you think that Joan will get *enough* physical training, ma'am?" said Johnny earnestly, shutting out the noises of Bach, Beethoven and Brahms with both forefingers. "Speakin' as an old all-in wrestler, ma'am, I couldn't take this matter more seriously. I——"

"Oh?" cried Miss Lipscoomb. "Were you an all-in wrestler? Tell me, where did you train?"

Johnny, in spite of himself, was flattered. He smirked and began to describe the difficult time he had had training with Laughing Cloudburst in Japan. In Ju-Jitsu. Before he had been talking for five minutes he was utterly side-tracked. Miss Lipscoomb was a wonderful listener. She was immensely impressed, hanging upon his every word. She often stopped him to implore him to demonstrate various holds and grips. By the time, therefore, that they had completed their tour of the school, Johnny was no nearer to discovering whether or not Miss Lipscoomb knew anything about a Mrs. DuVivien. It will have been observed, also, that had he been a little more polite about the school play he might well have been given some information about Miriam Birdseye. And this would have been a definite clue. But they did not come anywhere near to meeting Miss Birdseye herself, who was crossly looking through some linen-cupboards with the West House housekeeper.

Johnny, looking at the school, had assimilated a general impression of stale mutton, and was convinced he had drawn a blank.

Miss Lipscoomb, on the other hand, now possessed a delighted, if inaccurate, knowledge of the 'cross-buttock throw', 'the half-nelson' and 'the Westmorland wrist trick'. In the drive outside the school, as he said good-bye, Johnny put on his hat and waved the walking-stick in salute. Then he hung it soberly over one arm.

"Well, ma'am," he said ponderously, "many thanks for givin' up your valuable time——"

"Not at all, not at all," said Miss Lipscoomb in her gentlemanly way. "Many thanks for the interesting tricks you've shown *me*."

"Jest one thing," said Johnny. And he used all his magnetism and even switched on his famous 'damn you' smile. "You dance at all here? I mean——"

"An old woman like me?" said Miss Lipscoomb, responding to the magnetism only too well. "*Really*, Mr. Orr——"

"No, no, I mean—I meant," cried Johnny wildly, "do you have a dancing teacher at all? For Joan, you know. To help. Like the specialist says——"

"Everything is in a tiny bit of schemozzle just now," said Miss Lipscoomb quickly. She had been putting a good face upon things ever since Helena bbirch had left. She was only too well aware of the ephemeral quality of her talented temporary dancing teacher. "Personally, I . . ." She paused and looked at Johnny closely. "Particularly over the dancing," she ended confusedly. "Some days we do and some days we don't. That is, if you follow me. But *next term*, next term, when your Joan comes, I am sure we shall be able and *glad* to give her all she needs."

And with this reply, which made very little sense to him, Johnny was forced to be content. As he came away the post arrived and Miss Lipscoomb took a number of letters from the postman. Even Johnny, with his limited and unimaginative outlook, could see that they were likely to contain letters from parents announcing their intention of taking their children away from Radcliff Hall immediately.

CHAPTER FIVE

MIRIAM was buttonholed in the gymnasium by Miss Lipscoomb after she had left Johnny. The head mistress, no doubt as a result of her encounter, was in a passionately energetic mood. She had, she said, arranged a game of something that sounded like 'Bally Netball', because none of Natasha's dancing classes could take place.

"I want you," she said, "to arrange a staff team to play against the girls."

Miriam was appalled.

"But I don't have to play myself?" she said anxiously.

"Well . . ." said Miss Lipscoomb lightly. "It *has* always been obligatory for house mistresses."

"That was just what I was going to see you about," said Miriam hastily.

"You've thought it over, then?" said Miss Lipscoomb.

"In no circumstances whatever," said Miriam, "do I think I ought to accept."

Miss Lipscoomb looked disappointed. She was wearing a dark green jacket (very *chic*) with a rather lighter skirt. There was a faint suspicion of starch in the collar of her lilac cambric shirt collar. Then her face brightened again.

"Oh, well . . ." she said gaily. "That will make the sides right for Bally Netball. You can play for the staff."

There was a short silence while Miriam's enormous pale-blue eyes slowly lowered before the steely determination in Miss

Lipscoomb's. Finally Miriam said "All right." weakly, and asked when she began as house mistress.

"Good fellow!" said Miss Lipscoomb, and struck her a heavy blow between the shoulder-blades. Miriam spluttered and gathered her crochet-work sports jacket round her in her two fists. She had once again assumed her disguise. The shrieks of schoolgirls approaching their lessons died away gradually and a strange stillness enfolded Radcliff Hall. The morning's work had begun.

"Without Miss Fork-Thomas," said Miss Lipscoomb, "the time-table is still further disarranged."

"Of course," said Miriam. "No chemistry. I do see that one."

"Quite," said Miss Lipscoomb. "Like the B.E.F. at Dunkirk, eh? By Jove, we'll do 'em somehow!" Then she added, with a change of tone: "Wonderful opportunity for the right sort of physical recreation. Run like boys and girls won't think about boys."

Miriam said she thought this was rather a pity, and Miss Lipscoomb aimed another blow at her shoulder-blades. Miriam was too quick for her.

"And now," said Miss Lipscoomb, when she had recovered her balance, leaping from the platform to the floor, "d'you mind coming to see Matron with me? She's got some crazy idea she heard a shot last night."

Miriam's eyes, which during most of this conversation had been glazing in enforced detachment, now grew round and bright.

"Do *you* know," she said, looking hard at Miss Lipscoomb, "*what* has happened to Miss Fork-Thomas?"

"No indeed," said Miss Lipscoomb sharply. The corners of her mouth drew coldly down. "I can only suppose that she has been arrested. The police didn't say what had *happened* to her. Just that she would be unable to come to work today. I concluded the *worst*."

"Poor Miss Fork-Thomas," said Miriam.

"You're very charitable," said Miss Lipscoomb coldly. Her face had gone cruel and twisted and angry. "I *knew* no good could come to Radcliff Hall through Llandudno University," she said. "No good at all."

They were now walking through the main school, their feet thundering on polished linoleum.

"Why?" added Miss Lipscoomb. "Do *you* know what they are doing with her?"

"I?" said Miriam, with a start of horror. "Oh dear no!"

II

"Well, then, before we go over to the sanatorium," said Miss Lipscoomb, with a return to her former urbanity, "I wonder if you would mind coming to my room? There is a soccer football there that we shall need for Bally Netball."

Miriam reflected that she was an adult and therefore, in theory, not subject to these unnecessary whims of the head-mistress. Nevertheless she followed the neat flat back along the school towards East House and Miss Lipscoomb's sitting-room. As they went she grew angrier and angrier. This time she picked upon Natasha, the bolter, who gaily shelved all her responsibilities and as gaily avoided becoming a house mistress. Damn Natasha! She stubbed her toe against one of those scarlet fire extinguishers that litter all the most exclusive establishments and swore out loud.

"I beg your pardon?" said Miss Lipscoomb, with a laugh that was far from cosy. "House mistresses do not swear," she added. "Ha, ha! Much as they may want to."

She seemed quite serene again now that she had her own way. She looked at Miriam as though she were quite fond of her, bad language and all. Miriam did not care for this.

"Tell me," she said, "about Helena bbirch."

III

Among the little beast skins in her sitting-room, under the scowling painting of the first (and only) Baron Lipscoomb, Miss Janet Lipscoomb pursed her lips and put her hands in the pockets of her jacket. Her eyebrows met in a cross black line. Her heavy features seemed quite warped with anger.

"*Helena bbirch*," she said, "*betrayed my trust*. I would rather not speak of her."

"I do see *that* one," said Miriam reasonably. "But just the same, don't you think quite a lot of this"—Miriam waved her hand vaguely at the dead Miss Devaloys, the absent Miss Fork-Thomas, the disintegration of Radcliff Hall generally—"the whole Bally Netball," she said, "might be due to her? The . . . er . . . hidden hand," she suggested.

Miss Lipscoomb glared at her. She searched her jacket pocket for a pair of horn-rimmed spectacles. She now put them on and looked at Miriam. Her eyes glowed strangely. ('Like acetylene bicycle-lamps,' thought Miriam wildly.)

"Something in what you say," said Miss Lipscoomb surprisingly.

She bent and reached under her sofa and brought out a large cardboard box of netballs and bean-bags, coloured bands of braid and whistles on bits of string. It could hardly have looked nastier. She put it firmly on her desk and selected a large football and a bicycle-pump. As she picked up the bicycle-pump, a piece of scarlet braid became entangled in something. There was a crash. A heavy object fell to the floor. It lay between them. It was a heavy service revolver.

IV

"Oh, ha, ha!" said Miss Lipscoomb, picking it up. "Whatever will you think of me?"

"I suppose you use that for Bally Netball, too?" said Miriam, in tones of deepest sarcasm. "For shooting those who are off-side?"

"Don't be silly," said Miss Lipscoomb. "There is no off-side in Bally Netball. I've used it for the school sports for years. It's always loaded with *blanks* for starting the races."

"I *like* races," said Miriam gaily, in her most exaggerated public-spirited manner. "Three-legged. Egg-and-spoon. Bicycle races. Oh, I love them all!"

"Oh, so do I," said Miss Lipscoomb, and she crouched suddenly at Miriam's feet. Miriam, not unnaturally, recoiled. "Get set," cried Miss Lipscoomb. "*Go!*"

And she fired the revolver. In that confined space the explosion sang and sang and sang.

"If that revolver," said Miriam, "is loaded with *blanks* I am Stewart Granger."

An angry jagged hole had appeared in the window-pane.

V

Mrs. Grossbody rang the bell for Miss Bound.

"I heard it again," she said. "I heard it again."

"Now, Matron," said Miss Bound in soothing tones, "it was only a car back-firing on the Brunton road. Doctor Lariat *says* you aren't to fuss about strange noises you think you hear. It's very common after an overdose of that sort of drug, he says."

Frustrated tears rolled down Mrs. Grossbody's face. Dark and miserable shadows around her eyes made them seem older and more faded than usual. Outside, the pale sunlight and the rough grassy patch seemed mocking, iconoclastic, incredibly sinister to her fevered mind. (As a matter of fact they *were*, and it had nothing to do with her fever.)

"Doctor says, Doctor says, Doctor says," said Mrs. Grossbody passionately. "A fat lot of good that'll be when we're all murdered in our beds. What use was *he* when Gwen Soames had her appendix out last year? And why were those policemen beating about the bush in Lover's Loose this morning at seven o'clock?"

"Now, *Matron*!" said Miss Bound, as Mrs. Grossbody's voice rose shrilly.

"I want Miss Lipscoomb!" shrieked Mrs. Grossbody. "I want to take my Peggy away! I won't stand it a moment longer."

"Now, Matron, don't get excited," said Miss Bound.

"Excited?" said Mrs. Grossbody unfairly. "Who's getting excited? How do *I* know what harm you are doing in my absence? How do I know how many girls have chicken-pox and you not caring? Yes, and handing it on."

She sat up in bed and began to lay around her with the nice book (*The Forsyte Saga*) that Miss Bound had left for her to read. In the midst of her rising hysteria the door opened and Miss Lipscoomb stood there. She advanced towards the bed with a brisk firm tread and a flapping of fringed brogues. Miriam followed her, more slowly and with great distaste.

"Now then, Matron," said Miss Lipscoomb, without humanity. "What's all this I hear? *You* imagining things? You, who Miss bbirch used to say was the best spotter of a measles epidemic this side of Sussex?"

Matron groaned and muttered, turning over in bed. She was

heard to say that Miss bbirch had been a Real Lady, more than she could say for some.

"Now, now, Matron!" said Miss Lipscoomb. "Miss Birdseye is the new house mistress. We hope great things of her. You aren't being very polite." And Miss Lipscoomb grinned like a crocodile, turning her head from Miriam to Mrs. Grossbody and back again.

Miriam, whistling tunelessly, began to wonder which, of all of them, was just a little bit crazy. Mrs. Grossbody scowled and glowered.

"Then she's not long for this world," she said. "There's nothing but trouble and death in the cards just now."

VI

Miss Lipscoomb sighed theatrically. She crossed to the window and stood there, staring down on Lover's Loose. The little wigwam of corrugated iron that had been built round the bloodstains opposite Gull's Cottage was hardly visible. The plain-clothes man who lounged against the fence, guarding it, looked like any idler wasting time by the seaside in spring. Nevertheless Miss Lipscoomb winced and Miriam wondered why.

"So you tell the cards, Matron?" said Miriam tactfully. "Oh, I *dearly* love to tell fortunes."

"Matron's *wonderful*," said Miss Bound, with spaniel-like enthusiasm. "But she's even better with teacups."

Miss Bound smoothed the counterpane and Matron simpered. Miss Bound said should she go and *get* the cards?

"Don't lose your head, dear," murmured Miriam.

"Now then, Matron," said Miss Lipscoomb harshly. "There was no point in dragging Miss Birdseye and myself (I may say we are *very* busy) all the way over here to tell our fortunes. No indeed. And *what* exactly was it that you *thought* you heard?"

Miss Bound flushed and began to edge towards the door.

"You're all against me," said Matron, dabbing at her eyes with the sheet. "I know I heard a shot. And there were two deaths in the cards now and last Thursday. The ace of spades upside down and in a two. Eight o'clock last night. *Ever* such an unpleasant coffin in me cup."

"When was this?" said Miriam, sitting on the bed. "And what cup?"

"Ow! My feet!" said Matron, and moved them. Miriam *did* look very like the more irritating type of house mistress. She even contrived to keep her neck tightly strung like a harp. "I saw the coffin when I drank my tea," said Matron.

"No, Matron, when did you hear the *shot*?" said Miriam patiently. "And where did it come from?"

"Well, let me see," said Matron.

She began a long and rambling account of the evening as she had spent it, there in bed. She introduced fragments of broadcast talks to which she had listened (this *did* approximately fix the time, and Miriam bore with it, but Miss Lipscoomb danced with impatience). She made a great deal of incidents that had happened below her in Lover's Loose on other occasions. Eventually she produced the information about the shot. She had heard it (so near as she could judge) at seven or eight, she couldn't be sure which. Also, it had echoed around so, *ricochetting*, as you might say, she could not really tell *where* it had come from.

"You can see Gull Cottage very well from here," said Miriam, rubbing her nose with her forefinger. "What time did you go to sleep?"

Matron wasn't sure, but yes, she *could* see Gull Cottage well enough in the daytime.

"Oh, Matron," said Miss Bound indignantly, "you were sleeping like a baby when I brought your sleeping-draught last night."

Matron bridled and Miriam stood up hastily.

"What time did you do that, old girl?" drawled Miriam.

Miss Bound looked startled.

"Miss Birdseye is the new house mistress of West House," said Miss Lipscoomb, waving a hand. "You may answer her questions if you like."

"Oh!" said Miss Bound, and went on looking startled. "Well, I have been bringing Matron her sleeping-draught at 9 p.m., as Doctor Lariat suggested——"

"And let it be clearly understood," cried Mrs. Grossbody passionately, "I will not drink another drop of any medicine ordered by that man. Not after what I saw with my own eyes last night."

"Not," said Miriam suddenly, "that you could have used anyone else's eyes for the purpose."

"What?" said Matron belligerently.

"Nothing," said Miriam. "Tell us what you saw, pet."

"Miss Fork-Thomas, after dark, going towards his house as bold as brass."

"It's very difficult to see anything after dark, Matron," said Miss Bound.

"And you haven't got a very good view of The Lawns from here," said Miriam. "Now *have* you?"

"And in any case," said Miss Lipscoomb, "how did you know it was Miss Fork-Thomas?"

"By her head-scarf," said Matron sulkily. "Her white alpine head-scarf. The one Miss Puke gave her that she bought at the Bon Marché."

Miriam looked at Miss Lipscoomb and Miss Lipscoomb looked sour.

"It's quite true," said Miss Lipscoomb. "Miss Fork-Thomas *had* such a head-scarf."

Miriam wondered where it was now.

"I expect Miss Fork-Thomas is wearing it," said Miss Bound brightly.

VII

Miriam walked along the cindery path that connected the sanatorium with the rest of the school. Her head was bowed in thought, but Miss Lipscoomb, at her side, was chattering away like a tailor-made jay. A girl came towards them along the path. She was weeping bitterly. She wore the purple-and-white tie of Radcliff Hall and tears streamed down her face to wet it all unheeded.

"My *Dear Gel*," said Miss Lipscoomb. "We do not *cry* in Radcliff Hall. Keep a Stiff Upperlip. Brace Your Pecker Up. Where's your handkerchief?"

The girl continued to sob. She had a lank black fringe.

"Little horror," said Miriam pleasantly. "It is Julia Bracewood-Smith, isn't it?"

The girl stopped crying and sniffed and nodded.

"If you go on like that, you know," said Miriam harshly, "your nose will get even redder and more swollen and you'll look even *plainer*. What's wrong?"

The girl stopped crying and said it was Pongo, her daddy, who was wrong. Then she started crying again.

"Now shut *up*," said Miriam firmly. "What's the matter with Pongo, as you so wittily call him?"

More sobs. Finally:

"He can't have me to tea," said Julia. "Doesn't *love* me. Loves *everybody* better'n me."

Miriam could well understand this. Tears squirted from Julia's eyes. Miss Lipscoomb produced a man's large mauve handkerchief and handed it to Julia, who blew her nose noisily.

"Silly Old Juggins," said Miss Lipscoomb, and sounded exactly like Arthur Marshall. The child caught Miriam's eye and tittered. Miriam looked hastily away. "That's better now," said Miss Lipscoomb, not unkindly. "Now you Trot Along In to Miss Bound and take an aspirin. Say I sent you."

"Yes, Miss Lipscoomb," said Julia Bracewood-Smith, who now seemed to have her hysteria under control. She began to move away. One thick black woollen stocking slowly wrinkled round her leg. Her face was lumpy with crying. She was an unpleasant sight.

"Before you *go*, dear," said Miriam falsely, "how do you know all this about Daddy?"

"That I love him more than he loves me, do you mean?" said Julia, her lip trembling again.

"No, don't be silly. That he can't have you to tea," said Miriam sharply.

"Postcard," said Julia. She handed it out. It was a nice view of Zena Dare aged sixteen, and it said:

Sorry, Boopsi, have to go to Town, so can't give you tea as promised. Be a good kid.

Pongo.

It had been posted in Brunton the day before.

"He calls me Boopsi and I call him Pongo," said Julia.

"So I see," said Miriam coldly.

"I don't believe he's gone to London *at all*," said Julia. Her eyes were now hard and bright in her swollen little face. "I believe I just *bore* him *stiff*."

No one attempted to reassure the child about this.

"Look, darling," said Miriam suddenly to the head mistress, "I'll take Julia in to Miss Bound and get her aspirin *myself*."

Miriam's nobility, as she lifted her nose proudly and sniffed the air in a public-spirited manner, had to be seen to be believed.

"Jolly decent of you, Birdseye," said Miss Lipscoomb gruffly. Miriam and Julia turned away towards the sanatorium.

"See you on the Bally Netball pitch at half past two, then!" shouted Miss Lipscoomb over her shoulder. "And don't forget your gym-shoes."

Miriam looked at her feet, monstrous in large boat-shaped buttoned shoes stuffed with new supplies of paper each morning. She made no reply. Miss Lipscoomb went loping away down the path.

"My *Gawd*!" said Julia Bracewood-Smith vulgarly. "Miriam Birdseye playing netball. My Gawd! If the Ivy could see you now!"

VIII

"And how do you know," said Miriam coldly, "that Noel and Ivor will not be playing on the netball pitch this afternoon?"

Julia Bracewood-Smith looked suspicious.

"It's not *likely*," she said.

"It is not likely," said Miriam "that I should be here as a house mistress in Radcliff Hall. Still, here I am." She sketched a vague gesture. Julia Bracewood-Smith was silent. Miriam pressed her advantage. "Come," she said, "and get your aspirin. Tell me all about it. It must have been *torture* being their daughter."

IX

"Oh, it was absolute *hell*," said Julia. "It was appalling. Not that I really *liked* Mummy, you know. She was a *nagger*. And I suppose Pongo is pretty awful. I mean he does just as he pleases. But I do love him so very *much*."

And the tears started behind Julia's protruding eyes.

"Well, so will you be able to do just as *you* like, dear," said Miriam, firmly ignoring Julia's embarrassing emotion. "When you're grown-up."

"Do *you* do as you like?" said the child, with a sharp glint of eyes like black peppermint sweets.

"Er—yes," said Miriam. "Yes, I do."

"Then you must be *dotty*," said the child, "to have given up all those revues and everything, and the Ivy, and be a house mistress *here*." Julia Bracewood-Smith had a peculiarly adult sneer, and she employed it now.

"I expect I am," said Miriam cosily. "Most people are. It's just a question of whether they mind or not. I mean your father —er—*Pongo*, he is just a teeny bit eccentric, isn't he, for example?"

"I suppose so," said Julia, kicking at the cinders. "Going on writing those books that everyone thinks are such punk. Detective stories without any clues. Pah!"

"I can't read detective stories myself," said Miriam politely. "It is an intellectual exercise, like poker. Punk, are they?"

"Certainly Pongo's stories are punk," said Julia. "Everyone says so. Except it's fun reading them to see who he's put in. He put Mummy into *Death and the Archbishop* as a very nagging deaconess. *That* was why she committed suicide." Julia leered and put out her tongue.

"Get you!" said Miriam, aghast. "Have you read all your father's books?"

"Oh yes," said this gentle child. "He sends me complimentary copies. Since I've been at Radcliff Hall, though, there's only been one. *Death an' the French Governess.* That was confiscated by Miss Fork-Thomas."

"Oh!" said Miriam, abashed. "Are you in *my* house?"

"Yes," said Julia, with another leer. "Isn't it *hell*?"

X

Miriam, after her little charge had been fed several tea-spoons of bromide, walked back alone to West House and luncheon. Her mind was full of confusion.

Her mood was not improved by luncheon, which consisted of cold roast goat and a type of milk pudding known as 'frog spawn'. There were lumps of angry red jam in the pudding. They were very nasty. Sitting next to Miriam were two unwholesome-looking girls. One of them was dark and swarthy. The other had red hair. Both looked ingratiating, and the red-haired one looked as though she smelt.

"How long are you going to be here, Miss Birdseye?" said the swarthy one.

"Yes," said Red Hair, "and when is Miss Fork-Thomas coming back?"

"I really cannot *say*," said Miss Birdseye, ladling tapioca in all directions. "I shall be here until no one needs me any longer, I suppose. . . ."

(Natasha escaped to Cranmer, no doubt eating oysters, thought Miriam bitterly.)

"Oh, don't say that," said the swarthy one. "You taught us to say 'Where the Bee Sucks' the other day. I bet you've forgotten us. I am Molly Ruminara. And this is my friend Noni Postman. We are two of your prefects."

"Are you indeed?" said Miss Birdseye grimly. "And do we often unfrock prefects at Radcliff Hall?"

XI

After luncheon, Noni Postman drove Miriam into a corner in Miss Fork-Thomas' drawing-room and insisted on returning a book called *Death and the French Governess*.

"Curious," said Miriam absently, putting it on the table with some notes about the Upper Fourth's enunciation of the words 'O, to be in England'. "Curious. Someone mentioned that book to me only this morning. Is it any good?"

"It's no good as a detective story," said Noni Postman, "considering it from the strictest canons of the art."

"Oh?" said Miriam.

"But considering it's only by P. Bracewood-Smith," said Noni, suddenly becoming human, "it's jolly good."

Miriam opened it absently and glanced at the title page and the dedication. It was for 'T' ('Whatever "T" may be,' said Miriam to herself).

"Can I take this one, please?" said Noni Postman, like a mosquito in Miriam's ear. Noni had evidently asked that question before.

"Mm? Yes, if you like," said Miriam vaguely, opening *Death and the French Governess* in the middle. So she paid no attention to Noni Postman who, all unrebuked, hurried out of the room clasping James Joyce's *Ulysses* to her bosom.

INTERLUDE

JOHNNY spent a very dreary morning.

He walked slowly downhill from the school, past the sanatorium, avoiding the road. He passed quite close to Gull Cottage,
which (of course) did not mean anything to him. He observed,
but only vaguely, the plain-clothes man leaning on the fence
outside a hideous little bungalow. His only thought was that his
darling Natasha would never even admit to the existence of a
little red-brick horror like that. He turned his back on it. He did
not want to go back to the railway station to interview the disagreeable porter who had been so unkind to him the night before.
Maybe there was another school wearing purple besides Radcliff
Hall.

There were plenty of schools in and around Brunton-on-Sea.
The place was lousy with them. They got in Johnny's hair. Even
as he watched, some little crippled orphans from the little crippled
orphans' home hopped by him screaming down to the beach.

It was a moral certainty that two ladies and a woman with a
walking-stick and a schoolchild would not take a bus, except *in
extremis*. Probably a taxi had picked the party up at the station.
And the taxi-driver (if there were one at all in this one-eyed joint)
might remember Natasha. Hell, anyone who was not boss-eyed
couldn't fail to notice Natasha! *Someone* must have seen her
around. Perhaps this was the wrong place after all. . . .

He stretched his legs and began to step out more rapidly.
Soon he was almost running downhill, turning his ankles on the
steep, muddy path. The walking-stick was a hindrance to him.
Walking-stick . . .

Damn! Surely there was only one woman in the world (and
G. B. Stern) as madly addicted to walking-sticks as Miss
Lipscoomb? Why, she couldn't leave the things alone! Even
when she went through the hall she had taken one out of the
umbrella-stand and put it back again. Kind of wistfully. It *must*
be Eddie's walking-stick lady.

Blast the walking-stick! It now caught between his legs and
nearly tripped him. He was swinging down the path past the
gasometers. There was a nice ploughed field on his left that smelt
very well. It had been freshly turned. There were rooks skipping
about amongst the damp clods. They were picking things up with

their beaks. Beyond the ploughed field, well behind him now, was the piece of waste land known as Lover's Loose. Johnny knew nothing of its reputation. It sent him no subtle, sinister message.

He leant on a stile. He stabbed at a thistle with the stick. He lit a cigarette, protecting the flame of his match from the wind. He blew a cloud of light grey smoke that broke up instantly, swirling off towards the gasometers. He began to feel better.

The sea, for once, sparkled and beamed in the sunlight. It was smudged here and there with great purple cloud shadows. Towards the beach, over the rocks, it was creamed up with white foam. There seemed no danger of rain until the evening. The wind was holding it off. A lark, singing furiously, came down from a great arc of blue sky and began looking about for its nest. Johnny suddenly stopped feeling lonely.

A labourer, walking heavily, came up the path towards him. He swung an empty sack on one shoulder. He gave him 'good morning' as though Brunton were a true country place instead of the illegitimate offspring of the union between a seaside resort and conservative retiring-place. Johnny scratched his shoulders happily against the stile and looked back at the red roofs of Radcliff Hall.

It was a mysterious thing, certainly, the wilful disappearance of his wife into the landscape. No more mysterious, of course, than life itself. And Johnny, like all amateur philosophers, felt a deep melancholia descend upon him as he attempted to grapple, ineffectually, with the infinite. His melancholy was so pronounced by eleven o'clock that he walked briskly into Micah's, the chemist's, and bought himself some liver pills.

"Can you tell me," he said to young Mr. Micah, "if a Mrs. DuVivien has bought anything from you since she arrived here?"

This is the first time that Johnny had dared to ask directly for his wife. This was, possibly, due to Mr. Micah's extremely sympathetic manner. He shook his head.

"A vurry *beautiful* lady," pursued Johnny.

Mr. Micah smiled.

"There might have been a casual purchase," he said carefully. "But there has been no one giving that name to enter in the prescription-book. Of that I'm positive. I should have remembered."

He wrapped up the pills in white paper and sealed them with a neat dab of scarlet sealing-wax.

"Ah," said Johnny. "Good."

He walked blindly, backwards, out of the shop. He banged his foot against the weighing-machine as he went.

"Beg y' pardon," he said unhappily. Unkind Natasha had often said he was the clumsiest man she knew. *Extraordinary*, she thought him. How right she was. At the door he stopped.

"Does this place carry a taxi-rank?" he said. "Or a car hire?"

Mr. Micah was sorry for him.

"There is Creamline," he said, "and the Lipscoomb Garage."

"Which would meet trains?" said Johnny.

"They both do," said Micah. "The Lipscoomb taxi-rank is just inside the station yard. You can't miss it."

He called this encouragingly after Johnny as the street door slammed, shutting Johnny outside in the street, haunted. For a second he had thought he had seen something in the shining window. A charming face. Lustrous hair. Enormous eyes. It was a reflection of an advertisement for 'Craven A'.

Hell! So his *eyes* were playing tricks, were they? His practical nature reasserted itself. He undid his packet of liver pills and took three of them.

Two hours later, eating an excellent little luncheon of three dozen oysters and a pint of Guinness, Johnny thought wistfully of Natasha again. He hoped, in his maudlin way, that she was having enough to eat. He wished that she were sharing the oysters with him. She was so fond of oysters. And then he reflected that, wherever she was, she was probably very well supplied with everything she liked. It was a habit she had.

CHAPTER SIX

THE unhappy Miriam and the even more unhappy Johnny were only too right about Natasha. She was at that moment just finishing her twelfth oyster. The waiter, hurrying up with the champagne in its little ice-filled inverted top hat, was very excited by the whole thing. Roger Partick-Thistle, his golden hair falling extravagantly across his nose, was already more than drunk. but in the nicest possible way. He had been drinking in the bar, before Natasha joined him, with two silent soldiermen, who were dressed in tweed jackets with leather insertions. Now he was drunk enough to be indiscreet and extravagant, but not quite drunk enough to be uncivilized. Natasha, praising the oysters, asked him how long he had known Peter Bracewood-Smith.

"Peter!" said Roger, filling Natasha's glass and slopping a little champagne, fizzing, on to the table. "*Superb* character! So kind. Such shockingly bad taste, quite terrifying, my dear. I've known him about a year, I suppose. I met him first in the museum, you know, dear. He was doing research on forensic medicine."

"What museum?" said Natasha. "And what were *you* doing in it?" And she laughed.

"Let me tell you, dear, there is nothing funny about the *British Museum*," said Roger bitterly.

"No?" said Natasha.

"No," said Roger. "We met there in July, I think, when I was writing that little piece about my *organ* for 'At the Console' on 'How to Jazz Up Rimski Korsakov'. We sat side by side in *K. Such* a funny man."

"K?" said Natasha, surprised.

"The row we were both *lashed* to, dear, as readers. He was as much of a shark out of water as me, dear, I can tell you. No smoking. Terrible. So when I saw him stop one night in the portico and light *two cigars at once*, I knew he was a kindred—excuse me, dear—spirit."

Roger filled their glasses again and brought a small live tortoise out of his pocket.

"My Ever so Sorry Present," he said. "For Peter. Nice?"

The tortoise waved an elegant and wrinkled neck and accepted a small piece of lettuce with a flip of its leather lips.

"Oh, very nice," said Natasha hastily. "But do be putting him away before the waiter sees him. Tell me more about Bracewood-Smith and his *virile* beard. I am being told that his wife committed suicide."

"Ah," said Roger. "So she did, I *am* glad I was in Munich at the time, otherwise *I* might have been blamed. You know how *blamed* I always am. For *everything*, my dear. Yes, she fell out of a window, dear, I am *thankful* to say. A very tiresome woman. A spoil-sport."

"What a pity," said Natasha vaguely. She watched the

champagne flicker and bubble in the sunlight. "I hate people who are spoiling sport."

"Very British of you, dear," said Roger briskly. The waiter came with veal, cooked in white wine, with spinach and with the first new potatoes, swimming in butter. There was also quite a good salad, with hard-boiled eggs in it.

"No," said Natasha. "Russian. In Russia we used to love our sport *so* much. My cousin Vladima, my uncle Petrov——"

"Natasha," said Roger firmly, "you know quite well you've never even *seen* Russia."

"Tell me more about the Bracewood-Smiths," said Natasha instantly. "I am fascinated by his yellow eyes."

"Well," said Roger obligingly, "what else can I tell you? They had an affinity and it used to live in a magnolia tree in their back garden. Is that the sort of thing you mean?"

"You are knowing *damn' well* it is not, Roger," said Natasha angrily. "No. Why is Mrs. Bracewood-Smith committing suicide? What else does this man do but write books and drink and know you?"

"I don't know, dear," said Roger. "He used to hunt. He hunted with the East Sussex. That was before he grew the beard. Yes. He had a mistress, an opera singer. She's dead. He has one child——"

"I *know* about this child," said Natasha angrily. "*Why did Mrs. Bracewood-Smith commit suicide?*"

"I really don't know, dear," said Roger maddeningly. "By mistake, I expect. By mistake out of pique. To upset Peter, you know. A foolish thing to do, always, I think, don't you?"

Natasha suddenly recovered her temper and her sense of humour and smiled divinely.

"Now *I*," she said gaily, "will buy *you* a bottle of champagne and we will both get *stinking*."

"Oh, good!" said Roger excitedly.

The waiter came in with another bucket and another bottle of Bollinger. Natasha started to sing the 'Eton Boating Song', but quietly, beating lightly against her glass with her fork at the third beat.

"We'll *all* go *down together*," said Natasha. "Or wouldn't you say, Roger?"

"Don' mind if I do," said Roger, his speech suddenly blurred and indistinct. "Mind what I say, because it's true. Wouldn't tell everyone, but you're a pal. 'Tween you an' me an' waiter, dear, Mrs. Bracewood-Smith didn' commit suicide."

"No?" said Natasha vaguely. "Why not? 'Our bodies between our knees . . .' "

"She was pushed out 'f window," said Roger. "By her daughter, Julia Bracewood-Smith, aged fourteen years."

II

"Darling Roger, I simply am not believing you," said Natasha. "And how do you know this when you are in Munich at the time?"

Roger was now really drunk. He reached into the lining of his coat for his wallet, brought it out, and laid it on the table in front of him. He began to hunt through it, his eyebrows raised. He took out a Press photograph of two ladies in top hats at the *Grand Prix* (Paris, 1947), a postcard of a young lady dressed as a jockey, and a small invitation to a film Press show, showing two ladies striking each other across the face with whips. Then he found about fifteen pounds in notes and a book of stamps. Finally he produced some Press cuttings and a rude poem (rather badly typewritten) called 'The Good Ship Venus'. One of the cuttings, much tattered and frisked at the edges, he spread upon the table and looked at it with his head on one side. Finally he handed it across the table to Natasha. This is what it said:

BARONET'S DAUGHTER'S DEATH FALL

Mrs. Peter Bracewood-Smith (*née* Clarionet, only daughter of the late Sir Wilfred Clarionet, Bt., of Ricesteps, Herts) fell from the top floor of her Queen's Gate flat and cracked her skull, killing herself instantaneously, "When the balance of her mind was disturbed," said Mr. Biggs.

Evidence, given by house-parlourmaid Edith Johnstone (49) to the effect that Julia (13-year-old daughter of Mrs. Bracewood-Smith), was found screaming: "I pushed her! I pushed her! I hate my mummy," was to be disregarded, said Mr. Justice Biggs, summing up. "The child was overwrought," said Miss Johnstone, interviewed by our representative. "She obviously didn't know what she was saying. . . ."

Mr. Bracewood-Smith (author, of Brunton-on-Sea) gave evidence that he had been living apart from his wife for some time. "I need quiet for my books," said Mr. Smith as he left the court, a striking figure.

"It should surely say 'striking *bearded* figure'," said Natasha fretfully. "It *should* have said that."

"He grew the beard *afterwards*, dear," said Roger. "That is a three months' beard. Oh dear, I *am* drunk! What a pity."

"We will get a motor-car for you," said Natasha gravely. "And I will keep this cutting. But it is not being conclusive at all about the child pushing her mum."

"Well, *you* may not think so, dear," said Roger. "But *I* spoke to the maid, Johnstone, myself afterwards, when I came back from Munich. She said s' far from being upset about her mum's death, this baby Julia was tickled pink about it all. She couldn't have been keener. Oh dear, darling Natasha, we'd better not drink any more. She insisted she pushed her mother *out*. They wouldn't let her give evidence at the inquest, and I don't wonder. Poor old Peter was afraid she would be sent to Borstal. Oh dear, the room's fairly spinning."

Regretfully, Roger Partick-Thistle waved to the waiter and ordered strong black coffee. The waiter smirked and turned away.

"Roger," said Natasha firmly, "are you forgetting how Doctor Lariat finds this homicidal child crouching on the stage at that rehearsal? I can *see* you have forgotten."

Understanding struggled in Roger's eyes.

"My God," said Roger, "I believe you're right."

"I shall keep this cutting," said Natasha. "But where can I be finding the maid, Johnstone?"

"She's with a friend of mine, Major Bandarlog, as house-keeper," said Roger, drinking coffee in great burning gulps. "He lives near Brunton pier. Could put you in touch with them both *any* time. But, Natasha dear"—Natasha looked at him with large, incredulous, lustrous eyes—"however much you may *hate* children, you really don't honestly think a child of thirteen could procure a bottle of whiskey *and* inject it through the cork with a hypodermic syringe full of barbituric already dissolved in solution? And then re-cover the cork with wax 'n' tinfoil 'n' everything?"

Roger now looked bright-eyed and watchful and intelligent. He suddenly brought his tortoise out of his pocket again and tried to make it drink some coffee. Natasha sat in her chair, stunned and sobered.

"*Roger*," she said finally. Her lovely face was ravaged with distress. She wrung her hands together, writhing her fingers madly. "*Was* that being the method for the first murder? Because why should *you* be suggesting it? And if it *was* the method, how are you knowing?"

Owlish intelligence now peered from Roger's eyes and spread across his blurred, drunken features. He did not answer any of her questions directly.

"My word," he said finally, "and so it was!"

"But how are you *knowing*, Roger? *Please*, how are you knowing?" cried Natasha, with agony in her voice.

"I don't *know*," said Roger tartly. "Do stop nagging. For God's sake have a piece of bread."

He handed Natasha a roll. The spring sunshine suddenly seemed cold and comfortless. Natasha scowled at the champagne and refused the bread quite pettishly, pushing his hand so that crumbs fell on the table.

"Oh, heavens," said Roger Partick-Thistle finally, "*I* don't know whose idea it was that that was the method used. Gwylan Fork-Thomas', I think. Yes. Gwylan Fork-Thomas'."

III

Natasha and Roger left the Trust House, Cranmer, quite sobered and rather displeased with each other.

Roger had tried to recollect who had suggested the method to him and *when*. His forehead was quite beaded with sweat as he concentrated. Natasha had accused him point-blank of knowing more about the two murders than he admitted. Roger was horrified. His anxiety, on hearing there had been another death, was so genuine that Natasha was slightly mollified.

"But who," said Roger, walking delicately up the market-place towards the bus stop, "but *who*, dear, has been murdered? I do wish you'd tell me."

Natasha said that the police were obviously wishing to keep it all a secret and were hoping that the murderer might betray himself. Here she hung her head and said that she was not going to betray *this* to Roger from idleness, thank you very much.

"I shall guess, then," said Roger, his face lighting up. "I shall guess, and you will say hot or cold or *luke*. It will enliven the bus ride no end."

Roger was wrong. The bus ride was not improved by his attempts to guess the victim of the latest Brunton outrage. His choice wavered about capriciously between Miss Lipscoomb ('Aunt Janet', as he called her), or another attempt at Mrs. Grossbody, or Doctor Lariat. Natasha thought that the way he avoided any mention of Gwylan Fork-Thomas was *suspicious*. She regarded the smooth, childish face beside her, with no trace of vice upon it. She tried to guess a riddle in those unclouded turquoise eyes.

"I shall put Miriam on to you," said Natasha suddenly. "She knows you much better than I do."

"I wish you'd answer yes or *no*," said Roger fretfully. "Is it Peter Bracewood-Smith? Because if it is and you have let me buy him this expensive little tortoise when he is *actually* dead all the time I think it is most *mean* of you."

"How could it be Bracewood-Smith," said Natasha angrily, "when you have seen him this morning and the murder is happening yesterday?"

"Yesterday!" cried Roger excitedly. "That opens quite a different field of victims. Obviously another school-teacher, then, I should say. . . ."

Natasha, now thoroughly irritated by Roger, refused to play the macabre game any longer. She sat, looking silently out at Sussex, hating him. (It is perhaps a reflection upon darling Natasha's general instability that Sussex also had begun to *cloy*.) By the time that the bus approached the stop known as 'The Roman Camp' (perhaps a mile above Radcliff Hall School), Natasha was thoroughly tired of the whole set-up.

She clambered from the bus and announced her intention of *walking* down to the school. To her annoyance, Roger clambered down too.

The road was shaded ahead, downhill, by beech and oak woods. They came sweeping to the roadside, overhanging the ditches, filling them in September with beech mast and acorns. Occasionally a great scarlet toadstool reared its sinister head among the bracken, trimmed with white knobs like ivory. And the woods were not silent. Every now and then a frightened wood pigeon clattered and screamed near them, or there was a rustle in the undergrowth where a blackbird hopped. And once they saw a little brown toad legging it across the road for dear life. Natasha walked slowly, hating every minute of it.

"Goodness," said Natasha, as though she had reached the end of her tether, "how *very* nasty. I can hear children at play. . . ."

Roger, beside her, stopped, holding himself up by her elbow. "Yes," he said, "it is quite a distinct noise. Perhaps it is a school treat. We shall find charabancs drawn up waiting for them to finish their hard-boiled eggs and lemonade."

"While maddened dwarfs," said Natasha bitterly, "now tear around the countryside loose, destroying it and *picking* bits of it to take home to their classrooms. It is *all* the Government's fault."

"I see what you mean," said Roger. "Five bob for every extra one. Yes, it is unpleasant."

They came nearer to the noise every moment. Natasha had some justification for her bitterness. It was a terrible noise, compounded of screams and crashing undergrowth and (occasionally) sobbing. There was also tooting of whistles, and orders being given in a high-pitched voice.

"You see?" said Natasha coldly. "By blowing whistles these teachers delude themselves they have control. It is the same with railway trains. I have noticed it."

And so it was that they turned the corner of the road, and, walking more briskly, they were confronted with Radcliff Hall School playing Bally Netball. It was a truly bestial sight. In the centre of the game, which swayed all round her and often came dangerously near her feet, was Miriam, transfixed with terror. It was Miriam who was blowing the whistle.

IV

Bally Netball, according to Miss Lipscoomb, was brought to England as a result of the explorations of Mungo Park. Miss Lipscoomb was an authority on all the more obscure ball games and was herself a great exponent of stoolball. She said that Mungo Park had observed Bally Netball raging among the Zwartantos, the most vicious inhabitants of the Andes. Certainly the very name—Bally Netball—is a most hideous corruption.

Its American name is unpronounceable. Miss Lipscoomb claimed it to mean 'The Slaughter of the Innocent Squaws'. Some fascinating fertility rites, scheduled to take place at the beginning and end of the game, were always (advisedly) omitted by Miss Lipscoomb.

Any number of young women play: "So long as they are strong-limbed" (Mungo Park). The chief movement is the tossing of an inflated bladder over the left shoulder to ward off evil spirits, notoriously sinister. No player may catch or throw the ball except on the run, which leads to interesting sprains and contusions. When any one player touch another player 'in possession of the ball', it becomes forfeit, and 'possession' is given to the other side. Goals are scored by 'touching down' on the tips of the valley where the battle should rage. It is a very dangerous game indeed, and Miss Lipscoomb was crazy about it.

V

Natasha and Roger, horrified, stood near the top of the staff goal hill. This was defended by Miss Lesarum and Miss Puke (white- and black-speckled gym-shoes respectively). Miss Zwart was playing forward, eating an apple. They all looked apprehensive.

In the depths of the valley, Miss Lipscoomb pranced, flinging whole squads of prefects and leading girls to the ground. One or two of the younger ones were already severely bruised. They sat on one side recovering. No one seemed to think it odd that the head mistress had gone berserk. Play had resolved itself into a duel between the head mistress and Gwen Soames, who were encouraged by mixed screams of "G'w'on, Gwen!" and "Yours, ma'am," and "Rough old beast!"

Suddenly a horrid figure in a torn gym-tunic detached itself from the rest of the school and rushed at Miss Lipscoomb, waving its arms. It was quite out of control. It bit Miss Lipscoomb in the fleshy part of the thigh and fell into a gorse bush, dragging her with it. Miss Lipscoomb (who was 'in possession') flung the ball high in the air and cried, "*Would* you, Julia, by Jove!"

"Good God!" said Roger. "That's Julia Bracewood-Smith. She'll be *killed*!"

"Don't you believe it," said Natasha. "That child is *homicidal*."

"You'd never think," said Miriam, "that she has a teaspoonful of bromide inside her."

CHAPTER SEVEN

I⊤ is impossible to describe the remainder of the distressing Bally
Netball game in detail. Miss Lipscoomb (her habit for the last
fifteen years) remained berserk throughout. Even Miriam was
hurt by the football, which struck her a glancing blow on the
side of the face. And, half-way through the game, when Gwen
Soames had neatly 'sold the dummy' to one of her fellow prefects
and Miss Lipscoomb had applauded her 'running swerve',
Doctor Lariat drove up in his shiny black Rover. He stopped
beside the pitch.

"I got wind of the game," he said genially to Natasha and
Roger. He eased himself out of the driving-seat. "I *heard* it was
Bally Netball," he said. "There always *are* casualties."

And he smiled sadly at Natasha. He straightened his back
and walked towards the little line of girls with tear-stained faces
who sat by the pitch clutching battered ankles and swollen
wrists.

"That is not a bad man," said Natasha, watching his drooping
head. "Not that I am thinking *really well* of someone who is
wishing to be healing children, but you know what I mean."

Roger did not reply.

"Sergeant Tomkins think he · is, however," said Natasha
solemnly, nodding her head. "The circumstances inform against
him in a very *nasty* way also."

Doctor Lariat was now conferring with Miriam. He certainly
appeared upset about something, but whether it was the opinion
of him nourished by Sergeant Tomkins, or whether it was his
distress at the unnecessary suffering that he saw around him, we
shall never know. Miriam said she would give the game another
ten minutes.

Another black car appeared. It was as black as a hearse. It
was the police Wolseley. One or two children saw it and stood
still, open-mouthed. They watched Sergeant Tomkins and two
constables in uniform, who alighted and walked towards them.

When he came close enough it was possible to see that Tomkins
was vexed. His little face was puckered up with anxiety. He
seemed burdened with responsibility. He stopped beside Philip
Lariat, who was telling two children to go to Matron and have
laudanum put on their bruises as soon as they got in.

"Prescribing poison *as* usual," said Tomkins sarcastically.

"We can't go to Matron," said the child coldly. "She's very, very ill and mustn't be disturbed. That's Peggy Grossbody playing over there."

"No, of course not," said Lariat gently. "How *silly* of me. Go to Miss Bound, then."

Lariat turned away. He bumped into Tomkins.

"Oh, hallo, Sergeant," he said. "I beg your pardon. You wanted me?"

"Afraid so, sir," said Tomkins grimly. "*And* I have a warrant here this time. Want me to read it?"

The spring day suddenly became unbearably beautiful. The howling children were intensely sweet. They were, at least, alive. Behind Tomkins' neat head there loomed, for a second, the Old Bailey, the black cap. . . .

"No," said Lariat hastily. "Please not, please not. Not here, in front of the children. At the police-station. Someone can drive my car, if you don't trust me."

Tomkins relaxed. Constable Jones was told off to drive the Rover. The whole thing happened with very little fuss. Miss Lipscoomb, at the moment engaged in grinding the faces of two of her senior prefects in a gorse bush, did not even turn round. Only Miriam, Natasha and Roger seemed interested in the sombre little group. Miriam particularly galloped towards Sergeant Tomkins with all the subtle grace of a camel.

"Stop, Sergeant," she hissed as loudly as she dared. "Honestly, pet, I don't want to make a scene, but *you're taking the wrong one.*"

"Yes, you are, you know," said Lariat, with a sweet smile. He seemed to have a grip upon himself. His strange controlled detached manner was again in evidence. "You heard the extent of *my* foolishness last night. There isn't any more."

Tomkins said something about *that* being quite damning enough. Lariat sighed.

"But *truly*," said Natasha, opening her large eyes as wide as they would go. "Miriam is quite, quite *right*. And what is it with which you are charging him? Miss Devaloys or Miss Fork-Thomas? Or both?"

The howls of the little schoolgirls at play seemed to sweep over them in great waves.

"He doesn't want the warrant read, miss," said Tomkins,

cocking an eye at Radcliff Hall. "And I don't blame him. But since you ask, *both*, miss."

Lariat did not speak. He stood with his hands clasped loosely in front of him, as though he were already wearing handcuffs.

"There you are," said Miriam excitedly, while Roger sucked his teeth and tried to conceal his delight at the news. "I couldn't say whether Doctor Lariat is a *poisoner*, but I'm *positive* he wouldn't shoot the back of someone's head off with a revolver. He's too subtle."

"He might be subtle enough to have thought of that," said Tomkins. "Double bluff. See?"

"Oh, heavens," said Lariat wearily. "Take me away and let's stop arguing. Miss Birdseye, this is kind of you, but *please*——"

"But when Miss Fork-Thomas saw Doctor Lariat yesterday she was wearing rather a noticeable white scarf on her head," said Miriam. "Wasn't she, Lariat? Speak up, you fool!"

Miriam's nose and chin moved strongly and frighteningly together, like a nutcracker. Lariat looked at her in astonishment.

"That's quite right," he said angrily. "She was. But I don't see——"

His eyes filled with painful tears and everyone was embarrassed but Roger, who grinned with pleasure.

"What has this——" began Tomkins.

"To do with anything?" said Miriam. "Quite a lot, darling, and you, Lariat, you'll find that scarf the head-piece of your defence before long. You see, she left Lariat's house *wearing* the scarf. Didn't she, Lariat?"

"Yes," said Lariat slowly. "Yes."

"And you haven't found it, have you, pet?" Miriam turned to Tomkins, who said this was the first he'd heard of a damned scarf.

"Matron identified her by it. It's a fact," said Miriam. "And whoever blew her head off blew it off too and had to destroy it, or hide it. And it wasn't Lariat. Mark my words. Why, you and me, Sergeant, we were in his house by eleven, and he had to light the *gas-fire*. Remember?"

"Miss Birdseye," said Tomkins firmly, "what you say is fair enough, and we'll look into the scarf. But ten to one we'll find it in Lariat's boiler——"

"I don't have a boiler. I have Ascot heaters," said Lariat, in some triumph.

"Or stuffed down his drain pipe," went on Tomkins, unperturbed. "But meanwhile. I want my prisoner. On one side, *if* you please."

Miriam scowled. It was a most fearful thing to see.

"Very well, you silly little man," she said bitterly. "Arrest him. But I warn you. Natasha and I will brief ourselves for his defence. . . ."

The sergeant obviously considered this the grossest treachery. He said coldly that a fat lot of good *that* would do Doctor Lariat.

"I suppose you mean *subpoena*," he added, in sarcastic tones.

"Such language," said Roger Partick-Thistle.

And the Wolseley drove away towards Brunton-on-Sea.

II

The game of Bally Netball raged on unchecked. The little girls were inspired by such terror of their head mistress (now playing like a lambent flame along the ground) that they dared not turn their heads.

"Darling Miriam," said Roger, "has become such a steady girl."

And he looked at her appraisingly.

"The less we are hearing from *you*, Thistle, the better," said Natasha. "Do you *know*, Miriam, he has told me the way Miss Fork-Thomas has been saying the first murder has been committing. All over luncheon and all to do with his poor chum, Bracewood-Smith. . . ."

And Natasha, with many striking and dramatic gestures and her beautiful hair floating loosely round her face, described the process with the hypodermic syringe that Roger had said was too cunning to have been worked out by a child of fourteen. Roger sulked. He said again that he was sure it was that 'terrible old Fork-Thomas who had told him'.

"You mean that it points to Bracewood-Smith because he brought the bottle with him," said Miriam. "Well, it doesn't, darling. Just because he brought the whiskey. The bottles might have been switched."

"Well, then," said Roger, "we ought to have found a second bottle somewhere. And we didn't."

"But we are not *looking*," said Natasha.

"I was all *over* that stage, dear, and there was no second bottle," said Roger, losing his temper.

"Oh, to hell!" said Miriam. "Isn't homicidal insanity hereditary?"

"That is a scientific fact," said Natasha. "Miriam is at last being so *brilliant*. I have been thinking of Julia Bracewood-Smith *all* the afternoon."

"So what?" said Roger. He put one hand on his hip. He idled with his golden hair with the other. Miriam, looking at him with loathing, wondered what she had ever seen in him. "So you'll find it difficult to pin anything on old *Peter*, if that's what you mean."

"What is all this talk of pinning?" said Natasha. "I am going, since you ask, to call on Major Bandarlog, of the Pondicherry Parade. Or, rather, on his parlourmaid, Johnstone. She has been being parlourmaid to these Smiths," she explained to Miriam.

Miriam was instantly, rather touchingly, jealous.

"You are *mean*," she said finally. "You have all the *fun*."

"But, *darling Miriam*," said Natasha, puzzled, "you are so keen and public-spirited, becoming the house mistress, and I am keener on becoming the detective. Besides, there may be many, many clues still in Miss Fork-Thomas' drawing-room for the picking up. I see them there," she concluded maddeningly.

"I doubt it," said Miriam, with a shiver of disgust. A very junior child had run very near the hem of her garments. "And anyway," she added, and leered hideously, "I have discovered a *new vice* that will keep me busy until teatime."

"A new vice?" said Roger, his violet eyes dancing with excitement. "Oh, *what*? How *lovely*. . . ."

"I have," said Miriam (and she had the grace to look upset), "I have become a detective-story addict. I am deep in a terrible book called *Death and the French Governess*, by P. Bracewood-Smith."

III

By the time that Natasha and Roger had left the Bally Netball game no one had been killed. Natasha said her mind had now related several facts in a logical sequence. "I do not," she said, "wish to become confused with anyone *else's* homicidal tendencies." She therefore avoided Miss Lipscoomb and tiptoed from the Roman Camp.

"You must go away, Roger," she said, as they stepped lightly along the road together. "I have *work* to do."

"Oh, *why*?" whined Roger. "It's through me, after all, that you are getting the introduction to *Johnstone*. I do think you might let me play too."

"Roger," said Natasha sternly, "I am knowing that you were being scoutmaster in Brighton and that Thistle is not your real name."

"I wasn't a scoutmaster," said Roger. "I was a Grey Wolf."

But Natasha had made her point, and when they arrived at the gates of Radcliff Hall Roger said, "*Arividerci*." He began to run away up the drive, clutching at his hip pocket where the tortoise presumably was domiciled. He seemed to be holding it unnecessarily firmly. He ran with his golden head flung back, his feet shambling on the gravel. It was not until he had turned the corner that Natasha realized he might just as well have been carrying a revolver in that pocket.

IV

Pondicherry Parade was a short but noisome little collection of battered minarets improperly concealed behind the pier. Natasha had observed it several times during her stay at Brunton. Most of the members of the staff of Radcliff Hall could not conceal their contempt for it and its inhabitants. Anglo-Indian soldiers of an earlier and happier era than· this settled there, putting up screens of Benares brassware, umbrella-stands made from elephants' feet and Burmese gongs. They could be seen dimly, from Pondicherry Parade, moving cautiously behind the strings of beads that served them for window curtains. They looked like exotic newts in their tanks.

Here lived (and here had lived for the last fifteen years) Major and Mrs. Bandarlog, in Number Seventeen. This was remarkable for its lace curtains and its elegant frieze of sacred cows, if nothing else. As Natasha approached, a female hand drew a lace curtain aside and a face looked timidly out. Obviously Mrs. Bandarlog. Natasha paused before she rang the bell. She was apprehensive

(and rightly so), for out of the door there exploded an angry little
man, towed by an equally angry Welsh corgi. Major Bandarlog's
progress through life was obviously a series of such explosions.
His likeness to the dog was disconcerting. He had a big moustache
and choleric blue eyes. His collar was obviously too tight for him.

"Oh!" he said, and looked Natasha up and down. He did not
seem to like what he saw. Natasha decided serenely that he must
be a misogynist. "Canvasser, eh? M'wife doesn't see anyone."
And he pushed past her.

"Oh," said Natasha. "No."

"What d'ye mean, *no*?" said the major. He halted his face
about six inches from hers.

"No canvasser," said Natasha firmly. "It is being your
parlourmaid Johnstone I wish to see. Er—*non-politically*."

"Foreigner," said the major, in some triumph. "Maid's afternoon off. Good day to yer."

And he disappeared round the corner with his doggie. Both
of them bristled intolerance. Natasha sighed and shrugged her
shoulders. But the ghostly hand and face came back to the window.
And this time they beckoned. By and by Mrs. Bandarlog (a mere
travesty of a wife) appeared at the door.

"I hope," she began, "my husband . . . the major . . . pardon.
Very rude to you." She pushed a curl out of one eye. "Can
I help?"

"Not *very* rude," said Natasha, "just *rude*."

"Oh, dear!" said Mrs. Bandarlog. "You know what men *are*.
It's the steel plate in his head, you know. Heats up."

And she stood there, nodding and smiling, hoping for reas-
surance. Natasha reassured her.

"Of *course*," said Natasha. "*That* sort of thing is always making
the gentlemen so *irascible*, is it not?"

And Mrs. Bandarlog nodded and smiled and said indeed,
yes; but what was it, then? Natasha said it was her parlourmaid,
Miss Johnstone, then, and it was so *sad* it was Miss Johnstone's
afternoon off as she, Natasha, was knowing something *greatly* to
her advantage.

"Oh, how nice!" said Mrs. Bandarlog, quite brightly; and
then, as though she were writing one of Miriam's revue numbers:
"The pier, my dear. She always sits on the pier."

The door of Number Seventeen, Pondicherry Parade, shut
very gently behind her.

V

Brunton Pier was much as other piers, except that there was a sad lack of penny-in-the-slot machines. It did not, for example, compare with Brighton Palace Pier, or Bournemouth Pier, or even with Hastings Pier.

Natasha, however, was able to see with great pleasure All that the Butler Saw in Paris, and she also wasted some time over a machine that promised her (for one penny) 'A Picture of Her Future Husband'. Natasha thought it cheap at the price until she took a piece of cardboard out of the machine. In the middle of it were some horrid chemicals inscribed 'Spit on Me'. So Natasha spat. And instantly in the bright sunlight and in the middle of the card appeared a photograph of a man so like Johnny DuVivien that Natasha was quite horrified.

"It is a *judgment*!" she cried. She tore the nasty thing to shreds and flung it into the unheeding sea. "Saint Stanislaw, how *could* you?" she cried, in tragic tones.

"Nasty things, those fortune-telling machines," said a prim voice behind her. "Vulgar."

"Oh, aren't they?" said Natasha, spinning round. Immediately behind her was a thin lady with a tight mouth and a fawn face. She seemed to have indigestion. Whenever she hiccupped (which was quite often) she raised a hand in a cotton glove to her lips and said, "Excuse me." There was no one else on the pier. It was obviously Johnstone, the parlourmaid.

"I once knew a man, Peter Bracewood-Smith," said Natasha wildly, "who told his fortune on one of these machines and it says he will be free within the year, and he *is*. His wife commit suicide. So you see?"

"Excuse me," said Miss Johnstone. For a long time there was silence between them. Natasha sat on Miss Johnstone's bench and waited.

"Excuse me," said Miss Johnstone again. "Er—did you mention Mr. Bracewood-Smith? The novelist? I knew him and his wife, Mrs. Bracewood-Smith, over a number of years." There was a pause. "Ai was in service with them, ectually."

Miss Johnstone became very high-class indeed.

"Goodness!" said Natasha. She registered charm. "How wonderful. But how *sad*."

"Maind you," said Miss Johnstone, "much of it was Nanny's fault. Ai was never surprised it happened, reelly. Ai was only surprised poor Mrs. Bracewood-Smith kept alaive so long. Both of them."

"Oh, dear!" said Natasha. "How shocking that is being for you. *Do* let us be going and have a nice cup of tea somewhere. I am waiting," she added wildly, "for my little daughter, who is at school here. Yes. There is a café called the Itsy Bitsy Tea Shop quite near. We *must* have tea. It is so sad."

And such was Natasha's charm that poor Miss Johnstone, excited beyond words at an invitation to tell her favourite story in her second favourite teashop, spread herself to please Natasha. Natasha enjoyed the story enormously. She liked particularly the bit where Julia (it being Nanny's day out) flung her dolls from the attic window 'to see how far they would bounce'.

"Oh, I *do* see," said Natasha, "that after this it is not being a far step to real *people*."

"No indeed—excuse me," said Miss Johnstone. "Within the week, it 'appened. Seemingly. Mr. Bracewood-Smith was at 'ome for a change——"

"At home?" said Natasha, startled. "There was nothing being said at the inquest about this?"

"All's not 'eard at inquests," said Miss Johnstone. "*That* suited Mr. Bracewood-Smith's convenience. Ai should *hope* as *head* parlourmaid (they had kept three in those days) Ai knew my place. Ai did what he told me to save Miss Julia goin' to Borstal. Handsomely he rewarded me, I can tell you."

There was a pause.

"Oh, *good*!" said Natasha.

"Nowadays," said Miss Johnstone, "no one knows their place, not just the nursery as it used to be. Excuse me. I often wondered if I done—er—*did* wrong. Miss Julia, she went to one of these modern schools where nothing is repressed, so they tell me. Though mind—yes, I should like one of those pink ones, thank you—I've nothing against Borstal. My sister's niece was there and did very well for herself. Learnt dressmaking and married a naval officer."

"How *wonderful*," said Natasha. "There is no doubt?" she said, five minutes later, as Miss Johnstone drank her fifth cup of tea and ate her third pink cake. "There is no doubt at all? I mean that this child push her mum out of the window?"

"Oh, absolutely not, madam," said Miss Johnstone, madly

intoxicated by tea. "Absolutely not. Saw her with me own eyes. She said she wanted to see how far she'd bounce, miss—er—*madam*."

"Oh, dear!" said Natasha, who, though gullible, found this very hard to believe.

"Yes, indeed," said Miss Johnstone.

And here Natasha left this curious character, who had been prepared to perjure herself for an unspecified (but handsome) sum and yet was prepared to give the whole show away to a total stranger merely for free tea and a chat. Possibly it was very dull *chez* Bandarlog.

"And now," said Natasha to herself as she stood outside the Itsy Bitsy Tea Shop, waving good-bye to Miss Johnstone, "I must go and see Miss Helena bbirch, the h-hidden h-hand. We have delayed our meeting too long."

And Natasha, for no good reason that she could discover, sang the old-fashioned air of 'Greensleeves' to herself as she went, for the second time that day, to catch a bus to Cranmer.

INTERLUDE

IT is not my intention to try to show how the faults or virtues of a human being affect his destiny.

The fact remains, however, that had Johnny DuVivien *ever* attempted any direct approach in his search for his wife in Brunton-on-Sea he would quite possibly have found her at once. But his feelings of inferiority were so strong where she was concerned that subconsciously he felt that she would not want him when he *did* find her. So his approach was always hopelessly oblique and he was always handicapped by it. He always explained his feelings to himself as *altruistic*. He always muttered: "I want to know if the little woman is well. I want to find out if the little woman is happy." He never admitted that his true sentiment was: "I want the little woman to come home immediately."

Unpossessive, he thought, *that* was Johnny DuVivien.

He set out for the taxi-rank after luncheon in a hopelessly muddled state of mind. And here his mania for the oblique approach handed him over, bound and handcuffed, to Black Market Bob, the scourge of Brunton-on-Sea.

Black Market Bob was a very smart taxi-driver indeed. He was so smart that he looked like one of Hitler's S.S. Guards. He made cleanliness appear positively sinister. His bungalow in Brunton-on-Sea (he was a bachelor) was the scene of many pretty enterprises. After dark there was always the happy clatter of illicit petrol-cans and the merry rustle of nylons delivered by American soldiers. It was obvious to Johnny that Black Market Bob knew his way around Brunton-on-Sea. Johnny looked at him for a second from the opposite side of the station yard before he made up his mind. Then he approached. Black Market Bob sprang out of his taxi and stood rigidly to attention. He saluted.

"Cab, sir?" he said. Black Market Bob was certainly good-looking in a curious Germanic way. He only looked his best when wearing a peaked cap.

"Uh-huh," said Johnny, vaguely mistrustful. "But I want it for the whole afternoon. That be O.K.?"

Black Market Bob nodded.

"Long run?" he said laconically. Then he touched his hat again.

"Dunno," said Johnny, clambering in. He sank into the cushioned back seat. "Take me somewheres I c'n talk to y'."

"Very good, sir," said Black Market Bob, and let in his clutch.

He pulled up on the sea front. It was now getting on towards teatime. Natasha was already entertaining Miss Johnstone in the Itsy Bitsy Tea Shop. Nevertheless, the brilliant sun dazzled them and Johnny half shut his eyes.

"What did you want to ask me?" said Black Market Bob, slewing round in his seat. He had dropped his oily manner, and Johnny, watching him under lowered eyelids, asked himself what the man expected. Boy Scouts? Gin? Petrol? he asked himself vaguely. Bet he knows how to get it, whatever it is. Johnny's knowledge of human nature took him so far and no farther. He had an excellent worldly knowledge of weakness and vice.

"It's *information* I want," said Johnny. He steeled himself for the gigantic effort of self-revelation. "I'm lookin' for m' wife," he said, and blushed scarlet. "And I think she's round about here —somewhere. . . ."

He glanced up and down the empty esplanade, the shining, mocking sands, and sighed. Black Market Bob said nothing at all.

"Have a cigarette?" said Johnny.

Bob took it without a word.

"You don't say anything," said Johnny peevishly.

"Nothing to say," said Black Market Bob. "What does the lady look like?"

Johnny considered. His memory of Natasha's features and salient points had held him very near to tears for the last two months.

"Vurry beautiful," said Johnny, after a second or two. "Vurry, vurry beautiful indeed. About five an' a ha'f feet tall. About eight stone some'hing. Light ash-brown hair. Russian. Doesn't talk wit' an accent, but obviously not English. See what I mean?"

"*Easy*, in fact," said Black Market Bob, and he smiled an unpleasantly luxurious smile. Johnny made a note that Black Mark Bob's *thing* was ladies. He hurried on with his story.

"You carried anyone like this in the last fortnight?"

"No, *sir*," said Black Market Bob. "I'd have remembered if I *had*. But there, there're plenty of taxis in Brunton-on-Sea. I don't carry everyone."

"But you'd surely remember this one, now *wouldn't* you?" said Johnny. "If you pick her up in the future?"

"It sounds like it," said Black Market Bob. "It certainly sounds like it."

He relaxed utterly and tipped his peaked hat over his hard grey eyes. Johnny looked at his axe-like profile and felt cautiously in his note-case.

"What I thought," said Johnny unhappily, "was this. Here's the lady's photograph . . . an' here's a pound note. And if'n you ever see this lady anywhereabouts you nip to that-a telephone an' ring me at Brandy's Club to tell me. An' leave a message. O.K.?"

Black Market Bob looked at the postcard reproduction of Natasha and said, "Whew-woo!

"O.K. *indeed*," he said. "I c'n keep this?"

"All right," said Johnny miserably.

Black Market Bob smiled as he went on looking at Natasha's photograph. Johnny wanted to hit him. Then he took off his peaked hat and slid the photograph into the crown.

"Brandy's Club," he repeated. "O.K. I've got the number. O.K. I hope I'll be ringing you."

There was a long pause between them while the heartless sun illuminated a crocodile of nasty schoolchildren winding along the esplanade. Behind the children the shining sand (it was low tide) glistened pleasantly and a dog ran, hurpling over the shingle, to fling itself towards the sea, barking furiously.

"Now what?" said Bob. "After all, sir, you got the car and me for the afternoon. Better make use of us. Eh? What do you say?"

"Hell, I dunno," said Johnny.

"Why not try somewhere else?" murmured Black Market Bob with a wicked smile. "Why not Cranmer? Your wife's *just* as likely to be in Cranmer as here. And I've got a little parcel to pick up there myself."

"Oh, all right," said Johnny, resigned. "Cranmer."

And so it was. They must have passed and repassed Natasha in her bus at least twice on their way. Poor Johnny was congratulating himself on his astuteness. Black Market Bob knew all the gossip of Brunton-on-Sea with variations. That it was public-bar gossip of the most inaccurate kind, and no help at all, did not occur to Johnny. He was by now the drowning man who snatched at any sized straw. Any gossip about Brunton-on-Sea and Radcliff Hall was better than none.

"What's all this?" said Johnny, when he had heard how Miss bbirch had deserted Miss Lipscoomb and how strange Miss Lipscoomb was and how Bob's sister had overheard *such a scene*. "What's all this," said Johnny, "about a murder?"

Bob's sardonic mouth tilted slightly sideways.

"Two murders," he said. "Least, so they *say*. Two of the teachers at the College. One indoors. One out."

A spurt of fear cramped Johnny's heart for a second. It was an unreasonable thought. Damn! He had meant to be so reasonable.

The car was bowling along the road to Cranmer. Bob's hands were quietly impassive on the steering-wheel. The bright sun hurt Johnny's eyes. He shut them and tried to blot out his unreasonable thought. He tried a joke.

"Two teachers?" he said. "Thought there was a close season for 'em? Like grouse."

Bob did not smile.

"Knew 'em both *well*," he said grimly. "A Miss Devaloys, who liked 'er flutter on the 'orses. Yes. An' a Miss Fork-Thomas. Both quite young and charming. Funny thing. Most of the teachers at Radcliff are old trouts."

Johnny lit a cigarette. He tilted his hat over his eyes to keep out the reflection of the sun and the brilliant sea on their left. He also hid his relief.

"Did they have any other connection with each other?" he said. It was unbearable. *Why* should he think darling Natasha a school-teacher? Let alone a murdered school-teacher. No one should *ever* think thoughts like that. Devaloys. Fork-Thomas. What extraordinary names.

"Both sweet on the doctor," said Black Market Bob. "Doctor Lariat. Or so my niece who cleans up at the College says. They expect 'em to arrest the doctor any minute now. Interested?"

Bob shifted his hands on the wheel and half turned to stare at Johnny.

"Always like a good murder," said Johnny abstractedly.

"Who doesn't?" said Black Market Bob.

"You'd never believe it," said Johnny, suddenly anxious to impress this lean, unsmiling devil, "but I been employed as a detective in *four* murder cases."

And so, as poor Johnny thought, 'to while away the time' he gave him an account of the St. Anne Athaway murder, the Lawn Tennis case, and the strange things that had happened to him at Ardblarney and Schizo-Phrenia. And Bob still went on driving towards Cranmer and did not believe one single word. As Johnny embarked upon the more recent of his adventures, Bob cut sharply into the narrative. He pulled up outside a smallholding. They were quite near to Cranmer.

"This is where I got to pick up this four dozen eggs of mine," he said coldly. "Care to buy some yourself?"

Johnny felt the warm night-club proprietor's instinct for an illicit enterprise stir inside him.

"Take twelve dozen if your friend can spare 'em," he said largely.

"I'll try," said Bob. He was impressed. "But *you* must arrange delivery."

Johnny nodded. Then Bob set his peaked hat at a slant like Admiral Beatty's and disappeared towards the smallholding, whistling under his breath.

"Feller calls himself a *detective*," sneered Bob. "Can't even find his own damned wife. . . ."

He took off his hat to ventilate his head, and glanced down at Natasha's photograph smiling at him in the crown. Behind him in the car Johnny relaxed and congratulated himself on contacting the one man in Sussex who could provide the Bag of Tricks and the Cholmondeley Club with twelve dozen eggs. And it was at this precise moment that the bus containing Natasha rattled past to Cranmer.

CHAPTER EIGHT

bbirch Hall, originally Cheveley Court, and built by Sir Frank Cheveley, realized at his bankruptcy by Charteris and Co., of Brunton-on-Sea (auctioneers and estate-agents), was a nasty damp house of red brick. It stood in untidy grounds improperly cared for. There was a pond, for example, where mosquitoes bred and multiplied, and, as a result, most of the junior girls of Birch Hall were perennially covered in lumps.

No one answered the doorbell when Natasha rang it. After a little while she pushed it open and found herself in a dank little hall that smelt of mackintoshes. There were feet thundering overhead. There were one or two shrill cries that indicated schoolgirls. Otherwise, she felt she might have come to the wrong house.

"Can I help you?" said an exquisitely modulated voice behind her. Natasha turned uncertainly. The words had been spoken by a tall woman with neat black hair. It was caught into a bun. She seemed to have ear-rings on. It was too dark for Natasha to see any more.

"I am looking," said Natasha slowly, "for Miss Birch."

"bbirch," corrected the lady kindly. "I am Miss bbirch."

"Oh?" said Natasha. "How *splendid*. I am meaning, of course, can I speak with you somewhere?"

There was a pause while Natasha and Miss bbirch together observed the stirrup-pumps, the scarlet buckets of water, and all the fire-fighting apparatus necessary to a girls' private school.

"Not *here*," ended Natasha imploringly.

"Why, surely," said Miss bbirch, with much charm. "Come to my study."

And she led the way along dark corridors, past kitchen doors, through a lofty hall, panelled all with pseudo lacquer landscapes of horrid Japanese trees and ladies and gentlemen and pagodas. Here a drawing-class was in progress and fifteen small girls were crouched over desks with drawing-boards, making innaccurate representations of a geranium in a pot. The draught whistled through this hall and Natasha shivered. There was more light, and she had an opportunity of seeing what Miss bbirch looked like.

She had a thick white skin like a gardenia. And she wore trailing, *djibbah*-like garments of sage green. Natasha supposed that she was beautiful. She had not seen anyone do her hair that way since Monte Carlo, 1928. Miss bbirch suddenly opened a door on her left and they were in a small room that was mostly carpet and desk. It was very cold. The sun did not shine on it. There was no fire. Miss bbirch, Natasha suspected, was a cold fish.

"And now," said Miss bbirch, sitting at her desk and elegantly lifting a string of green soapstone beads that hung to her narrow stomach, "tell me what it is. Are you a parent?"

Natasha, mentally in conference with Saint Stanislaw of Lwow, had a great struggle. It would have been so enjoyable to be a parent for a moment or two. Mrs. Henfield, of Surbiton. But this would have entailed a tour of the school. Natasha could see it would be cold.

"No," she said. "I am a detective."

II

"My *dear* Mrs. DuVivien," said Miss bbirch incredulously, ten minutes later, refusing to accept the story at its face value. "For *whom* am I to understand you are working? *If* you can call this amateurish bungling *work*?"

Natasha grasped her temper in her two lovely hands.

"Your ex-partner, Miss Lipscoomb."

"Oh yes," said Miss bbirch. "Poor Janet!"

"She is hiring my partner and myself," said Natasha angrily, "for trying to find out who smashes up her school. And we see it is Theresa Devaloys who does all the tricks, turn the light out, draw the sexy drawings, wet the chalk, turn on the urn. But I know you, Miss bbirch. You tell her to."

"I?" said Miss bbirch faintly. "My *dear* Mrs. DuVivien."

"I am not," said Natasha smoothly, "being your dear Mrs. DuVivien. No. Even if you are knowing nothing of Theresa's prank it is still in your behalf it is being done. *And* we are knowing this. And we are reading the last letter she write you. And now please, let us make sense, shall we? These two ladies are being murdered. And you have the clue here. I know it."

Miss bbirch's eyes, large and black as grapes, opened very wide. Her soapstone ear-rings shook as she inclined her head. Then, very softly, she began to laugh.

"Of course," she said. "You will be the tart." And she laughed again, apparently in genuine amusement. Then she was grave. "Murder?" she said abruptly, as the laughter left her voice. "Who says murder?"

"Well," said Natasha, biting back the cold rage that consumed her, "the coroner will be saying so. And the jury. And the police are arresting the innocent Doctor Lariat."

"No!" said Miss bbirch delightedly, and jingled her ear-rings. "No! Theresa's *inamorata*. But *you* say Theresa was murdered?"

"And Gwylan Fork-Thomas," said Natasha grimly.

"My pretty chickens," said Miss bbirch.

"The new staff, perhaps, of Radcliff Hall," said Natasha coldly. "Meaning the new set-up that you and Theresa and Lariat shall run. In a house not so damp as this. I am knowing this one, too, in my bungling amateurish way."

Miss bbirch was silent, looking at her long white fingers, turning a jade ring on her little finger.

"You seem to know everything, Mrs. DuVivien," she said finally. "And I apologize. But what could I possibly tell you that you do not know already?"

And she raised her black eyes again and stared at Natasha, and Natasha felt Miss bbirch's formidable will-power and was surprised.

"Theresa is collecting money to assist in the buying of Radcliff Hall property," she said slowly.

"Miss Lipscoomb would never sell," said Miss bbirch briskly. "It is a false premise."

"We are all knowing how Miss Devaloys is persuading her," said Natasha. "And how me and Miss Birdseye, my partner, are hired to be stopping it. But I am knowing that Theresa has expectations of sums from various people. For certain reasons. Blackmail."

Natasha stopped and nodded her lovely head.

"Blackmail?" said Miss bbirch, as though she had never heard the word before. "You don't mean *blackmail*?"

Natasha was angry.

"If it is being blackmail," she said crossly, "then you will be bound to be prosecuted, you know. The law is being, oh, so harsh with blackmailers' accomplices."

Miss bbirch's jawline, under that gardenia skin, went tense.

"I swear by Almighty God——" began Miss bbirch.

"Save it," said Natasha. "You will need such oaths in the magistrates' court, not for me."

There was a pause.

"What do you want to know?" whispered Miss bbirch.

"Is Miss Devaloys expecting of £6,ooo from Peter Bracewood-Smith because his child, Julia, push her mum, Mrs. Bracewood-Smith (*née* Clarionet), out of a window?"

There was an astonished pause, and then through the cold study there was the sinister sound of Miss bbirch laughing happily, rippling with relief.

"Oh, my *dear*, no," she said gaily. "Come into the library and I'll *show* you why. . . ."

BOOK FOUR

A LITTLE MATTER OF PROOF

CHAPTER ONE

NATASHA left bbirch Hall in a rage. This was not improved by the telephone-box on the corner of Brunton Road, from which she rang up Miriam Birdseye. It had most of its door missing, the telephone-book had been wrenched from its string, the telephone itself was partly disintegrated. Someone had written 'Jerry P. goes with Edie L., the dirty cat' in lipstick on one of the walls. The whole thing smelt most unpleasant. Natasha did not even fancy her own reflection in the glass. She grimaced, as she listened to the clinking and banging that showed she was connected to Radcliff Hall School.

The new and hysterical parlourmaid, Greta, answered the telephone. After a quite maddening delay there were footsteps and Miriam growled at the other end.

"Look," began Natasha, without introduction, "I am now knowing who it is doing these murders for certain."

"At the most I hear, dear," said Miriam coldly, "and the murders have always been done for certain."

"No!" cried Natasha, gesturing wildly. "I have motive for this person. Of a sort," she ended, more doubtfully.

"Oh," said Miriam, "that's different. Well, tell me."

And Natasha, only occasionally interrupted by a pramful of insanitary children that bumped monotonously against the kiosk door, told Miriam everything that Miss bbirch told *her*, in the library at bbirch Hall. And, as I do not want to madden the astute reader of detective stories, who will already have worked this one out for himself, I will leave the rest of this page blank to indicate this information.

"Well," said Miriam, when Natasha had finished, "good for you, pet, and goody for our side and goody for Miss bbirch, who hardly sounds true, dear. But Tomkins says the inquest is to-morrow. And, when what he calls the Right Verdict has been brought in (Murder by a Person or Persons Unknown, and *not* by Doctor Lariat, as you might imagine) Lariat will come up at the County Assizes. Yes, dear, it *does* sound indecent. And *then* whoopee for the old Old Bailey and Mrs. DuVivien in dove-grey and the famous Miss Birdseye in black."

"Hyacinth blue," said Natasha crossly.

"What, dear?" said Miriam. "As you see, it's all very complicated and not a *bit* like a book by P. Bracewood-Smith."

"Were you ever finishing this?" said Natasha idly. "*Death and Whatever it is?*"

"*The French Governess*," said Miriam. "Of course. No, and I don't suppose I shall bother now. It got dull really when the murders and rapes stopped and there were just *clues*. . . ."

"I am so sorry for this Lariat," said Natasha.

The children, leering, withdrew from the door of the telephone-box. Natasha put out her tongue at them.

"You needn't be," said Miriam tartly. "It's *you* I'm sorry for."

"Me?" said Natasha. "Why?"

"Because there is no Valentine Brown for your Miss Phoebe, and Miss Lesarum says that she has learnt the part, *just in case*."

"Heavens!" said Natasha.

"And there is a rehearsal tonight, dear," went on Miriam, turning the knife in the wound. "And it will be *hell*, my dear, because the news is *out* about Miss Fork-Thomas. Half West House are prostrated. To say nothing of Miss Puke, who is locked in a lavatory in the staff wing, and is threatening suicide. She won't come out, and I have had to send for the fire brigade. It is all most disagreeable."

"Drama?" said Natasha, with some pleasure. "Then I will come back."

If the preparations for the Radcliff Hall staff play had before been feverish, they now became hysterical. To Miss Lipscoomb,

500 people pouring into the school hall at 2*s*. 6*d*. a head was an obvious symbol of prosperity and security. The fact that most of these people would come to Radcliff Hall in a spirit of hollow curiosity did not occur to her. The tickets were sold out. They were now being re-sold by spivs at 5*s*., or even 10*s*. 6*d*. Whenever she saw Miriam, Miss Lipscoomb told her about this and took her into her office to show her the playbills. These were already up all over Brunton-on-Sea.

Miriam looked at the playbills with complacency. The name *Birdseye* looked well, she thought. For once, too, she was actually getting as much publicity as she liked. Sergeant Tomkins' slogan, 'Straight at Last', had caught on. There was a second leader, two columns long, about her in the *Brunton Observer*.

Even the murders, which occupied the whole of the front page, did not detract from Miriam. The front page was illustrated with smudgy photographs of Sgt. Tomkins, C.I.D. ('in charge of the case'), Miss Devaloys ('the murdered French mistress') and Miss Fork-Thomas ('the murdered chemistry ditto'). There was even a photograph of the school taken from the prospectus. Soon the London dailies would have it and then the turmoil set in. Miss Lipscoomb did not realize that London reporters would be swarming all over her in ten hours, and all 'her' parents taking their children away in twenty-four. But Miriam knew it and she was looking forward to it. After the inquest, information about the murders would be exhausted. The London dailies would have nothing left to write about but Miriam Birdseye. This suited her very well, and she went into a happy trance thinking about it. She could not have cared less about who played Valentine Brown.

Perhaps the slogan 'Straight at Last' was truly a forerunner to greater things. Perhaps she could rent a theatre and do Ibsen. Or a quite, quite new play by a *young* and brilliant playwright . . . there were always such playwrights to be found in The Six Bells in Chelsea . . . a play like *The Eagle Only Barks Twice*, only better. Miriam very nearly rang up H. M. Tennant to tell them all about it. She was stopped by a child with a message.

"Miss Lipscoomb says, please, Miss Birdseye, that Sergeant Tomkins is in her study to see you."

"Thank you," said Miriam, with an alligator's grin. "Little horror," she added, as the child seemed to expect something.

"Yes, Miss Birdseye," it said hastily, and fled, a small scampering figure in purple and white with wrinkled black stockings.

Tomkins sat on the table in Miss Lipscoomb's study. It was a dark, cold cupboard of a room that led off her sitting-room. It was unused, except when Miss Lipscoomb gave some unhappy child 'a pi-jaw'. This is Miss Lipscoomb's phrase, not mine.

"Hullo," said Miriam, and scowled. She gathered her mauve lock-knit jumper-suit around her. Tomkins looked hastily at the floor and his mouth twitched. "You're making a great mistake," began Miriam.

"Now, Miss Birdseye," began Tomkins warningly. He smiled quickly, licking his lips and showed a pink adder's tongue under his little moustache. "That's just what I came to see you about. You'll be wanted for witness for the Crown at the Assizes. Like I said. Both you and Mrs. DuVivien. . . ."

"I don't care," said Miriam. "You've got the wrong man. We'll have proof before the Assizes. When are they?" she added angrily, as Tomkins continued to smirk.

"Now, Miss Birdseye," said Tomkins, with less assurance, "if you have any evidence, you ought to let the police have it. It'll be wasting time if you hold the inquest up. I can't say *when* we'll be called at the Assizes."

"We haven't got proof *yet*," said Miriam. "But we're getting it. We're getting it *fast*."

Tomkins was elaborately unimpressed.

"If you'd say who you're collecting it against I might help," he said, a little too casually.

"Oh, go to hell!" said Miriam. "Everyone knows *that*. Bracewood-Smith, of course."

"What a hope!" said Tomkins. He swung down his feet and stood up.

"Oh," cried Miriam, and stamped her foot. "I think you're beastly!"

It was from this moment that Miriam ceased, officially, to be Policeman's Pet.

CHAPTER TWO

THE rehearsal that evening was remarkable chiefly for the performance of Miss Lesarum, the girl-guide captain and mathematics mistress, as Captain Valentine Brown. She showed 'a fine turn of speed', as the racing papers say, and no other candidate had the smallest chance against her. Roger Partick-Thistle's reading of the part was uninspired and emasculated. Peter Bracewood-Smith refused to shave off his beard. Acting from the hip, Miss Lesarum swept all before her and Natasha finished the play more dead than alive. She and Miriam retired early, coughing, and repeating Miriam's early speeches to each other. Miss Lesarum, to their horror, was word-perfect.

Miss Puke did not appear, and Mrs. Grossbody, although well enough to sit in the stalls and criticize, said 'she would never, never, never, so help her, get up on that fatal stage again'.

"Two days to the night," said Miriam wearily. "Oh, dear! I feel like dear Ellen Terry at the last. I shall have my speeches pinned to your back, Natasha dear. Quite the new look. Very *chic*. And the inquest tomorrow. But perhaps I shall be able to learn my words then. While we are waiting about."

"While we are called," said Natasha vaguely. "Like the Salvation Army."

"It will be like getting divorced again," said Miriam.

"Only more tiring," said Natasha.

"It is very tiring being a *house mistress*," said Miriam, with a sigh. "I think it is more like the Oxford Group, or an early start from a hotel. 'Being Called.' I wonder if I dare ask Binkie on Saturday night . . ."

And Miriam was silent, gnawing her forefinger knuckle, staring into the middle distance.

Natasha was sad and silent. She had spent the evening (when she was not dodging the passionate performance of Miss Lesarum) in covertly observing Mr. Bracewood-Smith. He seemed to be starting a cold, but had no pocket-handkerchief. He had sneezed once or twice, glaring at everyone from bloodshot, rheumy eyes. He had wiped his nose on his sleeve. Miriam had dragged Natasha away.

"*We* can't afford to have colds, dear," she had said bitterly, glaring at him. "Nothing better than an old *murderer*. Damn' generous with his streptococci."

And, sarcastically, Miriam had recommended whiskey for a cold in the head.

"Kill or cure, I always say," she had said, teasing him.

233

"Rum, madam. Rum and veganin," said Bracewood-Smith, bowing.

"Oh, come along, Natasha, before you catch it," said Miriam. "I do think people are the limit who go about with colds. Bracewood-Smith will lose his voice, that's all, and then *I* shan't be able to hear him from the prompt-corner."

"We won't *all* find it necessary to try, Miss Birdseye," said Miss Phipps, appearing suddenly in the wings. "And I agree with Mr. Smith. I always say the best thing is to try and fight it on your feet."

Miriam had turned away, morbidly covering her mouth with a white handkerchief. Bracewood-Smith made an unattractive honking noise behind them.

II

In his flat behind Micah's the Chemist, High Street, Sergeant Tomkins now began to think that *he* was catching a cold. His case was accomplished and his day's work done and when he greeted Mrs. Tomkins (weak chest and all), he did not kiss her.

"Hullo, Mother," he said. "Startin' a cold. Bloomin' awful."

Mrs. Tomkins said she didn't suppose he *was* starting a cold. He was probably just wore out again, that was all.

"Why not get to bed with a nice book?" said Mrs. Tomkins. "I'll bring your supper up. Bit of plaice. It's nice."

Tomkins said he could fancy that, and kicked off his shoes in the hall. Then he reached towards the pocket of his waterproof.

"Got a library book?" said Mrs. Tomkins, from the kitchen. "I got one. *Clue of the Strangled Colonel.* Homicidal Hunchback and all. It's nice."

"No," said Tomkins. "Got a book. Been savin' it up. *Mamzelle of the Remove.* Said I wouldn't read it till the case was over."

And he went upstairs in his stocking feet and had a very hot bath. Later, wearing a pair of practically bomb-proof blue-and-white-striped pyjamas, he sat up in bed and ate plaice and chips and two slices of bread and butter. Finally he drank three cups of tea. Then he lit a cigarette and stretched luxuriously. He bent back *Mamzelle of the Remove*, opening it at the title page.

A letter fell out on his stomach. A typewritten, one-sheet

234

letter. It was addressed to Mr. Peter Bracewood-Smith by a firm of London solicitors. It said:

Dear Sir,

In representing our client, Miss T. Devaloys, we are instructed to inform you that £6,000 is the figure our client expects to get as damages and is the figure for which she would settle out of court.

In view of the gross libel, which we consider can easily be recognized in your current work Death and the French Governess, *and towards which our client can produce incontrovertible proof of her identity as Miss Lautrec, the murderess, you will appreciate that we should like an early reply, and are, dear sir,*

Yours faithfully,
P. Juvenile.
For Begby, Begby, Begby, Juvenile and Begby,
Solicitors.

"Well, Cripes!" said Tomkins, lying flat with horror. His pink face became pinker, his damp hair stood on end like a brush. "This beats all. I come to bed with me case nicely finished, to read a nice book. And what do I get?"

"A scorpion," said Mrs. Tomkins, entering with a fourth cup of tea.

III

"No," said Tomkins, five minutes later, turning restlessly in bed. He was now positive that he was swarming with cold. "No. It *needn't* bust the case wide open. But I can't afford to ignore it."

He slid out of bed. He took two aspirins. He wrapped himself in Mrs. Tomkins' pink flannel dressing-gown, which had been lying across the bottom of the bed. He flopped downstairs. He looked angry and undignified. He dialled the Radcliff Hall number. He asked for Miss Birdseye.

"As I see it . . ." he said confidentially into the telephone. He wrapped Mrs. Tomkins' dressing-gown more securely round his hips. "As I see it, a man would *hardly* commit a murder over a solicitor's letter. Not even to save six thousand pounds. . . ."

He waited anxiously for Miriam's reply, which did not come.

"*Natasha!*" said the voice in his ears. "Tomkins has a letter giving documentary proof of what you found out yesterday. *Just what you were wanting.* Theresa Devaloys *was* suing for libel and he couldn't afford to pay, so he murdered her to stop the case coming to court. Can't think why these lawyers, Begby and Juvenile, haven't complained before——"

"*Oi!*" shouted Tomkins, much disturbed. "That isn't what I said at all. There's no *proof*. This only shows motive. Just thought it would help you ladies"—Tomkins' voice changed and became maddeningly oily and ingratiating—"if you knew the police already *had* the evidence you're suppressin'."

"I am *not* suppressing evidence!" shouted Miriam.

"Keep your hair on," said Tomkins amiably.

Miriam slammed down the receiver.

IV

Miriam sat and panted a little, trying to get herself under control. She and Natasha were in the sitting-room that had formerly been Miss Fork-Thomas'. Already that day Mariam had confronted Noni Postman and Molly Ruminara. She had accepted, on behalf of Miss Lipscoomb, a term's notice from the heartbroken Miss Puke. On her desk lay a playbill, showing in blazing white and scarlet the words *Miriam Birdseye—Quality Street—Radcliff Hall*. Miriam looked at it proudly and then glanced guiltily away. The telephone began to ring. No doubt Tomkins, trying to ring her up again. Miriam looked at the instrument, which continued to ring.

"*I* shall not be answering it," said Natasha, watching it.

"*I* do not even hear it," said Miriam.

The instrument gave a convulsive ring and stopped. Both ladies sighed.

"It isn't enough," said Miriam. "Like I said, we've got to get proof."

Natasha shivered. She was more upset than Miriam. She had lit the gas-fire and now crouched over it, like a beautiful Siamese cat. She locked her arms round her knees and swayed to and fro. She stared into the little pale blue flames of gas. They settled and the asbestos at the back of the fire began to glow.

"We may be wrong," said Natasha eventually, "but none of

the Nevkorinas are having ever the legal mind. Not even my uncle Vlaslslav, the lawyer."

"Of course we aren't wrong!" snapped Miriam hastily. "We must just get evidence of possession of the *weapon*, that's all."

"I *am* so discouraged," said Natasha gloomily.

For a long time they were silent, looking at each other and at the gas-fire.

"If you sit *too* near the gas-fire, Natasha, you will get such awful marks on your legs."

Natasha moved her legs away.

"Roger is saying," said Natasha, "that Gwylan is telling him that whoever put that poison into that whiskey must have put it into the bottle *off* the premises. Like in an off-licence. With a hypodermic. And Bracewood-Smith *must* have done it because he brought in the bottle himself, or do you not follow?"

"How, with a hypodermic?" said Miriam. "Let's try."

"Do not be being silly," said Natasha. "We have no hypodermic."

"Well, if we could find Bracewood-Smith's hypodermic, then," said Miriam. "That would be proof. Proof positive."

"Perhaps he used someone else's hypodermic," said Natasha. "I am still discouraged."

And she rocked to and fro.

V

"Wouldn't you say," said Miriam, "that Gwylan had worked out all this business with the hypodermic?"

"And had been feeling the cork soft when she pushed in the corkscrew?" said Natasha testily. "Yes, that is what I am *meaning*."

"And then went and told him?"

"Who? Bracewood-Smith?"

"Well, that's what *we* think," said Miriam. "But *Tomkins* thinks *Lariat*, and of course Lariat has *hundreds* of hypodermics. Absolutely to hand. But anyway, went and told *somebody*."

"And this somebody is blowing the back of her head off with a revolver," said Natasha, with relish.

"Now, if we were to find revolver and hypodermic . . ."

"And Gwylan's head-scarf . . ." said Natasha.

"All *chez* Bracewood-Smith," said Miriam, "that would be something."

"Search Gull Cottage?" said Natasha, opening her hazel eyes very wide and smiling broadly at the prospect. "Why, we shall be murdered *ourselves* soon."

VI

So Natasha and Miriam laid their plans with great cunning. Miss Lipscoomb was to co-operate. She would invite Peter Bracewood-Smith to tea and would discuss his child, Julia, with him. Miriam brushed some crumbs from her mauve lock-knit skirt and said that she and Natasha could then 'pop across' Lover's Loose and investigate. Natasha was horrified.

"Miriam!" she cried. "You are catching this horrible expression 'pop' from Miss Lesarum."

"If that's all we catch from Miss Lesarum we'll be lucky," said Miriam.

VII

The next morning, after prayers, Miriam stretched out a claw for Julia Bracewood-Smith and dragged her into her sitting-room.

"Is it long, my dear Julia, since you have seen your—er—*Pongo*?"

"No," said Julia; "at least, it was my birthday this week, and he gave me a present." There was a pause. "Two presents," she added proudly, as though this, at any rate, were proof of Pongo's parental love. Miriam grimaced.

"But you haven't *seen* him?" said Miriam.

"Well, no," said Julia. "I haven't *seen* him."

And her chin began to tremble.

"Now, now," said Miriam briskly. "I only wondered if you mightn't like to have tea with him. In Miss Lipscoomb's sitting-room. Yourself, this afternoon. Miss Lipscoomb is quite agreeable. Er—so that you could meet, you know."

Julia's face lit up, and Miriam, to her annoyance, felt a bitch.

"Did you have nice birthday presents?" said Miriam.

"Well . . ." said Julia, still radiant, "*one* was nice. This watch." And Julia displayed it. "The other," she went on excitedly, "I shan't see till I'm twenty-one. But I expect it'll be nice."

"How singular," said Miriam. "You managed to avoid opening it? This present?"

"Oh yes," said Julia. "It is a little package. Addressed to the bank. I haven't had time to post it yet. . . ."

There was a pause, while Miriam thought furiously. She stalked to the window and looked out of it.

"Why haven't you posted it before?" she said menacingly.

"Oh, but I *have*," said Julia, wriggling. "I posted it yesterday."

"Oh, Julia, Julia," said Miriam wearily, in the accents of all the house mistresses in the world, "when will you learn to tell the truth? Bring the parcel and *I* will post it."

"Oh!" said Julia.

"And then you can have a lovely tea-party with *Pongo*," said Miriam, with a gentle sneer. "And now cut along to your translations from the Greek with Miss Puke. *After* you've brought me the parcel."

Julia Bracewood-Smith, her spirit broken, went away down the passage towards her bedroom. Miriam, watching her retreating back, decided against ringing up Tomkins to tell him. She stared down at the time-table on her desk. She realized, with a start of horror, that she should be conducting a class in elocution with the Lower Fifth. They were the most troublesome form in the school. By now they would be entirely out of hand, swarming in their classroom, breaking forms and desks. So she hurried out. She left little Julia Bracewood-Smith to put the parcel on her table by herself. This, as anyone may see, was a tactical error.

VIII

It so happened that this was the day upon which Mrs. Grossbody recovered from her *crise de nerfs* and returned to duty as matron. Once again she held the reins of office. The episode of the imaginary revolver shot was forgotten. She decided to hold one of her tours of personal hygiene.

Accompanied by Miss Bound, she progressed through the

bedrooms and dormitories of West and East Houses, peering into hair-tidies and under beds, pulling out drawers, glaring into drains and bathrooms. "Prevention," she said, as she did this, "is better than cure." Miss Bound was unable to discover exactly what it was that Mrs. Grossbody hoped to prevent.

By about 10.15 a.m. they had reached the top floor of West House and had prevented nothing except a large spider that was sitting in a vast cobweb in the housemaid's pantry. Mrs. Grossbody had thrown it out of the window. Everything else was in surprisingly good order. Mrs. Grossbody was rather cross about it. Miss Bound was already thinking wistfully of a half-hour with her mending and 'Music While You Work'.

It was at this moment that they observed a purple gym-tunic shooting into a bedroom door a little way ahead of them.

"One of the ge-als," said Mrs. Grossbody, quickening her pace. "On this floor in the *daytime*. Probably goin' into one of the *other* ge-al's bedrooms. Most unwholesome."

And, closely followed by Miss Bound, she twirled into the room after Julia Bracewood-Smith. Julia was laboriously opening the bottom drawer of her chest of drawers.

"Julia," said Matron grimly, "what are you doing up here at this time of day?"

Julia spun round. Even to Miss Bound, who wished her no real harm, she appeared guilty. Her damp black fringe was in her eyes as usual. A slip of white knicker lining was showing above her spindly legs.

"Please," she said, "Miss Birdseye sent me up."

"Don't tell lies, Julia," said Mrs. Grossbody promptly. "That isn't true. Miss Birdseye is taking Lower Fifth elocution. We saw her just now, didn't we, Miss Bound?"

"Yes, Matron," said Miss Bound cravenly.

"Oh!" Julia swallowed and tried to understand the peculiarity of adults, who always said she was lying when she told the truth, and applauded her most outrageous lies as honesty. ("Are you happy here now, Julia? Settling down now all right, eh?" "Oh *yes*, Miss Lipscoomb." "That's right, good gel.")

"*What* are you doing up here, Julia?" said Mrs. Grossbody savagely.

"I came . . . I came . . ." said Julia, with the right amount of hesitancy. "I came because I thought I had a rash. And I wanted to *look*——"

"Wanted to scratch, you mean," said Mrs. Grossbody grimly. "Where is this rash?"

"Please," said Julia, who had acquired at Radcliff Hall this unfortunate habit of beginning every sentence with this word. "Please, on my chest," she ended, standing up.

"*Take off your gym-tunic*," said Mrs. Crossbody. There was a pause while the wretched child began to disrobe.

"And your liberty bodice," said Miss Bound suddenlv.

Julia's torso was now displayed to Miss Bound and Mrs. Grossbody. It was a horrid sight.

"Well . . ." said Mrs. Grossbody, after a minute's intense satisfaction, "you certainly *have* a rash. Looks like scarlet fever."

And Julia glanced down at her chest and saw, to her surprise, an unpleasant, itching rash rising upon it even as she watched.

IX

"She must go to the sanatorium for isolation and instant observation, and everything she has been wearing for the last twenty-four hours must be held for baking," said Mrs. Grossbody, with sadistic pleasure.

She caught up a little parcel which Julia had been taking out of her drawer. It was wrapped in brown paper, rather heavily sealed. It was addressed to 'The Midland Bank, Brunton-on-Sea, per pro Miss Julia Bracewood-Smith'.

"Oh!" said Julia, starting forward, putting out a hand. "I want that. To post."

"Ha!" said Mrs. Grossbody happily. "Want to give everyone scarlet fever?"

"Mustn't start an epidemic, dear," said Miss Bound kindly.

"Sorry," said Julia.

It is a curious fact that this unpleasant and (as we suspect) homicidal child was as wax in the hands of Matron and Miss Bound. Some of this may have been due to the insidious effects of malnutrition. The remainder was certainly due to Matron's personality. Like most cowards, Mrs. Grossbody was a tremendous bully.

"Miss Bound will go and get your bed ready," snapped Mrs. Grossbody. "I shall stay and get your *things* ready for baking.

Anything that may shrink will, of course, be fumigated with the bedroom. Now, Julia, you are not to make a *fuss*."

Julia only partially understood the word 'fumigate'. Her sophistication left her. She was merely a terrified and unhappy little girl. (She was still, of course, rather unpleasant.)

"Oh . . ." said Julia. "My books . . ."

"Now don't be silly, dear," said Mrs. Grossbody, with enjoyment. "They should of course be *burned*. But we will only bake them."

"*Oh . . . !*" screamed Julia.

"Stop hindering, dear," said Mrs. Grossbody. "There are plenty of scarlet-fever books already. We can't have any more infected."

Julia said no more. A large fat tear rolled slowly down her pasty cheek as she realized that she wouldn't see her father that afternoon at teatime.

"Now, now," said Mrs. Grossbody. "No hysteria."

A sad little procession wandered towards the sanatorium, led by Julia with wildly flapping shoelaces. Her arms were full of eiderdown and the Bible and *The Pilgrim's Progress*, which were the only books Mrs. Grossbody had allowed her to bring. Miss Bound carried a suitcase with Julia's pyjamas. Mrs. Grossbody carried a heavier suitcase containing Julia's most precious possessions. At the door of the sanatorium they parted.

X

The baking-machine was a fearful iron engine that stood in the asphalt courtyard of the sanatorium. It was very like Stephenson's Rocket. It was heated by coal and coke for about fifteen minutes, when the metalwork inside became red hot and did untold damage. Objects placed in its stomach were, after fifteen minutes' steady heat, warranted free from germs, moths, lice or any semblance of their former appearance. Quite often they emerged covered with a light coating of rust; usually they were shrunk beyond recognition. However, they were sterile. The machine had been bought from the Royal Navy at the end of the First World War. It was the apple of Mrs. Grossbody's eye.

She crouched in front of it now, thrusting into it all Julia's little treasures. They included the paper parcel, a teddy bear and a small fur squirrel in a red coat. She stoked up the fire and put a match to it.

Instantly Julia's round pale face appeared at an upper window. She screamed loudly and beat on the window-pane. Miss Bound grasped her from behind and put her to bed. The match went out and Matron lit another.

XI

Miriam Birdseye listened to a spirited rendering of "We are thóse who ride faster than fate", in Classroom 19. She was bored and restless and she looked out of the window.

"*Pale Kings of the Sunset—Beware!*" announced Myfanwy Moon, the young lady who was reciting.

"Thank you, dear," said Miriam absently. "Do you know my sitting-room?"

"Yes, Miss Birdseye," said Myfanwy, surprised.

"Could you pop—er—*run* along there and get the brown-paper parcel that's sitting on my table?"

"Yes, Miss Birdseye," said Myfanwy, and left the room at a gallop. The Lower Fifth watched her with interest. Miriam pulled herself together.

"Next," she said vaguely. "You, dear, whatever your name is."

She pointed at a round, flaxen child in the front row.

"Verena Levinson," said the child, incensed.

"Oh?" said Miriam, bored.

"*Ai will araise and go now,*" said Verena Levinson.

"Leave out the expression, darling," said Miriam, "and try to pronounce 'I' as though it rhymed with 'Pie in the Sky' and not with 'Maida Vale'."

"Yes, Miss Birdseye," said Verena. When she reached her plans for 'bean rows' and a 'haive for the honeybee', Miriam drummed restlessly on her desk and looked out of the window again.

"*Dwell alone in the bee-loud glade,*" said Verena angrily, as Myfanwy entered with much clattering of feet. Without the parcel.

"Not there, Miss Birdseye. I'm ever so sorry," said Myfanwy. She squeezed back, past little Miss Levinson, into her seat.

"Hell and damn and blast!" said Miss Birdseye.

The bells shrilled all over the school. The First Lesson Period was over. Little Miss Levinson failed to make herself heard above the general cacophony.

"*Ai shall have some peace there . . .*" she shouted loudly as Miriam moved towards the door.

"Never mind that now, dear," said Miriam.

"*Hear lake water lapping,*" said Verena Levinson furiously. Miriam was too quick for her. She was through the door and the other side of it before Myfanwy told her little chums that the "Old Hawkeye wouldn't be able to get her own parcel herself whatever she thought, because it wasn't there and must have been stolen, damn and hell and blast!"

This seemed the height of wit to the Lower Fifth. Even Verena Levinson laughed heartily. The tone of Radcliff Hall was slipping.

CHAPTER THREE

As we know, the unfortunate Verena Levinson was only too right. Miriam now faced a vexing ten minutes in her drawing-room, hunting for a parcel that was not there. Eventually she stamped out into the corridor and caught the foxy Noni Postman, who was hurrying past.

"I want Julia Bracewood-Smith," she said, "and I want her at once. Can you get her for me?"

Noni was inclined to be lachrymose. She sniffed and said glumly that she would try.

"Good," said Miriam, ignoring all un-British displays of emotion. Noni's small blue eyes were watery and piggish. Miriam turned disdainfully away. She went into her drawing-room and stood by her writing-table. Here she consulted her time-table and found she was again ten minutes late. This time she was late for the Remove, and once more in Classroom 19. She might as well have remained there. She marched out of the room, seething with rage.

The inquest was that afternoon in the County Hall, Brunton. Miriam had hoped to examine Julia's parcel *long* before then.

She was now certain that Julia's disappearance (with parcel) was due to naughtiness, lunacy, disobedience and homicidal tendencies generally. It will be observed how well Miriam had entered into the spirit of her part as house mistress.

"*Good morning, Miss Birdseye,*" said the Remove, rising to its (collective) feet.

Miriam did not acknowledge this greeting. She pointed sourly at Molly Ruminara.

"You," she said.

"*Ai will arise and go now,*" said Molly Ruminara, startled. "*And go to Inisfree . . .*"

II

For once in Natasha's decorative existence at Radcliff Hall she had been pinned down to the extent of pushing the Lower Fifth through the less-flamboyant movements of the *Polonaise.* She was, as we may expect, already bored. She stopped twisting Verena Levinson's legs into a rough imitation of a true lover's knot and addressed Myfanwy Moon.

"What house is this Bracewood-Smith child being in?" she said.

The Lower Fifth was surprised. Several eager voices instantly supplied the information that Julia Bracewood-Smith was in West, or Miss Birdseye's, House. Verena Levinson rubbed one tortured ankle against the other.

"She could be found?" said Natasha vaguely.

The whole of the Lower Fifth now shouted that it could and would find Julia Bracewood-Smith. And so slight was Natasha's sense of public responsibility that she did nothing at all to stop them, but allowed them to stampede, shouting shrilly, out of the gymnasium, through the swing doors at the bottom of the hall.

"Thank God!" said Natasha.

She turned idly to Mrs. Pont, the accompanist, who sat, dazed, at the piano.

"God and Saint Denis for a little peace," said Natasha.

Mrs. Pont lit a cigarette and smoked it like a genteel dragon, blowing clouds of smoke round her face.

"Why do you want to see little Julia?" said Mrs. Pont. "*Not* a very intelligent little girl, I never think. No sense of rhythm."

"The good Saint Stanislaw has told me," said Natasha And with this obscure reply Mrs. Pont had to be content.

III

The Lower Fifth came raging back, pushing its neighbour and submitting not at all to its governor, spiritual pastor or master. One or two children were severely trampled on.

"Can't find her, Miss Nevkorina!" shouted some of the young ladies, and "Been over 'alf Radcliff 'All," said the others. It is a sad fact that most of these children had faint but unmistakable Cockney accents. It was the astute little Jewess Verena Levinson who announced that "Julia Bracewood-Smith was in the san". The other young ladies, whose errand had been sleeveless, were instantly jealous.

"Noni Postman told me so," said Verena.

Someone began to sing:

> *"Noni Postman told me so*
> *And Noni Postman ought to know. . . ."*

Natasha yawned.

"This rather boring noise," she said, "will now cease."

And curiously enough, it ceased.

"Mrs. Pont," went on Natasha, "will now play the whole *Polonaise* the whole way through. And you will oll be shutting up and sitting absolutely still and listening to it."

Natasha, unlike darling Miriam, had not the true teacher's vocation.

IV

By luncheon-time Miriam was told by Matron that Julia was in the sanatorium. Miriam then asked for Julia's little parcel and Matron said smugly that Miriam could not have it until the machine cooled down. Julia, she went on with a happy smile, was certainly the forerunner of a virulent epidemic of scarlet fever. Miriam said, "Oh yes, how nice," and this startled Matron.

At a quarter to two Miriam was still dealing with a distressing little institution called 'Sweets Thursday'. Each child, on this day, was allowed four chocolates, handed out by a house mistress and a member of the nursing staff. The sweets were kept in a small cupboard in the house mistress's drawing-room. There were often thefts from this cupboard.

At ten to two Miriam left with Natasha for the inquest. She was no nearer to opening and examining Julia's parcel. Her frustration was increased by Sergeant Tomkins, who talked all the time in a very silly tone of voice, with his eyes cast down and a pious, well-fed, catlike expression on his face.

"It is enough to be giving anyone the sick," agreed Natasha, in a passionate undertone.

The inquest was opened and then adjourned by the coroner. Afterwards, Sergeant Tomkins explained to them that they would next be required to appear before a magistrate to sign things, and Miriam said, "Wot, no Old Bailey?" and everyone was very shocked.

"We'll probably appear at the Old Bailey in about two months' time," said Tomkins, "*after* you've done all this at the magistrates' court." He was dressed entirely in green: greenish flannel trousers, green jacket, green tie. He swung a little brief-case maddeningly. "Care to have a coffee?" he said lightly. Miriam looked at him with hatred.

"No," said Natasha.

"Oh!" said Tomkins. "Hope you ladies don't *come* it over me, that's all," said Tomkins. "Suppose you'll be goin' round behind to see Doctor Lariat, will you?"

"He sounds as though he were a first night," said Natasha angrily.

"Go round *behind*, indeed," echoed Miriam.

"Well," said Tomkins wistfully, "you're *his* witnesses now, or so you say, not mine."

Tomkins sounded wistful, but Miriam had no pity. She said briskly that yes, she certainly was, and where could they find him?

"Cells," said Tomkins laconically. "Take you there if you like. Nice experience for you ladies."

"Tomkins," said Miriam, in a voice like a buzz-saw, "you seem to me to be behaving like hell, dear. I shall tell all your old chums in Kensington what the provinces have done to you."

And Tomkins hung his head.

Lariat was sitting in his cell in a deck-chair. He was neat and tidy and fairly cheerful.

His solicitor was with him, and also a youngish, fat K.C. called Charles Gracchus-Tiberius. Gracchus-Tiberius' head was florid and imposing and rather too big for his body. Tomkins muttered in an undertone that he was a wonderful prosecutor and a great bullier of witnesses.

"Must be thinkin' of 'is judgeship, takin' on this defence," muttered Tomkins in Natasha's ear. The solicitor was tall and dressed in grey. He was called Porson.

Tomkins introduced everyone with a brisk flourish of his brief-case.

"Two ladies," he said amiably, "convinced of your client's innocence. You'll be glad to know 'em. Be outside if you want me," and he slid through the door of the cell, which closed behind him with a neat click.

"I say," said Gracchus-Tiberius, in a powerful social manner, looking round him for chairs, "not *the* Miss Birdseye? Not *Miriam* Birdseye?"

Miriam and Natasha sat on Doctor Lariat's little bed. Porson coiled quietly up in a corner. Gracchus-Tiberius stood. Doctor Lariat went on sitting in his deck-chair.

"I expect so," said Miriam, looking pleased. "I am a school-teacher at the moment, however."

"And detective," said Natasha vaguely.

"Quite so, quite so," said Gracchus-Tiberius, before he realized what he was saying.

As usual, everyone found it hard to believe in Miriam and Natasha, and proceedings were held up for five minutes while the cell became full of Gracchus-Tiberius' hearty legal laughter.

"So you've come to help my client, have you?" he said finally. "Well, suppose you convince *me* of his innocence, then, eh?"

"We are not able to do that," said Natasha, a little foolishly; "but we are getting clues against the *real* murderer. Only we have not been getting it yet."

"It is very irritating," said Miriam.

Gracchus-Tiberius boomed and put his thumbs in his waist-coat pockets and asked, giggling, who the real murderer was, then, if it wasn't his client? Eh? His client began to fidget in his chair.

"Actually," said Miriam, "we think it is a man called Peter Bracewood-Smith. But we have no *proof*——"

"Peter Bracewood-Smith?" said Gracchus-Tiberius. "Oxford man? Balliol man?"

"I believe so," said Miriam. "You see——"

"My dear madam," said Bracchus-Tiberius coldly, "it is out of the question. *I* am an Oxford man. Peter was at Balliol with *me*, madam. He read the same schools that I did. It's unthinkable."

CHAPTER FOUR

MATRON had lied to Miriam when she said that she could not have Julia's parcel until the machine had cooled down. The machine, thanks to the east wind, some damp wood and a painful lack of paraffin, had never been alight. Also, by the time that a doctor had arrived, had looked at Julia and had definitely diagnozed scarlet fever, and by the time that the ambulance had taken her away to the fever-hospital, Mrs. Grossbody had been forced to decide that the child's possessions would be much better baked and fumigated down there at the hospital. So the parcel had been packed into the ambulance with Julia and, at a quarter to one, had gone with her to the fever-hospital.

'Caught (as Matron herself would have expressed it) bending' by Miriam, Mrs. Grossbody had evaded the issue. And only when she was faced by Miriam's most violent rage and Natasha's most sumptuous Slav explosion had she been forced to confess the truth. The parcel was at the fever-hospital. She could not say whereabouts. She was very sorry. She had thought she was only doing her duty.

II

"I am," said Natasha dramatically, "still doing of six things at once. This is how I am been going on ever since I am come to this place."

The performance of *Quality Street* was billed for 7 p.m. that very night. The fever-hospital telephone number was monotonously engaged. Miriam was unable to get a taxi to take her there. The *Daily Blast* had just rung up from Brunton railway station to demand an interview.

As usual, Natasha and Miriam were in Miriam's drawing-room. Matron, in tears, had just left to inspect all the West House chests and torsos. "An epidemic," she had explained to Miriam, "must be nipped in the bud."

"Very well, then, Mrs. Grossbody," Miriam had replied viciously. "Go and nip your buds. But please do not nip them here."

So Miriam, trembling with rage, had begun her series of abortive telephone calls. Every time she put back the receiver it rang furiously. More and more newspapermen and women were demanding exclusive interviews. Sometimes these telephone calls were toll calls, punctuated by pips and crackles and bangs; then Miriam was very rude. Sometimes they were newspapermen who knew Miriam already, saying that they were 'coming right up, Miss Birdseye'. Then Miriam was very polite. And then, just at the moment that Natasha connected with the taxi-rank and ordered a cab to take Miriam to the hospital *immediately*, Greta, the new and nervous parlourmaid, stood in the doorway and said, "the *Daily Glass*, please, miss," and ducked out of sight, quivering with emotion.

"I *had the Daily Glass*," snapped Miriam, "at breakfast."

But the *Daily Glass*, in this instance, was terrible old Meriel Juniper (well known as 'The Sob-stuff Scourge of Gray's Inn Road') in a fog of gin and angostura bitters and a very short fur coat.

She advanced on Miriam to wring her hand, and Miriam waved airily. She tried to shake hands with Natasha and Natasha ducked. Meriel Juniper sat abruptly in an armchair and gazed round the room with glazed and unfocused eyes. She looked like a performing seal, only more sad.

"This is magnif'cent," said Meriel Juniper. "Tell me all."

And she focused her right eye on Natasha.

III

Finally it was agreed that Natasha should stay and tell Meriel Juniper 'all' while Miriam rushed to the fever-hospital to secure the parcel.

"Don't forget *Quality Street*!" screamed Natasha after the taxi as it whirled away from the door. Inside, Miriam grinned and grimaced.

"Remember Scarborough or something?" said Miss Juniper vaguely, following Natasha back into the drawing-room.

"I am not knowing about *Scarborough*," said Natasha. "*This* is a play. Which we are doing tonight. Miriam and I are chief parts. It is a very *difficult* play."

Natasha, so far as she was able, contorted her lovely features in a scowl.

"Gracious!" said Miss Juniper, lighting a cigarette from the butt of the other and offering it to Natasha, who turned from it with a little cry of disgust. "Gracious, what a story! Dare we use it?"

Natasha led the way into the drawing-room.

"Please be sitting down," she said vaguely. "It makes us oll so restless when people go walking and prowling and pacing like this."

Miss Meriel Juniper was a confirmed prowler and pacer. She had stuck her two fists deep into the pockets of her little fur jacket, and now she pulled it tightly round her lean hips. She was very small and she looked very silly. She stuck her chin out and turned her profile to left and right continuously. It was a good profile, but this was no excuse. She went on in this way all the afternoon. Darling Natasha observed her covertly through long and tangled lashes and tried hard not to giggle.

First Natasha explained about the murders and the inquest, and Miss Juniper said yes, but the '*Evenings* would have that', so Natasha explained about their new suspect. And Meriel said, "Gracious, what a story!" and wondered if 'they dared'. Natasha explained why Miriam had gone to the fever-hospital and how they hoped for proof of guilt before the Assizes to rescue Doctor Lariat, and Meriel shook her head slowly from left to right.

"Too hot," she said grimly. She flicked some cigarette ash on the floor. "You got a drink?" she said wistfully, relaxing her profile for a second. Natasha was relieved.

"I am expecting so," she said. "The late Miss Fork-Thomas was being a gin drinker. She is now dead . . ." she went on vaguely, crossing to the cupboard.

Here she found the remains of a half bottle of Booth's. She poured most of it into a tumbler. Meriel took it and swirled it round and round in her right hand. She cheered up immediately.

"I know a thing," said Miss Juniper. "If you'll allow me to 'phone Jack—that's my news editor—I expect we can *use* this angle, without names. And put guard lines in. Yes. John—that's our crime reporter—he'll be furious. But there, he'll have the police angle anyway. John never stirs out of the police-station. And Johnny—that's the editor—*he* won't mind. Anyway, he's in Manchester."

Natasha, to whom this was so much gibberish, said oh yes, of course, politely.

If Miss Juniper were to *use* the telephone it might at least stop the incoming calls. All through this conversation the *World in Pictures*, the *Movietone*, the *Banner*, the *Sun* and the *Truth About the World* had all rung up. And each time that this happened, the ringing telephone bell had reacted furiously upon Miss Juniper, who had kept her profile working from left to right like clockwork.

IV

"Listen, Jack," said Miss Juniper, on the telephone to her news editor, "the whole Street is on to these girls like nine o'clock. But if you can guarantee two fifty, one of them will give us an exclusive."

"Why nine o'clock?" said Natasha, reasonably enough, in the background. "And what is the Street? And two hundred and fifty what?"

"Fleet Street," said Miss Juniper, without taking her mouth away from the receiver. "And Jack says how *can* he when he works for Lord Cute? *The Daily Glass* is Cute Press."

This still meant very little to Natasha.

"You please be letting me speak to Jack," she said, and held out a languid hand.

"O.K.," said Miss Juniper. She lit a cigarette, turned her profile from left to right, and stamped over to the window.

"Hullo, Jack," said Natasha caressingly into the telephone.

"Be paying no attention to your lady reporter's sordid money talk. *Oll* Miss Birdseye and I are wishing for is publicity. Publicity for play, for detective agency, for theory about new murderer. Particularly brilliant theory about murderer. . . ."

"I get it," said Jack, a long way off, and rapidly. "Publicity. O.K. Go ahead."

V

"I wish," said Miriam to the janitor at the door of the Brunton, Cranmer and District fever-hospital, "to see your boiler-man."

The janitor sat in a square glass case entirely surrounded by keys and lists and telephones and half-completed football coupons.

"Boiler-man, ma'am?" said the janitor. He was a dark purple man with a large square face. "What for, ma'am?"

He pushed a pair of gold-rimmed spectacles above his nose and balanced them on a highly flushed forehead.

"I am representing a famous newspaper," said Miriam, without much thought, "and your boiler-man has won a prize."

"We have several boiler-men," said the janitor profoundly. "Which one do you want?"

He pulled the glasses down on to his nose again.

"The one who's on duty now," said Miriam brightly. "Um. Ted . . . um . . . Bob. Oh, I forget his name. . . ."

"*Cyril* is on duty now," said the janitor suspiciously. "Cyril Bostock. What sort of prize has he won?"

The janitor was jealous. Miriam thought this charming of him.

"Ten pounds," said Miriam rapidly. "Cyril Bostock. Yes. That's right. *Such* a rotten memory. Thank you, dear. Of course, the newspapers are only acting as agents in this, of course. Like the police. You know Sergeant Tomkins, of course?"

"Oh?" said the janitor, bored. "Tomkins, eh? Well, then, I suppose it's all right."

And he reached above his head for a large and rusty key and handed it to Miriam.

"You don't mind if I *don't* come, miss?" he said. "I get comic palpitations on them stairs."

This confused Miriam, who had never seen anything comic in palpitations.

"Boiler-house staircase is over there, miss," he said, bored but polite. "Now excuse me, please. Two aways and four draws is . . ."

And he returned to his work.

Ahead of Miriam a flight of steep stone stairs wound down into the bowels of the earth.

VI

Miriam suffered very much from vertigo. She had never cared for staircase descents since that season in pantomime in 1926 when she had broken an ankle down fifteen feet of three-ply in the March Past of the Empire Fruits. Nevertheless, she hurried down the boiler-house staircase as though her life depended upon it.

Half-way everything became dark, and Miriam turned her ankle and swore. Three quarter way it was excessively hot and pieces of ceiling fell with a dry rustle into Miriam's hair. Miriam thought of spiders and did not care for her thoughts. After about two minutes she reached a square patch of electric light.

"Cyril the boiler-man—alone with his dampers," she sang gaily.

Cyril was small and lugubrious and twisty and dark, and, quite obviously, Welsh. Also, by his wheezing and frequent complaints, he was evidently an ex-hospital patient with a grudge. The air all around was full of sulphuretted hydrogen.

"Hello," said Miriam, halting at the door and arranging her legs (which were very good) with one knee bent.

"Hullo yourself," said Cyril, without looking up. He was crouched on the floor by a pile of sacks. "Another almoner, I s'pose?"

"That's right, dear," said Miriam quickly.

Cyril stood up and stared at her.

"You don't *look* like they usually do," he said. "But let me tell you, it's no use, whatever you say about Emily."

He was still staring at her as though he could not believe his eyes.

"Can't 'elp it if she wants to go on werking at the Co-op, with 'er chest. I'm 'er dad, that's all. An' nowadays no one 'as any regard for *parents*."

His voice became fainter and finally died away in a throaty

mutter. Then he suddenly looked her full in the face and smiled. He took half an inch of cigarette from behind his ear and lit it. He suddenly became a gay Lothario. He whistled gently, under his breath, like an American soldier. "Whew—whew. . . ."

"Been 'ere long?" he said, advancing slowly on Miriam.

"My first *morning*," said Miriam.

(No words of mine can adequately describe the fantastic sexual significance with which Miriam invested this simple phrase.)

"Fancy . . ." said Cyril. His mouth fell open.

"And this . . ." said Miriam, slowly and luxuriously, looking at him, "*this* is where you bake the scarlet-fever patients?"

She laid an arm along Cyril's shoulders and smiled cavernously. Cyril gulped.

"Not the patients, miss," said Cyril, but he did not move. He stood his ground while Miriam played with his ear. "Their *things*. . . ."

He sounded gloomy.

"Ah . . . *ha*!" said Miriam. "You will need *strength*, I am sure, to lift that shovel?"

She pinched Cyril roguishly in the bicep.

"Yes, miss," said Cyril.

The shovel was, perhaps, six inches long. Cyril expanded his chest.

"Ah!" said Miriam again. "And what is a—what is *cooking* now, dear?"

She reached delicately past Cyril's neck (which was slowly becoming suffused and glowing) and she opened a very small furnace door. There was nothing to be seen.

"Oh, *Cyril*!" said Miriam plaintively. She relinquished his ear with a sigh. "How disappointing! I was expecting hidden *fires*. You know. All banked *up* and smouldering."

"We does all that by electricity now," said Cyril sadly.

"So beastly," said Miriam. "Nothing like as good as the old-fashioned method. Show me, darling."

She ran one hand idly through his wiry black hair. It stood up like a lavatory-brush. Cyril spat on his hands. There was a second of uncertainty. Then Cyril stooped and picked up a trayful of objects from the floor.

"Well . . ." he began. "See this?"

Miriam nodded.

"Well, I shoves 'em up 'ere . . ."

And he opened another little door and slammed the tray dexterously into a tiny oven. He slammed the door.

"Then I does like this an' this, see?"

He turned two switches and regulated a little pointer.

"Good for an hour," he ended proudly.

"How wonderful!" breathed Miriam. She took hold of his ear once again.

"That's right," said Cyril complacently.

"Anything more to bake?" whispered Miriam.

"Only them things behind us on the floor," said Cyril. He began to blush again. Miriam grasped his neck in the crook of her elbow. Cyril gave a little cry.

"I'll 'ave them bakin' in two twos," said Cyril. "And then . . ." He stopped suddenly and looked at her, astonished. "Are you *sure* you're a lady almoner?" he said, puzzled.

"Oh, positive," said Miriam lightly.

Cyril breathed heavily.

Miriam raked behind her with her foot. She twisted her neck uncomfortably to see what she was raking at. She saw a small fur squirrel in a red coat. She saw a teddy bear. And she saw a square parcel done up in brown paper.

"Come on, miss," said Cyril. "Give us a kiss."

VII

"What is that over there?" screamed Miriam ten seconds later. "Cyril! A spider! Oh, how awful!"

Miriam had turned quite pale.

"Never you mind, my little chickadee," said Cyril fondly. "You stop 'ere. An' I'll kill um."

He advanced purposefully on the corner with the shovel. Instantly Miriam snatched up Julia's parcel. She had a moment of horrid panic when she found it would not go into her handbag. Then Cyril was back, swinging his shovel like a gladiator, whistling between his teeth.

"That's *one* spider that won't be troublin' my little chickadee no more," he said proudly.

"Oh . . . er . . . Cyril," said Miriam, maddeningly demure. "I must go now."

"*Can't* go!" cried Cyril. "On'y just acquainted."

He reached towards her. Under his dungarees his little chest rose and fell most purposefully.

"Oh, but I *must*," said Miriam. "You've no *idea*, Cyril. Matron's an absolute beast to all of us girls if we keep her waiting, and besides . . ." She looked round her wildly and extemporized. "It's Friday. Friday clinic. Yes, indeed. The clinic. I shouldn't have left it so long," and Miriam ran basely to the door, towards the staircase. She clutched the precious parcel. She began to run round and round, up and up.

"Oh no, you don't!" cried Cyril, maddened, leaping after her, his shovel raised.

VIII

It would be hard to say if Natasha or Miriam spent the next ten minutes more spectacularly.

Natasha's excitement over the imminent approach and the demands of the various newspapers was, of course, entirely intellectual. Otherwise there was little to choose between their nerve-racked and dishevelled appearance when they met again. Miriam's skirt was torn. She had a deep scratch down one side of her face. But she held the parcel triumphantly in her right hand. It was now six o'clock.

"What *are* you been doing, Miriam?" cried Natasha excitedly. Her nerves were becoming more and more tightly strung.

"Rather not say, rather not say, rather not say," muttered Miriam, glancing uneasily at Miss Juniper, who was curled in the armchair, fast asleep, like a cat.

"Be paying no attention to *her*," said Natasha.

And indeed, Miss Juniper's face was quite flushed with sleep and gin. Her mouth hung very slightly open, turned perversely down at the corners. Miriam stepped over her feet, folded in sleep in their heavy brogues, and opened her parcel on the table. It was heavily sealed with brown, gummed paper. There was a stout cardboard box inside with metal corners. There were a lot of shavings.

"Now what?" said Miriam dramatically.

She held one finger poised. She hesitated, about to stir the shavings.

"Oh . . . a man-eating tarantula or a praying mantis, no doubt," said Natasha, bored. "Just a suitable present for Julia on her twenty-first birthday."

But, of course, expected by one and all, the shavings surrounded a heavy service revolver.

IX

"Surely *this* is conclusive?" said Miriam, poking it. "Mum is sick of messing about. Mum wants to go home."

She stared at Natasha, who had become perfectly calm.

"Not entirely," said Natasha. "It only show that Bracewood-Smith wish to dispose somehow of a weapon that only might of been doing the murder of Miss Fork-Thomas. It prove conclusive he is crazy. But we all know *that*."

Natasha leant back in her chair and relaxed.

"You are lucky," said Miriam, who was far from calm. "We need the hypodermic." She glanced wildly at the clock, which said ten minutes past six. "Alas!" she said. "No nearer to proof, then, than before. And we have to change for flaming *Quality Street* any minute now."

"If we are sticking to original plan and searching Bracewood's cottage while he is out at tea with the child," murmured Natasha, ignoring Miriam, "we *might* be finding something. Our second thoughts are always worst."

"Eh . . . Wha'? Wha's 'at?"

Miss Juniper suddenly became most frighteningly awake.

"Peter Bracewood-Smith?" she said. "Who said 'Bracewood'? Where?"

She sat upright, lit a cigarette, flicked some ash on the floor and turned her profile from left to right.

"I am expecting in his cottage," said Natasha ambiguously. "But why?"

"Biggest swine in Chelsea," said Miss Juniper firmly. She lit a cigarette from the butt of her own and offered it to Miriam, who nearly fainted with disgust. "That's why. Most vicious man I know. Drugs. Dopes. Everything. No wonder his wife committed suicide."

Miriam leant forward.

"Did you say *drugs*?" she said.

"Certainly," said Miss Juniper. She bit off the word as though it was a piece of cotton. She did not seem to mind the fact that she was now smoking two cigarettes at once.

"Benzadrine tablets?" said Miriam.

"Oh *no*," said Miss Juniper gaily. "Nothing simple like that for Peter. Or, at least, not in the old days. Why, I can't write a feature myself without my benzadrine. I don't call benzadrine *drugs*. No. Morphia. That's *Bracewood-Smith*."

"You don't say," said Miriam.

"Yes, I do," said Miss Juniper excitedly. "What Sob-Stuff Meriel says *goes*. Why, Heather—that's a girl I used to live with—*she* knew Peter a long time. She says his arms are *pitted* with punctures."

"From a hypodermic," said Natasha slowly, getting the point.

"That's right," said Miriam. "But does everyone in the *world* know this but us? And Sergeant Tomkins?"

"Well, everyone in *Chelsea* knows it," said Miss Juniper. And she poured herself another drink.

"Forty minutes, please, Miss Birdseye!" called someone outside, in a very fair imitation of a callboy. Miriam and Natasha and Miss Juniper went silent and stared at one another. Then Miss Juniper turned her profile from left to right and reached for the telephone.

CHAPTER FIVE

ALL over Brunton-on-Sea people were getting ready for the Radcliff Hall play.

Mr. and Mrs. Micah shut up the shop and disturbed Roger Partick-Thistle in the bath as they did so. Then they buttoned themselves into their waterproofs and began their walk up to the school. Mrs. Micah lifted a small red umbrella with a yellowish handle and put her head down against the wind. There was another storm blowing in from the sea.

Great purple and navy-blue clouds swept in from the Channel, trailing plumes of mist and golden light. The tide swept in, too, sighing up the beach, picking restlessly at the shingle, snarling under the pier, and generally behaving like a wild beast.

Radcliff Hall (which, as the School Song says, is 'set four-square to all winds that blow') received the first rain with equanimity. It was, perhaps, more concerned with all the extraordinary things that were going on inside the school.

II

Peter Bracewood-Smith swore as he shut his kitchen window with a bang and split his thumb-nail on the catch. He felt dazed and surprised. Perhaps he had been overdoing it lately. Flaming difficult to make both ends meet. . . .

Perhaps if he sold everything he had *and* let the bungalow and went to the South of France this crazy tumult in his brain would cool? Perhaps his temples would no longer crackle and thunder? And then, and *then*, when everything was cool and quiet, in the mid-day, or in the siesta, he would be able to write a masterpiece . . . *his* masterpiece. A great sprawling masterpiece like *Anna Karenina*.

He turned on the cold tap. He put his thumb under it. It bled beautifully, staining the cold-water jet with a most brilliant, glorious scarlet. The sink spattered with bright red as the cold stung him. *Damn!* He sneezed, ear-splittingly. He *had* caught cold. He snatched at his sleeve. No handkerchief. He wiped his nose on the back of his hand. A trail of blood strayed across his nose. He picked up a scarf from the kitchen chair. He blew his nose furiously. Soft silk rag. It pleased him. The alarm clock went off and made him jump. Six o'clock.

"Hell!" he said, and stuffed the soft silk up his sleeve. "Only forty minutes to go!"

When he shut his front door, and put his head down to climb the hill to the school, the storm parted his black beard and swept it back behind his wide shoulders. He shook his head, but imagined cobwebs and shadows that always gathered before his eyes would not clear. He needed a drink. He would stop at the off-licence for a bottle of gin.

The rain, too, gathered fury. When he came to the gates of Radcliff Hall he was soaked through his shoulders. He sneezed again and again and again.

His strange conviction that writers were a race of Gods, owing allegiance to no laws, not even to the God of the Old

Testament, seemed less strong as the rheum started in his eyes. Perhaps writers were human beings after all? They were certainly subject to colds in the head. Perhaps they were also morally vulnerable? He would think that one out. . . .

III

Natasha and Miriam changed for *Quality Street* in their original bed-sitting-rooms. They shouted comments to each other through the matchboard partition that separated them. Their conversation was made more difficult by Miriam's radio, which played all the time at full blast.

"What do you suppose that poor gin-sodden Juniper is telling her editor now?" shouted Miriam. Her voice penetrated the confused noises of Dick Barton, Special Agent, and his friends.

"I am not knowing," replied Natasha, more indistinctly. Her petticoat was back to front across her face. She was tied into an irritable knot by blue baby ribbons. These, as lovers of Sir J. M. Barrie will know, form an indispensable part of Miss Phoebe's costume.

"I expect it will not be being anything libellous," added Natasha. "Not for this Cute Press. This Juniper is a newspaper woman of great experience. Also, she tells me she writes the Bright Thought for Today."

"Scandalous!" shouted Miriam, adding irrelevantly, "Tomkins is a ——!"

And she adjusted a distressing muslin cap trimmed with lace and other pieces of Victoriana. (Miss Susan, Act I.) She fumbled among her tubes of grease-paint and among the wet white which lay about on her dressing-table. There was a light knock on the door.

"*Who?*" bawled Miriam. She switched off the radio with her foot. "Can't see *anyone*."

In the comparative silence it was possible to hear a tiny, subdued little voice.

"It's Tomkins," said the voice. It sounded sheepish. "I've something quite special to tell you. We released Doctor Lariat at four o'clock this afternoon."

IV

"Is that Cute Press?" shouted poor gin-sodden Juniper accusingly into the ear of an offensive switchboard operator. "*Daily Glass.* News-room."

The simple word 'please' was unknown to Miss Juniper. Clicks and bangs indicated that the ringing telephone bell in the news-room probably interrupted an important mid-afternoon game of poker.

"Ah?" said a disgruntled voice eventually. It was the voice of a reporter who had obviously just cast away a busted flush.

"Meriel," said Miss Juniper powerfully. "Meriel here. That you, Fred?"

"Ah . . ." said Fred, agreeing with her.

"Well, tell Jack something's going to break here about that old drug-fiend Bracewood-Smith. Before evening. The weather's awful."

"Listen, make sense, will yah?" Fred was cold and unimpressed. "We ain't writing the weather report. You're on a murder near Eastbourne, ain't yah? What yah want me to say to Jack?"

Fred evidently turned to look at his boss, for there was a pause.

"Looks as though he's got a good hand," he said. "He's scowlin'. . . ."

Fred was the Light Touch reporter of the *Daily Glass.* His was one of the Lightest Touches in the whole of Cute Press. It was so light, I may say, as to be absolutely unnoticeable. Little humorous stories run up by Fred very, very seldom found their way into print. This may have been on account of the paper shortage. It was certainly the reason for Fred's indestructibly cynical manner.

"Say to Jack it's a front-page lead and we're the only ones on to it," said Miss Juniper, flicking ash on the carpet. "Tell him to get out all the Bracewood-Smith envelopes from the library an' look up that suicide case there was a while back. Wife tossed herself off a roof or something. Got the name? Bracewood-Smith. B for buttock, R for rupture, A for——"

"Yah, yah, I get it," said Fred, bored. "Brailsford."

"No, *no*, hold everything. Drug addict."

"Here, who're yah callin' names?"

"Smith, damn you, *Smith*!" shouted Miss Juniper. She looked around her for a drink, failed to see one and sighed. "The *hell* with all girls' schools."

"*Now* yah makin' sense," said Fred amiably. He held the quacking telephone at arm's length. "O.K., Bracewood-Smith. So what? I used to know him in Chelsea."

"You heard me the first time, then," said Miss Juniper. "Nothing's happened *yet*. But the 'whole length and breadth of Brunton-on-Sea holds its breath tonight' and 'terror stalks by day' and 'Many Bruntonians believe the arrests made by the police (whom God preserve) in the astonishing and macabre Radcliff Hall case have not yet gone far enough'. Oh yes. 'Your reporter has interviewed many prominent and unsatisfied citizens.' Get it?"

"Sure," said Fred, and laughed weakly. "I'll get all that roughed out. So the police have arrested the wrong man, have they? And our reporter will shortly clap handcuffs on him before midnight, will she? That it?"

"That," said Miss Juniper, "is about it."

"And what's the name of the new suspect, if it isn't asking too much?" said the voice of the news-editor suddenly. It was a gay, bright, booming voice. The voice of a man holding a full house, with kings high.

"*Bracewood-Smith!*" screamed Miss Juniper.

"All right, all right," said the news-editor faintly.

"At your service, madam," said an unusual, thick, rasping voice behind her. Miss Juniper turned quickly and saw Peter Bracewood-Smith swaying in the doorway. He had evidently called at the off-licence. There was a bottle of gin under his arm. Miss Juniper looked at this with interest. She even forgot to move her profile. She did not even throw away her cigarette. She stood and gasped.

"Who are *you*, madam?" he remarked, and advanced, blinking, into the light. "Do I know you?" he added, with soft menace.

"No, I don't think so," said Miss Juniper. She gently put the receiver back on its hook. She carefully turned her back on it. She moved her profile cautiously from left to right. She groped in the pocket of her little fur jacket for her engine-turned cigarette-case.

In London the news-editor said to Fred: "Well, the old gal ain't lost her grip yet, then. Oh well, it's my deal, I think."

"I'm a presswoman," said Miss Juniper, in Brunton-on-Sea. "I was telephoning the names of the cast and all that to the *Daily*—er—to my paper."

She stared at Bracewood-Smith. For some reason she was nervous. Bracewood-Smith noticed this and frowned. He wrenched the little metal cap from the top of his gin-bottle.

"Have a drink," he said, "fellow writer?"

He splashed the gin towards Miss Juniper's tumbler, where it stood on the writing-table. He missed, and the spirit stained the desk top.

"Why were you shouting like that," he said suspiciously, "if it was a local paper?"

There was a pause.

"They couldn't hear me unless I did," said Miss Juniper. "The storm."

"Drink up," said Bracewood-Smith, and handed her the glass.

He sank wearily into a little creaking chintz chair. His shoulders overflowed it. He threw back his great, soaking head and flung raindrops in all directions. He suddenly laughed, for no apparent reason. He sneezed.

"You've caught cold," said Miss Juniper.

"Don't be so silly, madam," said Bracewood-Smith. He wiped his nose on the sleeve of his jacket. "Rough. We authors always catch cold. Don't we?"

"No," said Miss Juniper, hypnotized by the power in his yellow cat's eyes. "No."

"Furthermore . . ." said Bracewood-Smith. He laid his head on Miss Fork-Thomas's writing-table. He swept his right arm around him in an unsteady arc. The desk-light crashed to the floor. The ink-pot, the glass tray of pens and pencils, followed it.

"Furthermore . . ." repeated Bracewood-Smith, "writers are not held by common considerations or *laws*. Repeat 'not'. Laws govern other people's lives, don't they? Conventions, so on, don't apply to writers. Artists, utterly amoral. Well-known fact. *Should* be, for great art. Conventions necessary for protection of *ordinary* human beings. Writers *mustn't* be protected. Down with ivory towers! Writers should buzz about the world."

There was a pause while Miss Juniper looked worried.

"Approachable," said Bracewood-Smith, and added inconsequently, "my head aches."

He took her tumbler of gin from her hand and drained it with a happy gulp.

"Free like the saints," he announced. "Particularly Saint Augustine. Eh? Wha' d'you say? Huh, fellow writer?"

Miss Juniper was astonished. She was confronted for the first time in her life by a bigger and more degenerate drunk than herself. Bracewood-Smith also seemed, if anything, more arrogant, more convinced of his own genius, more *boring*, than herself. Miss Juniper was jealous. She hit him on the knuckles with his pencil.

"Swiped my gin," she said sharply. She was no longer afraid. "Was a present. Give it back."

Grumbling, Bracewood-Smith poured her another stiff drink and looked round for a glass for himself.

"No tumbler for me?" he said. "Funny. Well, drink out of bottle, then, madam. Forgive me. Not very *chic*."

He tilted the bottle towards his fine black beard.

"What are your views, madam," he said, with sudden elegance and grace of gesture, "Of these conventions that hedge a writer, madam? Eh?"

"I'm quite conventional when it comes to *murder*," said Miss Juniper cunningly. "When it comes to taking other people's *lives* to protect my own interests. I don't follow you *that* far. That seems to me selfish to the point of lunacy."

The room suddenly was quiet. Bracewood-Smith's eyes narrowed. He seemed to try to stop the fumes of alcohol that rose to overwhelm his brain. The room was no longer full of those troublesome fogs and cobwebs. It was unbearably sharp and clear. It went reeling sideways, of course, but that was only to be expected. He focused the room. He focused Miss Juniper. *Damn!* He shouldn't have got drunk. *What* had she said?

"Takin' life, madam?" he said slowly. "That hardly seems to me relevant. It is, of course, an interestin' proposition."

"Come off it, old sport," said Miss Juniper, with horrid jocularity. "Come clean. *I* know you killed them."

Bracewood-Smith watched her breathlessly.

"I don't know what you mean, madam," he said slowly. He decided to be angry. "You burst in here. You break my lamp . . ."

He looked down for a second at the pieces of china at his feet.

They lay scattered all about the carpet, pink and blue. Now *that* was a tactical error. Never buy pink-and-blue lamp again. People might not believe you when you said it was yours. . . . He winced and looked up again.

"You make ridiculous accusations," he went on. "You try to stop my writing. You're jealous. My masterpiece. From jealousy. My *Anna Karenina's* better'n your *Anna Karenina*."

"Or Tolstoy's *Anna Karenina*?" said Miss Juniper coldly.

"You obstruct me an' talk about conventions."

"No," said Miss Juniper. "That was you."

She drained her tumbler.

"You drink my gin," said Bracewood-Smith, "and then you have the nerve to say I murdered poor Gwylan Fork-Thomas and Theresa Devaloys."

"I don't even know their names," said Miss Juniper happily.

"Hell!" said Bracewood-Smith, gathering pace and rhetoric. "Why should I *not* take the lives of these unhappy school-teachers? I am not saying, of course, that I *did*. Mercifully to release them from their thraldom in this vile place. But is it likely, madam? Do I look that sort?"

"No, cock," said Miss Juniper, turning her profile to the right. "But you *do* look the sort who'd do in a girl for six thousand pounds that you might've had to cough up for libel. Eh? *And* another one who might've found out what you'd been up to. Eh? You look *that* sort to me, cock."

She leant forward and stroked his face with one small, insulting hand. Bracewood-Smith panted with rage. There was a pause, filled only with Bracewood-Smith's heavy breathing.

"*Dear* fellow writer," said Miss Juniper happily, reaching for the bottle of gin.

"You've nothing on me!" screamed Bracewood-Smith. He shook his head from side to side like a bear at the baiting. "You can't prove a damn' thing. Nothing to prove. Keep my head. *And keep my mouth shut*. . . ." he added to himself, in a lower tone.

He suddenly glared up at Miss Juniper through his gummy swollen eyelids. Tears gathered in them. He sniffed. He wiped his nose on the back of his hand.

"Nothing to *prove*," he repeated. "Utterly nothing. You're jealous, that's all. Hellish newspapers! Hounding me."

He was suddenly quiet, regarding his feet and the pool that surrounded them on the late Miss Fork-Thomas' carpet.

"D'you call a revolver, posted to your bank for safe custody by your little daughter, *nothing*?" cried Miss Juniper. "Is your access to a hypodermic nothing? Is your bringing poisoned whiskey to a rehearsal nothing?"

Bracewood-Smith swatted at her as though she were a mosquito. He lurched to his feet.

"Yes, damn it, madam, I *do*!" he shouted. He sent the light chintz-covered armchair spinning across the room on well-oiled castors. "I damn' *well* do!"

So for a second there was the disgusting sight of two sodden, sordid, alcoholic wills grappling in frightful mental conflict. It was interrupted.

"Ten minutes, please!" cried the schoolgirl who was acting as callboy. She passed the drawing-room door and her light feet went away upstairs away from them.

"Attend to *you* after the play," said Bracewood-Smith.

"Like you attended to Fork-Valois and Thomas, I suppose," snapped Miss Juniper.

He swayed towards the door, an untidy but magnificent Elizabethan figure. His eyes were troubled, hunted, shaded again by the disintegration of madness.

"Wish," he muttered, as he banged his hip against the swing doors of the gymnasium, "wish I hadn't been fool enough to get drunk tonight."

V

The gymnasium had been filling ever since half past six with cigarette smoke and people and conversation. First came the early arrivals from Brunton-on-Sea: Mr. and Mrs. Micah, who had not missed a Radcliff Hall play since anyone could remember; and Major and Mrs. Bandarlog; and Mr. Intrikit and his horse-mad daughter. These all came early and were shown into excellent seats where they sat quietly, eating their sweet ration (Mr. and Mrs. Micah), torturing one another mentally (Major and Mrs. Bandarlog) or chattering (Mr. and Miss Intrikit). They all bought programmes from Myfanwy Moon and Verena Levinson. The programmes were tastefully decorated with a lady in a crinoline, holding a watering-can. They also bought copies of the school magazine (*The Radclifton*), and were presently lost

in wonder at the muse of P. Sykes (twelve and a half), which
announced on page 32:

> Child of my heart, o dream that I have loved,
> Why live you not as you were wont to do?

Major Bandarlog was irritated by Mrs. Bandarlog's enjoyment of
this little fragment and pointed out another, by P. Sykes (twelve
and a half), on page 70, beginning:

> Pretty little sunbeam, rising in the West,
> Drowsily you greet us in our downy nest.

which, the major said, had not even the merit of accuracy.
Everybody else sat quietly enough, their senses pleasantly titillated
by the proximity of the sinister stage.

VI

The later arrivals from Brunton and Cranmer came next—
those who burned entirely from idle curiosity, having bought
their tickets from spivs and were wishfully thinking of another
murder. It was thought that Miss Helena bbirch was there,
disguised in a New Look. And then came the reporters, not quite
so fast on to the story as the veteran Meriel Juniper. These
rippled like lice in the gallery. They were all a little drunk and
vexed to find themselves (at seven o'clock) so far from the Café
Royal and Regent Street. Eventually, looking rather small, the
school itself filed in, and then the house mistresses. The house
mistresses were to sit in special basket-weave armchairs half-way
up the hall. Everyone else sat and creaked on small cane-seated
chairs.

The arrival of the house mistresses was the signal for everyone
to leap to their feet and sing the school song, "The red cliffs of
Radcliff a beacon shall be". Because Miriam was in the play the
house mistresses made a meagre show. The special chairs were
filled only by Miss Lipscoomb and Miss Phipps and Mrs.
Grossbody and Miss Bound. Even so, Miss Lipscoomb and Miss
Phipps had to leave their places during the first interval to dress
for Act III.

The school occupied the first three rows of backless, splintery forms. Most of them wished that they were not there. Some, already, had appalling headaches. One or two of them (more particularly Daisy Stuckenheimer) had already been sick in the upstair bathrooms. But these were so anxious to see Miss Birdseye and Miss Nevkorina in *Quality Street* that they told no one of their alarming symptoms. They sat tight, with itching chests and running eyes giving scarlet fever to everyone else.

VII

Natasha arrived backstage, looking very pretty. Her hair had been elaborately dressed in the conventional ringlets (a little too long for the usual *Quality Street* manner) and, at this moment, she was looking forward to the evening's entertainment. She was secure in the knowledge that she knew her part perfectly. Stage fright had not yet claimed her.

"You needn't look for any clues—I mean *cues*—from me," growled Miriam, arriving five minutes later, a frieze cloak thrown over Miss Susan's unattractive garments. "I am utterly null and void. Tomkins has released Lariat."

"I wonder why?" said Natasha vaguely. She was seized, quite without warning, by the worst attack of stage fright she had ever suffered in her life. She went jet white under her make-up and shook from head to foot like a leaf. "I feel so sick," she wailed miserably. "I wish it were all over." She moved the curtains slightly apart to see who had come into the body of the hall. "Or else that someone would quickly murder us and we need not do it. Look, here comes Bracewood-Smith with a bottle of gin."

Miriam peered through the curtains above Natasha's head and said sourly that very well, then, Natasha needn't worry, they *would* be murdered now. In the doorway behind Bracewood-Smith appeared a slight figure, moving its head restlessly from side to side. Miss Juniper, posturing.

"There's that fly-catching exhibitionist, dear," said Miriam, suddenly in a better temper. "Do you think I could run about the stage holding the book of the play?"

Natasha pulled herself out of a downward spiral of misery

and self-conscious gloom and considered Miriam with her head on one side.

"I do not see why not," said Natasha. "It will be being much safer for *both* of us."

"It could be my Bible, you know," said Miriam anxiously. "Or that novel in the play itself about *the man* we read at the beginning?"

"That woman Juniper is being as near *d.t.* as anyone I have ever *seen*," said Natasha.

"Well then, you can't have been married very often," said Miriam sardonically. "All right. I shall read my part."

"I am meaning the nearest to *d.t.* with*out* actually having them," said Natasha. "I know many, many people who *have* them."

Natasha moved back from the curtains, saying to herself, 'Miriam, I mean of course *Susan*, I have met a certain individual', which was the first line of her part. Now Miriam began to feel very ill indeed. It was at this moment that Bracewood-Smith arrived and sank ponderously into the prompt-corner.

Without consulting anyone he threw the electric-light switches. The house-lights promptly went out and the footlights came up abruptly. The curtains jerked solemnly apart. The blue-and-white room of Miss Susan and Miss Phoebe Throstle was displayed to one and all. Roger Partick-Thistle came into the hall at the back.

VIII

Roger stood transfixed with the beauty of his own work.

Sergeant Tomkins came in and stood just beside him. He was wearing an unfamiliar (hired) dinner-jacket that cut him under the arms. Noni Postman tried to sell him a programme and a school magazine.

"In aid of Radcliff Hall's Sunshine Kiddies," she said.

"Don't be silly, dear." Roger waved her away. "If there's one thing the sergeant dislikes more than kiddies it's sunshine."

"Sh!" said several rows of heads, jerking round in front of them.

On the stage, Miss Lesarum, as Valentine Brown, swung about between Miriam and Natasha, remarking, 'No more mud on your carpet, Miss Susan. No more coverlets rolled into balls. . . ."

Natasha watched her closely with fascinated horror. The play, apart from this quite obvious antipathy that the leading lady felt for the leading gentleman, was going quite well. The audience relaxed.

"Reading her part," said Roger. "How sensible."

A small figure, full of energy and passion, rose from the floor at his feet.

"*You're* Roger Partick-Thistle," it said accusingly.

"Oh, lor' !" said Roger. He stepped nervously back out of the gymnasium through the swing doors. He took the sergeant with him.

"Meriel Juniper of the *Daily Glass*," said Miss Juniper, hotly pursuing him.

"This is Sergeant Tomkins of the C.I.D., dear," said Roger. "He's i./c. murders. He'll tell you everything. Meriel knew me in less-happy days," he went on, with a bright smile.

Roger fled away from them, along the passage from the gymnasium, leaving them both together. His memories of Miss Juniper were exclusively confined to the write-up she had done of the Wolf Cub scandal in 1934. Miss Juniper had interviewed Roger's mother. The *Daily Glass* had published Roger's mother's opinion of him, which should really not have been printed.

The gymnasium doors swung behind Sergeant Tomkins and Miss Juniper. The little crackle of applause swelled to an ovation. The first act was over. Miriam and Natasha were taking their bows.

"Come on, *quick*," said Miss Juniper to Sergeant Tomkins. She held out the cigarette that she had just been smoking and offered it to him. Sergeant Tomkins took it in a trance. "Come round *behind*," said Meriel Juniper. "That's where my story is."

IX

Natasha was prancing about backstage, tossing her ringlets and cramming them into a mob-cap for Act II. She was somewhat odiously pleased with herself. Miriam, on the other hand, was suffering an agonizing moment of self-doubt. She sat on the floor with her head in her hands. Miss Lesarum was hurrying into Captain Valentine Brown's uniform, as hired from Nathan by Doctor Lariat. It was not wildly becoming.

"Do you think they like us?" said Miss Lesarum wistfully.

"Of course not," snapped Miriam, without raising her head from her knees. "I feel sick," she said, adding in funereal tones that she was damn' glad she hadn't allowed Binkie Beaumont to come.

The stage was a turmoil of frayed nerves and fuss. Sergeant Tomkins and Miss Juniper arrived at the moment when Brace-wood-Smith was trying, drunkenly, to superintend the rearrangement of Miss Phoebe's and Miss Susan's blue-and-white room as a school.

Bracewood-Smith was now aggressively drunk. He swayed on the spot and quoted irrelevent passages of verse from the more obvious of Shakespeare's tragedies. He had accounted for the whole bottle of gin. He was now outlined against the string-coloured curtains, a wavering ponderous shadow, shouting, 'Toes *Out—So*, Chest Out, Georgy', the immortal line that starts Act II of *Quality Street*. From time to time he lashed out at the trembling children from West House who had been allowed to make up Miss Phoebe's dancing-class.

"'For God's sake,'" he suddenly remarked casually to the sergeant, who stood in the doorway, "'let us sit upon the ground and tell sad stories of the death of kings.'"

"Okidoke," said the sergeant amiably.

He moved towards him through a general pandemonium, consequent upon the fact that Maud Stuckenheimer had at last been sick. There was a sudden silence, as though a signal had been given.

Bracewood-Smith kicked a form into position with one un-steady foot. To him the whole scene was small and sharp and reeling, as though he saw it through the wrong end of a telescope. There was danger, certainly. Who *was* this man? He wore an ill-fitting dinner-jacket. He was jealous, of course. *Everyone* was jealous.

"Moss Brothers?" he said, sneering. He flapped a large hand to keep him away. He blew his nose.

"Uh-huh," said Tomkins, staring at him.

The man was staring at him. Why did he stare so? He still came towards him. And why did he stand up straight when everyone else swayed about so? How did he do it? Anyone could, if they stared like that. . . . But he must keep his head.

The stage spun faster and faster. Actors and actresses, waiting for *him*, Peter Bracewood-Smith, chattered and giggled and spun in the doorway. How *could* there be discipline when such irrelevancies interrupted him? Good God! The cobwebs were coming back. He groped to brush the film that was forming in front of his eyes. He brushed at the man in the dinner-jacket to get him out of the way.

"Miss Fork-Thomas' head-scarf, I presume?" said the man in the dinner-jacket.

The man in the dinner-jacket took the handkerchief out of his hand. He stared at it stupidly. It *wasn't* a handkerchief. It was a white silk scarf, worked all over with a pattern of edelweiss.

The man in the dinner-jacket shook it out in its luxurious folds.

"Lovely bit of stuff," said the sergeant. "Miss Fork-Thomas', I presume?"

In the distance Bracewood-Smith heard his own voice, scarcely human, growling, barking, wailing. He could not stop it. It said:

"A scarf? Gwylan Fork-Thomas' scarf? How *can* it be hers, you fool? I burnt Gwylan's, I tell you . . . I burnt it."

INTERLUDE

THE following day Johnny DuVivien sat in the office of Brandy's Club, Brunton-on-Sea, in a frightful rage. He had spent an utterly useless two days chasing false clues up and down the coast to St. Leonards and Hastings and Eastbourne, and the final arrangements for the purchase of Brandy's Club had been concluded. He now felt that this had been a mistake. He would have given a lot to be able to re-sell, immediately, to someone else.

He slopped some gin into a tumbler and drank it neat. *That* would hold his headache off. He swallowed two aspirins and glared round at the untidy little room which would shortly be *his*. Perhaps it was for the best. Once he were a *bona fide* resident of Brunton-on-Sea, Natasha would not be able to elude him.

Even Black Market Bob was now convinced that she was here. His niece, or his married sister, had seen someone answering the description, and looking just like the photograph, talking to Mr. Intrikit of the Brunton Hotel. But when Johnny had called on Mr. Intrikit he had gone to the school play, damn it all. . . .

The gin and the aspirins were taking effect. He felt very much better. His head now only felt bruised.

Henry appeared in the doorway in his shirt-sleeves.

"Sorry, dear," he said, "to disturb you when you feel so *rotten*, but Black Market Bob wants you on the 'phone. *Here*, do be careful!"

For Johnny was gone, banging Henry savagely on the hip as he went by him, flinging himself at the telephone like a bolt from a crossbow.

"That you, sir?" said the voice. "Bob here. Look, sir, hurry. I'm at the station now. There's a party very like your missus leaving for London on the 4.15. . . ."

CHAPTER SIX

"Yes," said Tomkins that same afternoon, handing Natasha's and Miriam's luggage into the Pullman car of the 4.15 Victoria Express. "Yes. Bracewood-Smith panicked over that second murder all right. Reely was no necessity for Mrs. DuVivien and you to chase about that *way*. Looking for clues."

He tipped his gent's fur felt and lifted Natasha in, holding her under her elbow. In his other hand was a copy of the *Daily Glass*. Meriel Juniper's article was prominently displayed.

"I was finding clue looking a little dreary myself," said Natasha.

"We lost our heads, dear," said Miriam. "What I can't understand is why Miss Lipscoomb took back that bbirch bitch as partner. She lost *her* head, too."

"It was love, dear, love," said Natasha.

Their luggage was impeded by a presentation electric clock with an inscribed plate *For Birdseye et Cie, which came to Radcliff Hall in hour of need*. A contingent of the school, with Miss bbirch and Miss Lipscoomb, stood on one side of the platform to see them off.

"Be careful of our clock, Tomkins," said Miriam, stepping into the carriage in her turn. "Good God!" as he leapt up beside her. "Are you coming too?"

Tomkins followed them smoothly into the Pullman car, swinging his little brief-case. Through the windows Natasha saw the last of Brunton railway station, the porter, the milk-cans, the weighing machine, the little knot of purple schoolchildren.

"Indeed I am," said Tomkins. "Not often I get a case likely to go to the Old Bailey all on me own. Goin' up to celebrate. Gor', what's that?"

For a terrible wailing now burst out all along the platform where Radcliff Hall, in all its royal purple, fluttered white handkerchiefs in a last good-bye. Natasha ran childishly to the window to look, and observed Miss Lipscoomb and Miss bbirch and the choir (Gwen Soames and Molly Ruminara much in evidence) under the clock. Miss Lipscoomb carried a tuning-fork. She plucked it once and nodded to Miss bbirch. Their reconciliation was evidently complete. And to everyone's consternation they broke unsteadily into the chorus of the Radcliff Hall School song, known and shuddered at by Radcliftons all over the world:

> "Go Slow—Radcliff Hall!
> Steady and Strong, Radcliff Hall.
> *Pro Bo-No Pub-lic-O!*
> Four-square to winds that *blow*!
> (*Pro Bono Publico*)"

sang Gwen Soames and her little friends *ad nauseam*.

The ragged chorus gathered volume as the 4.15 began to glide away from the little station. An obsequious man in a white coat took the sergeant's order for three coffees. The last triumphant shout of "Radcliff Hall!" went sighing away on the wind.

" 'The red cliffs of Radcliff a beacon shall be'," quoted Miriam. "Not a very good little number. Well, well. That's over."

And she glanced furtively down at the cheque in her bag, payable on Coutts and Company for £300.

"Cheap at the price," she murmured.

"I am not knowing so much about all of *that*," said Natasha gravely. She threw back a lock of hair and watched the sergeant with the innocent, limpid gaze of a startled fawn. "How do you feel? I was thinking you were going to be most seriously ill since last night."

"Mum's tum is still not right," remarked Miriam. "She will never play with a straight bat again. Tell us, Tomkins, what made you release Lariat for that terrible mad old Bracewood? You didn't tell us, you know. My head aches," she added inconsequently.

"Reely don't wonder, miss," said Tomkins.

Lewes station swam up towards them and they paused there, chugging and shuddering gently, long enough to allow three greyhounds in leash to clamber, barking, out of the guard's van.

"As a matter of fact," went on Tomkins, "it was young Mr. Thistle convinced us. Young Mr. Partick-Thistle and the bicycle."

"Thistle?" said Miriam angrily. "What do you mean?"

She drank her coffee and put her chin on her hand. Outside the window the glorious English spring, garlanded all with chestnut blossom and white dusty may, came flowering with fury. Natasha looked at it with loathing.

"I am thanking the good Saint Stanislaw," she said, "that I am going back to London."

"Mr. Partick-Thistle came into the station, madam," said Tomkins, "after that there Bally Netball game. In a bit of a taking. Said he'd been drinking with Bracewood-Smith the night of the Fork-Thomas murder and got so drunk he passed out. So drunk he couldn't walk, and Bracewood-Smith pushed him all the way up the hill on a lady's bike. *And* he couldn't find it anywhere the next day. Seems it was *his* bike."

"Rodgy would ride a lady's bicycle," said Miriam. "So *louche* of him."

"He didn't like to come forward because . . ." Tomkins hesitated.

"Because you locked him up on account of the Wolf Cubs?" said Miriam. "We know all that. Don't spare us."

"Apparently something *you* said to him, miss," went on Tomkins, turning to Natasha, "made him think he was on the spot of that murder, as you might say."

"I?" said Natasha, dilating her eyes. "Now what the sweet hell could I possibly have been saying? I am being the soul of valour always. Discretion, I mean. And I am agreeing with you *so much* about Miss bbirch," she added, turning to Miriam.

The sergeant lit a cigarette.

"Don't doubt it, miss," he said. "Very discreet you always are. It was just your interest in the Bracewood-Smiths that set him on thinking, some of Mr. Bracewood-Smith's behaviour being a bit odd. Thistle said he had the screaming heebies.

Thought he was covered with cobwebs or something when he was sober. Suggested we might keep the old eye on the gentleman for his own good."

Tomkins flicked ash into the round bowl provided by the Railway Company. He flicked ash with almost as much passion as Miss Juniper.

"Rodgy did rather well, then?" said Miriam, surprised. She glared out at Haywards Heath. "Gracious," she said, "I feel ill!"

As this was Miriam's usual form no one paid her very much attention.

"Well, yes, miss, he did," said Tomkins grudgingly. "Drew a map of the field. You know, Lover's Loose. Found that the . . . um . . . blood-stained patch of grass was about equidistant between Lariat's house and Bracewood-Smith's cottage. And it was even more likely, you know, that whoever it was ran after her."

"The housekeeper of the doctor's would swear he had not been out, I am supposing?" said Natasha.

"Well, yes, she did. But she'd so obviously been in bed asleep that I wasn't inclined to accept her statement at all."

Miriam shuddered fastidiously.

"I mean, the murder obviously hadn't been *premeditated*," went on Tomkins. "And it wasn't likely that Lariat would have acted so ca'm. And Mr. Bracewood-Smith was acting peculiar by the time we caught up on him. We were quick there, mind. He'd been on the roof."

"Doing what?" said Miriam.

"*You* had gone home," said Natasha accusingly.

"Disposin' of that velveteen jacket of his," said Tomkins. "You may 'ave noticed he hasn't worn it since. If you'll excuse me."

"I feel terrible," said Miriam, looking out of the window.

"When you are saying 'bloody'," said Natasha, "I suppose you mean it. Covered with blood, I suppose you mean?"

Miriam shivered again. Tomkins stubbed out his cigarette end.

"Yes," he said. "Very disagreeable. He tore it up as best he could and shoved it down the soil-pipe in a hurry. No time to *burn* it, and he didn't dare go up on the roof the next day on account of we had a plain-clothes man on guard of the whole of Lover's Loose. Soon's 'e set out for the play that evening we nipped out an' in an' up on the roof, I can tell you. An' there it was. Stuffed in the soil-pipe. Pity how drink affects a man, i'n't it? Now, the *first* murder (if I can call it so, just between ourselves, like)—*that* was a lovely job, that was."

"What an awful thing to say, dear," said Miriam.

"No, but reely," said Tomkins, "it was *clever*. More like a thing in a book than real life, if I may say so. That give me an inkling, too. Once Mr. Partick-Thistle suggested it was done by punchin' a hole through the cork with a hypodermic, an' then gettin' someone to draw the cork, we were certain of him. *Really* clever, y'know. Couldn't prove a *thing*."

"Clever," said Natasha.

"It'll take us all our time to get a jury to accept the evidence for that one, that's all, miss," said Tomkins enthusiastically. "But the case for Miss Fork-Thomas is a push-over. Absolutely. Or I hope."

He suddenly stopped and leant over towards Miriam.

"Penny for Miss Birdseye's thoughts," he said.

Miriam pressed her aching head against the cool glass of the Pullman-carriage window. She was wondering deeply if it were not possible that the two murders had been committed by different hands. Her fevered mind threw up an image of Roger Partick-Thistle earnestly explaining the method used to kill Theresa Devaloys and hurrying round to the police to tell tales.

"Wondering if Roger mightn't be the murderer," she said.

Sergeant Tomkins' mouth fell open.

"After all," said Natasha, delighted at the twist that events were taking, "Roger is telling *me* that Gwylan is telling *him*. And I think he is so *right*."

"I *do* think that is what happened, miss," went on Tomkins serenely, recovering his balance. "I think Miss Fork-Thomas arrived at Gull Cottage when Mr. Partick-Thistle was there, too, as drunk as a lord."

"I am knowing three lords," said Natasha, "and all of them are always very drunk. I have noticed it."

"Yes," said Tomkins. "And Miss Fork-Thomas accused Mr. Bracewood-Smith of the murder of Miss Devaloys, in front of Mr. Thistle. I expect she thought she had a witness, you know. After all, Mr. Thistle is a very deceptive drunk. Remembers everything 'e hears, you know, but can't remember where he heard it. That's very usual, you know, miss," he said, turning to Natasha, who became angry and distant.

"Is it?" she said coldly. "I am seldom, if ever, drunk, thank you very much."

"Too many drunks in this case altogether," said Tomkins quickly, watching her, bright-eyed. "Good thing you and Miss Birdseye stayed so sober. Your findings were all quite correct, I think," he went on. "Even if you did reach 'em all the wrong way. And quite haphazard. Only thing *I* don't understand *is*, if that wasn't Miss Fork-Thomas' scarf, who the hell's was it?"

"It was *mine*," said Natasha sweetly. "But I have not been having the *remotest* idea how it is getting there. It even has my laundry mark on it."

II

The train ran into Victoria, jiggling merrily. Porters ran, trolleys clattered, sexless voices spoke through loudspeakers, telling them that the Golden Arrow was one hour forty minutes late. Miriam stood still in the carriage door, sniffing the smoky air as though it were heaven.

"My heart overflows," said Natasha.

Sergeant Tomkins only parted from them in Baker Street, outside the office. He insisted on going there in the taxi with them, clasping their presentation clock in his arms till the last possible moment. Finally he stood bowing on the pavement, while Miriam (utterly bored by him) fumbled with the house door key. Eventually he clambered back into the taxi, took off his hat repeatedly, and drove away, shouting that he would see them all at the magistrates' court and then the Old Bailey.

"You must pay our expenses," said Miriam.

"And we are so very, very expensive," said Natasha. She smiled her sad, gay, heart-piercing smile. Tomkins did not know which of them he loved more.

III

The office was just as they had left it. Miriam took down the ticket that had announced, during the last week, OUT—GONE TO CRIME. She went upstairs.

Natasha idled towards the telephone to ring up the kennels

about Amy, her little pekinese dog. As she reached towards it to pick it up, it began to ring.

"Are you Birdseye et Cie?" it said angrily, as she picked it up.

"Yes," said Natasha cautiously. "That is—er—*yes*."

"Wall," quacked the voice, "this is Peep, Peep, Paul and Pry, detectives, London Wall. We got a client who's exhaustin' us Care to take him on? He wants to trace a missin' relative."

"What sort of relative?" said Natasha. "A rich one?"

"Pays a fifty-quid retainer," said the voice. "Wants to find his wife. Care to cut in?"

"What is being his name?" said Natasha. "I am not caring for handling other gentlemen's wives."

There was a pause while the voice looked up its card index. It returned to the receiver full of hope.

"DuVivien," said the voice. "Mr. Johnny DuVivien."

"No," said Natasha instantly. "We cannot be helping you." She put back the receiver rather too quickly.

"Natasha! *Natasha!*" shouted Miriam, upstairs in the bathroom. "Hey! Come up here. This is *terrible*."

"Wrong number," said Natasha, on the stairs. "What is terrible?" she ended gravely.

Miriam was bending and twisting, staring at herself in the bathroom looking-glass. She was stark naked. She pointed to her back and chest. The violent, unmistakable rash of scarlet fever had risen there, and was still rising.

THE END

LOVE CHILD
Maureen Duffy

'A macabre tale of jealousy and possessiveness'
– *Daily Telegraph*

Kit's mother has just embarked on an affair with Ajax, her husband's secretary. Kit is murderously jealous, but of whom, her mother or Ajax? And what gender is Ajax, or Kit for that matter? It is impossible to tell. Why is the reader uncomfortable not knowing? Whether boy or girl, it is clear that Kit is a monster: a mini-adult whose freakishly sophisticated brain knows 'everything' and whose stunted emotions know nothing. The combination is, inevitably, disastrous . . .

Love Child, Maureen Duffy's teasingly brilliant explorations of the meaning of gender, was first published in 1971.

Maureen Duffy is one of Britain's most admired contemporary writers. Her work includes novels, biographies, plays and poems. Virago also publish *That's How It Was* and *The Microcosm*.

WINTER LOVE
Han Suyin

'A stunning novel – resonant, penetrating and unsentimental'
– *Georgina Hammick*

Red is a married woman with children. But since adolesence she has been desperate to conceal from herself and others the true significance of her feelings for women. Now, with middle-age approaching fast, her thoughts turn insistently to her student days in that bitterly cold winter of the last year of the war when Mara offered – and Red rejected – love, desire, and trust. Painfully, Red relives the past, and comes to see the part that cruelty, loss and fear have played in the formation of her frozen sexuality. And with enlightenment, comes the possibility of thaw . . .

Han Suyin, born in China in 1917, is best known for her novel *A Many Splendoured Thing*, and for her volumes of autobiography. *Winter Love*, her beautifully written and perceptive novel, was first published in 1962.

THE CHILD MANUELA
Christa Winsloe

The novel of the film *Schoolgirls in Uniform*

Manuela von Meinhardis has a loving mother and a callous, egotistical father, an officer in a crack Prussian regiment. On her mother's death Manuela is sent to a repressive school for officers' daughters where all affection is outlawed. The harshness of the regime reflects the iron fist of Prussianism and the Hitlerism already well entrenched by 1932 when Winsloe was writing: the cruelties practised by female staff upon their pupils foreshadow the complicities and horrors of Nazism. In such an environment, only Fräulein von Bernburg offers tenderness and love, and for that both she and Manuela must suffer.

Available in Britain for the first time in more than half a century, *The Child Manuela* is the remarkable and passionate novel on which the famous film *Schoolgirls in Uniform* was based.